The Sinner's Reckoning

A Vicky Donahue Novel

Steve Dwight Nichols

This book is a work of fiction and the product of the author's imagination. Names, characters, places, events, incidents, business entities, religious entities, and organizations are used fictitiously. Any resemblance to actual places, organizations, business entities, religious entities, incidents, or persons is entirely coincidental.

ISBN: 978-1-7365728-0-1

Printed in the United States

The Sinner's Reckoning

Books

1. Murder and the Preacher's Wife
2. The Sinner's Reckoning
3. The Good Samaritans

Steve D. Nichols

Prologue

"The CIA has done bad things over the years trying to help our country, while the meek in those other countries have been sacrificed. The CIA has supported dictators and other leaders over the years: The Shah of Iran, Ferdinand Marcos in the Philippines, and Manuel Nortiega in South America. To stand back and close your eyes to these unnatural and unjust acts to the innocent makes you just as sinful in God's eyes as the senator for allowing that young girl to be raped. You should go ahead and rape her yourself. Our Lord will judge us all."

The man walked up to her and looked her directly in the eyes, and Vicky knew she was going to die. She stared him in the eyes without blinking or fear, and she said, "I am the good shepherd and the good shepherd lays down his life for the sheep."

"Are you quoting Apostle John to me?"

Steve D. Nichols

Chapter 1

Where there is one Cheiracanthium Mildei spider, there are two. They witness all from the vantage point in their transparent webs and transparent bodies on our ceilings and the tops of our walls. They have been observed in every state and, basically, every home in America. They mean us no harm, and they desire to cohabitate with us. They feel the shake and vibration in the structure and move to the corner of the web to better conceal themselves. They know the evil is coming.

The small girl woke up crying, and the pain was non-stop. The lady had actually smiled at her when she violated the girl. She remembered seeing the older man sitting in the chair, smiling and watching. She hoped she would be okay once they let her go, and that she could find help. She hoped to see her parents. At this point, hope was all she had left. She could not recall how many days it had been. She remembered being moved to a second home in the same cage. The cage had become her home since she left her family, traveling by boat and truck. She was only allowed out of the cage for one thing. She had hated the man with the cold hands who was extremely mean and did things to her that she had not conceived were possible. She now was in a basement without windows. She did not know if it was day or night or how long she had been in this basement. She had no clothes or cover to keep warm. She cried for her mommy and daddy. Then, the devil showed up, and he seemed to enjoy cutting her and burning her with the fire after he violated her. Her body was hurting all over. She was not certain how many fingers had been cut off and burned. She was too scared to look at her hands. The pain from the burning never stopped. She prayed for death. She could not sleep for any length of time due to the pain. She could hear the door opening and him coming down the stairs. He walked very fast to the cage and pulled the quilt off, and she could not look up. She just lay in the cage. She prayed for death. He reached in and pulled her out by her hair. He was never gentle. He pulled her head up and placed a plastic bag over her head. She did not resist. She thought the pain finally would stop as she could no longer breathe and was happy to die.

Chapter 2

Delores was the newly appointed district manager over most of the southern region for the FBI. She was now stationed in the Atlanta Office. She had graduated from New York University in Political Science and earned a law degree from Harvard Law. She was five foot, four inches and was very pretty with her dark hair, dark brown eyes, high cheekbones, fit athletic-looking body, and a lovely smile. She also possessed a photographic memory with a competitive result-oriented personality. She had been fast tracked at the FBI. No one had ever been promoted to a district manager level at her age of thirty-three, and being a single black lady, she was an anomaly. Her dedication to her job and her country had never been in question. She could have worked in the private sector and made five times more money. She had been promoted above several men who had been at the job longer. She was well aware she was expected to produce results. She had met with her two top agents, which she had handpicked, Roger Henagar and Tracey Vaughn. She wanted the best to work on this case, and now she was told she could not share all the information about the case with them. It was clear from history that if the CIA was involved, she might never know all the details. She also knew from dealing with the CIA in the past, she would need to step back and let them operate. They normally were very able and efficient to clean up their mess with a plausible explanation once the dead bodies started turning up. The saying in Washington, when she worked in that area of the country, was no one could spin a story like the CIA. Delores did not like the thought, but she had to be untruthful and misleading to her two agents about what she knew.

When they called and told her they were going to Nashville to meet with the former sheriff of Butler, Tennessee, who had just accepted the position as a special agent with the Tennessee Bureau of Investigation (TBI), she normally would have been in total agreement. Now, she had been told by her boss and the director of the FBI, Alexander Bass, to pull back on her investigation into missing Asian girls. While sitting in the meeting with the two men in the Washington office, she could feel her anger boiling over. She was told, in so many words, to stop the investigation. She was furious with the order. Finally, Director Bass mentioned that the CIA had an operation ongoing, and her investigation might be counterproductive. When she still pushed back and mentioned she had lost Kelly Stephenson, a young agent, who was her responsibility and was brutally murdered at a water tower in Butler, Tennessee and her killing might be related to the Asian girls, Director Bass then surprised her, and said the decision had been made above his pay grade. At that point, Delores knew the only person above the director was sitting in the White House. The director made it clear she was not to tell her agents about who made the decision to pull them pack, and it was imperative the local law enforcement in Tennessee would not be provided any information about the federal case. This was a dark operation being handled by the CIA. She knew she needed time to consider her orders from Director Bass. She also knew she never wanted to make decisions when she was mad. She wanted time to calm down. She sent the e-mail, telling her agents she wanted a virtual meeting the next day to discuss the investigation, and to hold off on going to Nashville to meet the former sheriff.

The next day, while she was still in Washington, she was talking with Tracey and Roger by video link. They told her they were going to Nashville to meet Wayne Tipton, the former sheriff of Butler. She told them to meet her in her office the next day when she returned from Washington at 9:00 a.m. She now had to make a decision to either pull them off the case and risk them going behind her back and losing her respect and confidence, or allow them to proceed with their trip to Nashville. She felt, at this point, the meeting with the former sheriff would be very short, and the death of the FBI agent killed by the rogue highway patrolman may not be related to the serial killing of the girls. Her specific orders were to pull back the investigation on the serial killing case and when she mentioned Bill Cramer might be part of the case, Director Bass said to hold off on investigating Cramer if they were related. Either the former sheriff knew something that was not in his report that she had read while monitoring the case from her office in Atlanta, or he didn't. It was a basic 101 investigation.

The investigator always talked to all possible witnesses in person in order to pick up on body language and personal insight. The subjective items were sometimes the case breakers, and all personal insights that were left out of the written factual reports could lead to discovering the killers. Officers across the country had always been trained not to write anything in a report but the facts. A defense attorney could spin all the subjective items if the case ever went to court.

When they came into her office the next morning at 9 a.m., she was not surprised Roger had taken a seat across from her, and Tracey had remained standing near the door. It was like they knew how to make someone feel uncomfortable, and there was no way to make eye contact with both of them at one time. She had figured one of them was always watching for body language while the other one was engaged in the conversation. They had become a very good team at hunting down serial killers and criminals. She asked, "What do you hope to gain with the trip to Nashville? You have a copy of his report."

Roger said, "The former sheriff is the only person to talk to Cramer, and maybe something was said in person which is not part of his report. Cramer never talked or made friends with any of the other Tennessee Highway Patrolmen. They all said he was a loner and not sociable. His neighbors hardly knew him. The former sheriff might be our only hope."

Delores knew, by that comment, they had been investigating Bill Cramer. She had asked them not to look into him. She knew they had anticipated the location of the next body and where it was going to be buried. The plan was to catch the killer burying the body. Instead, Kelly Stephenson, the young agent assigned to monitor the possible next location, had been brutally killed. Delores said, "He is going to want answers."

Tracey spoke up, "We can tell him about the agent killed at the tower and the missing girls. He might be willing to assist us if we provide him with some facts." Tracey hesitated, and then said, "We might need his help. We need a break in the case."

Delores could tell where this was headed, and she knew she had to stop it. She had her orders. She also knew her agents had spent countless hours and days on the case, and they were emotionally invested in finding the culprits. She knew asking them to pull back was not going to work. They were dialed into solving the case. They had one objective, which was to find the killer or killers. They were not going to pull back, even if she ordered them. Delores said, "Okay, you two can go to Nashville and ask the former sheriff what Cramer told him, and you can tell him the lady was an agent for the FBI. We had discovered two young ladies from Asia, one in a shallow grave and one in the river, and we want to keep the investigation quiet and keep the media in the dark. That is all you can tell him. Do I make myself clear? The locals are not to be updated any further than that." She then held up two fingers and repeated herself, "Just two of the Asian girls who were located. Nothing more. They won't suspect a serial killer being involved if you just mention two have been located, and we will stand a better chance at keeping this quiet. You can suggest Cramer may have been the killer of the young Asian girls. Do you understand?"

Delores knew the former sheriff, Wayne Tipton, would have his suspicions and demand cooperation and additional information. They were not going to share any additional information. That is the way this process had worked over the years, and that was the way this was going to work now. The local law enforcement would have to accept it. She just wanted to make certain they did not go to the media. All this had to be kept quiet until her boss said it was okay to release a statement to the media.

Roger glanced at his partner, Tracey, and then looked at Delores and asked, "What's up? What are you not telling us?"

Delores looked at both men and said, "That is a direct order. Do you understand?"

The two men looked at each other and understood the meeting had been finalized with her firm remark. They both walked out of the office. They were planning to drive to Nashville that afternoon and go to the TBI office in Nashville before 4 p.m. without scheduling an appointment. Not giving Wayne, the former sheriff, time to think about possible questions to ask them, and catching him off guard, would work the best for them. They also were aware something was going on above their rank. They had not worked for Delores but a few months, and they were not certain why they were being asked to pull back on a murder investigation, especially a serial killer case. They needed to determine if Cramer was involved with the killing of the girls. The standard procedure was to run down every clue and rule it out and then move on to the next one. Meeting the former sheriff should have been on the top of the list.

Tracey asked, once they were well out of hearing range and walking in the hall leading to the elevator, "So, what do you think is up?"

Roger shook his head no. Tracey immediately understood to wait to discuss the meeting once they were out of the building and make certain no one could hear what he wanted to say.

Steve D. Nichols

Chapter 3

Wayne Tipton was sitting in his new office on the first floor located on Cherry Street in Nashville, Tennessee, where he finally decided to accept the job offer working for the Tennessee Bureau of Investigation (TBI). He liked being a sheriff of Butler County, Tennessee, but like most jobs, there are always trepidations. His old friend, Dale Hunter, had recommended him for the opening with the state police (TBI), and after a week of considering his options, Wayne accepted the State of Tennessee offer. Dale had worked for the TBI in the office located in Memphis, Tennessee, for the past seventeen years. He and Wayne had stayed in touch over the years, off and on, after they had graduated from college together, and both joined the Border Patrol Office in Brownsville, Texas. They worked as Federal Border Patrol Agents on the border with Texas and Mexico for a couple of years. Both became disenchanted with trying to keep poor people out of the country who were looking for employment to support their families. They had wanted more challenging careers where they could make a difference. Both had decided to move back to Tennessee and secured jobs with the Metro Police Department in Memphis, Tennessee, as patrolmen, with the hope of moving up as law enforcement officers. Dale had accepted a position with the TBI three years later, and Wayne worked as an officer for three years before becoming a detective for the Memphis Metro Police Department. After twelve years total working for the Memphis Police Department, Wayne was asked by the governor's office to fill in for a temporary period as the sheriff in Butler, Tennessee, located northwest of Nashville. The sheriff in Butler had unexpectedly died with a heart attack, and the only other officer on the force at that time qualified to be acting sheriff was in his twenties with less than two years' experience. In order to fill the need for a sheriff in the small counties on a temporary period, the State of Tennessee would assist with recommending experienced law enforcement officers. Wayne fit that description and had been recommended by the governor's Office to assist Butler County. Wayne had served with honor and received several awards from the mayor and police department in Memphis during his career. He had built a solid reputation in Memphis, and with the State Attorney General being from Memphis, Wayne was asked to assist. He ended up working as sheriff in Butler for almost eight years, in which he had been credited with solving three murders committed by a rogue Tennessee Highway Patrolman, two weeks prior to transferring to the TBI.

Wayne now had just completed his first almost full week of work at his new position as special agent for the TBI. It was Friday afternoon, and he had met several of his co-workers. Most of the first

18

week was spent learning and becoming familiar with the automation system, which was somewhat different from the computer system he was accustomed to where he was the sheriff in Butler, Tennessee, for the past eight years. Wayne thought to himself that he was tired of being updated on court procedures, updated laws, and review of cases the TBI frequently worked. He was ready to start receiving new assignments and moving forward with his career. He wanted the cases involving multiple counties, investigating drugs, and corporate crime. He wanted cases that were more complicated, so he could assist the county sheriffs. As he was sitting in his chair, he felt bored for the first time in several years and thought the state job might be too lackluster after working as sheriff and continuously being pulled in several different directions at the same time for the past eight years.

He sat back in his chair and started thinking back to the last couple of weeks in Butler. He smiled when he thought about Randy Evans. Evans was the town's mentally challenged handyman who drank too much, and the rogue highway patrolman by the name of Bill Cramer had set him up to take the fall for the murder of the unidentified lady. Cramer had listened in on the phone calls by bugging both the office phone to the sheriff and two deputies' phones. He learned when Brian Foster would be driving on Highway 12, leading from Nashville to Butler, to meet with the sheriff to discuss the lady killed at the tower. Wayne had assumed Cramer had pulled Brian over on Hwy 12 and they fought, with Cramer breaking the neck of Brian Foster.

He leaned forward in his chair and placed both elbows on his desk, reminiscing about the shooting of Highway Patrolman Bill Cramer. He never really thanked Vicky Donahue for saving his life. She just seemed to appear out of thin air, holding a gun. Vicky and her husband, Matt, had just moved to Butler, Tennessee, from San Diego the third week in January. Matt was the new preacher at Middlebrook United Methodist Church. Matt was an overnight success with a rock star status in Butler. Matt had a very joyful personality with a great deal of charisma, which enabled him to connect with the kids, the parents, and the elderly people of Butler. He had the type of personality that no one he met was a stranger and everyone was a friend. Vicky was his stunningly beautiful wife who worked gratis part-time at the church doing whatever was needed. Matt and Vicky were a team. Wayne's deputies had talked about Vicky and commented in the sheriff's office that whichever room Vicky walked into, she would always be the prettiest woman in the room. No doubt, everyone noticed her natural beauty, and she always was dressed in flattering, updated apparel.

Wayne still lived in Butler and talked to the citizens in passing. He understood, after talking with Mark Wilson last week at the Fast Jet convenient store in Butler, that Vicky often went to his shooting range on Friday afternoons and had achieved several belts in her Karate class, which was also located in Butler. Wayne realized, sitting at his desk, that he needed to tell Vicky personally how much he appreciated her saving his life and putting a stop to the torture. He remembered hearing the gunshot, which came from behind him, entering Bill Cramer's mouth and blowing out the back of his skull. The gunshot almost scared Wayne to death with surprise, as his entire body jerked when the gun was fired. Cramer had just shoved the end of the needle-nosed pliers under Wayne's big toenail, twisted, and pulled off his toenail during the start of the torture, which caused Wayne to nearly pass out. The pain was excruciating, and nothing like Wayne had ever felt. Wayne was hoping he could pass out, so he did not have to endure any additional torture. When Vicky fired the shot, he remembered thinking he was never so happy to see someone in his entire life when the new preacher's wife, Vicky Donahue, stepped out from under the water tower steel structure supports with a pistol pointed at Cramer's dead body. Wayne was so happy to be saved, he felt like crying with relief. He had given up hope and wanted to die due to all the pain. He was not sure how much more he could take, and Cramer had said they had just gotten started. He had also said he was going to castrate Wayne. He knew Cramer was looking forward to torturing him and then killing him. He could tell Cramer was a sadist, psychotic maniac. After she cut the plastic ties and freed him, Vicky made it clear he was never to tell anyone she was involved, and made the scene look like Cramer had used his pistol to shoot himself through the mouth. Wayne had called his deputies and TBI Special Officer Hunter as soon as Vicky left the scene. The TBI notified the FBI, since an officer had been killed, which was standard procedure, and both departments investigated the death and agreed it was a suicide by gunshot. Wayne had explained to the TBI and FBI agents that his office had received a crank call about a possible suicide at the tower. He told them that, as he was driving to the tower to check the call out, he saw Cramer turning onto the road leading to the tower and followed Cramer to the water tower, questioning him about the two killings. Before Wayne could stop him, he shot himself through the mouth. He thought Cramer had been looking for a spent shell casing when Wayne approached him. He never really said why he had returned to the scene of the murder of the young lady. The TBI secured warrants to enter Cramer's apartment in Chattanooga and discovered Cramer had a second apartment in north Nashville. When they acquired a second warrant for the apartment in Nashville, they located the surveillance equipment he used to listen to the sheriff's office and phone calls. They also located illegal high-tech bullets just like the one Wayne had discovered in the water tower while investigating the unidentified woman's murder. The case was considered a federal case, and the FBI team in Nashville seized all evidence with intent to the identity the young lady Cramer had killed at the water tower, and how Cramer had obtained the illegal bullets while working as a highway patrolman. Where and how he had obtained the illegal bullets, which were found in his gun and his apartment, were very concerning and baffling to the federal investigators. The FBI stopped sharing information on the Cramer investigation with the TBI, but Wayne had understood the ATF had been called in to assist the FBI with the investigation into the bullets and how a Tennessee Highway Patrolman had obtained military grade bullets. Once the federal authorities took over the case, the local law enforcement office was seldom kept updated on the investigation unless there was an arrest, at which time the chain of command would update them. And that is the case with this investigation. There had been no news from the FBI or the ATF about anything to do with Officer Cramer. No one had mentioned the fact that the young lady's body had disappeared from the Butler County Hospital during the night. Wayne had his suspicions, but no evidence. As Wayne sat in his chair, he realized he was going to always be in Vicky Donahue's gratitude. She asked for nothing in return but to be anonymous with the shooting.

Wayne had no open cases in Butler, with the suicide and confession of Bill Cramer. With Cramer admitting to killing the lady, the FBI had taken over the case concerning her missing body that had been stolen in the middle of the night from the local Butler County hospital. The citizens of Butler were pleased with what Wayne had accomplished as the sheriff. Wayne had strongly recommended Vince Newsome to be the temporary acting sheriff until the upcoming election, and then the voters could decide. Wayne had noted Vince had the skill set and deserved the right to be the interim sheriff until the election schedule for the next year. Vince had worked for Wayne as a deputy for the entire eight years, as well as two years under the prior sheriff. They had a good working relationship based on mutual respect. The State of Tennessee agreed with Wayne, and Vince was named acting sheriff until the scheduled voting took place the next year in which Vince had already decided he would start campaigning for the election to be the next sheriff in Butler County.

Wayne rubbed his hands over his face and smiled to himself again, as he thought back to the look on Randy Evans's face when he told Randy the murder had been solved, and he was a free man. Randy looked pitiful, with the missing front tooth and the two black eyes had almost healed. When he had first been arrested, he had a big red cherry-looking mark on his face, two black eyes from the broken nose, the missing front tooth, and having not showered in two days. Wayne looked around in the office to see if anyone was watching him, laughing to himself.

Randy was truly happy to be released from the county jail and not facing murder charges where he had said all along that he was innocent. He had thanked Wayne, and said as he was going out the door, "I am going to buy myself a cold beer, and the hell with all of you."

He recalled how happy he was for Randy to be released from jail. He had known Randy was not the killer earlier into the investigation. Officer Cramer had done a masterful job of setting up Randy. Wayne needed to try to figure out who the real killer's identity was, and he used Randy as a decoy.

He remembered meeting with Brian Foster's parents and telling them the killer had been discovered, and that the killer committed suicide when he was faced with being arrested. This seemed to help the parents feel a little better, knowing justice had been served. Wayne had further explained that Brian must have either seen Cramer pick up Randy from the bar or drop Randy off at Liberty Street while Randy was unconscious. Brian, at the time, had not connected the highway patrolman to the murder of the young lady. The death of Brian, who was the Fosters' only child, was devastating to the parents, the extended family, and the community. The church family, led by Matt Donahue, worked with the parents to assist with coping and moving toward a recovery resolution. The recovery period would take years. Most of all, Wayne was thinking about how he never had the opportunity to thank the angel who saved his life, Vicky Donohue.

Wayne snapped out of his daydreaming when he noticed three men approaching his desk. One man he recognized as his new boss, John Hayes, with the TBI. John had been with the TBI for close to twenty-three years. He had been a manager for almost seventeen years. He started in Knoxville, Tennessee, as a patrolman, where he was promoted to a detective for approximately two years prior to signing on with the TBI. John was overqualified for the job. He was the only employee of the TBI that had passed the bar exam after graduating from the Memphis State Law School. The TBI was his life, and he was proud to have been a TBI agent. He expected everyone else to be in love with the job and follow the orders. The other two men Wayne had never seen prior, but Wayne could tell by the way they were dressed and by their demeanor that they were most likely federal agents. One man was a tall, thin black man with wire rimmed glasses, sharply dressed; the other was short and stocky with medium-length hair parted in the middle. Both men appeared to be in their fifties, wearing suits and ties. John introduced special agents with the FBI Tracey Vaughn and Roger Henagar, both from the Atlanta Office. Tracey was the fit but slimly built black man who looked similar to O.J. Simpson. Roger was a middle-aged white guy with hair parted in the middle, about 5'9" in height. Tracey immediately walked up, as Wayne was standing with his hand out, and congratulated Wayne on his excellent police work dealing with the rogue highway patrolman. Wayne said, "Thanks," and shook Tracey's hand and then shook Roger's hand. Roger then asked if they could have a private word with him. Wayne said, "Certainly," as John led the group to the conference room. The four men walked into the conference room, and John closed the door. There was a large table with twenty chairs in the conference room, and Roger elected to remain standing in the corner leaning against the wall while the other three took a seat. Once they sat down, Tracey explained that the young lady killed at the water tower in Butler was Special Agent Kelly Stephenson. "Kelly had just graduated top of her class from the FBI training school in Quantico a few weeks prior and had volunteered for this assignment in Butler. We set her up with a cover at the Butler newspaper as a reporter, but this was not going to be a dangerous undercover operation for her. It was designed to be a safe assignment without any perils. The newspaper would give her certain freedom to move around. Her assignment was to observe and report back to her handler. The handler did not hear from her on the first check-in scheduled that day, and she missed the second twelve-hour call to check-in with the handler. Missing one sometimes is not that concerning, but two gets the wheels in motion to double-check on the field officer. The next thing we knew, your office was reporting a murder at a water tower of an unknown young female."

Wayne had been listening with anger, raging with every word. He glanced over at Roger, standing in the corner, who was staring at him. Wayne leaned forward and in a very furious voice said, "You were running an undercover operation in my county and did not tell me. If you had told me, an eighteen-year-old man would not have been killed."

Roger irately said, "Wait a minute, Wayne. We had just lost a twenty-three-year-old FBI agent who had just been on the job for a few weeks. We had to tell her parents how she died. We had to tell the boyfriend she was engaged to marry that his unborn baby was killed. You saw what he did to her. We tried to talk the grieving parents out of viewing the body. The mother passed out in the morgue after the sheet was pulled back for viewing. Do you have any idea what that was like? We wanted blood."

Wayne said, "So you came into Butler and took her body in the middle of the night and did not mention it to anyone. What kind of bullshit is this?"

Roger said, "The parents had the right to have her body, but we did not want anyone to know about our ongoing investigation. Leaving the body in the hospital in Butler was not an option. We were going to tell you as soon as our investigation would allow us."

Wayne hit the tabletop with his fist and look directly at the agent sitting across from him. He said, "That is bullshit. What gives you that right? Why not be transparent now about what in the hell is going on?"

There was a pause. The two FBI agents were hoping John would step in and calm Wayne down by taking their side. John just sat in his seat and stared directly ahead.

Wayne's face was red with anger, and he asked, "What were you investigating, and don't give me the bullshit that you can't tell us?"

Roger said, "Missing girls."

Wayne looked at John, and John seemed very surprised with this revelation and asked, "What missing girls? We don't have any missing girls in Butler, Nashville, or anywhere in Tennessee."

Roger said, "The girls are not American citizens, or at least that is the way it appears. We suspect they are being brought into this country through the Gulf of Mexico from places like South Korea, North Korea, Vietnam, Cambodia, and other Asian counties. This is part of the human trafficking and sex slave problem going on all over the world. The people that are the masterminds behind this have gone unnoticed for decades. They are very smart, and we do not know a great deal about this since it is mostly outside our borders. They know no one would ever consider looking within the United States for these missing kids from the third world countries. There is no record of them ever being kidnapped. We believe they are being raped multiple times before they are being disposed of permanently. They are being purchased on the dark web in a very sophisticated, covert system. The president has been asked by the third world countries to assist with the human trafficking problems around the world. All the NATO members are being asked to consider a worldwide movement to solve the human trafficking problems. This issue is a lot larger than any one nation. This issue is being moved up on the list with NATO. The president is considering the direction our country should take, and it is under review to ascertain how our country can best assist with this global problem. Most of these countries do not have records and have no way of knowing how many people are being sold into slavery. If a family member leaves for a job in another country, the family may never hear from them. Sometimes parents are selling their kids in hopes they will have a better life. The kids are never heard from again, and there are no records of any of this. The reports are staggering; estimating over twenty thousand a year are missing, and a large number are kids. They are not showing up later in other foreign countries; it is like they are just disappearing in thin air."

Tracey looked at John and then Wayne, "But, we know for certain we have located two dead Asian girls, one in the Tennessee River east of Nashville and one south of Nashville in a shallow grave, in the past year. We were lucky to have found the bodies. Their ages were ten to thirteen years old, and the remains were in bad shape. They were missing some fingers, which indicated possible torture. The bone structure and tests suggested malnutrition, which would suggest not American citizens but kidnapped kids from third world countries. There had been nothing related to anyone in Butler County. We were just checking out a lead which we did not feel had a strong possibility. We had not considered Cramer being involved until he turned up dead. We started looking into him and discovered Bill Cramer died in 1990 in Iraq. We do not know who committed suicide at the water tower."

Roger looked at Wayne and asked, "Is there anything Cramer said to you that could help us with our case?"

Wayne started to calm down, and said, "No. Once I had him cornered, he was trying to find out if I was aware of any additional witnesses to the killing of your agent. I had explained we were aware of the listening equipment he placed in my office, and my deputies were headed that way. We had him boxed in. I guess he wanted to know if I had ever talked to her, and with whom else she might have discussed the facts of her investigation. I guess he assumed she was working for the paper as a reporter and never considered her being an agent for the FBI. He did say he wanted to torture her for information. She hit her head and was knocked out. He had indicated she might not have been able to remember anything due to a possible concussion in the short term when she awoke. He was pushed for time, and he killed her. He must not have had extra time for her to come to because he killed her before he got started with torturing her. He indicated prison was not a place he would ever consider, and he then pulled his gun and ate a bullet. He confessed to three murders, your agent, the eighteen-year-old, and an old army buddy that recognized him from Iraq. He mentioned right before he shot himself, "What were the chances of running into someone in Butler, Tennessee, who knew him?" All this information is in my report. I have nothing else to add. I do have a couple of questions. Did you locate the agent's car and computer?"

Roger said, "Computer. Her work computer was at her office."

"I am talking about her Apple computer."

"How do you know she had another computer?"

"When my deputies searched her apartment, there was a charger for an Apple computer lying under the couch."

Tracey said, "No. It may have been in her stolen car."

Wayne asked, "What happened with the investigation into the bullet I discovered in the water tower? I understand it was an experimental type of technology and had not been approved for consumer use."

Roger looked at Wayne and said, "The bullet was turned over to the ATF, and they have not reported their findings back to us."

Wayne said, "You indicated the man was not Bill Cramer. Who is he? You are the freaking FBI. If you do not know who an American that has served in our military is, who would?"

"We are checking into his identity. We are not allowed to discuss that with you."

With that statement, they all stood and said goodbye. They did not offer to shake hands. The FBI agents could feel the ill contempt from the two TBI officers. As the two FBI men were walking out the front door of the TBI office, Wayne said to John, "They are only telling us about forty percent of what they know."

John said, "It is more like ten percent, and no, they are not ever transparent about a case like this. The only time they mention the facts of pending cases like this is if they need our assistance." The two men stood and watched the door close behind them.

John then added, "The FBI has been beneficial with assisting in the investigation of chop shops, online bank fraud and other types of multi-state cases. They have their job to do, and we have our job to do. I certainly hope they catch the people responsible for human trafficking. I am certain we will start hearing more details about the human trafficking problem once the folks in the White House announce their plans. Did you hear when those agents introduced themselves? They indicated they were out of the Atlanta office. My liaison with the FBI is located in Nashville, and his name is Seth Burns. Those two men might be with a specialized investigative unit and not the average agent. There might be a lot more going on."

***

Tracey looked at Roger as they were walking in the garage to get into their car for the drive back to Atlanta, and asked, "What do you think?"

Roger said, "This all is shit. I believe Wayne, the sheriff. He is very frustrated with us for not telling him what is going on. Beyond that, I did not pick up on anything he is holding back. I suspect if we had been in his old sheriff office and not standing in front of his new boss, he would have cussed us like you have never heard. He was genuinely mad. He was not faking his anger, and I believe our boss is holding a substantial amount of information back from us. I have never worked a case where I just did not trust my boss. I believe Delores already knows who Bill Cramer is. I figured in our meeting she would have told us. I am glad we did not tell her or report we know Bill Cramer is not Bill Cramer. We gave her a chance to tell us, and she did not. I know she has to be holding back significant details about the case." He smiled and looked at his partner, "Hell, I do not know if I can trust you."

Tracey looked over at Roger and said, "That is also my thoughts. We should be able to identify who Bill Cramer really is, and we should be able to interview the manufacturer of that bullet, or at least see the copy of the interview. The TBI lab noted in their report the bullet was made of chromium, the third hardest metal on the planet. Someone in our government knows something and is intentionally keeping us in the dark. I believe Delores has that information and is not allowing us access. Something is going on, and we may have to ask Dolores to be forthcoming with her agenda. I was also wondering about one thing when listening to Wayne about all that information that Cramer provided before he shot himself. They must have talked for five to ten minutes before the suicide. To spend that much time with someone you caught and had boxed in, and to talk for that length of time, just does not seem plausible. But the former sheriff seemed to be telling the truth."

Roger said, "You can leave me out of that meeting with Delores. She will chew us up and spit us out if we question her. Have you read her Bio describing where she has worked and what she has accomplished? She did not make regional manager because she was a pretty black lady. The upper level of management has seen her skill set and have fast tracked her up the management ladder. She has done the job. If we question her or go over her head, we will find ourselves unemployed or stationed in the wastelands of North Dakota. Besides, all we have is the former sheriff's statement. We cannot refute it, but you are correct; that is a lengthy conversation to have with someone prior to them shooting themselves."

Tracey smiled, and said, "Hell no. I would be the only brother in the state of North Dakota. Do you really think she would reassign us to the wastelands of North Dakota?"

Roger said, "You know what I mean." He then looked at Tracey and said, "I do not see the wife and kids leaving Atlanta to live in North Dakota next to you." Both men laughed, and Tracey said, "Let's see what happens next."

Tracey said, "Cramer killed our agent. The question is why? The murder of our agent is nothing similar to the Asian girls. I would have liked to ask Wayne about the notes we received with the location of the girls. What did the killer mean when he said, 'I saw the captured prey?' There has to be more to the phrase than what we told our boss."

Roger said, "I agree. I don't think the death of our agent is related to the Asian girls. Wayne's report reflected that they could not locate most of agent Stephenson's notes, and they had no clue what she was working on. Her boss at the paper was of no help, but he indicated that she was working late and doing research into the history of Butler County. I have looked at every possible meaning of that saying. My best guess is the face value of what is being said. He saw the prey. He trapped the prey. He then killed the prey."

Tracey asked, "You don't really believe she had been working undercover for two or three weeks and was killed for discovering something unrelated to the Asian girls' murders?"

"I am not certain what to believe. Her assignment was to scout out the point we felt the next body was going to be placed and make certain the cameras were not discovered. There is something going on that we can't see, just beyond the horizon, and I feel it is right in front of us." He looked over at his partner, "Someone is playing with us with the notes they sent, but I feel there is something else we just can't see or touch. It is like an intangible object. It is right in front of us. The way the new regional manager is acting tells me something is up."

"You are the brains on our team. You need to figure this out. I am just here for the single, good-looking women."

Both men laughed.

***

Wayne told John he needed to talk to someone in Butler and was getting ready to leave. John said, "Okay. Come Monday, you will be getting your first assignment."

"That sounds good. I was starting to get bored."

John said, "I will see you Monday and, Wayne, do not let the FBI and their procedures get under your skin. Believe it or not, we are all in this together."

Wayne drove to the shooting range and saw Vicky's Nissan Maxima sitting in the front parking lot. He entered the door to the shooting range and saw Mark at the front desk. The two men had ridden horses together and dove hunted with each other for the past seven years and had become close friends. Mark had always helped Wayne with his campaign for sheriff by installing signs around town asking people to vote for Sheriff Tipton. Mark had also talked Wayne into joining his church, Middlebrook United Methodist Church, about eight years ago. Mark was a retired army sergeant who purchased the indoor shooting range more as a hobby than a career choice. He always liked to provide pointers on shooting all types of guns, and he was a regular church member at Middlebrook United Methodist Church. Several church members would practice shooting on a regular basis. The church members would compete in tournaments at the shooting range, which was a fun way to fellowship together. During the fall, they would have a turkey shoot in the back area to raise money for the youth trips. Mark was always helping the church with projects. He was sixty-two years old, about 5'11 with very little hair, stocky built, and always chewing on a cigar except when he was in church. Mark also trained and provided the necessary instructions for citizens to obtain the gun carry permits in Tennessee.

Wayne, without saying hi, said, "I noticed Mrs. Donohue's car in the lot," as he came through the door. Mark smiled and shook his head, pulled his cigar out of his mouth, and replied, "Hi, Wayne. It is good to see you, too."

Mark kept the smile and said, "Vicky obtained her permit a few weeks prior, with excellent shooting. She shoots weekly, and yes, she is shooting in lane four. I showed her how to shoot two pistols at the same time. She borrowed the 9mm Beretta, and she did very well. I hooked up the mobile target and had it traveling at high speed across the back of the shooting range, and with the 9mm, she shot lights out. At fifty feet, even I was impressed. She is a natural with a pistol. Hell, she is better than I am. I tried to convince her to enter some shooting tournaments in Nashville. I sell her the bullets at a discount, which I load on my own. Now that you are with the TBI and updated on all the high-tech bullets, I guess you know the metal casing is the only part of the bullet that can be traced by law enforcement to the manufacturer, and I keep reusing the casing to reload."

Wayne smiled at the information, not knowing if that was true or not. He said, "I need to start shooting more often. I seem to have more free time with the new job. I might start coming to shoot once a week. I hate to go into the state shooting range in Nashville and be the worst shot in the place. I will buy half a box of your reloaded shells and shoot a few rounds." He gave Mark the twenty dollars for the fee, and he then walked through the range door, placing his ear protection device on. He found an open lane and took a position beside Vicky, who was standing and target practicing. He started to shoot one at a time. She looked over and saw him, and she stopped shooting.

She asked in a loud voice, "How is your toe?"

Then she added, "I still have not seen you at church."

Wayne said, "The toe is going to be good as new as soon as the nail grows back. Thanks for asking." Wayne still did not like to think about the violence of having his nail ripped off with pliers. He would never admit that he still had nightmares about the episode, waking in the middle of the night, yelling, and covered with sweat. He also wanted to hide the fact that the toe had gotten infected, was an eye sore to see, hurt when he walked, and taking additional time to heal.

He intentionally did not mention church. They both loaded their guns. Wayne was shooting a 9 mm Beretta, and Vicky was shooting a .32 Smith and Wesson with a medium barrel. They attached the new targets, both holding down the lever that hauls the target down the range. Both kept looking at each other without taking their hands off their levers. Vicky grinned and raised one eyebrow. Finally, Wayne released his lever, and then Vicky hesitated a couple of seconds and did the same. They both turned, squared their bodies, and started shooting at their targets. Once the guns were emptied, they both pulled the switches to bring their targets to them. Wayne's arrived first, and he was pleased with his target. He felt relieved that the target looked as good as it did, with all the sixteen bullets being accounted for (with sixteen holes). He secretly wanted to impress Vicky. He smiled and said, "Sixteen shots and sixteen holes. Look at it and weep."

He had remembered Mark saying she shot regularly. He also figured he was joking about her being better than himself, and she should enter tournaments. He figured she might be average. He looked over at Vicky's target and his smile disappeared. He was surprised to see how much better Vicky was at shooting than he was. He had hit his target, with the holes randomly being spread out all over the target, but Vicky had placed all her bullets in a tight group inside of each other, right in the nose of the target. The holes were so tightly fit together, one could not ascertain if she had shot four bullets or nine. From fifty feet that was considered excellent, according to Wayne as he reviewed her target. She smiled, while he compared the targets. He felt very humbled and dropped the targets in the trash. He then said "Your target looks okay. I tried to spread my bullets out all over my target." She smiled. He then asked her to step out the back door to the side where the rifle range was located; he wanted to talk to her.

Once the door shut behind them, and they removed the earmuffs, Wayne turned and looked Vicky in the eyes. He told Vicky how much he greatly appreciated her saving his life. He said, "I was about to die a very painful death at the hands of a mentally ill, psychotic, sadist killer. Thank you for being there for me. I owe you my life."

Vicky said, "You are welcome. Just remember I was never there."

Wayne smiled, looked questionable at Vicky, and said, "The preacher's wife was the last person I thought would save my life by shooting Cramer. You seemed to have appeared from thin air. By the way, why were you there?"

Vicky considered telling him the truth, about placing the GPS tracking device on both his vehicle and Cramer's vehicle, and setting the alarm on her I-phone to buzz when the two vehicles were within fifty feet of each other. She would then also have to explain that she did not trust him, and this could lead him to be very suspicious about whether she was the one at the tower the night of the murder with Brian Foster, and that was something she would take to the grave with her. Vicky loved her husband, and she knew if that ever got out, it would destroy his career. Instead, she said, "I was considering taking the youth group from church to the water tower as a field trip on Wednesday night to look at the stars. We try to take them to different places and meet at each other's homes when we can. They seem to like field trips. I heard the kids talking about the water tower. I think Holly indicated she had been on top of it when she was fourteen years old. I was checking it out while Matt was in a meeting at your church." She looked him in the eyes when she had said your church. "The hill leading to the water tower is a very challenging jog, and I needed some exercise. I get tired of jogging around the subdivision all the time."

Wayne thanked her again and said, "You still have my card with my cell phone number. If you ever need anything, please call. I owe you my life."

Vicky said, "I have you loaded as a contact on speed dial on my cell phone. Don't worry, I will call if I need anything."

Then Wayne said, "One more thing. The FBI had identified the young lady at the water tower. She was an undercover agent who had just graduated from the FBI academy a few weeks prior to working in Butler. She had been working for approximately two weeks undercover, with no prior experience working undercover, and her handler did not check up on her after she missed the first twelve hour scheduled call. The two FBI agents that came to meet with me at the TBI office indicated they have an ongoing investigation and are trying to locate missing Asians girls being brought into this country, raped, and then killed. They had located two bodies with some missing fingers in middle Tennessee, near Nashville. The bodies had been in two different locations and had been dead for several months. They are part of the world-wide human trafficking problem. They were not American citizens, so there is no record and no released information to the news media. So far, the FBI has been able to keep this out of the media. They asked me not to repeat the homicide information. My boss felt they most likely do not want the killer to know they have discovered the bodies. They are not very forthcoming with an ongoing investigation. They did not mention why the undercover agent was in Butler, but we assume it had to do with a possible placement of an additional body. The two agents arrived in my office unannounced and left very quickly. They did not leave a call back number nor did they volunteer one, and they provided very little information about what they knew. My boss, John, felt they were part of a special task force out of Atlanta. He knows the local FBI agents. He did not know these two men. They were not asking for help into the investigation of the girls; they were trying to find out what I knew about Officer Cramer."

Vicky said, "That sounds weird. Are there any suspects?"

"No suspects. The lady agent did not report to her handler what she might have discovered before being killed. Cramer, before he killed her, wanted to know who she was working with and what she had discovered. He wanted to know who else might know whatever it was she had discovered. He told me, while he was torturing me, that he had to kill her prior to torturing her for the information."

Vicky felt repulsed at the thought of what she had witnessed, and she did not think she could have watched the lady being tortured. "Does the FBI believe Cramer was involved in killing the girls?"

Wayne said, "They did not say for certain. They did not comment about whether or not they felt Cramer was the killer, but they said they are now looking into him. This whole thing is very unorthodox. The entire actions of the FBI and this investigation are not normal. I am not certain why I was never informed of their investigation, being that I was the sheriff in Butler. Also, why was my new boss at the TBI never updated? The normal procedure is to keep the local law enforcement in the know concerning pending investigations, if for no other reason, so we don't run into conflicts with ongoing investigations or even accidently arrest their undercover agents and ruin their case. I could understand if they were investigating me or someone in my office, but they weren't. They drove all the way from

Atlanta to ask me in person about Cramer and nothing else. They have access to my report. It just does not make sense."

Wayne looked perplexed and shook his head, while looking down, and said, "The FBI only shares the information they want to share. They are never transparent with an ongoing investigation. The problem with the FBI is they look for informants or spies. They are not willing to have their agents crawl around in the gutters with these types of people, and that is what must be done to capture the really bad scum. In order to be successful, an officer must build a rapport with the scum in order to arrest other scum. The FBI listens in on phone calls and scans the internet, but the FBI agents will not do the dirty work in the gutters of our society to catch these people. My guess is they will find out that Cramer was killing the Asian girls. Why else would he have killed the agent? There is nothing else going on in Butler County to warrant an FBI undercover investigation."

Vicky could tell Wayne was frustrated with the FBI agents. They both said goodbye, and Vicky went back to finish shooting her last few shots before leaving to go home and meet her husband, Matt, for date night. She thought about what would make someone do these things. She thought she would do some research into the mentally ill, psycho-type killers. The internet had to be full of information about them. She smiled to herself when she thought about how much better her target looked compared to Wayne's target, and he was shooting a gun with a better range that was proven to be an overall better pistol.

She was going to ask Matt to buy her a Beretta 9mm for her birthday. She really like the one she borrowed from Mark.

Matt called Vicky as she entered their home and said he would be home in about twenty minutes, and that they could go out to eat and maybe catch one of the new movies. She told Matt, "That sounds great! I am going to take a quick shower and be ready." She washed off fast and started getting dressed. She ran into the laundry room, retrieved her stockings, and laid them over the kitchen chair. She then ran back into the bedroom and put on her pink bra and matching panties, as Matt walked through the door. Matt was always in a hurry to eat dinner and liked to beat the crowds. Matt had just walked into the family room, which opened into the kitchen, when Vicky asked, "Do you see my stockings? I can't find them anywhere." Vicky walked through the hallway into the kitchen, carrying her white dress and high heels. Matt said, "Here they are, on the kitchen chair."

Vicky took a seat in the chair, and slowly placed on and fastened the top of the white stockings one snap at a time, with Matt watching. She made certain Matt could see every inch of her legs, her polished pedicure, and her manicured nails with matching polish. She remembered this was one of the colors Matt had purchased for her when they had become roommates and lovers. After she pulled her dress over her head, Matt said, "I am so blessed to have you as my wife."

While driving to the restaurant, Matt mentioned he thought he would apply to the University of Tennessee, the University of

Alabama, and a couple other schools in order to obtain a master's degree in physics.

Vicky looked at him, wondered if he was considering changing careers, and said, "I thought you liked being a preacher?"

Matt said, "Physics would be a hobby. I am not considering changing careers. I love my job and these people. I have always enjoyed science, and I can take the classes remotely, all online. I might not ever even have to visit the school. I will know if I have been accepted in the next thirty days."

Vicky said, "That sounds very interesting, and I think that is a great hobby. I wish I were smart enough to understand physics."

After dining out at the upscale steak house in Nashville, they decided against seeing a movie. They returned home, where Matt told Vicky he was going to take a Viagra. He led her to the bedroom and slowly unzipped her dress. He set some baby oil by the bed on the nightstand. Vicky acted like this was the first time, and Matt pulled back the covers. Vicky laid down, placing her hands above her head near each of the bedposts. Matt took off her high heels and started unhooking the stocking on her left leg. Once removed, he used the stocking to tie her left hand to the left bedpost. He removed the stocking from her right leg and told Vicky that this was why men liked stockings so much; they can be used in bondage. Vicky smiled and her body started rotating, with her foot rubbing back and forth on the mattress, getting into the bondage as she moaned, "I surrender." After the prolonged lovemaking, both were so happy and so much in love with each other. They both agreed to make certain to be free next Friday for date night. Matt knew he had quenched Vicky's sexual needs. Matt had always explained to couples in marriage counseling sessions, sponsored through the church, the importance of setting aside special time for each other, and this was theirs. Matt had focused to make the time special for Vicky. He knew about her past and her desires.

Chapter 4

Saturday afternoon at about 4:30 p.m., Vicky was driving home from Nashville, where she went shopping, and noticed Frank Vitola in a red truck crossing the street in front of her and turning into the Wet Spoon Bar. She remembered how upset he was when she met him at the church for marriage counseling a few weeks prior, and he was in a different truck with a camper on it when he entered the church parking lot. Matt had asked her to sit in for him because he was at the Foster's home, meeting with the family after Brian Foster's death. During the meeting, Frank had talked about stoning his wife, and he had quoted scripture out of the old testament about how an adulteress wife should be stoned. He finally agreed to try to forgive his wife, but Vicky did not buy the act. She reached up and rubbed her cross around her neck. She had not thought much more about Frank, but now seeing him brought back the negative vibes. She remembered how she had trouble sleeping that particular night after her meeting and told her husband the next morning that Frank might be a killer. She could not put her finger on what bothered her about Frank other than Frank possessed a possibly hidden, evil personality, with maybe even some depression. She remembered how he kept balling up his fist in anger like he wanted to hit someone, and she had told Matt that Frank just did not appear normal. He seemed to be full of hatred and was manipulative and very cunning. She was very concerned about his wife, and what he might do. It was almost like he had already decided what he was going to do, and he needed an alibi with a character witness. She remembered asking him if they had kids, and he had said no. Vicky recalled how thankful she was that no kids were involved. She thought he just seemed to have an angry and violent temperament, but it was the cunning part of his personality that scared Vicky. She knew something was not right, with him seeking help from the church. She thought, during the meeting with him, that he really needed to be treated by an expert, like a psychiatrist. He did not attend church and had not in years. She thought, he could be very violent, and his end game may be to kill his wife and her boyfriend. That was her gut feeling. He came across as someone who would kill and have an airtight alibi and not get convicted. He seemed sly, cunning, and the type of person who would strike when one's guard was down, not using a frontal assault. He was going to use the church meeting as proof that he was trying to work things out with his wife, and he would need an alibi out of town. He had figured no one at the bar would know who he was, and he was just building up courage by adding alcohol to his plan and waiting for the time to pass.

Frank, during the meeting, had shown Vicky the tracking device he had used, and downloaded the app on the iPhone for Vicky. He had used the tracking device to keep track of his wife, while he was out of town driving his truck, hauling cargo across the country. He placed the tracking device on his wife's vehicle, under the frame, without her knowledge. He would stay gone for ten days at a time, working as a long-distance truck driver. Vicky was surprised at the revelation and said to herself, "That's it! He needed to get rid of the tracking device, which, by doing so, provided him with an alibi." The manager at the Verizon Store had explained to her that the tracker had a reverse history and would note the location in the area of the country where the iPhone was located. The iPhone could always note time and place. Vicky speculated he had left his iPhone located out of town in an out-of-state location, and the tracer he gave Vicky provided him with an alibi. She would be his witness. That is why he was upset that Matt was not at the meeting, because what better witness than a preacher.

Vicky pulled off the side of the road, sliding in the gravel on the shoulder while looking in her rearview mirror for traffic coming up from behind her, and repeated the logic to herself, thinking, "That is why he gave me the tracer." She decided she would give it back to him by turning around, sneaking up, and placing it under the frame of the truck he was driving while it was parked at the bar.

She turned around, drove back to the bar, and entered the parking lot very slowly, where there were ten vehicles. She made certain no one was watching or in the parking lot. She walked behind the truck and placed the tracking device on the metal frame, toward the rear near the tow package. She quickly got back in her car and pulled out, making certain her iPhone was now tracking the tracer.

She remembered how to set the alarm to go off on her iPhone when the tracking device got within fifty feet of either the entered address or another tracking device. She remembered the address was 205 Elm

Street, where Frank had said the boyfriend lived. She entered the information into the iPhone and set the alarm with the address. She had driven by the home a few times over the past couple of weeks and had seen Frank's wife's car parked in the driveway and figured Frank's wife might not be aware that Frank knows about her affair. Vicky drove home, where Matt was watching television. He told Vicky he was going to review his notes for the Sunday morning sermon. Vicky began to wonder, over the next couple of hours, if maybe she was over-thinking the situation, and perhaps he was not going to kill his wife. She tried to downplay what she had done and thought to herself that she must be becoming paranoid. She laughed to herself and thought that maybe she was the one who needed the psychiatrist.

At about 8 p.m., Vicky's alarm went off. Her phone was set on vibrate in her pocket. She told Matt she was going to the store for some coffee and breakfast items while Matt was preparing for the church sermon in the morning. Vicky knew Matt was always looking things up on the internet to use in his sermons and reviewing the bible to quote certain scripture. He always wanted to present the sermons with current information and refer to the bible to support Christianity, where other preachers used the same sermons over and over from years past. Elm Street was only a quarter of a mile from her home. Vicky drove fast at first, then slowed as she approached the address. In the distance, she could see the truck once she had turned on Elm Street. This was the old section of Butler, with small homes which lined both sides of the street. She pulled over to where she could see Frank's red truck behind another vehicle on Elm Street. She could see Frank's silhouette sitting in the driver seat. He appeared to be staking out the home. She lifted her iPhone and called Wayne, who answered on the second ring. Vicky said, "Sheriff, I need some back-up at 205 Elm Street. I have followed Frank Vitola to this home where his wife might be inside with her boyfriend, and Frank is sitting outside in a red truck. He appears to be staking out the home."

Wayne knew a lot of people still called him Sheriff. He figured that was going to be a nickname in Butler. He did not hesitate and said, "Vicky, I will be right over, and I will pull in behind you. Who is Frank Vitola?"

"I will tell you when you get here."

"You need to stay in your car. Do not get out of your car if he gets out."

"You better hurry."

About four minutes later, Wayne pulled in behind Vicky's black Nissan with his headlights off and walked up and slid into her passenger seat. Vicky said, "Do you remember the marriage counsel meeting I had scheduled when you came to my home? Well, this is it. Frank has been drinking for at least four hours. I passed him when I was coming back from Nashville, and he had turned into the Wet Spoon Bar." Vicky did not want to mention the tracer and iPhone. She never wanted Wayne to know or suspect she had tracked him and Cramer to the tower a few weeks prior, where she had shot Cramer and untied Wayne. She had to live with the death of Brian Foster every day, the young man that was killed by Cramer, and she felt responsible. Her sinful action had led to the untimely murder of an innocent eighteen-year-old man who had his entire life in front of him. Wayne had accepted her excuse, which was plausible, about the possibility of a youth field trip and about her jogging in the area. Vicky had struggled with the heavy burden of her guilt. She felt she did not merit God's grace.

Wayne said, "I will call Vince for backup. If Frank gets out of his truck, I will move to cut him off. You do not get out of the car."

Vicky was listening as Wayne called Vince and said, "Hi, Vince. I am sitting at 205 Elm Street, watching a drunk man who is outside a home in a red truck. The boyfriend and his wife may be in danger inside the home. Yes, that is correct. She and her boyfriend are in the home."

Wayne looked at Vicky and said, "Backup will be here in about ten minutes, maybe sooner. Vince indicated he would call Denny and Darrell for additional backup."

Vince remembered what Wayne had always told him back when he was the sheriff, saying, "The more police officers present, the more likely the suspect will give up, and no one will get hurt." The domestic cases were the most dangerous because emotions were always running high; additionally, they were coupled with thoughts of betrayal, consumption of alcohol, and thoughts of suicide, which could lead to bad decisions. The FBI had posted several articles about the need for the police departments across the county to go in numbers and be careful. The domestic cases, based on statistics, were known to be widowmakers for police officers' wives and their families.

After about seven minutes had passed, the lights in the home were turned off, and suddenly Frank opened the door to his truck and stumbled, getting out of the truck. Wayne told Vicky to stay in the car, and he jumped out to cut Frank off in the road. Wayne walked toward him and, in a very commanding voice, shouted, "Frank, stop and put your hands up. I am a TBI officer."

Frank looked surprised, confused, mad, and drunk. Wayne closed the gap. Vicky remembered how cunning Frank was at the church meeting. She reached up to her neck, and unconsciously started rubbing the cross on her necklace. She said to herself, "Do not get too close. Do not get too close." Wayne kept walking toward Frank, closing the distance to within ten feet. She had an ominous feeling about the situation. Frank glanced around and acted like he was drunk. Vicky could tell he was making certain no one else was in the area, waiting for Wayne to get closer, without his gun pulled. Vicky unsnapped her seat belt, pulled her gun from under her seat, and opened her door.

Wayne kept walking closer and closer, and she could not hear what they were saying. Vicky walked in the shadows of the trees on the sidewalk. It was starting to get dark. There were no streetlights in the area and no moonlight. She kept hoping Wayne would stop approaching Frank. Frank kept acting like he could hardly stand from drinking. All of a sudden, Frank sprang at Wayne, bent over in a bull rush. Wayne tried to step to the side and allow Frank to pass. In doing so, Frank was able to hook his right arm around the left leg of Wayne. Both men fell to the asphalt in the middle of the street. Wayne tried to break loose. Frank had fallen partly on top of Wayne and was reaching for his hands and inching further on top, with the weight difference making it more difficult for Wayne to escape. Wayne reached for his gun. Vicky could not tell where the gun was, as she was approaching from the rear of the two men. They were fighting for control of the gun, and the two men were still rolling on the asphalt, hitting each other with their fists. Frank had partially stood up, bent over, with his legs apart straddling Wayne, who was on his back. Vicky saw the gun slide under the car parked on the side of the street. Vicky took off running down the middle of the street. As she came up behind the men, she had planned to target Frank's knee, but he was bent over, preparing to hit Wayne a second time with his fist. He was holding Wayne by the neck, choking him with his left hand and preparing to hit him in the face with his right fist. Frank had the leverage and had positioned himself to keep hitting Wayne. Wayne tried to cover his face with his left hand and remove the choke hold with his right. He was also kicking up at Frank. Vicky planted her left foot and drove the top part of her right foot into the crotch of Frank Vitola. He moaned with the shock of the pain and raised his head up, as he reached for his groin area. Vicky then hit him full force in the back of the head with the grip of her pistol. He fell like a large sack of grain, face down on top of Wayne. She could see Wayne moving from under the big man. She bent down in Wayne's face as he was worming out from under the limp body, gritted her teeth and said, "What in the hell are you doing? Were you trying to get yourself killed? He came here to kill his wife and her lover. What did you expect?"

Wayne looked up, while pushing out from under Frank, who was out cold. "I had the scene under control."

The sirens were getting closer. Vicky shook her head and said, "I was never here." She turned and ran to her car, started it up and drove off.

Vince arrested Frank for public intoxication and had Denny place him in the back seat of his car, after putting handcuffs on him and searching him. Frank had started to come to, but was very drowsy, rubbing the back of his head. Denny removed a pistol from Frank's waistband. As Wayne walked back to his car, he noticed Vicky had turned around and drove off without anyone else seeing her. Her car was gone before the neighbors and other officers arrived. He was surprised that she was able to turn her car around and leave without at least one of the neighbors noticing her drive off.

Vince told the couple in the house that Frank was being arrested. Frank's wife was very shocked that he was in town and knew she was with another man. She said, "He should have been in Colorado with a delivery." Vince told her she might want to obtain a restraining order, and an attorney to represent her in a divorce. Vince told the wife that her life and the man's life could be in danger. She asked how they knew to watch Frank. Vince said, "We had an anonymous tip. A man in a red truck was sitting in the street and looked very suspicious."

Vince said, "I called the highway patrol. They will send the on-call highway patrolman over to secure the red truck and check it out. They said he would be here in a couple of minutes. They will have it towed to the garage on Main Street. They will let us know if anything turns up."

Denny drove Frank over to the sheriff's office. Frank seemed startled, and said he had a headache. He asked what happened. Denny explained, "You are under arrest for public intoxication, and other charges are pending."

Vince asked Wayne if he needed to go to the hospital. He could tell Wayne had been hit. His shirt was ripped, and his face was red and scratched. He assumed, somehow, Wayne had knocked Frank out. Wayne said he would follow them over to the office. They searched Frank a second time and found another pistol in his boot. Frank, who is about 6'2" tall and weighs 260 pounds, with long hair and a dark beard, walked over and literally fell into the bunk and immediately was asleep, snoring. During the initial search, they located a pistol in his waistband, a .38 special, and Denny had discovered the 2nd pistol hidden in his boot, a small .22 Remington, before leading him to the cell. Wayne said, "That is why you always complete a thorough search. Denny, you did a good job finding the second pistol."

As the four men were talking about old times in the main office, Darrell inputted a search on the guns. Based on the serial number found on the one in his boot, it was stolen during a murder in Bloomington, Indiana, almost twelve years ago. He almost yelled at the guys and said, "Look what I just discovered."

Wayne suggested that while Frank was in jail, they needed to obtain a warrant to search Frank's home. Wayne also suggested that Denny call the police office in Bloomington to obtain a copy of the investigation report to see what else was stolen and verify the facts. Wayne started to recall how Vicky said there was something not right about Frank, and that he seemed to have a very violent nature with a possible mental issue.

Darrell completed the warrant and called Judge Myers to explain they needed a warrant signed, and it was urgent. The Judge said to bring it on over, and he would review it. Darrell drove over to Judge Myers's home to obtain the needed signature on the search warrant. Wayne, Vince, and Denny met Darrell at the home, with the warrant. Denny had gotten Frank's keys when they searched him, and he used the house key to enter the home. Ken had the police report emailed to him on his iPhone. He explained to Vince that it was a double homicide that had not been solved, and that there was a list of items stolen. During the search, Denny was reading over the list of the items that were stolen, and Wayne located in the bedroom a double-barrel Browning shotgun. The shotgun had the matching serial numbers to the list, and Darrell found a diamond ring in the bottom of the chest in the bedroom. Denny said the diamond ring also appeared to be listed on the police report. The initials were engraved "RD" in the band.

Denny said, "They have DNA according to this report. Her name was Renee Snodgrass. We will need to verify what her maiden name was prior to marrying her husband to verify if the initials "RD" are hers. The elderly lady was raped and then killed by being hit over the head with a baseball bat. Her husband was also killed by blunt force trauma. He was also hit on the head in their home."

Vince carefully picked up Frank's toothbrush and hairbrush and placed them in a plastic bag to run the DNA test. Wayne suggested a plan of action on how they should question Frank tomorrow, once he wakes up. Wayne knew the sheriff and deputies had no experience with murder cases. The county was just about crime free. They needed to get him on tape and record him lying as much as they can before they ask him about the shotgun and the ring. The lying would help in court; jurors hate liars. Vince called the police department in Indiana and talked with the on-call captain, explaining what they had discovered. The police captain from Indiana said, "We will be sending a detective to question Frank. We have an unsolved double homicide, and we have had no leads until now. The detective will arrive Sunday at about 11 a.m., since you can hold Frank for twenty-four hours only for public intoxication. The detective will arrive as soon as possible. Please do not mention the guns and ring to him. The lady's maiden name was Renee Dandridge. Her family was very upset and would periodically contact us about possible developments in the case. Let our detective interview him about those items and the double homicide. Thank you very much for contacting us."

Vince said, "We understand. We will hold him until your guy gets here."

Wayne had contacts at the TBI, and the state crime lab would work extra hours a day, seven days a week, if needed. Since they could only hold Frank for twenty-four hours, the test had to be pushed through the crime lab. Wayne was concerned about Frank being a flight risk, since he travels to the mid-west and to the border of Mexico and has crossed into Mexico for work. Wayne was able to drive the hair and toothbrush samples to the lab in Nashville first thing Sunday. He told Vince the DNA test should come back from the lab by Sunday midday.

The next day Vince updated Wayne on the arrest, and the detective from Indiana arrested Frank for the double homicide. "He was going to kill his wife and her boyfriend, although he never confessed."

Wayne thought that was very possible, and then said, "Good police work got him." They both said goodbye.

***

Wayne walked into his office at 8 a.m. Monday morning and his boss, John, noticed him and asked him to come into his office. John always started the workday at 7 a.m. and worked to 6 p.m. if needed. He motioned for Wayne to sit down and asked him what he had been doing over the weekend, and Wayne said, "I was working in the yard and riding my horse."

John asked, "Did you arrest anyone over the weekend?" John then smiled, and before Wayne had a chance to answer said, "The state police in Indiana called my boss to express their appreciation and say thanks for the help with the double homicide case in Indiana. That is how I found out about your weekend activities. You need to keep me in the loop on what you are doing, so when my boss calls me to congratulate me and my employees on good work, I am not sitting in my chair wondering what in the hell he is talking about."

John then congratulated Wayne for solving the double homicide. John said, "I am impressed that you have only been in the new position with the TBI for one week and have already solved a double homicide; that has to be a record. I also called our lab and thanked the techs for rushing the DNA test through on a Sunday. They were glad to hear how their efforts produced the results and the arrest of a man in a double homicide."

Wayne said, "I had help from the sheriff's department in Butler, and everything happened so fast. I will try to update you in the future."

John smiled and said, "Your first official assignment is to work with two federal agents."

"Okay."

John said, "They are ICE officers, and I will introduce you. Come with me. They both have worked in immigration for years and are part of the regional group completing a sweep through Tennessee."

Wayne thought to himself that this is not what he figured he would be doing, but he assumed this was part of the job. The new TBI

60

officers probably get these assignments. John led him to the conference room, where he said, "Wayne, I want you to meet Rex and Stan."

Stan was a sixty-one years old with long gray hair and, at one time, had been in good shape. He now looked like he needed to exercise and work off the middle-age spread above his belt. Rex, on the other hand, was twenty-nine years old, a weightlifter, 5'11, and had a crew cut. Wayne figured he weighed about 230 lbs. He looked like a large stump. He was as wide as he was tall, but not fat. John said, "They can brief you on what they need. I've got another meeting." John smiled, walked out, and said, "Good luck," as he was turning to exit the door.

Stan and Rex both stood up and shook Wayne's hand. Stan looked over at Wayne and said, "This job really sucks and is very political, but unofficially we try to arrest just the single males who can slip back across the border without too much trouble. We must meet a quota and fill out a lot of paperwork."

Wayne thought to himself, this might not be too bad after all. Rex then said, "We need to check out your old area in Butler, starting this coming weekend. Right now, we need to finish up in Nashville. We have been checking out each county in Tennessee. The TBI has been assisting with the county inspections. We started in West Tennessee and moved east across the state. We understand you used to work for the border patrol in Texas?"

"Yes, I did, but that was a lifetime ago. I am certain things have changed since then."

Stan smiled and said, "Not really. We catch some, and they come back across the border to be with their families. We miss some, and they stay put. Same ole same ole. The automation and the procedures have changed, but the people have not."

Wayne said, "You guys just need to let me know how I can assist."

Stan said, "You can ride with us in Nashville, and then we will schedule some site investigations in Butler. Your state has requested a state employee be part of the task force as we cross Tennessee."

Chapter 5

It was the week for Vacation Bible School at Middlebrook United Methodist Church to begin. Several of the members had been meeting and preparing for the week of fun for the kids. Matt and Vicky had worked with the youth who had volunteered to lead some of the classes and play with the kids on the playground. Vicky noticed and met a lovely little Hispanic girl who was eight years old, named Valerie. Vicky watched her play soccer with the older kids and was surprised by her skill set at such a young age. Through the week, Vicky became attached to Valerie and learned that Valerie enjoyed playing soccer and played with one of the other little girls, whose family was a member at the Middlebrook United Methodist Church. Part of the routine was that Vicky always hugged all the kids and met the parents when they came to pick up their kids. She met Valerie's mother and told her, "You have quite the soccer player," as she hugged Valerie. They talked about Valerie's upcoming game on Saturday morning at 8 a.m. Vicky had agreed to come and watch.

After getting out of bed at about 6 a.m., Vicky jogged five miles and took a quick shower. She told Matt she would be going to the soccer game, and Matt indicated he was asked to play golf with three of the church members. Vicky smiled and looked up, trying to conceal her smile, and asked, "So you play golf?"

Matt said, "I am trying, and we will see how this goes. You know my history, and how sports have always come easy for me. One of the guys has an extra set of clubs that I can borrow, so I am certain everything will work out."

Vicky thought she'd better wait to laugh when she got in her car. Vicky arrived at the soccer fields, and she noticed two teams of Spanish men playing on the large field. Vicky had not realized that there were so many Spanish people in this community.

Vicky walked over to the smaller field and started watching Valerie play soccer. She stood back from the sidelines and allowed the parents and grandparents to walk back and forth and yell for the kids. During the second half, Vicky heard some crying and commotion coming from the larger field, which was located behind the small field. Vicky saw Wayne Tipton with two officers. The two officers had jackets on, with ICE noted on the back. They appeared to be asking for the identification cards and driver licenses. They had blocked the entrance gate to the soccer field, with another officer stationed at the gate. The officer had stayed at the gate and was allowing people to enter, but no one was being allowed to leave without showing ID. The parking lot was surrounded with large telephone poles lying on the ground, and once you entered the parking lot, there was only one way to leave. They cuffed four Hispanics, three men and one woman (who was pregnant), for being illegal immigrants, in order to arrest them and transport them to a detention facility in Nashville. Vicky thought to herself, "I can't believe they are doing this in front of the kids and families!" Vicky jogged up to where Wayne was standing and stood within one foot of Wayne, stared into his eyes with a very stern look on her face, and said, "Is this what I think this is? You need to release these four individuals."

There were a lot of upset Hispanics standing nearby, and everyone got quiet and watched Vicky and Wayne. They had been crying and were very upset, and even some of the local Caucasian residents were upset and watching. The audience seemed taken back by Vicky's action and her direct challenge of the authorities.

Vicky was giving Wayne a look that inferred, "You owe me."

Wayne looked uncomfortable, and after a brief pause, he walked over to Stan and Rex and asked them to release the four Hispanic individuals who they were attempting to detain. He said, with his hands out, pleading, "Their ID cards are okay. They have the correct identification. Now that I looked at them a second time, I noticed they are correct."

The officers at first hesitated, but to everyone's surprise, uncuffed the four people and then got in their vehicles and drove off. Stan told Wayne, as they were driving away, that happens a lot, and they end up releasing several people a year after realizing the cards and identification were okay. Rex and Stan then laughed as they headed back to Nashville. There must have been an inside joke. Wayne just sat in the car seat with a stern look on his face. He was somewhat concerned about what the report would say about his actions.

The four Hispanic people were so happy, and their friends and relatives hugged them. The entire soccer game had stopped, and some of the players had walked over to witness what was happening. Vicky started to walk back to the small field and watch the remaining of Valerie's game, when an elderly Hispanic woman walked up and stepped in front of her, cutting her off, and asked, "Who are you?"

"My name is Vicky Donahue."

"No, who are you? Those federal agents changed their minds and tucked their tails between their legs and left. Who are you?"

"I am the minister's wife at the Middlebrook United Methodist Church here in Butler."

The elderly lady, with a sincere look on her face said, "My name is Maria, and I wanted to thank you from the bottom of my heart for helping my people and friends. I know where your church is located; some of my friends cut the grass and work on the landscaping."

"They do a great job. The landscaping is always very pristine."

Vicky looked at Maria and tried to judge her age. She had a very pretty smile, with very few wrinkles. Maria had a very difficult accent to understand, and Vicky had to listen very carefully to every word. Vicky thought to herself that Maria must have been very pretty when she was younger. Her hair was jet black, with very dark brown eyes, and a beautiful smile. She stood about 5'6 with a weight about 140 lbs. At about that time, a flash came running up to Vicky in the form of Valerie. Vicky immediately picked her up, hugged her, and announced, "How pretty this little girl is!" Valerie asked, "Did you see me score?"

Vicky said, "Did you score? I got involved in something over at the adult field and missed you scoring. I guess I will have to come back next week to watch you."

Vicky looked at Maria and said, "This is the prettiest little soccer player that I have ever seen."

Maria said, "I know she is. She is my granddaughter. Her father and three uncles were playing soccer on the larger field. She also has some cousins playing."

Vicky set Valerie down, and she ran over to her parents, who were walking in their direction. "No wonder she is so good with all those family members playing."

Maria said something derogatory about the U.S. President, who she said was trying to deport as many illegal immigrants as could be located and did not care about families. Vicky did not understand everything Maria had said but understood enough. She replied, "Well, that's the policy of the U.S. Government. The government wants to deport the bad people, and some good people are now getting caught up in this mess and are having to be deported. If you see bad people, let the police know. We are all in this together."

Maria thanked Vicky again for helping. Then, several other Hispanic people thanked Vicky and told her they owed a debt to her for standing up for them. Vicky, who spoke Spanish quite well after living in San Diego, answered in Spanish to the people who did not speak English, "You are welcome. De nada." Vicky went to the store and then she was going to hurry home, where she had agreed to meet with some of the girls in church youth and sit out by her pool with them. She wanted to buy sandwiches and drinks at the store and hurry home. The four girls showed up with their towels: Cindy, Holly, Jennifer, and Angela. Vicky asked if anyone else was coming. Jennifer answered, "Nickie wanted to, but she was busy with family. Mary went to Nashville."

Vicky said, "We are going to have the youth meet here one Wednesday before the end of the summer and enjoy the pool."

Holly asked, "Can I bring my boyfriend?" Vicky said, "Certainly, you can. Why has he not been coming to church or youth with you?"

Holly smiled and said, "I am working on it."

Angela said, "I wish I could get Tim Thompson to come to church or youth."

Cindy said, "He is very good looking; is he a sophomore? Do you like him?"

Angela said, "We talk a lot, and we have been to movies together, and yes, he is a sophomore." Then, she added, "He does not go to church. I am not certain he believes in God."

Vicky said with a smile, "Bring him to youth and let Matt have a debate with him."

"Tim is smart and likes science. He says he wants to be a scientist, and they do not believe in God."

Vicky said, "Matt majored in Physics and knows all about science-related classes. He loves to have friendly debates."

Angela said, "I might bring him here to the swim party."

Vicky said, "That sounds good to me."

Cindy asked, "How did you meet Matt?"

Vicky explained, "We met in the doorway to the library where I broke my bracelet, and the beads poured all over the floor. He was coming in the door, and I was running out the exit door. The bracelet broke because the bag I hung around my shoulder with some heavy books slid off my shoulder and broke the bracelet. Matt helped me pick up all the beads and offered to have the bracelet repaired. I took too many difficult classes during my first semester. I was a cheerleader, and I was about to have a nervous breakdown. Matt was a sophomore and had already taken the classes, and he agreed to help. I was a damsel in distress. I discovered he was very funny and very nice. He was not self-absorbed and never has been jealous. He is a very caring person. He is brilliant. He scored a thirty-five on the ACT in his sophomore year of high school, missing a perfect score by one point. We somehow fell in love. You just don't know when you are going to fall in love. It was the last thing I thought would happen, but when it happens, you need to stop everything else going on in your life and focus on the love." Vicky smiled and shook her head, while looking at the girls.

"How old were you the first time you went all the way with a guy?" Vicky smiled and said, "You need to ask your mother those questions.

Your parents love you all very much, and they glow when they talk about you. You all do realize parents live vicariously through their kids. I noticed all of you are wearing two-piece bathing suits. Do you know my father would not allow me to wear a two-piece suit when I was your age? I also could not wear nail polish. He was very strict, but now as I look back, he did it because he loved me and wanted what was best for me. He did not want me to grow up too fast and be faced with making adult-type decisions too early in life."

Vicky realized the girls were looking up to her. Vicky said, "I can give you advice on dating." She noticed the girls really acted like they wanted to hear what she was about to say. Vicky said, "It is not whether you cheat on your significant other, but whether the significant other thinks you cheated. So, do not put them in that position. Show respect and be nice, and don't flirt with other guys. You guys will figure it out; you will want to date nice guys, not mean or not self-absorbed guys, as you get older. Plus, I can also tell you that you guys will become better looking as you get older, and all four of you are very pretty."

The girls all smiled, and Holly said, "Thanks for saying so."

Vicky sat in her lawn chair and was thankful no one had mentioned Brian Foster's death. Just the mention of his name brought back a feeling of guilt. Most of the kids had been able to move forward in their lives. She, on the other hand, had considered her sins unforgivable, and she knew how her heart felt. She wanted a reckoning because of her sins. She blamed herself and her actions for his death. She had seduced Brian because she could not control her urges, and now he was dead. He was a kid who had just turned eighteen, and he would still be alive if it were not for her. She could have told the authorities what she saw and protected Brian. She felt so guilty. She kept thinking back to the apostles, and how most had died painful deaths, knowing they could be tortured, but they still preached Christianity. The apostles were selfless and true believers. As Vicky sat in the chair, she understood what she wanted to do was help these kids in making life choices and help the people who needed help and could not help themselves. She thanked God for providing her the fortitude to pull the trigger to kill Bill Cramer. She actually felt good about the end result, and him dying in the parking lot of the water tower, next to the sheriff. She felt his death was part of her reckoning. As she sat in her chair listening to the girls talk, she figured her soul was lost, and she did not deserve to be forgiven for seducing Brian. He was dead because of her. She hoped her future actions could atone for her sins. She thought about how the articles she had read about how apostle Phillip died while being carved to pieces in front of the town of people, who were present to watch and cheer his killer on because he was trying to teach them how to worship in the name of Christ. He was aware of the dangers, and he went to the city of Hierapolis anyway. She prayed to God to provide her with the same courage and conviction. She also told God while she was praying, she did not believe killing the highway patrolman was a sin, and she hoped God agreed with her reckoning.

* * *

Later that afternoon, around 2:30, all the girls started getting their towels together and told Vicky thanks for the food and for allowing them to sit by the pool, as they left to head home. Matt came home about 2:45. Vicky asked him how the golf game went, and Matt replied, "I did great; I outscored everyone else with a score of 123 on 18 holes, with nine mulligans. I thought it was funny listening to the three guys talk about cheating and how best to cheat when you play golf. Tyler actually said, 'If you ever hit a ball in a gorge, ask for help to find the ball and then drop a ball out of your pocket near the gorge and let one of the other three golfers find it. Then, say I could have sworn my shot went into the gorge. They won't suspect a thing.' By the way, he is the president of the church council."

Vicky smiled and said, "It sounds like you had fun."

Matt asked, "Do you want to go out on a date with me? I feel good about outscoring all the other guys, and they have been playing for years. We need to celebrate. I believe I have found another hobby. I am a natural player. It came really easy for me."

Vicky started laughing, and then said, "Yes. I will be ready by 5:00."

She understood and knew this was her time with her husband. She pulled out a tight-fitting dress and got somewhat excited because they hadn't been out in two weeks. They both had been working so much in their church and Vacation Bible School. They had missed their Friday night date night. They agreed to go to a Mexican restaurant on Main Street that Matt had been wanting to go to since they had moved to Butler. He loved Mexican food and had really missed it since moving from San Diego, where he ate Mexican food three to four times a week.

Once they walked into the restaurant, which was over half full, Vicky and Matt noticed that there was a lot of whispering between the hostess and waitress. The hostess was extremely nice to them. All the employees smiled at them. The waitress came up to their table and gave them a very warm greeting. She then told them their meal was on the house. Vicky recognized one of the cooks from the soccer field, and she thought the other waitress was also at the field that morning when the ICE officers and Wayne Tipton were making an arrest. She was very much aware of why the food was on the house, but she wanted to let Matt believe it was his status in the community. She had not mentioned to Matt what occurred at the soccer field.

Matt thought that someone at church had told the manager to put Vicky's and his meal on the church member's tab. Matt started looking around to see who he might recognize. Matt said, "I do not recognize anyone and do not recall any Spanish folks coming to the church." He looked at Vicky and asked again, "Do you?" Vicky was excited to be out on a date with her husband. She looked at Matt and thought of all the wonderful times they'd had together. She smiled and removed her high heel shoe off her left foot under the table and placed her foot in the center of his lap. Matt felt her foot, but just as he turned to smile at Vicky, the manager walked up. He warmly greeted and welcomed them and repeated that their dinner was of no charge to them.

Matt said, in a joking expression, "I am a big eater and might order some expensive food and wine," as he looked around again to see who from the church was paying for the meal. The manager assured Matt that was okay. Vicky smiled and said, "Thank you."

Matt then felt Vicky's other foot slide up in his lap.

As the manager was leaving, he said, "Let us know if you need anything, and your meal is on the house." The waitress returned to take their order.

Vicky asked, "May I have enchiladas?" Matt ordered the beef fajitas.

Once the food was promptly brought to the table, Matt and Vicky dug into the food. Matt said, "This was very delicious, and I love this meal. I am surprised at how good the food tastes." Matt looked at Vicky, feeling her foot move slowly in his lap, and smiled, "Is this going to be a Viagra night?"

Vicky smiled a seductive smile, "Honey, it might be a two Viagra night. I love you very much."

His smile grew bigger.

* * *

Sunday morning, the church service went fine. There was nothing unusual that happened. Sunday school class was nice and fun-loving. Vicky attended the adult class, and Matt went to his office, worked on the Sunday night sermon, and reviewed his upcoming sermon, which was scheduled after the Sunday school class. They both agreed to go home to eat lunch; normal was great for a Sunday after all they had been through with the death of Brian Foster and then the busy week of vacation bible school. Vicky said, "I might sit next to the pool and take a nap."

Matt said, "I might take a nap in the bed. I am still tired from last night. You were a real tiger last night," as he smiled at Vicky.

Steve D. Nichols

Chapter 6

Roger Henagar read the note, and his anger spiked. He thought, "Dammit, we need a break." The FBI crime lab had already checked it for prints, and the note and envelope were clean and had no prints or DNA. Roger thought, "What can I do to create a break on this case?" Tracey Vaughn, his partner, looked up the longitude and latitude location. Tracey said, "You are not going to believe the location of number five."

Roger looked up from the note. Tracey said, "The location is in a graveyard at a church on Locust Street in Butler, Tennessee. We were right. We knew the next buried body was going to be in Butler, Tennessee. I just have no clue where number six, the next one, will be. The body is fifty-two miles from the center point in Nashville. I wonder why the change and not sixty miles like the other bodies. Everything has been so exact with the killer. The notes are all the same and the prior body locations have been very precise, even checking the difference between the bodies in the perimeter locations, not just from the center point in Nashville. The unknown subject is very anal and now he has broken his routine. He might be aware we were watching the next projected drop point, but how would he know?"

"I will call the boss. I am going to recommend we send a crew in tonight to recover the body and cover the grave back up. They can take some sod with them and make the scene look normal."

Roger pulled out his cell phone, and when she answered, said, "This is District Manager Bailey."

Roger did not bother to repeat his name. He said, "We've got another body and location in Butler. I would suggest we send a crew in tonight to retrieve the body and cover the ground with new sod."

There was a pause, and the cold hard voice asked, "Where?"

"The note has the body located in a graveyard at an old Baptist church in Butler. It would appear to be random time intervals between the bodies being placed in the ground. There is no discernable pattern. It has the same comment as the other notes, 'I saw the prey in the web.'"

Delores could hear the fatigue in the voice. She knew her guys had been working seven days a week without much sleep, if any. "Okay. Send them in and let us retrieve the body. Is there any chance this was the first location picked, and all the other locations were picked after this one? A graveyard cannot be a coincidence. I wonder if all the locations were picked months ago, and he is waiting for the girls to place them in the prepicked areas. Is there any way to predict where the next body will be placed?"

The pause was intentional. "We have tried to guess his next move. This one was eight miles short of where we predicted, and we have no clue why. We felt the next body would be in Butler, sixty miles from the center point. This body is a distance of approximately fifty-two miles from the center point of Nashville. We do not know why the change in eight miles. He might be on to us. Now we will have to start over. We have gone through all the notes from the agent that we were able to locate in Butler. There is no helpful information. Her computer is still missing. We were hoping someone would turn her laptop back on, and at that point the tracer would send out a location beacon. It has not been powered back up. We had a tracer hidden on the computer, and we are monitoring it twenty-four hours a day. We are speculating that she knew nothing about this killer, and someone else took her hand-written notes. Her killing might not be related to the girls being killed. She was not cut and tortured like the Asian girls. We figured two different killers, and like I said, they might not be related. We are still monitoring all phone calls in and around Butler. We have nothing."

"What is the next step?"

"We will retrieve the body tonight and keep twenty-four-hour monitoring on Kelly Stephenson's laptop. She was the dead agent found in Butler."

"I know who she was," snapped Delores. Delores knew too well who the young female agent was that died in Butler. She woke up every morning and went to bed every night thinking of her. Her death was on Delores's hands. She was the one who recruited the young agent and explained how simple the assignment was going to be. Then, she was mutilated in Butler. Telling her parents was the hardest thing Delores ever had to do. She wanted this killer more than anything. She also knew placing any additional pressure on her two lead agents was not going to help. They were giving her everything they had, and they had help from other units when they asked for assistance. She knew her two agents on this case were very smart, well-trained, and most of all, fully invested in finding the killer.

"We are also checking into the highway patrolman that committed suicide at the water tower. We know he confessed to killing our agent, Kelly Stephenson. His military file has been sealed. We are trying to go through the normal channels. We have not been able to retrieve the information. We know he is not Bill Cramer."

"I have told you two to back off on the investigation into Bill Cramer. He is not to be investigated. How do you know he is not Bill Cramer?"

"Corporal Bill Cramer died June 25, 1990, in Iraq. We talked to a couple of men in his unit, Corporal Anthony Ferguson and Private Jerome Benfield. He went missing and was never recovered. We emailed the photo of the man at the water tower, and both men said that was not him. They did not recognize the man in the photo. We have no way to know if the man at the tower was involved in the murder of these girls because he did not confess to killing any of them. He did confess to killing our agent, the teenager on Hwy 12 in Butler, and an older man by the name of Roger Turner who may have been in the Marines with him in Iraq. Neither Corporal Ferguson nor Private Benfield knew Private Roger Turner. Like I said, he did not confess to killing the Asian girls."

The pause on the phone was very noticeable. "I will get you the file on Bill Cramer. This is starting to sound like a CIA problem gone bad. I will be in touch. You need to watch your backs. I'm not certain who we can trust, but I want the killer. After you have the girl picked up, let me know her condition, and if there are any additional leads on the case. Do not investigate Bill Cramer. I will see what I can locate on him and let you know if the information relates him to the killings." They both hung up. Delores knew Director Bass had asked her to pull her agents off the case with regards to Bill Cramer being involved with the death of the girls. The request was an unofficial request, with very little explanation except that the CIA had an ongoing investigation. She knew she needed to be careful. Someone in the government was not playing ball and might be on the other team. Why else would the CIA be running an operation inside the country? According to guidelines carved in stone by Congress, the CIA had to have an FBI agent attached to their team when operating inside the country. This was the official rule, and everyone was well aware that rules were not always followed.

Delores picked up her personal phone and called a very old contact. She was aware that she was to call only in time of emergency, and this was it. The person answered the phone by saying, 'Hello' in a deep, harsh voice. No names were mentioned. Delores said, "We need to meet. I will text you the time and location with a name. I need some information, and this is very crucial. I would not be calling and asking for help unless it was a life and death situation. I had no other place to turn." Delores knew the spook. She had worked with him in Washington ten years prior, when she was stationed in Washington on her first assignment. They had fallen in love, which both knew was taboo and not in the best interest for either of their careers. She also knew she had better be careful. Once the CIA was involved, people might turn up missing. The CIA could not afford for a former spook to talk in court, to Congress, to reporters, or anyone. The information they knew just could not be leaked to the American people. The CIA had the hunter-killer squads, who made people and problems just disappear. She was planning to catch a plane to Washington and meet her boss, the operations director, to review her caseload, which outlined how her managers over the different units had performed. Some of the cases were pending court dates and some were in the midst of trials, with some being settled out of court. There was always a large number which had to be reviewed with the weekly reports from her unit managers. She would meet her contact at her corporate furnished apartment. The only lead they had was the name Bill Cramer. She was determined to discover his true identity and find out if he was involved in the Asian girls being killed. Why would an ex-CIA agent or some former federal agent kill her undercover agent? Yet, he had confessed to killing her before he shot himself. Delores reminded herself that Director Bass had mentioned to her not to investigate Bill Cramer if he was involved with killing the girls. The CIA had a black operation in play. She looked up at her ceiling while sitting in her chair. She started rubbing her temples. Her headache was starting to become uncomfortable. She repeated the thought. Why would director Bass tell her not to investigate the person, Bill Cramer, who murdered her agent? Was he involved with the Asian girls? She thought they might be related. None of this made sense to Delores. Some of the puzzle pieces were missing.

Steve D. Nichols

Chapter 7

Monday, about 10 a.m., Maria called the church and asked to speak to Vicky. The church secretary took the message and sent a text to Vicky. Vicky called, and agreed to meet Maria at the church at 4 p.m. Vicky arrived earlier and was helping clean the Sunday school rooms. The normal cleaning lady had called in sick. Vicky suspected she was working another job to make additional money, and the church job was a second source of income. Vicky asked Maria to come into the conference room when she heard Maria knocking on the church office door. Maria immediately started talking very fast while still standing on the sidewalk. Vicky said, "Wait, just a minute. Let us go to the conference room, and please slow down."

Maria talked very slowly, over-pronouncing each symbol once Vicky closed the conference door behind them and motioned for Maria to go ahead. Maria told Vicky that she had learned that several police officers were meeting at the local motel on I-24, and she was concerned that they were going to arrest and deport the immigrants who did not have their papers. She did not believe this was fair, and she was scared for the local hard-working families. She asked, "Can you help?"

Vicky held up her hand and said, "Wait a second." She picked up the phone and called Wayne Tipton.

"Hi Wayne, this is Vicky. I need to ask you a question."

She asked him whether her information was correct, and he confirmed that they were planning to raid the chicken processing plant on Western Avenue. The plant hired over two hundred people; most were legal, but close to twenty-five were not. The plant worked three shifts and supplied a large percent of chickens to Nashville and the surrounding cities. The fine for hiring illegal immigrants could be as high as $10,000 per employee. The owner, Nate Burns, was always concerned about this but made certain no one was aware in the news media or the police departments of his hiring practices. Nate seemed always to be worrying about something. That was his nature. He looked like Jimmy Carter when President Carter was sixty. His family had owned the business for sixty-five years, and it was started by his grandfather. The business had been very profitable, but like most businesses, it became more and more challenging to retain and locate good employees. He had started hiring the immigrants ten years prior, to keep up with the demand for chickens. He found out the immigrants he hired provided a great workforce without a lot of the headaches. He did not provide them any benefits, and everything was done in cash. Consequently, the immigrants did not pay income tax, and that was the rub with the rest of the taxpaying nation. The laws had changed over the years, making it more difficult to issue the payroll for undocumented employees, and the fines had increased, but that was the risk he accepted. He was paying the workers as subcontractors and not employees, which was against the labor laws in Tennessee.

He figured he saved money each year with the payroll expense, but now the fines would almost double the saved amount.

After Vicky hung up with Wayne, she told Maria that her information was correct. They were going to raid the chicken plant on Western early in the morning. Maria looked very worried and said that she needed to leave so she could tell everyone to leave work and not to show up at the plant.

Vicky said, "Maria, I have an idea. I think everyone in the community who has a green card or is a citizen should show up because if no one is there, the authorities will know that someone has tipped off the workers about the raid, and they will return days or weeks later. Besides, the owner may not want to hire the undocumented people if there is a chance the authorities might come back for an inspection. The fines for the owner can be expensive."

Standing there looking at Vicky, finally, Maria understood Vicky's point. The next morning when the additional agents along with Wayne, Max, and Stan showed up for the raid, the manager told the owner that they were getting ready to get raided, and he needed to act surprised. The owner, Nate, immediately spilled his coffee and was very concerned because he could be fined for working illegal immigrants. The fines might force him to shut down the plant. Nate started to cuss and worry at the same time. Nate said, "How do you know this, and why are you just now telling me?"

The manager smiled and said reassuringly, "I have everything under control. Just act surprised."

The officers drove in tandem. Five vehicles rolled slowly to a stop after entering the parking lot, which was inside a 6-foot-tall chain link fence. Two of the vehicles were large vans. Stan and Rex walked into the office, and explained they were going to check everyone in the plant. Nate acted very surprised and asked why. He put on a show that could have won him an Oscar. At least, that is what the manager later told him, as the vehicles were leaving through the gate after the inspection.

The authorities lined up all the workers and checked them, but none of them were illegal. The process took about fifteen minutes. They left, after telling Nate Burns, the owner, that everybody checked out. Nate Burns said, "Of course everybody checked out. I do not work illegal immigrants." Then, he added that the authorities could come back anytime.

Wayne thought to himself, "That is a lie. I know for a fact he has hired illegal immigrants." He wondered how the management was made aware of the inspection. He had his suspicions that Vicky had somehow alerted everyone and planned that all present be legal. He was not going to tell Stan or Rex of his suspicions. There were times in law enforcement where an officer had to look the other way and keep on going. This was one of those times.

Chapter 8

Later in the week there was a bank robbery in Arkansas, with the bank manager being shot and killed by an unknown gang of four. A group of White Supremacists was thought to be involved. They robbed a bank and shot three other people present in the bank, then killing the manager with a head shot. The robbers fled with an undisclosed amount of money. The national news had mentioned the bank robbery as the feature news report on Monday morning. There had been no arrest since the robbery on Friday. The reporter was asking for help to identify the group, and for viewers to call the FBI hotline number listed on the screen. The only information about the robbery that the FBI and the Arkansas State Police were releasing was the names of the manager, who was married with two kids, and the other three people that were shot. The report did add that the robbery was well planned and seemed well organized, and it might be linked to several bank robberies in the Midwest. Monday morning, Matt was listening to the news while eating his breakfast, and Vicky walked in the kitchen, preparing to make herself some coffee. The Channel 9 news was repeating the main story about the shooting in Arkansas from the prior Friday. There were no leads, with the robbers wearing disguises, so they could not be identified. The information suggested a White Supremacists group might have been involved. The FBI and the Arkansas police were not releasing any additional information.

Matt told Vicky that another one of the people died while in the hospital. Evidently, the robbery might have been an inside job, according to the rumor on the other channel by an unnamed police source. The money was laid unprotected behind the counter, waiting for the private truck delivery company to pick up the two bags of money. The money had been removed from the vault and placed behind the counter by the associate branch manager, which was not the normal procedure.

Vicky said, "It is amazing what people will do for money."

Vicky told Matt she would drive by the church and help clean up, and then go to Karate class. On the way to church, her cell phone rang. She recognized the number and thought, "I wonder what Maria needs?" She smiled to herself and answered the phone. "Hello, this is Vicky."

Maria started talking very fast, and Vicky asked her to please slow down. Maria said, "I want to meet you. It is very important. It cannot wait. Please, can you help me?"

Vicky asked, "Can you come by the church?"

Maria said, "I will be there in fifteen minutes."

Vicky thought this must be important. Vicky also figured she was not asking for any personal help because Maria seemed to always be trying to help the Spanish undocumented people in the community. Maria was coming over to meet, and she was so animated. Vicky opened the church, turned off the alarm, and started cleaning the front of the church. She saw Maria pull in the front parking lot, in the old brown Pontiac with the two hubcaps missing. Vicky opened the door and asked Maria to come into the front conference room. She asked Maria how she was doing. Maria burst out and said, "The killers were coming to Butler, and I want the three illegal immigrants protected. They are good people and should not be deported. Please can you help?"

Vicky raised her hands in total surprise, and asked, "Wait a minute, Maria, what are you talking about?"

Maria slowed down and pronounced every word very slowly and said, "The killers from Arkansas are riding through Butler and will be staying in 1419 Walnut Street. They are hiding out after killing the people in Arkansas and robbing the bank. They are very mean people."

Vicky was in total shock and asked, "How do you know this, and where is Walnut Street?"

"One of the gang members has come to the home and is waiting for the others. They push my people around because they cannot ask for help. They are not legal. Walnut is in the north, near Kentucky."

"So, Maria, how do you know this?"

"Because one of the people at the home told my cousin. Can you help?"

"Is there any chance they are going to rob one of our banks?"

"I do not know what they are going to do. Can you help?"

Vicky pulled her cell phone off her belt loop and hit Wayne's number. Wayne had just walked back to his desk while drinking his second cup of coffee. His phone rang, and he hit the answer button on his cell phone.

Vicky said, "Wayne, it is Vicky."

Wayne said, "Yes. What's up?"

Vicky said, "The bank robbers in Arkansas are going to be in Butler County at 1419 Walnut Street at 11 a.m. tomorrow. They already have one man here, making certain the home was safe for them to hide out. We do not know if they will hit a local bank or not."

Wayne nearly dropped his coffee, reaching for his pen to write down the address and time. Wayne asked, "How do you know this?"

Vicky said, "There is one important thing you need to make certain does not happen."

Wayne asked, "What would that be?"

"There are three non-Americans at the farm, if you know what I mean, and I want to make certain the three men are not deported and are not hurt. They are being forced to allow the gang members to stay at the farm they watch over. The Owner of the farm moved out of state and left these three people in charge of his farm. They do not have anyone to help them."

Wayne did not hesitate and said, "I will see what I can do. I will call you back." He figured Vicky's source was a local Spanish person. Wayne hung up, walked into his boss's office, and announced, "John, we need to talk."

John was talking with two other agents about another ongoing case. John asked, "Can it wait?"

"No, it is important."

John said, "Okay, what do you have?" The two other agents turned to look at Wayne.

Wayne said, "You know about the killers and bank robbers from Arkansas? They are going to be in Butler at about 11 a.m. tomorrow at 1419 Walnut Street."

John said, "Hell, yes, that was important!"

Wayne mentioned, "We need to let three illegal immigrants, who are not involved, go and not deport them." John waved his hand and announced he would need to call the FBI. Wayne asked, "Why don't we handle it?"

"The feds are better set to take care of something this big, and if something goes bad, it will be them that gets shot and not a TBI agent. We will be present for support. I need to call my liaison with the FBI and give him a heads up. They will want to get one of the SWAT teams up and running."

John opened his contact phone book listing and called Seth Burns, who answered on the first ring. Seth has never been social, and he always wanted to get right to the point. Seth answered, "This is Seth Burns, special agent for the FBI."

John introduced himself, and then abruptly announced that the Arkansas killers and bank robbers would be in Butler, Tennessee at 11 a.m. tomorrow. Seth did not say anything, and John asked, "Are you still there?"

Seth said, "Hell, yes, I am still here. How did you come by this information? How reliable is your source?"

John held his hand over the mouthpiece of the phone and asked, "How reliable is your source? He wants to know the name of the source."

Wayne said, "The source was very reliable, and I am not telling."

John looked at Wayne, and said, "Very reliable, and we are not telling our source. Do you want in or not?"

Seth said, "I will make the call, and we will meet you in the Butler County Sheriff's Office later today."

John said, "We will call Butler Sheriff Vince Newsome. We want to make certain the locals are made aware of any FBI agents in the county." He smiled at Wayne when he said it.

They hung up. Seth immediately called the fast response team commander in Atlanta and told him what he had. The chief indicated he would call the SWAT team out of Washington. Dan Hopper is the team commander who is a former Navy Seal commander. Dan took the call and indicated his team would be up and running in twenty minutes. He said his team would be on the plane, and they would be landing in Nashville in less than two hours. Dan spent three years as a member of the 82nd Airborne, and then passed the Navy Seal training and spent the rest of his seventeen years as a Seal member, and captain for the last twelve years. He looked the part, and all his team members had bought into his leadership style. The entire team was handpicked by Dan and were all ex-military, from different branches of the armed forces. Once he retired from the Navy, he was not certain what he would do; but, when the FBI came calling and offered him a position with the fast response SWAT team out of Washington, he decided he could not turn down the job opportunity. The bylaws of the FBI dictate that as soon as Dan and his team land, he would assume total command of the operation. They landed at the Nashville International Airport, and they had three black SUVs waiting to take him and his team directly to Butler. Wayne had called Vince and updated him on the meeting scheduled at his office. The TBI command team and the FBI team would be present. Wayne and John walked into Vince's office and shook hands.

Linda had set up the office with extra chairs, extra coffee, and drinks. Denny and Darrell were present, and they all talked for a few minutes. Linda had a large map of the area laid out on the table; in addition, they looked at the satellite image of the farm on the internet Ping Maps. They were studying the roads and the terrain. Linda looked through the foyer glass door and announced the Feds were here, and she released the lock on the front door from her desk as they walked through the foyer door. Wayne, John, and the sheriff's employees stood back and waited. The door abruptly opened, and Dan walked into the office with Seth Burns and three other SWAT members. The other members of Dan's team stayed in their vehicles. They were going to check into the motel and would be briefed later in the follow-up meeting, along with the FBI and TBI agents. Dan and Seth took charge, with an urgent nature, and started looking at the map on the table while discussing the situation, without saying hi to anyone. Dan started telling his unit leaders what they were going to do, and how they needed to deploy around the farm. Then, Dan turned to Seth and asked, "How do we know the gang members are going to be arriving at 11 a.m., and how many members are there?" Seth pointed to John and said, "John, here is the manager of the TBI out of Nashville." Dan looked at John, who was leaning against the wall. John told Dan, while pointing at Wayne, "Wayne is the special agent with the TBI, who has a source." Dan turned and looked at Wayne. "Seth had mentioned on the drive over that he had not worked with you on any prior cases. How long have you been with the TBI?"

Wayne said, "I am on my third week."

Dan smiled, and said, "You are joking, right?"

Wayne said, "No, I am not joking."

Dan laughed, and asked nonchalantly, "Who is your source?"

Wayne looked at Dan with eye contact and said, very sternly, "I am not telling you." Wayne knew he would never mention Vicky's name. Either they would accept his answer, or they would not, but he knew where he stood with Vicky.

Dan figured he could intimidate a new employee and said, "Excuse me? What in the hell do you mean you are not telling me?"

Wayne said, very angrily, while not taking his eyes off Dan, "Fuck you and the rest of the FBI! You were running an undercover operation in my town which caused an eighteen-year-old kid to get killed, so for all I care you can pack your shit up and leave. I did not want to invite you to this party. We don't need you."

John stepped in between the two men and said, "Everyone, please calm down. Wayne was the sheriff here in Butler, and he has contacts."

Dan realized this was not the military, and not everyone could be bossed around like in the military. He looked at Vince, and then at Wayne, and started to say something. Wayne took the opportunity of quietness and said, "There are three illegal immigrants at the farm, and you need to make certain they are not harmed, and they are not to be deported."

Dan started laughing again, and said, "Sheriff, do not tell me not to deport illegal people."

Wayne then said, "I was listening to you discuss the alignment of your men, and you need to place a couple of men on top of this ridge, which overlooks the farm. You can also relocate the command center to this other farm, located here. We know the owner." Dan looked at the map.

Dan looked at where Wayne had pointed and asked, "Why would I want to take two men all the way out there? That is a quarter of a mile away."

Wayne said, "Because the leader of the gang will pull his bike on that spot and watch for a signal from his soldiers before he comes into the farmhouse yard."

Wayne was so upset, he turned and walked out the door.

Dan asked, "How the hell does he know this?"

John said, "I would suggest you take his advice."

Dan turned to Seth and said, "We need to hide four additional men in the woods and place two of them so that they can block the road leaving that area, and the other two in the woods. They can work with two of my men, who will have the responsibility of stopping the leader. I want to make certain we catch the leader. We will set up at 3 a.m. in the morning, and I will make certain we have lookouts on the roads coming into the farm. We need to try to maintain radio silence until the members arrive at the farmhouse."

John followed Wayne out the door and met him in the parking lot. John said, "Wayne, this is the way this works. We do our job and turn the heavy lifting over to the FBI."

"I just don't like being pushed out. We are handing them the perfect setup, and they act like ungrateful pricks."

John explained, "This is like playing football, and a player on the other team hits you after the whistle. You don't get up and fight. That will do nothing but penalize your team and teammates. Or it's like sliding into a base, and you know you're safe, but the umpire calls you out. Or like in basketball when you're standing your ground, and the guard on the other team runs over you. You are called for the foul when he obviously charged. You cannot yell at the umpire or ref. That is what sports teaches all of us. Hell, it is not fair, but this is the way it works. Listen, Wayne, I have several agents who will be watching the roads and providing support. You can stay with me at the command center located approximately a mile from the farm and watch this go down on video links."

Wayne could feel his blood pressure start to ease upward, and said, "Okay. I understand. I will do my part. I will get word to the three immigrants that help is on the way."

He called Vicky and asked her to tell her source that the police would help, and that they just needed to cooperate with the officers. He did not go into specifics of the help, or when the help would arrive. He told Vicky it was critical that this does not get out. Vicky listened, and said, "I understand. What about the immigrants?"

"I will do all I can to help, but I cannot make any guarantees."

There was a pause on the line. Wayne said, "The FBI is calling the shots, and to be honest with you, they come across as pricks. This is a lot bigger than dealing with immigration. We are dealing with cold-blooded killers, and we have to make that the priority."

"Okay, I understand."

She called Maria and told her that the good officers would help.

Maria said, "Thanks. I am so worried, but I trust you, Vicky," as she hung up.

Vicky felt a sting in her gut when Maria announced she trusted her. She hoped the undocumented people would be okay.

The next morning, in the darkness with cloud cover, the FBI SWAT team entered the barn and secured their positions. The unit leader communicated on the secure line that unit one was in place. Dan replied, "Roger, unit one." Unit two entered the home and arrested the one gang member, who was still in bed. They had pushed the wire lens under the door threshold, which provided a view of the interior. This provided the needed information about the occupants, and that the door was not booby-trapped and was clear to enter the home. They woke the Spanish men and walked them outside, as they had the lens placed under his door watching the suspect sleep. They noticed several tats on his upper body where he was sleeping shirtless. When they entered the room, the man went for his gun, but the two first SWAT men had entered the bedroom and had him bound before he could aim and shoot. He would not cooperate. They removed him from the scene by vehicle, and Seth had him taken to the Nashville federal lock up. Dan said, "So far, so good."

The snipers were in place and had radioed to Dan that they were ready and on standby.

The gang members started rolling into the farm driveway on their Harley motorcycles at about 10 a.m. The illegal Mexican men waved at the gang members, presenting a normal condition. They slowly drove two of the motorbikes into the barn. The unit leader kept the command center updated on the secure radio channel, as the two bikers approached. When they got off the bikes, they were faced with six very prepared FBI agents. They were cuffed and laid face down in one of the barn stalls. The unit leader secured photos of some of the money found in the saddlebags, with the serial numbers, and texted the copies to the command center. He announced that photos were on the way. Breanna was set up in the command center. She was the computer tech for the FBI. She reviewed the serial numbers and ran the cross-check on the serial numbers through her laptop, which was taken in the robbery in Arkansas, and after about one minute announced, "We have a perfect match." Dan opened the channel on his walkie talkie, and said, "We have a positive match on the currency."

Wayne had whispered to John, "I am surprised the one in the home had not been conferred with prior to them riding into the farm driveway."

"The FBI is blocking the cell phone signals in the area. Their two-way radios are on a separate channel. One of the concerns, according to Seth, is one of the gang members will get away and cause a car chase, and innocent bystanders could get hurt. We want to keep this entire engagement in this area."

Wayne said, "The call must have been made yesterday. The trap has been set and seems to be working." There was a male and female, FBI agents, on highway 12 at the Tennessee-Kentucky line, who were pretending to be having car trouble. They were updating Dan on the gang members as they passed. The riders were spread out, no doubt not to raise suspicions as they crossed into Butler County.

The unit leader inside the home did the same, updating the command team. They saw the next two riders approaching about four minutes later. They tried to keep the chatter down to a minimum, especially as the two men were approaching closer to the front door. The two other members got off their motorcycles out front and walked into the farmhouse, and as soon as the door closed, the FBI agents overwhelmed them with their numbers. The seven agents had been hidden in the bedrooms, kitchen, and utility room. They had a small camera hidden, watching as the men closed the front door. They rushed out in unison and handcuffed the two men, placing them face down on the living room floor. The unit leader radioed to the command center, "We have apprehended two males." Dan showed a little sigh of relief and turned his attention to the two agents on the hill.

Overlooking the farmhouse from the perch on the hill, like Wayne had said, the leader pulled into the open area. He was watching the farm home and barn located down below. The two agents were hiding in the dense foliage. They spoke into the mic to the command center; the rider had turned his bike off. They very quietly kept Dan informed. The rest of the unit was listening in, as they announced in a whisper, "He is just sitting on the bike, watching. He has tried to use his cell phone and seems to understand he has no signal in this remote area. He has now pulled out a pair of binoculars and is looking at the entire area. He might be concerned with the two members who went into the barn and never came out."

Dan interjects, "We want everything to look normal. Team two leader, ask one of the immigrants to walk on the front porch of the home and then walk back into the home."

The agent said, "This is Unit 3. We can advance from his rear area and stay clear of his mirrors and use the immigrant as a distraction. We are approximately fifty yards to his left."

Dan said, "What other choice do we have?" It was a rhetorical question, and no one answered. Dan then gave the go-ahead. The team two commander had one of the Spanish men walk on the front porch, stand still for a few seconds, and then walked back into the home. The two agents took the opportunity to advance toward the leader, knowing the man on the front porch would provide a distraction. The two agents kept low to the ground and ran at a full stride, bent over until they were twenty feet to the left and behind the bike. They started a fast walk to be stealth, with their guns pulled. The two FBI agents walked up from behind him, putting their guns in their holsters, with the bigger agent lifting him off his bike with a full body slam. They wrestled with him for about one minute before they were able to cuff him. They called the command center and reported. They removed two pistols from the back of his pants waistband and his jacket pocket. They opened the saddlebags on the motorcycle and located fifteen rolled-up bundles of money. They called Dan on the mic to confirm, "Unit 3 has the suspect in handcuffs."

Dan felt a big sigh of relief, and said, "Roger that, Unit 3."

They searched the other gang members' motorcycles, parked in front of the home, and they located several guns and money rolled up in rolls. The spotters, located on the incoming road, had verified there were no more bikers spotted. Since the FBI already had the serial numbers of the money stolen from the bank in Arkansas to verify if these were the bank robbers, it seemed to speed up the entire process. The FBI team uploaded some additional serial numbers, which produced a perfect match on the laptop computer Brianne was working on, and they noted all the serial numbers had a match. When the matches of the numbers were being continuously confirmed, the agents all seemed to celebrate with each announcement.

Dan said, "I want to hear each suspect being read their rights," with his speaker up to his ear as they were being mirandized.

The plan was that Seth's unit would process them in the federal facilities in Nashville, and the SWAT team would return to Washington.

At that point, John motioned for Wayne to leave by the rear door of the old farmhouse, a half-mile from the arrest location. Both men walked to John's vehicle and drove off. John half smiled, and indicated that in this line of work, it is about building relationships. The FBI will get all the credit, but they know who made all this possible. The arrest will be all over the national news tonight and tomorrow. The folks in Arkansas will be relieved that the murderers have been arrested. The FBI needs good press every now and then. It helps their image and with the recruitment of new officers.

Wayne called Vince and told him the job was done. "We got six total men arrested, and the FBI will process them. You guys can go back to the routine operations." Vince said, "Thanks."

Vince radioed his deputies and updated them; they could stand down and go back to regular activities. They were stationed on backup, watching the secondary roads around Butler for any additional gang members who never showed up. Vince had been watching one of the banks in Butler, located on Main Street, and the TBI agents had been watching the other two banks.

Dan turned and noticed John and Wayne had left. He had not noticed in all the excitement that they were no longer in the command center. He looked out the window and noticed their vehicle was gone. He asked, "Breanna, when did the two TBI officers leave?"

She shook her head and said, "I do not know. I was so busy confirming the serial numbers on the money and confirming the money was part of the bank robbery in Arkansas." She looked around the large living room, and then added, "I did not realize they had left."

John and Wayne entered the sheriff's office, where Vince asked, "How did it go?" Wayne started updating Vince, Denny, Darrell, and Linda on the take-down and the arrest. Wayne said, "It could not have gone smoother. I figured there might have been some shooting, and with the FBI snipers, which are all ex-military, it would not have been pretty for the suspects."

The men were talking when Linda announced the FBI was coming through the parking lot. She buzzed the door open, and Dan Hopper walked into the quiet office. He walked up to Wayne and said, "Thanks for the help and the great police work. I certainly appreciate your position and thank you." He then said, with a mischievous grin,

"We did not locate any immigrants, and the SWAT team is headed back to Washington. The FBI men out of Nashville have also agreed that they did not locate any undocumented people. I just wanted to thank you in person for the assist. Those men were some very violent and nasty people we just took down, and we could not have done it without your help."

Wayne could tell his entire demeanor had changed. He was very relaxed, unlike the previous meeting yesterday. Wayne shook his hand and said, "You are welcome."

Wayne wished him a safe flight back to DC. Dan said, "Seth's office in Nashville will handle the arrest and paperwork. We did our job." They waved goodbye.

John said, "Not bad for a few weeks of work, Wayne." Then he added, "Seth will be easy to work with since we have built this relationship. Like I said, this is how this works. The only time the TBI is ever mentioned about any arrest is when they arrest a sheriff or a policeman, which normally the FBI is called in on those cases also, and they still get all the credit."

John shook his head and said, "If you want credit for your work, the TBI is not the place to be."

Wayne said, "Seth does not act very friendly."

John said, "Hell no. He is not. He has a personality like a cucumber, but I know what to expect from him."

They walked out and got in John's car to return to the office in Nashville. John said, "If someone stuck a piece of coal up Seth's ass,

I guarantee you that he would produce a diamond in the bathroom. He is pushing for advancement, and he has really drunk the FBI cool-aid."

Wayne thought, as they were driving down the road, John might not be too bad to work for after all. The first three weeks have been okay.

John said, "You know, Wayne, if you were the SWAT team leader, you would want to know the source. That is a logical question."

Wayne did not reply and stared directly ahead while they were heading for the interstate. He thought about Vicky and how she seemed to have an in-depth understanding of people in general and was very intelligent. Her father was a pilot in the United States Air Force, and he had heard, from listening to the folks in the diner talking, that her mother had a Ph.D. in English. She had inherited some very good traits from her parents. Wayne asked, "Have you heard any more about the missing girls mentioned by the other FBI assholes?"

John smiled and said, "No, Wayne. I have not heard from the other two FBI assholes."

They both started laughing. "I did ask Seth, while in the command center, about that issue after the arrest. I felt that maybe he would be a little more open to having a conversation after something positive happened. At first, he did not say anything, and I thought I was going to get the usual response, "It is under investigation, and I cannot commit on a pending investigation." But, he surprised me. He indicated he had been left out of that loop, and the unit in Atlanta was handling it. He said I knew more about that case than he did. He said his team was in the dark. He was told the Atlanta unit was more centralized to the entire operation, since there are several southern states involved or might be involved. The unit is being handled by the regional manager out of Atlanta, and she handpicked her team of agents just for that assignment. All of what they do is restricted and on a need to know basis, and Seth indicated no one had access to the investigation files other than the one unit. He said the agents were not local, and he had not been able to pick up on any chatter or rumors. He made it sound like it was all dark. The unit had agents located in Nashville, which were not part of his team. Then, he really surprised me, Wayne, when he said the president was considering tasking the CIA with the global crisis of human trafficking. The CIA would work with the FBI inside the states on domestic cases. Normally if something is being considered, it is going to happen. The powers to be are just establishing the framework and structure to have everything lined up. This could provide the CIA with the perfect cover to operate legally in almost all foreign countries. They are always looking for loopholes and how to take advantage of situations. That is the most Seth has ever said to me, totally, since I have known him for nine years."

Wayne said, "I was the sheriff for eight years, and the prior sheriff was here for fifteen years before his heart attack, and there was not one single murder in Butler County. He had a man die in a home fire years ago, who fell asleep drinking and the cigarette fell in the floor.

The smoke killed him. There was a car wreck years ago with a fatality, and a hunting accident, and I had a suicide and a car wreck on Highway 12. In the past few months, look at what all has happened here in Butler County."

John said, "Frank Vitola was a random event, and we don't know if he would have killed his wife and her lover. Those bank robbers were also random. They might have been sneaking in and out of Butler for years without anyone knowing, until the undocumented people told you. The other killing, with officer Cramer and the FBI involved, I just have no clue what that is about."

Wayne said, "The reason the mayor never would vote to increase the deputies' salaries was because there were no murders, and the crime rate was well below the national average. He always brought up how little crime we have here in Butler. The large subdivisions in Nashville are now extending out to the county line and the people in that area are driving to Butler to shop. There are three new subdivisions being built or in the planning stages, with over one thousand homes inside Butler County off Highway 12, near the county line with Nashville. The county is starting to grow, and with it will be more crime. There is no telling what all these undocumented people know and see. They cannot come forward for fear of being deported. The FBI will not send their agents undercover into the gutters of our society." The two men rode in silence, contemplating what they had discussed.

Chapter 9

Linda answered the phone. The man on the other line introduced himself as the preacher at South Side Baptist Church on Locust Street. Linda took the report and told Vince. Vince asked Denny to ride out to the church with him. On the ride over to the church, Vince explained how the arrest of the bank robbers three days ago was being reported as a teaching lesson on how to have several different police departments converge on a single target. Denny said the entire process could not have gone better.

Vince said, as he was pulling onto Locust Street, "Someone dug up a grave a few nights ago in the graveyard. The church had just installed a small security camera, which provided an overview of the cemetery. They kept having vandalism issues, and to protect the tombs, the camera was installed in hopes of catching the kids. They have reported the problems over the years, but we were never able to catch the kids. They were preparing for Halloween in a few months, which is when the graveyard has been visited every year by teenagers. They started adding the graveyard to the fun of Halloween by decorating it for trick or treat, but this time they noticed that someone had dug up a grave." Denny smiled and said, "That does sound unusual. They just installed a camera, and a few nights later, someone dug up a body. I can't wait to hear this story."

As they pulled into the church parking lot, they both got out of the cruiser and walked over to the two older gentlemen standing in the graveyard. One of the men had on overalls, and the other one was dressed in a flannel shirt with jeans. One of the men turned and said, "Hi. I am Reverend Cagle. Thank you so much for coming out."

Vince introduced himself and Denny, and said, "I understand you have reported a stolen body,"

"No. We don't have a stolen body that we the church had placed in the ground, but we had someone pull into the parking area in a white van with no plates. Two men walked out here to this tomb and removed a body, and then placed it in a large clear bag and hauled it off. The two men went to a lot of trouble to place the sod back and make it look normal. When they shoveled the dirt up, they placed it on plastic, so the area around the grave would not look disturbed. Once they pulled the body out of the ground, they placed the dirt and new sod over the grave. They picked up their plastic and carried the body wrapped in clear plastic to the van. The body was wrapped in clear plastic prior to being buried. They made it look perfect except the sod they used was a different type of grass. The man in the overhauls said, "The cemetery has all Bermuda grass, and the sod they used was Kentucky 31."

"So. You do have a body that was stolen."

"No. The body that was buried in this grave was buried in 1954. Look at the tombstone. They did not dig near deep enough to get to the casket and that body. We have the disc from our newly installed

112

security camera, and we can provide you a copy. We have no information on who would do this or why. The camera was just installed last week on the light pole under the light." Vince and Denny both turned and looked at the light pole and camera. It was difficult to see the small camera under the light. "We felt we needed to call the police," Reverend Cagle continued. "We have no information about the body that was removed and hauled away. We do not know when it was buried. Our camera did not catch the body being buried. It must have been buried prior to our camera being installed last week."

Vince said, "We will watch the tape, but are you certain they took a body and not something else? How do you know they did not dig deep enough to reach the casket?"

"Like I said, they had a body, with skin. We could see it clearly through the clear plastic. This was no skeleton, and they did not open a casket. The disc we handed you will answer those questions."

"Are there any other activities noted on the tape?"

"No. We went over the recordings, and there is nothing until two days ago. We thought something was not perfect with the ground around this area. The grass is a different type of grass."

Vince noted the cemetery was covered in Bermuda grass except for this grave. "We watched the recordings and saw this."

"So, you have no knowledge of the body being buried, and how it got in your cemetery?"

"That's correct. We started wondering what else might have happened here in our graveyard. The camera was just installed last Tuesday."

Denny had taken notes. He and Vince thanked the two gentlemen and said goodbye. Once in the car, Vince said, "File a report, and we will see if it happens again. It must be a joke someone is playing on the church and preacher. I guess we will look at the tape sometime tomorrow. I had Linda check when the report was first filed. There are no missing bodies in our area, and Linda checked in the surrounding states. There are no missing persons unless we expand the search back two months, and that report was filed in Jackson Tennessee, dealing with a young adult who may have run away from home."

Denny said, "That is what I was thinking. It was all I could do not to laugh. Did you see the look on that other man's face when Preacher Cagle said skeleton? I bet the youth director and a couple of the youth are behind the joke."

Chapter 10

Tracey called. Delores answered by saying, "Delores Bailey, Regional Manager, FBI. How may I assist you?"

Tracey said, "We got the body. There are several fingers and a toe removed. The body has been taken to the FBI forensic office in Nashville. The investigation is restricted to just the agents listed on your list. They will send us the report in a few days. The girl had been raped and tortured before being suffocated. The body was sealed in the large plastic clear bag. It was the same as the other girls, but this one had nine fingers cut off, with the digits cauterized, and one toe removed and cauterized. She must have gone through living hell. We will forward the medical reports. I am sorry we have no further information."

Delores could tell by his voice that the agent was very frustrated and wanted help. They had reported that the body would be buried in Butler County. They had expected it to be buried eight miles further away from the center point in Nashville and now they had no explanation for the deviation. She had been ordered to tell them to pull back on the case into investigating the girls, but they had set up surveillance against her orders. Her gut had been telling her Bill Cramer appeared to be ground zero with the serial killing of the girls, but he had committed suicide weeks ago.

They did not know when the body was going to be buried, just the location, but their trap did not work. Delores shook her head in thought, "The body was actually eight miles closer, but on a straight line from the central point in Nashville. She hated her job at times like this, and she had secretly hoped their trap had worked. She thought, since the trap had not worked, her boss and Director Bass may never know. She hated to impose disciplinary actions against her men for doing the right thing; however, her orders came from the top. This was the price of being in management. She also knew managers covered for their agents all the time and intentionally left facts out of reports. She knew her two lead agents wanted a break in the case. She said, "I will review the information and get back to you. Do not share this information with anyone else. This has to be kept quiet. Like I said before, do not share this with any other FBI employees and do not file your report electronically. I want the written original report and all copies sent to me sealed in overnight mail.

"Do we have a security breach inside the FBI?"

"Do as I request, and don't give up. That is an order. We will find the people behind this."

"Roger that. We will not give up," Tracey replied and hung up.

Chapter 11

Vicky and Matt agreed to open their home up to the youth, with hot dogs and swimming on the following Wednesday. The Vaults had mentioned it in the previous youth meeting, and the Sunday School class teacher had reminded the class the prior week. Vicky had mentioned that Angela wanted to bring a friend who does not believe in God. Matt said, "That is great. That is part of what we are commanded to do is help non-believers learn about God. The book of ACTS 1:8 commissions us to spread Christianity. We need to tell and show all people, with our actions of love, kindness, and grace, how Christianity can help people with life and life choices."

"I want to help those in need. Maria introduced me to an undocumented young lady at the soccer field today that was pregnant. I arranged for a doctor to see her. I found out later she was pregnant with twins. The doctor said this was a high-risk pregnancy, and I may have made a difference. What I want to do is help. Of course, I had to get stung by a bee on the foot first, before I was able to meet the lady." Vicky laughed. "Did you know a bee sting can be treated by chewing tobacco?"

Matt smiled, "No I did not know that was a medical treatment for a bee sting, but in Tennessee anything is possible."

"I will tell you about it later. For now, let's get ready for this party."

***

The pool party was planned, and it was a very hot summer day with no rain in the forecast. The party was scheduled for 5 p.m., and hotdogs would be grilled. The youth started showing up, two and three at a time. There was a total of twenty-seven youth that showed up. Some were friends of members, who had been invited. Matt had said, "The more, the better." Angela walked in with a very good-looking young teenager, holding his hand.

Vicky asked, "What is your name?"

Angela said, "This is Tim Thompson, and I told him he was invited to come over with me to swim."

Vicky said, "It is nice to meet you, Tim, and be our guest. Jump in the pool. It will cool you off."

Joe Vault and his wife, Brenda, sat at the table with Vicky and Matt, and talked about how much fun they had at the church sleep over that the kids had enjoyed the prior Friday night. They were watching the kids play pool volleyball, as Joe said, "After you two left, we finally got the kids in the church, where we all agreed on a movie for the boys and one for the girls. We told them the theme of the movie had to be a 90's movie." Joe then added, "The boys picked a western movie with Val Kilmer playing Doc Holiday, and the girls picked an Officer and a Gentleman. I liked both of those movies."

Brenda said, "I will be your huckleberry and be a daisy if I do." She started laughing.

Joe said, "The boys repeated those lines at least one hundred times after the movie. That was the two lines Doc Holiday said when he was ready to shoot someone, or after he had shot someone. The boys would act like they were in a gunfight, and they kept saying those lines over and over."

Joe then turned to the swimming pool and shouted out at Cody, "I will be your huckleberry." The kids started laughing.

Vicky said, "I might have to watch that movie. I like Val Kilmer as an actor."

Joe said, "I will let you borrow it. It is in the van."

They all swam and ate grilled hotdogs. The Vaults volunteered to bring a large cake and ice cream. They started gathering for the lesson, and Jennifer asked, "Tim, do you go to church?"

Tim, who had been having fun, said, "No, not really. I believe in evolution, and you do not."

At that point Matt, who had been quiet most of the afternoon, said, "I believe in evolution."

Tim said, "You're the preacher."

Matt smiled and said, "Is that a question?"

Matt then said, "I still believe in evolution."

Holly asked, "Really, do you, or are you just pulling our leg?"

Matt said, "Yes. The fact that humanity is taller than we were on average, one hundred years ago, is evolution. Evolution, simply put, is just change. But evolution does not explain everything." Matt said, as he looked at Tim, "Darwin left too much out of his teaching of evolution."

Tim asked, "Like what?"

Matt replied, "Why would mankind lose their body hair and then have to kill animals and wear their fur to stay warm? Why lose body hair? That does not sound like evolution to me."

Tim said, "They most likely started out in a hot region like Africa and migrated to colder climates."

The other kids were listening with a great deal of interest. The entire group was quiet. Matt knew he had everyone's attention and said, "The other animals in those regions did not lose their body hair or fur, and people in cold climates do not have more hair on their bodies than people in warm regions." Matt looked around at the group, and then added, "Why are humans the only animals on planet Earth building spaceships? You would think another type of animal would have gotten smarter in ten million years and be splitting atoms alongside humans. No other animal on planet Earth shows any traumatic signs of intellectual development, other than humans."

Tim looked perplexed and did not say anything. Matt looked at the group and said, "Evolution does not explain creation, but it is an on-going process."

Matt then noticed all the kids were still listening and very much dialed into the conversation. He said, "The bible can be somewhat controversial."

Cindy asked, "How so? It seems fairly straight forward to me. We need to follow the great commandant and the golden rule."

Matt looked at Tim, and said, "The bible said the planet had been visited by extraterrestrials." This brought on a lot of laughter from the kids.

Holly said, while laughing, "Now, I know you are pulling our leg, Preacher Donahue."

Matt said, "Genesis 6:4 says, "The sons of gods came down and had sex with the women on earth, and this action produced famous people. Some people think the astronauts are the reason the intelligent level on Earth with humans increased, which catapulted mankind ahead of the other animals on Earth, and if that is not controversial, what is?" Matt had a broad smile on his face, watching some of the kids pull out their bibles and read the verse.

Matt then said, "You can't put God in a box. Anything is possible with the Lord."

Vicky noticed some of the parents had arrived to pick up the kids. They were parked in the road near their driveway. Since this was a swim party, the lesson was going to be short and impromptu. The Vaults had decided to assist at the swim party but had agreed to let Matt and Vicky handle the lesson if they wanted to have one. Vicky decided to forgo the planned lesson. Vicky also seemed to think the debate had gone on long enough, and said, "Let's have our prayer. It is getting late." They all thanked Matt and Vicky for allowing them to swim and eat. They started leaving after the short prayer.

Vicky said, after the last of the kids had left, "The kids are all very well behaved and are a true blessing."

Matt shook his head up and down, and said, "Yes, they are. I hope we are able to provide a Christian foundation for them as they move from being teenagers into being young adults, and on to parenthood. I also hope I hooked Tim Thompson on coming back to youth, maybe even church, and reading the bible."

Vicky smiled and said, "They seemed to all be very well-balanced, loving, caring, young people. My mother said when I was growing up, that is what a parent should hope for most in a child is to have a child that is caring and loving."

"Yes. I believe with the Lord's help; parents can reach that milestone."

Vicky said, "You are correct. If I allow God to direct me and place the problems in God's hands, I seem to be able to deal with life. I pray every day for God's help and read my devotional daily. I have also found out that if I stay very busy, I seem to do better. I know helping the young immigrant lady with her pregnancy and planned surgery was a blessing for me. Helping these kids is a blessing. Plus, taking all the Karate classes, jogging, and the shooting classes help. I shoot at least two boxes of shells a week. I do better if I am not bored. Plus, having you as my loving husband is the biggest blessing."

Vicky remembered her Social Science class in college where they discussed problems in America such as alcoholism, drug addition, overeating, anorexia, gambling, sex, and several others. She recalled the professor had said that sex was a $48 million industry, and no one claimed to know anything about it. She had become aware that her sexual desires were not normal. She recalled how everything seemed so normal and innocent when they first started dating. Matt had said he was turned on watching her with other male partners, and she had acted out the scenes as he requested. He seemed to like the bondage scenes, with her tied up, the most. He was thorough with the entire process. He would make her stay in the apartment for two days without allowing her to leave, and he would sleep on the couch. Before the scenes with the other men, she remembered how frisky she would become and how all the tension in her body would be on edge over the two-day period, waiting for the encounter. Matt always wanted to make love to her after the encounters and would tell her how turned on he was, watching her. Then, Matt went through an awakening with God. He wanted to change and become a preacher, and he made the transition. Now, she just could not adjust, and all that excitement was still part of her. She now was presented with an ongoing internal struggle. She could remember how the sinful life was so fun and exciting. She knew San Diego, California, was the wife-swapping capital of the world, and what Matt and she had done was very minor in comparison. She now was happy to live in Middle Tennessee, where the people were a lot more conservative. She had hoped that lifestyle was behind her, but still she was aware if a man looked at her with desires or commented on how pretty she was, and this caused her desires to start pulsating in her body. The best therapy was helping other people, having devotion by reading the Bible, praying daily, and exercising.

Matt had noticed that, with all the workouts, Vicky had actually become even prettier. He could count her stomach muscles, and her legs had become more developed and more attractive. She was just so pretty, and it would be impossible for her not to be noticed. Matt accepted this and became accustomed to men going out of their way to notice her and talk to her. Matt knew he was going to support her the best he could. He felt his love for the Lord would show him the grace and understanding to support his wife through the difficult times. Marriage was never easy. There were always good times and bad times. Being a Christian is not an easy life. Being a Christian, however, helps a person deal with the bad times and accept the good times in a humble manner. Matt had committed himself to Vicky, and he was not going to let her down. Matt said, "You know, Vicky, I love you more than ever."

She looked at him and said, "I love you, too." She thought a preacher's wife should not have these desires. She wouldn't let him down.

Matt said, "Don't you worry, we will get through life together with God's guidance. If we have a set-back, we will work through it. I truly love you."

Chapter 12

On Friday morning of the next week, Maria called Vicky; but, she was talking so fast, and with her accent, Vicky had to asked her to please slow down. Vicky finally understood that Maria wanted to meet her at the church. Vicky had been jogging around the neighborhood when Maria had called. Vicky agreed to meet Maria in fifteen minutes. She took a quick shower and headed out the door. She figured there must be another pregnant female that needed her help. Maria seemed to know all the Spanish people in the community, and she had become a citizen several years ago when the laws were more relaxed. Vicky had noticed at the soccer field that every one of the Hispanics said hi to Maria. Vicky thought she would check with an attorney to see how difficult it would be to assist with helping the undocumented people to achieve citizenship.

The two vehicles drove into the church parking lot at the same time. Vicky had her solid black Nissan Maxima, and Maria was driving the old model brown Pontiac with two missing hub caps and a dent in the right front fender. Vicky got out of her car and opened the locked door to the church, while turning the security system off. Fridays were typically slow at the church, with no one working other than the lawn service group, who was scheduled later that day to mow the grass and pick up any trash that may have been thrown in the churchyard or parking lot.

The church secretary and Matt were off on Fridays. However, Matt normally would still schedule visits with the elderly and do hospital visitation on Fridays. The elderly loved for him to visit them. He always tried to point something out in the bible that was unusual. He liked to ask them trivia type questions.

Vicky asked Maria and her friend to walk into the conference room through the front entrance. Maria introduced the woman with her as Emma. Emma barely could speak English, with a very limited vocabulary, and was talking very fast. She seemed very nervous, and obviously upset. Vicky noticed the black rings under Emma's eyes, and she noticed Emma did not appear to be pregnant. She, however, looked very stressed and fatigued. Vicky had trouble understanding anything being said in Spanish. The accent was nothing similar to the accent she was accustomed to in Southern California, and the speed and low tone of what was being said hindered her understanding. She asked Maria to explain in English.

Maria held her hand up to Emma for quietness, and she said very slowly and calmly, "She saw a small girl that was in a locked cage at the judge's house. It looked like a large dog cage, and it was covered with a heavy moving blanket. The cover came off for a few seconds when the men were taking it out of the van."

Vicky was very astonished, and excitedly asked, "What judge, and where is this home located? Why have you not called the police? When did this happen?"

"The judge is David Larkin. His home is a mansion near the lake, where Emma works cleaning the home. Emma has no papers. She is from Nicaragua and is afraid she will be deported. She is even scared to tell the co-worker because the lady will tell on her. The co-worker is afraid that if she keeps quiet, the employer will have her arrested and deported for not telling on Emma. Emma's husband told her to say nothing, or she might never get to see her kids again if they are deported. Her husband has no papers, either. If she is to be deported, they could be separated from each other, and her kids would be by themselves. The other employees are constantly living in fear and are scared they all could be deported for any number of reasons. Not telling the employer on a friend, a co-worker, or family member for some reason could get a person deported. That is why we have to watch our kids, especially our teenage girls who do not have legal papers. They can be sexually mistreated. Vicky, I trust you, and I do not know who else to talk to about the girl. Please do not mention this to anyone, but can you help? The girl was naked."

Vicky asked some additional questions, like who else saw the girl, the time of day, and asked for a description of the girl.

Emma said, "She looked to be about twelve years old, and she was Asian."

Maria translated. She said, "She saw the girl in the garage being dropped off out of a van while she was housed in the cage with her hands tied. She had never seen the two men prior to the cage being delivered. They were dark-skinned but not Spanish-looking, more like

Europeans. Emma had not felt good, and her child had been sick with a high fever the previous few nights. She had very little sleep the prior Wednesday night. She indicated they were cleaning the home on Thursday, and she fell asleep upstairs in one of the guest bedroom closets. When she woke up the two ladies working in the kitchen and the other maid had all left. They must have felt she had left early, because she had told the new maid she was not feeling good and had very little sleep. It was getting dark outside when she woke up. She walked quietly down the stairs and through the home, trying to figure out which door to leave through without anyone knowing she was still in the home. She said she was terrified. She knew the home had a security system, and she knew she needed to leave before it was turned on by the judge. She knew she would be fired and deported if the judge found out she was still in the home and fell asleep when she should have been working. She was going to leave through the side door in the garage. She noticed the light on the security camera in the foyer was flashing red. She had noticed in the past, when they were cleaning, it was always flashing green. She was on the verge of turning the knob to the door when she looked through the glass in the interior door into the garage, and she saw the large white van pull into the garage. She was afraid to move. Then, she saw the door to the van open, and the cage with the little girl was dropped off. Emma said she was not scheduled to work at that time of day, and they thought she had already left when the other maid and cooks had left. She saw the judge in the garage, talking with the two men. He appeared to be angry and maybe cussing the two men, for not taking better care of the girl. There were no other witnesses. Thursday was the only day they were scheduled to clean. When one of the men bent down to set the cage down on the concrete floor of the garage, his shirt rolled up his back, and she could see his gun in the back of his pants, secured in his waistband. At that point, she hid in a coat closet in the hall, near the foyer and front door, for over an hour. She said she started to shake and could not stop trembling. She heard them carrying the cage upstairs. Then, the two men and the judge came back down the stairs and stood in front of the hall closet. She heard one of the men thanking the judge and saying they would make certain the next girl would be fed and bathed before being delivered. Once the two men left and the judge went upstairs, she waited and finally eased out the back door, hoping the security system was still off. She said she does not know anything about the security system, and she was afraid they saw her. Some of the cameras on the exterior appeared to be flashing green and some of the ones on the interior were still flashing red. The one in the garage where she exited was flashing green. She placed a trench coat from the closet over her head and hid under it. She ran across the field until she made it to the shore of the lake and woody area. That is the area where the fence does not extend all the way to the lake, and she could exit the yard. She walked back to the road through the woods in the dark, and walked home, which was a few miles. She has been crying ever since. She's afraid for her life and her family's life. She does not know what happened with the girl after she hid in the closet.

She worried she would be killed or deported, never to see her kids again, but she was worried more about the girl in the dog cage. Since she does not know if the security cameras were on, she does not know if they filmed her leaving the home. She wants to do the right thing, but she is scared for her family. I told her you can be trusted, and you could help. We trust you Vicky."

Maria then explained that Emma and three other ladies were preparing the home for one of the judge's parties. The two cooks stayed in the kitchen, until they left with the new maid. The other maid was new, and Emma did not know her. Her English was not very good. The judge works out of state in Ohio, and only visits the home a few times a year. He used to visit more often, but he has slowed down over the years. They explained that the judge had one of his parties planned this weekend, told Vicky about the parties, and answered the rest of her questions.

Vicky glanced at Emma while Maria was talking, thought about how Emma was dressed in her black work shoes, and realized the security people would be able to identify that a maid had left the home. She had scratches on her forearms and a large one on her ankle. Vicky assumed she got the scratches from walking in the woods. Vicky told Maria she would help. One way or another, she would help that child. She said she would not mention Emma's name, or how she found out about this information; they did the right thing by telling her. She asked Maria, "Can you provide her family another place to stay or could she stay with other family members until they hear back from me? This is a safety measure, and even with the raincoat, the security people might be able to identify her as a maid."

Marie looked concerned but understood. She said "Emma has family in Nashville. I will tell her to take her husband and child, and what she needs for a few days, and go stay with them."

Vicky pulled two hundred dollars from her pocket and gave it to Emma, and said, "This should help. Please leave as soon as possible and do not tell anyone where you and your family are going." She said goodbye to the ladies and reinforced to them she would not mention Emma's name. She explained to Maria not to mention this on the phone. The authorities might be listening, and she would call a good policeman that could help.

Vicky contacted Wayne by phone as soon as they left the church. She told Wayne they needed to meet as quickly as possible at the church or wherever was closer, and that this was very important. Wayne indicated he would be there in thirty-five minutes and hung up without saying goodbye. Wayne came directly to the church from his dentist appointment, where he was undergoing a routine personal dental visit. He called his boss and told him that his visit with the dentist was taking a little longer than expected. Wayne drove into the parking lot and walked into the conference room. Wayne asked, "What's up?"

Vicky was sitting at the table, deep in thought. Vicky looked up and explained what she had heard. She explained that there was a party planned at Judge Larkin's house tonight.

Wayne said, "Without her statement to the police, we cannot obtain a search warrant. Then, if she's not legal and does not speak English, I doubt any judge would sign off on a search warrant, especially since we are talking about an Federal Appeals Court Judge. Those positions are selected by senators."

Vicky understood that it was a select invitation-only party. She told Wayne that she planned to attend the party to see if she could locate the young girl. There was no other way, and they had to help the child.

Wayne asked, "How credible is the lady?"

"There is no doubt in my mind that she saw the girl in the cage in the garage. She has a very limited English vocabulary."

She hesitated, and then said, "You know, Wayne, this has to be related to what the two FBI agents told you about the murdered Asian girls and their two bodies found here in middle Tennessee."

Wayne said, "Wait a minute. You are talking about a federal judge. Again, there is no way we could obtain a warrant based on what an illegal person was saying about a federal judge; and, it might be related, but we need proof. Judge Larkin might not be involved, but someone else could be using his home to hold the young girl. Does this lady know for certain it was, in fact, the judge and not someone else? Plus, the FBI has not told anyone about the missing girls and the graves. We have no proof there are any missing girls. We cannot assume the FBI will substantiate that for us or reveal their case and information about the ongoing investigations. We have nothing."

Wayne hesitated, and looked around like he was in deep thought. Frustrated, he said, "Dammit. However, that would explain the undercover agent working for the newspaper and being killed at the water tower. They know they are looking for one of their own."

Vicky said, "The lady will not give a statement. She is afraid she would be deported and never see her kids again. I don't blame her for not wanting to give a statement. I am surprised she told me what she told me. You know that no one in law enforcement will believe her, and off she'd go back to Central America without her family. She said that she saw the judge talking with the two men, and then one of the men promised that next time the girl would be fed and washed before they dropped her off. The woman speaks very little English, but she said she understood some of what was said when the man was talking to the judge in the hall, while she was hiding in the coat closet. She said she was trembling uncontrollably and was afraid, because she would have been killed if discovered. The men left by the garage door, and the judge was upset when he first saw the child because she had not been bathed or fed. You are right. We need proof. Then, we can obtain the warrant. We don't have a lot of time, and I am going to figure out how to get inside that home."

"If you can get inside and see any signs of the young girl, you can then exit, and I will block the driveway if I have to. I will wait for Vince and his deputies to get there with a search warrant."

Vicky asked, "If we have probable cause, would we need a warrant?"

Wayne changed the topic and asked, "How are you planning to attend?"

"I am working on it."

Wayne said, "We need an excuse to obtain access to the home. Do you know who is catering the party? Did Maria indicate if the cleaning staff was going back to the home?"

Maria and Emma had explained to Vicky about the cleaning and cooking type of work performed at the judge's residence. Some were employed as housekeepers and cooks, while others were employed for the lawn care. They were finished with the cleaning of the home for the upcoming party. Maria explained that Emma had said that they all were told that their services would not be needed during the party tonight, and that they were to leave the house by 4:00 p.m. on Thursday. If they were requested back to the home before the party for any reason, they would be contacted. So, Vicky continued, "I will not be able to enter as a maid unless there is a need for additional cleaning required, and then I would need to hide inside the home. But, I am certain they would count the number of maids entering the home and watch them. We can't wait. We cannot count on me entering the home as a maid. We need some other method. There is a child in that home that needs us, and no, they did not know who is catering the party. They said when the judge has a party, he normally hires Dillon Hayes to supply working girls for his male guests. Dillon normally tries to persuade the young Hispanic girls to work for him, and Maria said they try to keep their kids away from Dillon. Dillon Hayes drops off women at the party. Do you know Dillon Hayes?"

Wayne said, "I have had the privilege to arrest Dillon many times, mostly for public intoxication or driving under the influence. He has been arrested twice for assault. He got off because the young ladies would not press charges. Both times he had been rough with the females, and he drinks and parties too much. He has the reputation of selling drugs to make a living, and he was busted several years ago for selling weed. He has managed the strip club in Nashville for a few years, where he allegedly makes money on the side, dealing with the dancers and setting them up with private dates. He lives near Interstate 24 in a trailer park on the east side of the interstate, but he runs his illegal business in Nashville. He deals in drugs and women in Nashville. He is small-time and stays under the FBI radar. Like I said, he does not deal in Butler County, or I would have arrested him. It was well known that one of his enterprises was his group of women, so I am not surprised he would be the pimp for such activities. The strip club makes it difficult to catch him running a prostitution ring through the club. I will go talk to him."

Vicky raised her eyebrow and said, "You mean, threaten him."

"It works. There might not be a better way to get inside that home in such short notice. Maybe you can enter with his women. Look around and call me. I will be stationed outside."

Vicky said, "I will do it. We are the only chance that child has. I don't see another way, and we don't have time to figure something else out." She repeated, "The only hope that child has, Wayne, is us, and I not going to let that child down."

Wayne left and drove toward Dillon's home near the interstate. He agreed with Vicky; he did not want to let the child down and wanted justice. He had always hated when people who were sworn to uphold the law took advantage of their position and benefited illegally. He knew Dillon would not be working this time of day and would most likely be at home, after working late the prior night. He also remembered how he did not like Dillon. After talking with the two women Dillon had hit, he felt Dillon was a jerk for using the young women. They backed out of signing their statements, and both times Dillon walked. Dillon tried to stay out of the center of Butler when he could. He knew how Wayne felt about him.

Wayne saw Dillon in his nice, older model Chevy Camaro on Highway 40, and turned the unmarked car around. His unmarked vehicle was set up with the lights on the grill and headlights like the unmarked traffic cop cars used by city police in Nashville. He accelerated and pulled his car behind Dillon's, with the lights on. Dillon pulled over, and Wayne could tell Dillon was not happy being pulled over. Wayne walked up to the car and said, "Dillon, I need you to step out of the car."

Dillon had figured he would not be asked to exit the car. He assumed he would be asked for license and vehicle registration and could stay seated in the car; at least, that is the way his last speeding tickets were handled. When Wayne asked him to step out of the car,

Dillon knew he would need to hide his gun. He figured if he was asked to step out of the car, the car was going to be searched. He knew, if an officer asked him to step out, that was not a good sign.

"I was not doing anything wrong; besides, I heard you aren't the sheriff no more. This is harassment. If you are going to give me a speeding ticket, then give me the damn ticket."

Wayne said, "You swerved, and I need to verify you are not under the influence, ... and I said, step out of the car."

Dillon stepped out of the car, and Wayne aggressively pushed him up against the car and frisked him, finding a pistol in his waistband.

He said, "You've got to be kidding. You are a convicted felon, and you have a gun in your waistband. Dillon, I am going to arrest you, and you are correct; I am not the sheriff. I am a special agent for the TBI. You know it is illegal for a felon to carry a gun. You have violated your probation." Wayne had not figured Dillon was stupid enough to carry a gun, with him being a felon; in addition, he was still on probation for drug charges. Wayne smiled, standing behind Dillon, and knew now he had leverage on Dillon. He would be very cooperative with a deal.

Dillon ducked his head, and said, "Damn, Sheriff. There's no harm. Come on, let me go. Please. I am not doing anything wrong. I don't want to go back to jail. This just isn't fair. I have been straight for two years, with no drugs."

"No. I am going to arrest you and put your ass in jail for three to five years, and I am going to confiscate your nice sports car. We can use it to ride around when we are looking for bad guys."

Dillon said, "Shit, this isn't fair."

Wayne took him and put him in the back seat, with handcuffs. Dillon looked like he was going to cry. Dillon was a thirty-two-year-old high school dropout who had avoided hard labor. He had always tried to get by without working and made his money off others who worked. Wayne had always considered him a con man. He had short, brown hair and was about six foot two in height. He was overweight, with a flabby belly.

Once they settled into the car, Wayne looked in his rearview mirror, watching Dillon, and said, "Well, maybe we could work something out."

Dillon seemed to be too eager, and said, "What would that be?"

"I understand you will be dropping some women off at Judge Larkin's party later today."

Dillon seemed irritated, hesitated, and finally said, "Where did you hear that bullshit?"

"Okay, let's go." Wayne acted like he was going to call in to have the highway patrol tow Dillon's car.

Wayne started the car with the mic in his right hand, and Dillon said, "But what if I was? That is not illegal, if some folks want to have a good time."

Wayne said, "So. Is that a yes?"

Dillon looked down, and then looked into the rearview mirror, into Wayne's eyes, and said, "I have been asked to bring one very lovely lady to the party and drop her off at 6:55 p.m. on the dot. The judge is exceptionally anal about his timetable, and the lady I drop off."

Wayne clarified, "One lady."

"That is right. Just one special lady."

Wayne said, "I want you to drop off a lady working for me, with no questions asked. All you are required to do is get her in the home and leave. I will forget about your pistol, but I will not give it back to you. You can keep your wheels and stay out of prison."

Dillon said, "The lady needs to be special, or the judge can be mean. The judge is paying top dollar at two grand. I assume she will need to strip dance."

"The lady will be special. Don't worry. Do we have a deal?"

Dillon said, "Yes. I will be ready at 6:45, at the grocery store. She needs to look good and be special. I promised the judge I would deliver a special lady. She needs to be very pretty."

Wayne said, "Dillon, you are not to breathe a word of the arrangement to anyone, because if anything happens to the woman, I will personally come after you. I will arrest you for carrying this pistol, and your ass will go to jail. Do you understand?"

Dillon said, "They are having a masquerade party, so tell her to have a mask of some type. She needs to dress very expensively. He likes high-class looking women at his parties."

Dillon seemed thankful to be let go and not be going to jail. He realized Wayne had him, and there was no other option.

Wayne said, "You better make this happen, or your ass will go to jail. Do you understand?"

Dillon said, "Yes, boss man. I will do this one favor, and we are even."

Dillon figured he would stay out of Butler after this, and this would blow over. He could drop the girl off, and the judge would not know about the TBI being involved with him or the girl. He thought to himself, "I am fucked if I don't help the TBI, and the judge may never know I was aware that she was some type of undercover agent. I will have to take my chances and lay low for a while."

***

Wayne immediately called to ask Vicky to meet him at the church. Vicky agreed to meet him in the parking lot. He told her the arrangements, but he mentioned this might not be the best plan, and she should not be doing this. "I am not certain I trust Dillon Hayes. I hope I was able to clean off home plate with him, to make certain he understood he'd better not double-cross me. I suggest we think of something else."

Vicky said, "Okay, go ahead and get a warrant."

"You know no other judge is going to sign a warrant based on a non-citizen who cannot speak English without some proof, especially since we are dealing with a federal judge."

Vicky said, "Exactly. That is why I am going into that home as a stripper, and we better not let this girl down. We are her only hope."

Wayne knew they did not have time to set up surveillance on the judge's home. Plus, he knew his new boss with the TBI would never agree to it. Not with a federal judge being involved, and by the time the FBI got involved, the girl would be moved to another location. Wayne said, "The best way..."

Vicky interrupted Wayne, and finished the sentence, "Is me entering the home as an invited guest, and you ready to come in as backup, once I find the girl. We really have no other choice if we are going to try to save this girl, which I am going to do one way or another, with or without your help."

Wayne, at this point, realized Vicky's conviction, and he knew he owed her his life. Wayne could tell she was not going to sit back and allow a girl to be raped and maybe even killed. The more he thought about this girl, the more he agreed it did sound plausible, with what the two FBI agents had described regarding the two Asian girls found near Nashville.

Vicky said, "It is time for action. If you don't feel comfortable, then say so. Either you are in or not."

Wayne nodded his head, "I am in. Let's get this done, but you'd better be careful. We are dealing with killers. Cramer was a killer, and he may have worked for these people. They would have hired someone else to replace Cramer, so be on the lookout. The quicker you can look and leave, the better." He looked at Vicky when he said, "look and leave", making certain she understood. He wanted to emphasize that point, so she would not take it on herself to take any unnecessary chances. He would call for backup if needed, and he knew that was the only way this could work. People like this were always prepared, and he was not certain Vicky understood how dangerous this was going to be.

Vicky looked at Wayne very sternly and said, "Yes. Cramer was a killer, and we took care of him. I will be okay. We have to try to save that child. I will not be able to live with myself if I do nothing."

Vicky told Wayne that she would go as a stripper. Wayne understood; he really did not like that idea, but he came around. He couldn't imagine that anything deadly was going on during a party hosted by a federal judge. These were rich and powerful people, most likely, invited to the party. Not all of them would be involved in human trafficking and raping a child. No one would know her, and she could act sick and call him for back up if she needed to be extracted.

Vicky said, "Listen, I can handle a sixty-year-old man. I looked into Maria's friend's eyes. There is no question: she was not bluffing. She saw a child in a cage. I could detect fear and anguish in her. She has no reason to lie. She has risked everything and her family by coming forward. She would be killed if they knew what she saw, and

Wayne, we would also be killed if they thought we knew. This information is toxic. Matter of fact, I asked the maid to leave the area with her family until I get word to her that it is safe to return. I understand the danger. I also understand no one is in position to help that girl but us."

Wayne felt he was out of options. "I will stay outside, parked down the street at the pull over at the large field, and you have your phone set with my text number, and I will be ready to bust into the place."

Vicky said, "Listen, Wayne, I will do what is necessary to locate that little girl. We may be the only hope she has. They cannot afford to allow her to live. She is the proof of the crime. You most likely will not have to enter the home. Dillon can drop me off at the front door, and I will walk out the front gate and call you when you can pick me up, if I can't locate her. I should be able to look around in the home while a party is ongoing. I figure it'll take two hours once I walk through the front door. They will have a meal planned for the guests and while everyone is eating, I will walk through the home. This is like you mentioned to me days ago, about the FBI not crawling in the gutters of our society to build rapports with people. I have tried to help the Spanish people in Butler and look what we have discovered. They helped with the bank robbers from Arkansas, and now this. It is hard to tell what these undocumented people know and see across our country. When they see law enforcement, they think deportation, and run."

Wayne said, "Yes. This is case in point. I will be on standby for two hours, then I will be knocking at the front door." Wayne thought to himself, these people are killers. They will be especially careful. She has made up her mind, and she is going into the home, with or without me. Maybe this is the safest plan. Finding proof will be very difficult. On the other hand, the judge might not have any security personnel inside the home. After all, who would work for the judge under these circumstances?

They said goodbye, and Wayne drove to his office in Nashville.

Vicky went to Nashville and purchased the outfit and mask for the party. She tried on several different outfits before settling on the jumpsuit. She purchased a very tight-fitting, white shiny jumpsuit that was low cut in the back and barely covered her breasts. She made certain she could conceal her iPhone in the front of the jumpsuit, inside the band of her panties. The jumpsuit was baggy in the area just below her navel, where the material was sewed together, and hung loose fitting from the strap around her neck. The jumpsuit was designed to be fastened in the back of the neck with a button, leaving her upper back exposed, and was designed to be worn with no bra. She would wear a high cut thong panty that would hold her iPhone tight against her belly. She decided she would wear a long blonde wig with a tiger mask, covering her eyes so that if anyone in attendance was from Butler or even went to their church, they would not recognize her. When Vicky got home at about 4 p.m. from shopping, Matt came up to her and kissed her and asked, "What did you buy?"

Vicky showed him the one-piece, and Matt said, "I cannot wait to see it on you. Maybe we can have date night next Friday night in Nashville, but not in Butler. You are not allowed to wear that outfit in Butler."

She smiled and said, "I was going to wear it to church Sunday."

Matt looked surprised and horrified.

She smiled and said, "Don't worry. I am just kidding."

He reminded Vicky he would meet with the church council after 5:30 p.m. They were going to discuss the possibility of hiring an assistant pastor or a youth part-time pastor. The membership was starting to climb. Every week at least two families were joining the church. Vicky did not want to mention the need for a more reliable janitor, but at some point, the church would need to address that, also. She was going to start looking for a full-time job and not be able to assist the church as much as she had been. Matt smiled and said, "I am not going to hold my breath on the church council making a final decision at this meeting. The reason they were meeting on Friday was because Gordan and Alice Phillips will be back in town Friday afternoon, and everyone was busy on the weekends. Gordan and Alice wanted to be part of the discussion on hiring an additional pastor. Hey, maybe you can model that silk looking jumpsuit for me later tonight."

Vicky smiled and said, "Maybe." She thought about telling Matt about the long, blond wig which hung down to her waist, but thought she might just surprise him with the wig and the tiger mask.

Matt left for the church meeting at about 4:30 p.m., and Vicky got dressed in her outfit, with a long, baggy buttoned dress shirt of Matt's to cover her up. She drove to the grocery store and parked away from the other cars. Wayne had told Dillon to look for a black Nissan Maxima in the parking lot. She did not want anyone to see her in the outfit or the wig. She knew she could not explain her attire and the wig to another church member.

Chapter 13

The personal phone buzzed. He always hated the phone. For years he had been bullied and chastised. He knew he had no alternative. "Hello." He waited.

"You're a damn fool!" The harsh, direct voice announced, "You listen to me: you better take care of your security problems before I take care of you."

He felt the pit in his belly turn. He felt flushed. The voice was so stern, he became frightened. "There was someone videoed leaving your home after the package was delivered. How could you not have known? If this blows up on you, I better not have any blow back."

He was able to meek out in a surprised voice, "What?" He was truly alarmed.

"We think it was a maid. She was covered in a trench coat, which did not cover her legs and shoes. Only a maid wears shoe like that. We did not detect anyone else entering the home except for the two cooks and the two maids. Only one maid is seen leaving with the two cooks at 4 p.m. I have dispatched someone to interview the maids."

The judge knew what that meant. The maids would be interrogated, and the one from the video would be tortured and then killed. Her family would also be killed in front of her. There would be no mercy. The judge said, without considering who he was talking with, "Can we just deport the family? Who is she going to tell if she even knows anything? These people are very easy to intimidate and control."

"Listen to me, you incompetent imbecile. If this happens again, I will have my men interview you. Now don't tell me what I am forced to do because you are such an incompetent ass. You are turning into a liability." The phone call ended.

The judge thought to himself, "That poor family!" He knew what the man on the other end of the telephone was capable of doing, and his men were all trained to execute the orders. He had lived in a constant state of fear since they met in the Army decades ago. The colonel was responsible for all those killings over the years. When was it going to stop? He felt empathy for the maids and wondered which one had caused the problem. The judge also remembered thinking, that night at the election so many years ago when the colonel was elected to the United States Senate representing Tennessee, that his power would become enormous if he stayed in office unchecked; and, he also realized he would never be released from being the senator's pawn.

Chapter 14

While sitting in the edge of the cornfield in his truck, Wayne looked at his watch. He had been walking around, acting like he was surveying the field for dove hunting. When his phone rang, he was hesitant on answering it, but he knew the Butler County Sheriff only called him if it was important. Vince had never been the type of person who called just to be friendly. Wayne answered. Vince said, "We just received a call an hour ago, and I just pulled into the wooded area north of town, off Highland View. Someone dumped the body of a young Spanish lady. She has been beaten and maybe raped. The body was not hidden. It was easy to locate. A woman coming home from the store called it in as she was driving on Highland View and thought she saw some exposed skin of a body about fifteen feet off the road. It is not nice to see, but it is nothing like the body we worked at the water tower. We could not locate any identification. She might have been a maid. The only clothes she had on were her shoes."

Wayne felt anxious about Vicky, and what she was prepared to do. He said, "Listen. I am on a call. You need to call the TBI office line and request Doctor Parker and Dallas to investigate. Both men worked for the State of Tennessee Medical Examiner Department and the Forensic Department. Thanks for the update. I will call you later to check on the case." Wayne hung up immediately and thought, the lady had been tortured and killed and left to be found. Someone is sending a message to the other Spanish people in the community. He thought, dammit, Vicky is mostly likely en route with Dillon. He knew now that this was a bad idea. These people were killers, and they needed to abort. He hit her preset speed dial number.

Vicky looked at her phone and knew Dillon would be pulling into the parking lot at any time. She answered the call. Wayne said, "We need to abort. The local sheriff's department just located a young Hispanic lady's body off Highland View, just north of downtown." There was a pause, and then he said, "The lady had been tortured and left in the open to be found. They are sending a message to us, with that body."

Vicky said, "The person I met with took her family to Nashville, hiding with her extended family. It must have been the other maid. My contact said she was new to the job and new to the area. She was trying to save money to send to her family in one of the South American countries, so they could join her. I am not stopping. We are not going to abort. Dillon just drove into the parking lot." She hung up and thought, "Her death was my fault. I never considered her as a possible target. Emma had said the lady was filling in for the other maid that injured her hip. Please God forgive me for not protecting that innocent lady." The guilt she felt was almost

150

overwhelming. Maria and her friends trusted her to make the right decisions and protect them. She got mad and looked straight ahead in thought. She accepted what she had to do.

Vicky said to herself, "I am not going to let this girl down." She punched in delete on her iPhone to delete the entire call history for all her recent calls. She figured her phone might be seized at the door. She had already deleted her contacts, and her phone was clean and new. She had memorized Wayne's number, and hoped she would have an opportunity to call him.

Steve D. Nichols

Chapter 15

She waited for Dillon to pull up next to her, and she told him to follow her to a wide area on Lake Road where fishermen sometimes park and fish from the bank. She would leave her car.

Dillon, still worried about double-crossing the federal judge, glanced at his watch, and said, "Okay, but we need to hurry."

She drove off, with Dillon following. She left a change of clothes in her front seat and left the key in the floorboard. She knew she had a backup key hidden under the rear bumper.

Dillion didn't know who she was when he met her at the grocery store parking lot, but he wished she worked for him. He was just able to see her face, blond hair, and dark perfect suntanned complexion through the rolled down window, and thought she was stunning, with her perfectly bleached white smile. He could not wait to see the rest of her. When Vicky pulled her car over, got out, pulled off the button-down baggy shirt (leaving it in her front seat), and walked around to get in Dillon's car, his jaw dropped. She was perfect, with the long blonde hair hanging down past her waist, dark brown eyes, and the dark bronze skin with the perfect athletic-looking body. He was genuinely stunned, watching her walk around the front of his car. Her dark, suntanned skin looked more like a bronze color in contrast to the white shiny jumpsuit, which presented a perfect picture. He had been worried about the lady not being pretty enough, and he now realized she was drop-dead gorgeous. The judge had made it clear how pretty the woman had to be. He had emphasized her looks twice. Dillon knew, after dealing with the judge in the past, what he expected.

Vicky jumped in the front seat and said, "Let's go."

He thought, she might be a prostitute. He then said, "Wow! Does the TBI have a secret side business? Where did he find you? You surely aren't a cop, are you?"

Vicky smiled and said, "Your job is to drop me off. No more, no less; and thank you, Dillon, for taking this job working for the TBI." She knew Dillon would not want anyone to know he was helping the police. In his line of work, that could be very detrimental for business, and maybe his health. "I would suggest you not mention this to anyone. I believe Officer Tipton made that clear to you. Did he not? Do you understand?"

"Yes. That part was made crystal clear. I will drop you off at 6:55, and leave."

Dillon kept glancing over at her as he drove to the judge's house. He could smell her perfume, which just added to the perfect picture. Dillon said, "After this job if you were interested, give me a call. I manage the strip club in North Nashville. Some very nice men come in on a regular basis, and we just added a shower on the back part of the stage with glass walls and a glass door for the audience to watch the dancer while bathing."

Vicky cut him off and said, "No thanks."

"I am just saying. You could really make a lot of money. He caught himself and thought, "I might be talking to a cop." Then he said, "There is nothing illegal about taking your clothes off on a stage in front of a lot of men. It is perfectly legal and can be very lucrative for a dancer as smoking hot as you."

Vicky smiled to herself and thought, it is a wonder he is not in jail for being so stupid. They rode the rest of the way in silence to the judge's home. Wayne was sitting in his older black truck. Vicky saw him and thought, "I wonder where he got that truck?" as they drove by. Dillon did not seem to notice Wayne, which was good. Wayne assured Vicky he would wait for a signal from her, either a text or a call from her cell phone. He agreed that she had two hours, then he would come to the front door. They had figured she would be able to walk through the home at some point, and they had hoped the opportunity would be as soon as she arrived. In and out, very fast, was the plan.

Steve D. Nichols

Chapter 16

Matt was at the church that evening to meet with some of the church council to talk about the church's finances and possibly hiring an associate pastor. He never knew who would show up at these meetings and who would not. He had left early to see what information he could provide during the meeting about the increase in the new memberships, the number of people now attending the Sunday morning church service, and how much the Sunday school classes had grown. Preacher David, Matt's mentor, had always said the church council could understand numbers, and always be prepared for any type of meeting in which your career is concerned, because no one on the council will have the numbers and be prepared to represent your interest. Most people in the church only think a preacher works one day a week. Matt felt the growth in the church would provide the information needed. It was self-evident to Matt that the need to expand and have two pastors was obvious. At least, that was his opinion.

After the board members had taken their seats in the front conference room, they had a short but nice blessing. "The church has been growing, and the finances are improving," said Robert Bowers. "We are here to address the need to hire an additional pastor or youth director. Then, Tyler will address several other ongoing projects." Robert had been the church treasurer for the past ten years and kept his fingers on the pulse of the church's financial commitments. "But do we really need to hire another preacher?"

Matt looked around the table, and then realized no one was present to represent his position of needing help. He remembered what his mentor had said and was thankful he was prepared for this meeting. Matt wanted to remain calm and not show any emotion, but he wanted to emphasize his point to the committee. After all, he loved these people and the community, and was so thankful for the opportunity to be their pastor. Matt said, "Most churches this size have two and sometimes three full-time preachers. The church has grown, with more members routinely showing up to church than in the past decade."

He handed out copies of the prior ten-year records for attendance and mentioned the numeric results. He then provided the church council a copy of the records since he had been the preacher, and the growth noted was forty-seven percent. He also handed them a list of churches in Nashville, on which he had outlined the larger churches which had multiple preachers. The list had forty-five churches with two or more preachers. "We had twenty-seven kids at the swim party at the youth meeting," he said, giving them a copy of the records showing the increase in Sunday school attendance since he had been there. "We even have people driving up from Nashville and driving south from southern Kentucky to attend the church service and Sunday school classes." He named off several families. "Look, I am working seventy to eighty hours a week, and Vicky is working about forty hours a week, and you do not pay her. So yes, you need to hire another person. The only reason I showed you these records is to stress the need for additional help. It is about being able to meet the needs of the flock and grow the church. It's about meeting the needs of our community, and helping the youth obtain a strong Christian foundation which will support them the rest of their lives."

Matt knew that by showing the list of churches with two or more preachers, along with the records of growth on three different pieces of paper, it would have more of an impact with him introducing each item before sending the paper copy to each of the council members.

Tyler smiled and said, "Maybe we should put you on a timecard."

Matt, knowing Tyler was joking, said, "No way you are putting me on a timecard. Jesus said in the book of Mathew, talking about taxes, to give Caesar what is Caesar's, but I do not want to have to keep track of my work hours even if I made more money and could pay more taxes." Matt looked at Tyler and then Robert because he knew they were the leaders who made the decisions for the church. Matt then said, "Sometimes meeting with families away from church is work even though it also is social."

To change the subject and move the meeting along, Tyler said, "I have been a salaried employee my entire career. I honestly was not aware of the difficultly of keeping accurate records for a preacher." He then asked, "Do we need a youth minister or associate pastor?"

Matt said, "Both. We really need to start considering having two Sunday morning services. The church will be over capacity soon with just one sermon. By providing two services, we are reaching out to the members and the community by being more accommodating. I do believe Joe and Brenda Vault are excellent youth directors and do great things with the kids. The church is very blessed to have them, but most churches pay a full-time music director, who also works as the youth director. At some point they may want to step down, and consideration needs to be made on their replacement. We cannot expect someone to take on all that responsibility in the church, gratis. The church does not need to be caught totally surprised and without an action plan."

The meeting continued for another thirty minutes, with Matt thinking that at least he had said his piece. He planned to eat out with Joe Vault and two of his older sons after the meeting. He was pleased with the way the meeting ended, with consideration being given on hiring a second pastor who could work with the youth and assist with the community outreach programs. Mr. Bowers commented, "Matt, you certainly are a very prepared person." Matt smiled.

Chapter 17

Dillon drove up the driveway at a slow speed. Vicky was taken aback and stunned by the home, the size, the material used in construction, and the landscaping. The home was magnificent. The cost of the home had to be way over a million dollars. He stopped the car and got out, and walked around to open her door, dropping her off as requested by the judge at 6:55 p.m. He told Vicky to walk into the judge's home; there was no need to knock. "He will be waiting for you. He is very punctual about his parties and the time in which things are scheduled. It is 6:55 on the dot." Dillon had mentioned for her to expect to be electronically scanned as soon as she walked into the home. Vicky got out and adjusted her top to make sure her breasts were covered, and her iPhone was securely in place and concealed in the band of her panties. She had planned on saying, if the iPhone were discovered, that she would need to call a taxi for a ride home. The front of her outfit was split down past her belly, with excessive ruffled-type material below her navel. Everywhere else, the fabric was very tight fitting. She thought to herself that her outfit was showing too much cleavage, as she walked up the front two steps. She had hoped she could enter and immediately start looking around inside the lower level of the home. As soon as Vicky opened the door, the elderly man, who looked like the picture of the judge Wayne had provider her, walked up to her and said, "You are the prettiest lady I have ever seen. I am truly privileged to make your acquaintance. I am your host. Please come into my humble home." He took her hand and kissed it. He repeated, "I am so honored to make your acquaintance."

Vicky smiled at the elderly man. Her first impression was of a grandfather figure, who was polite and sympathetic. Standing in the foyer, she noticed the solid wood oak paneling, the marble floor, and the large oak staircase leading to the upstairs. The exterior of the home was all over-sized brick with a pea gravel concrete driveway and sidewalk. Vicky wondered how a federal judge would be able to afford this mansion. She saw the pictures on the wall of the judge when he was a young man in the Army and college. She noticed several other soldiers in the group photos. There were photos of the judge receiving some awards, but no recent photos, photos of children, or of a wife. Vicky thought the lack of photos of a wife and children might be alarming. He might have a hidden dark side which a wife or grown children may have forced him to keep in secrecy.

The judge asked her to walk up the stairs to the second floor, and they proceeded to the balcony. "The fun is about to begin, and my guests are expecting to be entertained," he told her.

As he gently took her hand and led her up the stairs, she stated, "This is a very lovely home. Do you have two levels or three?"

The judge steered her out onto the balcony once they reached the top level overlooking the back yard and the lake, and finally replied, "I have a small man cave in the basement. There are three levels, my dear." He then explained that his guests had already eaten and were ready for some entertainment. She noticed a hot tub with a small pool in the east area, with another balcony and another steel spiral staircase leading to the pool. The balcony overlooked the pool, which had French doors opening from the foyer area of the second level of the home. She walked up beside him on this balcony and noticed about thirty people, or fifteen couples, in the patio area below. She could see the lake and another home, which was larger than the judge's home, over on the other point of the lake, which must be past the judge's home on the small road off Lake Road. There were no other homes visible, and the view of the lake extended for close to a mile. The view overlooking the stone-covered patio, pool to the right, and the lake was beautiful. She was very much surprised at the money spent to build these two homes, and no one had ever mentioned them in church. She focused on the people attending the party, trying to recognize those in attendance. She noticed the way everyone was spread out; she could not ascertain if these were couples or random friends. She noticed a very pretty blond lady who appeared to be in her thirties, talking with several other women. With the masquerade masks on and the distance from the top of the balcony, it was difficult to guess the ages of the women, and Vicky thought that most, no doubt, have had enhancements completed by plastic surgeons. Most of the guests were in their fifties or sixties, maybe even seventies. She looked for the obvious wrinkled skin on the hands, arms, and necks, trying to judge the ages of the women. Vicky did not recognize anyone at the party. The men appeared to be older gentlemen with gray hair.

The women were wearing their masquerade masks, which mostly just covered their eyes, but a few wore masks that covered their entire faces. The men were in tuxedos, and all talking in groups of three or four. She noticed the women appeared to be drawn to and wanting to talk to the pretty blond.

Vicky figured she must either be the alpha female of the group or was with the alpha male of the group. The judge was just standing and looking at his guests. Vicky figured she would stand there and wait for his instructions, and her opportunity to search the home. She had not seen a door leading to the man cave in the main floor foyer when she entered. Vicky and Wayne had agreed that the girl was most likely being held in the basement. Wayne had repeatedly told Vicky to be careful and not to assume anything. "Someone is raping and killing girls. You will be in danger, and I will be your only backup," he had reminded her. She was aware she needed to locate the stairs and cover as much area as possible, as fast as possible, and then act sick and leave. She wished she could have secured photos of everyone at the party. Being able to identify these people might come in handy. They had not considered trying to secure a miniature size camera to her outfit. Dillon had indicated the women in the past were always checked at the door for electronic items with a scanner by private security men. He had mentioned to her in the car on the drive over to be prepared to be scanned, but they had not scanned her. She had her cell phone, but she could not start taking photos with the judge standing next to her. She did not want anyone to know she had a phone, but if it were discovered, she could easily explain why she had it.

She wanted to walk around in the house, especially in the basement, but the judge had told her not to move. She glanced behind her, and there were two men dressed in suits that looked like security men. They had ear devices and appeared to be working. They were not trying to talk to the other guests, and they were now watching her. She had not noticed them until now, and for some reason they had not scanned her and located her cell phone at the door. The men must have been stationed upstairs. She figured if she asked where the bathroom was, one of the guards would have to escort her to the bathroom and straight back to be with the judge. She didn't want to draw attention to herself, but she wanted to see what she could find. She and Wayne had figured she would arrive prior to the meal being served, but the judge had just mentioned that the guests had already eaten. She had planned to use the food as an excuse, saying either something got spilled on her and she had to go and clean it off, or acting like she ate something that did not agree with her. She kept running over different scenarios, but nothing seemed plausible. She finally decided she was going to have to ask the judge where the restroom was located; that was her best excuse. She would hope the guard was not tasked with escorting her. She could use that as an opportunity to do a little surveillance. She figured if she were caught in the basement, she would act drunk or high, and say she made a wrong turn. She knew she had to do something fast.

The guests had gathered into the patio area below the balcony, and Vicky saw two men standing off to the side, dressed in nothing but shorts, with no shirts and no shoes. They had white tape around their knuckles and wrists. The judge told Vicky he would be right back and told her not to move. He told the two men behind her to watch her and not to allow her to wander off. The judge walked down the outside spiral stairs, telling everyone the fun was getting ready to start, and he walked to the center of the patio, which was cleared. The patio was twenty feet by twenty feet of tile-covered concrete. The judge asked his guests to stay clear of the patio floor area. "We need some room," he said with a big smile. The judge always seemed to be smiling. The judge announced he would cover all bets, and that his man was the big man. They all laughed, with a couple of men making bets on how long the match would last. No one seemed to be wanting to bet against the judge.

Vicky realized that the men were going to be contestants for an upcoming tough man competition that was getting ready to occur. Vicky had never like watching the fights on TV, and she had never considered going to watch a fight in person. She had always thought they were too violent. Someone always got hurt, and it was not necessary.

Once the floor area was cleared and the guests had formed a circle around the center of the patio, the judge announced the fighters. He then pointed at Vicky as the honored guest. She thought that was weird. Vicky smiled and noticed the two security men still were watching her, standing behind her. Vicky thought the judge must want everyone to think she was dating him tonight.

The two men entered the area. They were ready for the "tough man competition." The one man was one of the largest man Vicky had ever seen. He stood about 6'9" and probably weighed 300 pounds. He looked like he had been lifting barbells for years. His dark-colored skin gleamed with perspiration. The other man was Hispanic and quite a bit smaller, but he was still well over 200 pounds and over 6'3" tall. He acted like he was hesitant and had questions about fighting the bigger man. He had a trainer or friend, who kept talking to him in Spanish. The trainer was Spanish-looking with jet black hair and dark skin. He looked to about fifty to sixty years of age. Finally, the trainer pulled a bottle of baby oil out of a bag and rubbed it on his shoulders, back, and arms. The man still did not look too eager to fight. The trainer kept whispering to the contestant as he rubbed the baby oil on his shoulders and arms. He looked at the judge, and said, "We are good." The other big man just stood and patiently waited, staring at the tile pad below his feet.

Vicky took this time to look at the guests. She was trying to notice additional details about the guests. They were elegantly dressed, men in their tuxedos and women in long evening dresses. Many of the women had expensive jewelry and were wearing diamonds. Vicky was grateful she did not recognize anyone. These people were from out of state, and maybe from other countries. She figured they were all multi-millionaires, or maybe billionaires. No one she recognized from Butler was attending the party.

The judge announced the fight would start in just a few minutes. The judge started walking back up the stairs, with a wide smile on his face. He walked up next to Vicky and started to rub her shoulders. Vicky looked down and noticed several of the guests were watching. The judge said, "The Spanish man wanted to back out of the fight when he saw my man. His trainer rubbed baby oil on him and told him it would make it hard for the big man to hold him, with his skin being slick." The judge then started to laugh and said, "The guy fell for it."

One of the judge's friends waved to the judge, walked into the middle of the ring, and announced the fight was ready to begin. The fight started with the two men squaring off. The Spanish man kept trying to run around the big man and hit him and retreat. The big man just kept walking after him, sometimes with his guard up and sometimes not. The Spanish man hit the big man with both his fist combinations, right, then left in the face, and the big man just covered up. The big man had blood starting to appear from his bottom lip. The spectators started yelling, getting into the fight. The Spanish man just kept punching and running. The big man had not landed one punch, and the Spanish man had landed several to the face, ribs, and head. Vicky thought the big man had no speed and did not know how to fight. Both men were covered in sweat. The heat was in the mid-eighties, and humidity was in the seventies. Vicky watched as the sweat just poured off both men. The judge kept rubbing her shoulders, and Vicky thought she needed to break free as soon as the fight was over. She needed to look for the girl and the cage. During the fight would be the perfect time when everyone was occupied, watching the contest. She noticed there were no waitresses, just an open bar for the guests to help themselves. The first round ended at the three-minute mark, and both men walked away, with the Spanish man walking under the edge of the balcony below where she and the judge and two security men were standing. The big man walked toward the railing of the patio. The trainer rubbed more baby oil on the shoulders of the Spanish fighter, and he kept talking to him in Spanish, urging him to hit and retreat. He was saying, in Spanish, "Do not try to wrestle the big man. Do not allow the big man to grab you. Keep your distance. He is big, slow, and does not know how to fight. This will be over soon. You are doing great. Keep trying to hit him in the mouth where he is bleeding. Remember your family needs you. This is a three-round match. You have finished one round, and you are ahead. Just hang in there two more rounds."

Vicky could understand the Spanish, and she was certain no one else understood. He drank a lot of water. The big man just stood still, looking down at the tile floor, showing no emotion. He had rubbed the blood away with a rag he had next to his backpack and clothing. He was huge, very muscular, and covered with sweat. He drank bottled water and never looked at anyone, keeping his gaze on the tile floor. He had no trainer and did not appear to be concerned. The second round was getting ready to start, and some of the men started betting on the smaller fighter. The judge stopped rubbing Vicky's shoulder and acknowledged the bets. The judge asked if there was anyone else wanting to bet? The very pretty blond lady said in a loud voice, "I will bet $25,000 on the Spanish man."

Two more men matched her bet, and all were betting against the judge. The judge asked if there were any more wanting to bet? He hesitated and made eye contact with most of the men. When no one said a word, the judge waved to one of the men to start the second round, and all the betting was concluded. He whispered to Vicky while standing behind her, "My dear, this is better than the horse races in Kentucky." He had moved up directly behind her, and she could see the smile on his face as he leaned forward next to her. With his left hand, he slowly rubbed it across her backside, allowing his finger to trace the thong, and now placed it on her waist. She acted like she did not notice, and stood frozen, watching the contestants. The second round started as the first round, with the smaller man throwing punches and backing up. The men in the audience began yelling for the Spanish man. The big man did not know how to block the punches, and he was too slow to avoid getting hit. Most of the blows were to the body. After he took a punch to his ribs, he would drop his guard, and the Spanish man was able to land several punches to his face and head. It had become clear the Spanish man was going to win the fight; it was just a question of how long the big man could keep taking the punches.

About two minutes into the second round, surprisingly, the big man showed a burst of energy with agility and quickness, and jumped very quickly toward the Spanish man, cutting him off from his retreat. The Spanish man was off balance, stumbled and was trying not to fall. The big man caught him in a headlock. He then twisted around to the back of the man and picked the smaller man up off his feet, over his head and body-slammed him into the tile patio floor. The man's back hit the patio floor very hard, with the back of his head bouncing off the hard surface. The man looked like it knocked the breath out of him, and at that moment, he looked scared. The big man placed one of his knees on the chest of the Spanish man, holding him down, with his left hand choking his opponent's neck. He acted like he was going to hit the smaller man in the face with his fist of his right hand, when the Spanish man's friend suddenly entered the ring, slid next to the fighter, and tapped out. The trainer looked scared for his friend. The trainer was looking at the big man, pleading, saying, "Please no. No more, please." The crowd all got quiet with anticipation of the man being knocked out or worse. The big man stood up slowly and raised his hands in victory. The Spanish man turned on his side and was gasping for air, while lying on the concrete pad, trying to get his breath. He looked stunned and injured. He was not faking; he was in pain. Vicky thought the big man knew he was going to win all along. He was trying to be merciful and must have been told by the judge to act like he was going to lose, so that the judge could make money gambling. Even still, the big man had to allow the other man to punch him repeatedly, which had to hurt with all those punches. After the fight, the friend who had stopped the fight helped the Spanish man up. The fighters left the patio and walked under the balcony. The guests begin mingling again. The judge told Vicky to walk down the stairs with him to the lower patio, as he gently rubbed his hand across her bottom a second time. He took her by the hand and led her down the spiral metal staircase. He wanted her to meet someone. She noticed the two security men followed.

She felt the judge was a cold man. His eyes had no warmth. When they walked down the stairs, he asked, "My dear. Did you like what you saw? What do you think about the competition? I thought it was very exhilarating."

Vicky asked, "How much did the men get paid?"

The judge said, "My dear. It always goes back to money with you. The winner gets paid a lot of money. He is very well rewarded. In addition, he will receive a very nice bonus for winning. The other man received a fair deal. The big man is the one I had my money on, so I am glad he won. I just made $750,000.00."

Vicky thought the fight was rigged. The judge was a con artist. He just swindled his guests out of $750,000.00. He had the smug better-than-you attitude and must feel he is above the law. She started wondering what her role was going to be. Was she going to have to strip dance in front of the guests? So far, she had not been able to search the home. He had kept the security men watching her the entire time. She had never considered the judge having security men at his party, watching her. Why would they not be watching the girl. There must be a reason. Vicky thought the girl must be here, somewhere very secure.

Vicky had accompanied him to the lower level. When they arrived at the bottom of the stairs, he held her hand and walked her to the area under the balcony. The Spanish man and his trainer were in a hurry and were walking around the side of the home, headed for the gate and the driveway on the west elevation, to leave. The fighting was over. The big man was standing in nothing but a jock strap, with water running from a garden hose attached to the upper wall, over his body. He had a very blank look on his face and still had some blood on his lip. The pretty blond had walked over in front of him, watching him cool off under the water. Up close with her mask removed, Vicky could tell she was close to fifty years old, but she looked thirty. Vicky turned her attention to the judge, and he then explained to Vicky her part in the night's festivities.

He looked at her with a big smile on his face and said, "My dear, you and the winner are part two of the entertainment." As the judge was looking at her, he held up two fingers, his smile grew bigger, and he said, "You will now perform in front of our guests. I will have my men move the large table into the open area."

Vicky began to feel sick to her stomach, and at first, she did not understand. She was in total disbelief. After a second, she finally understood what was getting ready to happen. She was going to have to provide a live sex show with the boxer in front of all these rich guests. She started thinking and considering all her options. She knew there was no way she could leave, and she still had not located the little girl. She had come here to locate the girl. She was the only hope the girl had. The security men stood between her and the way out through the home. There were two additional security men under the patio, and they went and picked up the large table and placed it in the middle of the patio area. Vicky thought back to her college days and some of the things she had done, but she knew this was different. She also knew somewhere there was a small, scared girl whose life may depend on her, and what she could discover. She remembered what Wayne had said about the two bodies located close to Nashville. She surmised that this was bigger than her, and she had to do whatever was necessary to locate the girl. She got mad and despised the judge and these people. She accepted what she was going to have to do, to try to save that girl. She thought back to the Apostles, and how most of them were martyrs for Christianity. This was just a fraction of what the Apostles went through or what the little girl was going to endure. She knew she had no choice. If she did not try to save this girl, she could never forgive herself. All these images ran through her mind, and she conceded she only had but one choice.

The judge then walked to the center of the floor. Vicky took the opportunity to walk over to the big man, and said, "I got this."

She then motioned for him to lean forward and whispered in his ear, telling him what to do and when to do it. He had no sign of emotion one way or another. Vicky thought, he is noncommittal. He must also be forced to fight and perform with her in front of these people. She told him she did not like this any more than he did, but they have no choice. It will be over soon. He nodded that he understood.

The judge had finished addressing his guests and now asked that Vicky and the big man enter the area. He said, "I believe this is going to be a big contrast to the fighting. I wanted to make certain everyone was going to be entertained. The first part was for the fighters, and this part is for the lovers."

Vicky took him by the hand, and they both walked into the center of the deck. Everyone was watching. Vicky seductively began to undress. She palmed the I-phone and placed it under her jumpsuit as she turned her back to the audience, and laid it in the empty chair, so that no one could see it. With everyone moving in closer to watch, and most seeming interested in the show, the pretty blond walked within two feet of the side of the table like she was very excited about part two of the entertainment for the party. The men were all standing around the patio, watching Vicky.

Once she was undressed, she walked over to the boxer and removed the big man's jock support.

She then led him by his hand over to the table and urged him to lie down on the large table that had been moved into the center of the patio. Vicky had him lay on his back on the table, where he took up most of the top surface.

She began slowly kissing him from his head to his feet. She remembered how Matt had trained her to go around the world on a man, and how doing so really elevated the anticipation and the climax for the man. She then returned to his erection and took him in her mouth. After a few seconds, he gritted his teeth and said, "Oh God."

Vicky pulled her head back and allowed his ejaculate to fly in the air, onto the blond lady's face, neck, chest, and dress while she was standing next to the table. She had walked next to the table and acted like she loved this type of entertainment. Vicky had obviously done this intentionally.

The oxygen seemed to be sucked out of the patio area. No one made a sound or moved. Then, the blond lady started to laugh, as she wiped off her face and dress.

She very loudly announced, "This is the best party I have ever been to. I want to see more."

The other guests started to join in the laughter, and the atmosphere in the room relaxed. One of the other women started helping her wipe off her neck and face with a napkin.

Vicky then jumped down from the table and walked over to the corner table next to the house, where she picked up the bottle of baby oil that the trainer had used on the Spanish man in the fight, and she jumped onto the table very quickly and effortlessly, where she stood over the big man. She started rubbing the baby oil on her stomach, lower back and chest while making eye contact with the audience. She was trying to give him time to recover, while providing entertainment for the audience. She knew he had to be tired from the fight, and she was not certain how old he was. She certainly did not want the women to walk out and leave her in this area with all the men. She felt she needed to do a little more to complete the show.

She placed her left foot on his stomach as she stood on the table next to him, and she poured a generous amount of the baby oil on her thigh and allowed it to run down her leg, dripping off her toes onto his stomach. She then started rubbing in the oil on her leg. She then switched legs and slowly did the same. She noticed the big man was starting to get erect. She got on top of him and moved to straddle him. He penetrated her, and she started moving on him. She moaned more than she probably needed to, but she wanted a good show for the audience. She understood what was expected of her.

Her body released, and his body released into hers, and then she immediately slid off him, with a tear coming out from under her mask. She looked him straight in the eyes and matter-of-factly whispered, "Get your money, clothes and leave. We are done. I am truly sorry about all this."

She then walked over to where her clothes were and started dressing. She felt relieved it was over, but she felt horrible for what she had to do. She thought, "I am going to look through this home one way or another." She was able to place the I-Phone in the top band of her panties like before, without anyone noticing. She had her back to the audience. She got dressed rather quickly.

The good-looking, very distinguished older man walked over to the blond as Vicky was getting dressed and said with an urgent tone, "My package has been delivered, and we need to go."

The blond responded, "Certainly, honey. Let me make certain I have wiped all his nectar off my face first." She kept wiping her face with the napkin. She looked at her husband and asked, "Did I get it all? Is there any in my hair?"

As he turned to leave, he said, "You can shower when we get to our home. The chopper will wait for you once you are ready to leave."

Vicky knew she had seen the man somewhere prior, but she could not place him. She was certain now, after listening to the people talk, the rest of the audience were from out of state or from other countries. The blond must have been his trophy wife. She did not recognize anyone else. She made a mental note to remember the faces of the men at the party. She wondered how many of these people knew a child was being held in a cage. These people were repulsive, with all their wealth and privileged attitudes. They were very rich, which made them feel they were entitled, and they must feel they were above the law, given the impression that they were very egotistical.

The party was over. The guests started to file out of the patio area. None of the guests were leaving through the interior of the home, and most seemed to have already walked around the sidewalk to the other side of the home where the vehicles were all parked. The big man must have got dressed rather quickly and was handed an envelope from the judge. He then walked at a fast pace on the sidewalk, toward the parked vehicles. He never opened the envelope. After he turned the corner at the garage, Vicky heard a motorcycle start up and thought that it must be him leaving.

The rest of the guests told the judge what a great party it was, and he was smiling and thanking them for coming. One man said he wanted Vicky's number, and the judge said, "No problem." An elderly lady with a French accent, who could have been in her eighties, said, "I want the big man's number."

The judge said, "No problem," and they all started laughing as they were leaving. The elderly lady then said, "Maybe next time you men can shorten your meeting. I have been here since 2 p.m., but I really liked the last two parts. The judge just smiled.

The men who had placed bets with the judge paid with smiles on their faces and congratulated the judge on his winnings. The judge told them the fight could have gone either way and that he just got lucky. Vicky thought, "He is such a liar. The fight was rigged."

As Vicky stood off to the side, she noticed the four security men had left and the area was nearly empty. All of the guests had also left. She was hoping to get a chance to walk around and look through the mansion for signs of the girl. The judge walked up to her. Vicky thought he was going to ask her to leave, but instead, he told her that it was his turn and that she should not have gotten dressed.

Vicky, very business-like, said to the judge, "You owe me two thousand dollars."

The judge said, "Wait a minute now. What about a discount?"

"No, you owe me two thousand dollars; give me the money, and then we can talk more about your discount."

The judge smiled and said, "You certainly drive a hard bargain, and with what I just witnessed, you know you've got me at your mercy. I have no doubt you know how to entertain an elderly gentleman."

The last of the guests had now left, and a petite Asian woman walked up and placed her arm around the judge. Vicky had not seen the lady prior. She was not wearing a mask. Vicky was somewhat intrigued by the action of the woman. She was very well dressed, pretty, and looked a few years younger than the judge.

Vicky didn't realize it was the judge's wife, and instead thought that he may be cheating on his wife.

The judge introduced Vicky to his wife and then asked his wife to give Vicky three-thousand dollars, as he held up three fingers. She drives a hard bargain, but based on what I know, she will be worth it."

The judge's wife said to Vicky, in an Asian accent, "I would love to give you three thousand dollars. You certainly are beautiful. Come with me, please."

She took Vicky's hand and led her inside the home. They walked up the wood stairs, through the hallway, and into another part of the house. Vicky was still very mad about what had just occurred, but she was hoping at last for an opportunity to search the home and, most of all, save the girl. The security men were nowhere to be seen, and she thought to herself that the fewer people in the home, the better. Vicky said, "This is certainly a beautiful home. I would love to walk around and see it."

"Maybe later, my dear. Right now, I want to show you the upstairs and give you your money." She led Vicky into a large, almost empty bedroom with a high vaulted ceiling. The French doors at the end of the bedroom were partially opened, which led to the deck and the second exterior steel spiral stairway on the rear of the home. The large room was empty except for a king size bed with hooks hanging from the large wooden bedposts, a large wooden armoire, and one chair. The bed had a large mirror as a headboard and a large mirror installed on the top of the bed attached to the six-foot-high bedposts. The judge's wife closed the door and opened the double doors on the large wooden armoire. Hanging in the armoire were several sex toys.

Vicky was disgusted when she realized what was expected from her. The judge's wife indicated that she wanted Vicky to be put in bondage, while holding up a pair of handcuffs with a smile on her face. She thought, "These people are perverted, and he is a federal judge." Vicky smiled at the lady and walked up to the armoire, looking at the array of items and acting like she was interested in the assortment. She then lifted a bullwhip from one of the pegs. Before the judge's wife could realize what was happening, Vicky quickly wrapped the small part of the whip twice around the judge's wife's neck and pushed her backward into the large chair, which was facing the bed. Vicky positioned herself behind the woman and the chair, and started pulling on the whip, cutting off the airflow to the wife's lungs.

The whip was close to eight feet long, and Vicky had it pulled tight, holding the middle of the whip, with the handle lying on the carpet floor.

Vicky gritted her teeth and said to the woman, "Your only chance to escape this is to tell me NOW what I need to know. The FBI is waiting outside. Your husband is not going to take the fall for you. His career and reputation are much more important to him than you are. You are on your own, and you make me sick. Tell me NOW where the girl is being kept."

Vicky could tell by the look on her face when she mentioned the girl that the judge's wife knew she had been caught. Vicky pulled the whip even tighter and kicked her high heels off, while holding the whip tight. She wanted to be able to run or fight, and the shoes would hinder both.

The judge's wife started crying and telling Vicky that they had not hurt anyone, as she looked at the armoire. She reached up to her neck and tried to loosen the whip. When she realized that was futile, she motioned to Vicky that she would cooperate. Vicky knew she only had a little amount of time before the judge walked into the room. She also knew she would not be able to restrain and question two people at the same time.

Vicky allowed the woman to stand, because she had motioned to Vicky that she was going to show her something. She suddenly pushed Vicky, who fell backward, releasing the whip when the lady yanked it. Vicky had figured the wife would run to the bedroom door and jumped in that direction to cut her off. Instead, the wife ran to the French doors. The judge's wife turned to run out the back of the room, where a balcony overlooked the back of the property through the French doors. She started to turn to take the steps down the steel spiral stairs when the handle of the whip that was dragging behind her bounced upward and flew into the top of the handrail. The handle of the whip wrapped around an iron spindle as she went around the corner to go down the stairs. The wooden handle to the whip got caught sideways in the metal spindle and the top rail. As she ran down the top two of the fourteen steps, she was jerked backward when the whip pulled tight, causing her to fall over the side railing. The staircase was a spiral staircase made of steel three-foot-high railing, set in the concrete balcony at the top and tile covered pad below. The whip broke her fall from landing on the tile-covered patio, but in doing so, it broke her neck. Vicky chased after her and saw her fall over the rail as she ran out the doors. She looked over the rail and saw the woman hanging by her neck, with her feet about two feet from the ground. She was swinging back and forth. Vicky thought to herself that there was no question that the woman was dead. Vicky looked around the patio and the pool. She did not see anyone. She did not have time to check to verify if the wife were dead or if she could help her. The way her head was hanging sideways, Vicky was certain of the outcome. The cervical bones in the neck that holds the neck upright had snapped, and the woman's head was lying over to one side in a very unnatural manner. She glanced at the body swinging back and forth and turned and ran back into the room.

Vicky heard the judge whistling as he was coming down the hall, so she quickly positioned herself next to the armoire. The judge entered and smiled with anticipation. He said, "I am ready to be entertained. I want to see three thousand dollars' worth of entertainment." He then looked around and asked, "Where is my wife?"

Vicky said, "Judge, please sit. We can get started without her."

He smiled and sat down in the chair. He seemed truly excited with the pending adult entertainment. Vicky picked out the small fourteen-inch baseball bat that was hanging in the armoire and acted like she wanted it to use in the upcoming event.

Chapter 18

Wayne was sitting in the 1999 Ford F-150 black truck he owned and used to pull his horse trailer with when he went riding. Otherwise, the truck was randomly used. He kept thinking how dangerous this plan was, allowing Vicky to be alone, undercover, with no training, and no support. He recalled what the two FBI agents had mentioned about the Asian girls being transported from Asia to the US. He thought Cramer might have been employed by the judge. Cramer had been a highway patrolman with training from the Army, and maybe Special Forces. Wayne thought, "People like that are always prepared for all unforeseen circumstances. If that is what we are dealing with, we are in over our heads. Vicky has no training and backup, except me." He felt the pit of his stomach starting to turn. He thought about calling Vince and telling him what was going on. At least then someone might be able to intervene if this went sideways. He wished he had not allowed Vicky to go into the home by herself, but he knew he could not stop her. She had said she was going, with or without his help. She was going to try to save that girl. He thought that this might be a suicide mission for her. He pulled a second pistol, with an ankle holster, from the glove box. He strapped the holster to his ankle and pulled his pant leg down over the pistol. He refocused, when he noticed a couple of Mexican fellows had driven by in an old

Datsun pickup. He figured they must have been the hired help, maybe the bartender or waiters, and he hoped Vicky would be okay.

There was nothing he could do. He had been in the cornfield since 4 p.m., and the only people that entered the driveway were the Datsun Truck and a big man on a motorcycle about ten minutes prior to Vicky being dropped off by Dillon. Everyone else had arrived at the home prior. He had figured just the opposite, that the guests would have arrived after 6 p.m. Vicky's contact with the maid service had provided them limited information about the party. He cursed the plan. He knew he had to act normal at work, so his boss would not suspect him being involved if this plan went sideways. He had a scheduled appointment with his boss at 2 p.m. He had wished he had been able to stake the home out prior. He knew his boss would have never allowed any of this to have occurred.

The plan was in motion. Nothing else happened for about fifteen minutes, and then he saw a black Cadillac drive out and turn right, followed by a black Suburban. Both vehicles were heading away from the exit of the dead-end street and the toward the end of the road, in the opposite direction from him. He thought the road was a dead end, not far from the judge's driveway. He wondered if the two vehicles had gone the wrong way. He had never been this far out on this street and was not familiar with this area. The windows were tinted, and he could not tell who was in the two vehicles. Then the motorcycle, followed by a third vehicle, and then one vehicle right after another pulled out of the driveway, past him and headed for Lake Street and the interstate. Wayne assumed the party must be over. He looked at his phone to make certain Vicky had not tried to call him. He noted thirty-seven minutes had expired since Vicky entered the home. He figured the fewer people at the home meant fewer possible witnesses and a more dangerous situation for Vicky. He decided he would walk up the road and watch from the tree line across the street. He did not see another vehicle in the driveway, and the gate was open. He thought to himself that the alarm and cameras might be off at the gate and the home. He knew, after reading reports about professional thieves in Florida, that they would commit the crimes during parties because the alarm system was always turned off to the homes that were hosting the parties. Wayne heard and saw a helicopter taking off from the home at the end of the street and flying south toward Nashville. He crossed the street and jogged the approximate one hundred yards to the front step. He was listening for noise. He was considering walking around the home. He checked his watch and forty-six minutes had passed since Vicky had entered the residence.

Steve D. Nichols

Chapter 19

Vicky walked over next to the judge, who had turned to look for his wife. He called for her. He had not noticed that Vicky had walked over next to him. She slapped him on the temple of his head with the small bat, and then slammed the bat down on his right hand, crunching the bones in his hand. She took the end of the bat and punched down on the bridge of his nose, causing it to split open and bleed, and his glasses were knocked to the floor.

She immediately started interrogating the judge. He started to cry and moan. He wanted to know where his wife was. He acted startled and confused, looking around the room. Vicky ignored his questions and told him that the FBI was waiting and planned to question him. She told him not to move, or she would beat him with the bat. She then said that he was going to be arrested. She asked him the whereabouts of the young girl that was in the locked cage. "We know about the cage and the Asian girl. Where is she?"

He looked around in the room and asked again, "Where is my wife? Did you hurt her?"

Vicky gritted her teeth and said, "Listen, you piece of filth. No child should be placed in a locked cage. You made me do that disgusting stuff in front of those people, and you rubbed your filthy hands on me. Do you really think I won't beat you with this bat? What type of human waste are you?"

Vicky then added, when the judge kept looking around the room, "She hung herself rather than go to jail," as she pointed to the balcony. "She knew she had been caught, and your cleaning lady has been discovered butchered into pieces."

The judge could see the handle of the whip around the top rail, stuck between the two iron spiral pickets on the railing through the French doors. The whip was still swinging back and forth, and he could tell it had tension on it. He could not see the other end of the whip, but he assumed Vicky was telling the truth. A tear ran down his face. He kept acting confused, like he was helpless.

He said, "We had not hurt anyone. It's not us. We had no choice. We did not kill the maid." He was pleading that they had not hurt anyone, with tears in his eyes, as he, too, looked at the armoire. Vicky thought he looked pitiful and innocent, like he could not hurt another person. Then, she refocused on the girl and how the judge had taken advantage of his status in the community. He was a federal judge, appointed to uphold the law.

She said, gritting her teeth, "You are a federal judge, and yet you have parties like this and place kids in dog cages. You are a disgrace, and you do not deserve to live. Now tell me where the girl is."

She swung with force and hit him on the shin of the right leg with the bat. He started crying in pain and leaned over in the chair to rub his shin. He said, "Please no more. I have rights. I want my attorney.

Vicky gritted her teeth in his face and said, "You don't have any rights with me. I am not a cop, and I am going to beat you with this bat until you tell me what I want to know."

He could tell, by her voice and facial expressions, that she meant what she said. His right hand was throbbing with pain. He figured his index finger was broken, and now his shin might be broken or at least have a chipped bone with a deep bruise. He said, "I will tell you. I am sorry about the girl. My wife has an unusual appetite for young Asian girls, but we never hurt anyone. We have been forced to do these things. I am sorry."

"Listen to me. You need to tell me where the girl is RIGHT NOW!"

He leaned back, sat upright in the chair, and suddenly reached in his vest with his left hand and pulled out a small derringer. His entire demeanor changed. He went from acting helpless to taking charge. He aimed the pistol at Vicky and demanded that she step back. Vicky was surprised and paused. Before she moved, he looked straight ahead with a look of determination on his face, a look of resolve, and pulled his left hand up and started to aim the pistol at his left temple. Vicky quickly reacted and hit his arm with the bat, by swinging downward. The gun discharged, and the bullet hit the judge in the throat, exiting the neck and landing in the upper part of the drywall near the ceiling. The judge leaned back in the chair and was looking up at the ceiling.

Vicky immediately ripped the pillowcase off a pillow and attempted to stop the flow of blood from his neck with the pillowcase.

Wayne was not certain where the gunshot originated, other than it came from inside the home. He was instantly scared for Vicky's life. He knew she had no gun. He rushed in the front door with his pistol drawn and started yelling, "Police!" at whoever was in the house. Vicky yelled that she was upstairs.

Vicky kept working to try to stop the bleeding but was also trying to persuade him to tell her where the girl was located. Vicky said, "If you have not harmed anyone and it is not you, you do not want to die with the girl not being safe. Tell me where the girl is. Now is the time to confess your sins." Vicky was pleading with the judge. He was choking and gasping for air. His face was turning whiter and whiter, as the blood kept pouring out his neck. Wayne opened the door and entered the room.

He finally gasped the word, with a hoarse low tone voice, into Vicky's ear, "Ed." He shook his head no and tried to repeat himself, "ED."

His head fell to the side, and he then died, choking on his blood. Wayne tried to see if he could provide first aid, but realized he was dead; the hole in his neck had caused too much blood loss. Plus, the bullet had pierced his throat, and there was no way to force air into his lungs with a hole in his throat. The bullet had also pierced through the side of the Carotid Artery in his neck. Wayne and Vicky stepped backward and looked at all the blood, glancing at each other.

"He shot himself, using his left hand, when I asked him about the girl in the cage. I told him the FBI was waiting to arrest him. I did not realize he was left-handed. He had the gun hidden in his vest. I hit his right hand with the bat, trying to bruise his hand and his fingers, so I could control him."

Wayne looked down and saw the small pistol, and without an expression, Wayne asked, "Is there anyone else in the home?"

Vicky said, "No. We need to search the home. His wife hung herself off the back porch when I cornered her and asked about the girl and threatened her with being arrested. She ran out the door, and the whip got caught in the railing, which pulled her over the rail, and she appeared to be dead."

Wayne walked over and looked at her hanging by her neck with the bullwhip. He glanced around the rear of the home and did not see anyone. Vicky said, "We need to look through the home. We've got to find that child."

Wayne said, "We do not have time; someone might have already heard the gunshot and called the police. The people at the large home next door would have heard the gunshot if they were outside, and I saw two vehicles head that way after the party. Let's allow the police to complete the search. We have done our job."

Wayne then added, "Just to cover our bases, I am going to call this in, and the guys will be here in ten minutes." He then said, "I mean Vince and his deputies."

"Both looked at this armoire when I asked about the girl."

Wayne walked over to the side of the armoire and kept looking at the side and the back and said, "It has a false back. There is a hidden compartment in the back part."

Wayne pulled his pocketknife out of his pocket and pried the back panel off, and Vicky said, "Oh my God."

They saw several photos of young Asian girls naked in this bedroom, with the judge's wife doing horrible things to them. The pictures were attached to the back of the armoire with thumbtacks.

Wayne said, "You need to wash the blood off your hands and wipe your fingerprints off everything you have touched, and you need to run to your car and change clothes. You can put on a shirt and flip flops from my truck. If you're seen running from here, someone will think you are running from a crime. Once you get on Lake Street with a change of clothes, you will be just another jogger." He looked at her bare feet and her holding her heels, and then said, "Or someone out walking bare foot in the grass on the side of the street."

Wayne called Vince, and Vince answered saying, "Hello".

Wayne immediately said, "I have two apparent suicides, and I am going to give you the address. I am also going to call John, my boss, since one is a federal judge."

Vince, very excited, said, "Ten-four. We will be headed that way."

Vicky started to leave, after washing her hands in the bathroom and wiping down the handle to the whip and the bat. She said, "I have not touched anything else." She turned and asked Wayne, "How does a judge afford a home like this? This home is worth well over one million dollars."

Wayne said, "We will check into it. Now get going."

Vicky picked up her shoes and ran down the stairs to the patio. She wiped off the baby oil bottle and the table. She then ran around the west elevation of the home and down the driveway.

***

Vince and Darrell had arrived about fourteen minutes after the call from Wayne. Vince, Wayne, and Darrell had placed gloves on and walked through the home. Wayne had mentioned to Vince and Darrell that they needed to complete a walk-through and clear the home, but they need to let the TBI handle the forensic investigation. They cleared the house. About twenty minutes later John and four TBI agents arrived. The highway patrol cars had also arrived, and the officers were installing the yellow and black crime scene tape and watching the exterior of the home. Wayne had told John that he, Vince, and Darrell were careful not to touch anything, except doorknobs, with the plastic gloves. Then, the FBI guys, Tracey Vaughn, Roger Henagar, along with several other FBI agents, walked into the home about five minutes after the TBI agents, and told them that this was a federal case. They needed to leave immediately because the FBI had full jurisdiction. Tracey yelled, "They all need to leave right now." Tracey yelled it a second time. The TBI men had walked through the home a second time looking for anyone else in the home and had just started to look through the home for evidence, when they were told to leave. One of the agents had carried a large dog cage out of the garage to the front porch area. They left out the front door and, when Wayne saw the cage, he yelled at the FBI crew, "You need to look really close at that cage and have it tested for human DNA. The judge does not own a dog. See those photos we found behind the back of the panel in the armoire."

Wayne got madder by the minute, and he cussed the FBI under his breath.

John looked off balance by the request from the FBI. He had tried to explain what Wayne had discovered and that he was the manager for the TBI. He knew something was not kosher. He had never been ordered off a scene by the FBI and was totally dumbfounded by the request. He looked at Wayne and said, "Let's go."

Darrell and Vince also headed for their vehicles. They were all very upset and were cussing the federal officers under their breath.

Wayne said, "I am done with this shit."

John said, "I will see you in the morning. I know it is Saturday, your scheduled day off, but you will need to complete the report. You will need to take your time and write up the precise, factual, comprehensive report. This will go directly to the top."

Wayne thought about what he would write in the report, as he walked back to the field to his truck and drove home. He knew he would report that he heard the gunshot as he happened to be walking the field across the street, where he was looking at the large cornfield for hunting dove in the upcoming dove hunting season starting in September. Since he thought he heard a gunshot while in the field, and the gate was left opened, he felt he should investigate the low caliber gunshot. He walked around back and saw the lady hanging by the rope from the rear rail, with her neck broke. He proceeded up the spiral staircase and entered the home, where he found the man sitting in the chair with the gunshot to the neck. He tried to stop the bleeding with the pillowcase. He was already dead and could not be revived. There was no one else in the home when he arrived, and he had noticed several vehicles leaving the home when he was in the field. He had not paid any attention to the cars. When he heard the gun shot, he felt something might not be right, since all the guests had just left. He would write that both died by apparent suicide. One hung herself, and the other shot himself. If anyone noticed the judge's nose, he would suggest he must have fallen on the stairs after the wife hung herself.

Steve D. Nichols

Chapter 20

As soon as the TBI and sheriff's officers left the residence, Tracey walked to the swimming pool area out of range of being heard, and made the call. Delores Bailey was with friends she was meeting for dinner. She was not surprised by the incoming phone call and answered on the first ring. "This is Delores Bailey, District Manager, FBI office in Atlanta."

Tracey said, "We are here. We have what appears to be two suicides. We asked the locals to vacate, and they cussed us. At this point, we are not certain if they will cooperate with us or not. We did not ask them how they discovered the two bodies before we forced them out, but it appears the former sheriff, who now works for the TBI, was looking at the field across the street for a possible dove hunting field and heard a shot. He walked over from the field and around the home and saw the judge's wife had hung herself off the rear balcony. He walked up the spiral staircase and looked into the bedroom through the open door and found the judge bleeding from the neck from a self-inflicted gunshot from a small-caliber gun. The bullet appears to have traveled through his neck and stuck in the top of the bedroom wall. The gun was on the floor next to his body. The agent with the TBI tried to stop the bleeding, but he was too late. The bedroom only had three pieces of furniture. One is a large bed with a mirror on the headboard, and one large mirror attached to the four bedposts located above the bed. The second item is an armoire with several adult toys, and the third piece of furniture is a large leather chair, which is facing the bed. The TBI officer located some very disturbing photos of young Asian girls, hidden in the back concealed compartment of the armoire. We will also need to have the forensic team check out the dog crate for DNA. They yelled at us when they were leaving that the judge did not own a dog, so what was the dog crate being used for? They must suspect something. The judge had a party, and all the guests had just left. We are trying to obtain the names of the guests, but no luck so far. There is no one left to interview. We will try to figure out who catered the party. We suspect the judge used undocumented employees to clean the home, and we may never be able to obtain their statements. It will be very difficult for us to locate the maids without seeking the county sheriff department's assistance. The workers will be concerned with being deported."

Delores had walked outside of the restaurant by herself and asked, "Are there any girls?"

"No one else is in the home."

"Are you certain we are dealing with two suicides? Is there any reason to believe we have a homicide?"

"We will have our forensic people investigate, but based on what I am seeing, we are dealing with two suicides, and we may have just solved the case of the girls' murders."

"Dammit. This is a federal judge. All his prior cases could come under review if he is found to be linked to kidnapping. I want the property searched inside and outside and make certain nothing is leaked to the press. We will provide the press with a plausible report once we determine what has happened. I mean, do not leave any stone uncovered. I will call Washington. It might be best to report a double suicide and leave the killing of the Asian girls out of the report to the media. We will have to obtain cooperation from the locals. I expect to be updated daily." The phone call ended.

Chapter 21

The sheriff had an extra-large blue tee shirt in the cab of his truck and a pair of flip flops. Vicky quickly pulled off the jumpsuit and put the tee shirt on, and left carrying the flip flops, wig, and jumpsuit. She left the sheriff's pickup truck, running barefoot in the grass on the side of the street. She arrived at her car and pulled the hidden key from under the bumper of her car. She jumped in the front seat and laid down in the passenger seat, as Darrell and Vince went flying by her with the sirens and blue lights flaring. Vicky quickly changed into the spare set of clothes that she kept in her car and drove off. She threw away the blue shirt, flip flops, wig, heels, and white jumpsuit, which were all rolled together and stained with blood, in the diner's garbage dumpster behind their building, on her way home. She drove home, and immediately took a shower after entering her home through the garage. She quickly toweled off and put on her favorite tee shirt, with the Mickie Mouse logo on it. She sat down on the couch, crossing her legs. She had not had a lot of time to process what had just taken place, but she felt very relieved that no one knew she was involved in what happened on the patio. All the security cameras were flashing red and turned off, not recording. She was confident that with the wig, mask, and the fact no one appeared to be from the Butler community, that she had total anonymity and her identity was safe. She kept wondering what could have happened to the child. She was not going to tell Matt what she had done, and she did not want anyone else to know. She was always so careful how she acted in public, with Matt being a preacher. She heard the garage door start to open, and she knew Matt had pulled his truck into the garage. He announced, once he entered the home, that it had been a very tough and long day. Vicky could tell he was frustrated and tired.

He said, "I cannot believe how conservative these people are with the money at a non-profit institution. I finally had to tell them that I am working eighty hours a week, and then I asked them how many of them were working eighty hours a week."

Vicky smiled and said, "I just got in from a long jog."

Matt said, "I am sorry, how was your day? I am just a little frustrated with not being loved."

"I love you. I really love you a lot."

Matt said, "I love you too. I am exhausted, and this was going to be our date night."

Vicky asked, "Do you want me to get you something to eat?"

Matt said, "No, I ate with Joe Vault and two of his sons. That seems to be our routine after these meetings."

Vicky said to herself that it was alright, as Matt sat with his head back and fell asleep on the couch. He had said he was going to have to go to bed because he needed to catch up on his sleep, and Vicky thought, "He did not make it." She went into the kitchen to get herself something to eat and thought about the missing girl. She placed both hands on the countertop and stared in thought. She did not feel any remorse for the judge or his wife. She wondered how they had gotten by with this over the years, and where was the girl? How long had this been going on? Why have the girl in the cage the day before the party? None of this made sense. She knew Wayne would let her know what they discovered. She thought back to Maria's friend, and how she looked so convincing when she was telling her story about seeing the girl. She seemed to recall the smallest of details, things that someone would not make up. She had no reason to lie about what she witnessed. Those photos of the girls in the back of the armoire proved they were involved. Vicky surmised Maria's friend had to be telling the truth and thought about that poor, helpless child.

Steve D. Nichols

Chapter 22

The TBI agents had planned to take the cage for testing, when the FBI agents told them to leave. Wayne had hoped they could have gotten it loaded before the FBI showed up. They needed proof of the other girls. He had not removed the photos either. He thought the TBI forensic team would handle all the evidence. They were forced out by the FBI so suddenly, and now they still had no evidence. The next day, Saturday morning, John called Wayne and told him the FBI wrote it up as two suicides. The wife and husband had been having problems and had health issues. His best guess was they did not want the investigation into the federal judge and his wife to become public because they knew this went beyond the judge. They wanted to catch the ultimate ringleaders and all the other associates in the child trafficking ring. They still had not located a child or anyone who attended the party. At this time, all they had were the photos that were found. Their lab techs would secure every print in the home, and they would turn that house upside down, looking for evidence.

Wayne asked, "But they will not share anything with us, will they?"

John said, "I am working on cooperation, and I will get the governor involved if I have to. I will do everything I can to make this a joint investigation, but this is a federal case. We have no proof there are any missing girls, with none reported in Tennessee. See you Monday."

Wayne sent the report by e-mail to his boss and walked out of his office in Nashville. His boss was working from home, and they could talk more about the case Monday.

Chapter 23

Jeff Burton and his old high school buddy, Ross Carmichael, had been fishing together since they were fifteen years old. They had decided they enjoyed the night fishing compared to day fishing about twenty years ago. They basically had Cheatham Lake to themselves. The lake was very tranquil, and they enjoyed drinking beer while they trolled for the crappie, which during the summer months would be schooled up in the middle of the lake and traveling around the points, staying out of the warmer, shallow hollows. With their fish-finder, they would try to stay directly over the fish, and catch their limit before midnight. Jeff had always prided himself on being great at fishing. Over the years, he had learned the best bait to use and what depth to troll. The crappie looked up and fed on food in the water directly above them. The lure, which looked like a small caterpillar that glowed in the night water, would vibrate as it was being pulled by the fishing line directly positioned above the fish in the water. The depth of the lure, in conjunction with the fish, was the key. Jeff had figured that out years ago and had kept it to himself. He would always tell someone, if asked, the type of bait and the area he fished in the lake, but he never mentioned the depth of the bait, which was the most critical aspect to catching the crappie. The bait could not be too shallow, but also could not be too deep. This time of year, the fish would be about twelve feet deep in the cooler water, and his fish finder confirmed this depth. The key was to know how fast to troll in the boat so that the bait would drop right above the fish, at about eleven feet. It also helped to have bait that glowed in the darkness and created a vibration as it spun through the water. While fishing on weekends, they also would drink most of a twelve-pack apiece of Coors light. The joke Jeff always told was, "I hope catching fish doesn't interrupt our beer drinking."

Ross was heavier and taller than Jeff, and always seemed to drink more beer. He was fair skinned, with very light-colored hair. His nickname in high school was Marsh Mellow. He knew Jeff would have the responsibility to drive the boat onto the boat trailer and drop him off at his home. Ross did not have to be concerned about driving under the influence. This particular night, Ross had drunk his beer and borrowed a couple from Jeff. They had been on the lake since 6 p.m. and drank a couple of beers while driving to the lake. Each had a large ham sandwich to eat at about 8 p.m., with chips. Jeff was using this opportunity to catch his limit of fish and some of Ross's. Ross was having trouble working the rod and reel like he normally would, due to the fourteen beers he had drunk. As the boat came around point number 17 at about 10 p.m., Ross had moved to the front of the boat. He was looking up at the stars, noticing his head was spinning, while sitting in the front swivel chair. He told Jeff, "My head is spinning like a top."

"Yes, you are drunk. You better stay seated before you fall into the lake and scare the fish. Let me catch a few more of your limit, and we will go."

Ross seemed to relax, looking out the front of the boat with Jeff looking out the back of the boat, running the trolling motor by moving the foot pedal, while the trolling motor pulled the boat slowly through the water. Jeff also had moved the portable fish finder to the back of the boat, while glancing at the fish finder from time to time to make certain they were staying above the fish. Jeff would drink a beer, while at the same time watching three rods, trolling, and listening to Ross talk. Ross had given up fishing and looked at the shoreline out the front of the boat. He was surprised. He wiped his eyes. He said, "Hell, fire! Jeff! I just saw a naked Indian woman running down the bank and into the woods."

"Shit. I know you are drunk. Your wife is going to be pissed at you for dreaming about an Indian woman."

"No, I know what I saw. She was near the tree line."

"You are drunk." Jeff turned around and said, "Show me."

"She was over there at that point, and she ran into the woods. She was naked and bare foot, running across the rocks."

Jeff said, "That is over seventy-five yards away. You are full of shit. You do know that don't you, Ross?" Jeff noticed Ross did not have a line in the water, and his rods were broken down and ready for the trip home.

"Okay, I get it. You are ready to go home. Let's go."

Ross said, "So you don't believe me? She might be camping in the woods and skinny dipping."

"Hell no. I don't believe you. You have been making shit up for years, and you are drunker than a skunk."

Ross felt sick at that point, and he felt the chair screwed to the fiberglass hull give way. He looked down at the screws, which had backed out of the metal bracket holding the chair to the fiberglass hull. He knew Jeff would be pissed. He got up, and in one fluid motion, started puking in the middle of the boat.

Jeff turned around and looked at Ross with a smile on his face, and said, "You got to be fuckin kidding me. You got the entire lake to puke in, and you missed it by hitting the floor of my boat."

Ross, while on all fours, had tears coming out of his eyes from puking so hard, and he said, "I was afraid I might fall in the lake, and I knew you would understand. It must have been something in that sandwich. Are you feeling ill?"

Jeff said, "Let us head to the dock, and hell no, there is nothing wrong with the sandwich. Hell no, I don't understand."

Ross talked about the naked Indian all the way home, with Jeff just shaking his head and laughing. He dropped Ross off and said, "Say hi to Pocahontas for me."

Ross said, "Kiss my ass," as he stumbled and stepped out of Jeff's truck. Jeff shook his head as Ross struggled to walk up his driveway to get to the back door of his home. He left his fishing equipment in the boat and told Jeff he would get it later. Jeff said,

"You can get it when you come over and clean up your puke." Jeff watched as Ross stopped about halfway up the driveway to take a piss in the yard, then he laughed and drove home.

Jeff walked into his bedroom, and his wife Maggie was reading a novel and asked him, "How was the fishing?" Jeff said, "I caught most all the fish and had to clean them all. Ross got very impaired, and he kept saying that he saw a naked Indian running down the bank of the lake into the woods."

Maggie said, while laughing, "Dear God, how much did he drink?"

"He was on a mission to get drunk, and he did. I bet he was glad he does not have to go to work tomorrow. He upchucked in the boat, but he said it was caused by the ham sandwich which we bought at Rooster's Deli." Jeff cleaned himself up in the bathroom, climbed into bed, kissed his wife, and went to sleep immediately.

***

The following Sunday morning, Vicky walked into Sunday school class as the classmates were laughing. Maggie was telling how Ross was very drunk at the lake Friday night, and saw a naked Indian lady at the lake running down the lake bank into the woods. Maggie said, "Jeff called him yesterday in the middle of the day and asked if Pocahontas had been over at their house. Then, he would tell Ross there was a report on the news of a naked Indian running across the top of the lake without getting wet."

The entire class was laughing. The class leader walked into class a few seconds behind Vicky, changed the subject, and started the class lesson. Vicky looked at Maggie and Tiffany, who had been laughing so hard they had been crying. Tonya and Donny Freeman, who had been coming on a regular basis to Sunday school and church, had also been laughing hysterically along with several others.

They walked to church from Sunday school class an hour later, and the classmates were still talking about the fishing trip with Jeff and Ross somebody. Vicky was always looking at the church to see how many people were in attendance. She arrived in the auditorium close to ten minutes prior to the start. Vicky, to her surprise and dismay, saw Jimmy Sterns, the big boxer that she had seen at the judge's home Friday night, sitting partway back in the middle aisle by himself. She remembered his name from when the judge had introduced him. He was smiling at everyone, and he made eye contact with Vicky. Vicky felt very uncomfortable. She felt flushed and nauseated. She thought, how did he know where to find me? How did he know I went to this church? She thought Dillon Hayes must have told him. She should have never allowed Dillon to follow her. He must have gotten her tag number. Why else would Jimmy be at the church?

She assumed he was there to blackmail her. She didn't want to talk to him. Vicky realized she had a few minutes prior to the service, and she went out in the hall, called Wayne, and said, as soon as Wayne answered the phone, "I have a problem."

Wayne asked, "What is going on?" Wayne thought she was going to talk about the judge. He had told Vicky to watch what she said on the phones. Someone might be listening.

"I need some help. At the party that night, there was a tough man competition, and one of the men must have recognized me. He is here in the church. Dillon may have told him who I was, and where to find me."

Wayne thought at first, what difference would it make, but he could tell Vicky was upset and said, "I will drive over and follow him from the parking lot. I will check him out and have a talk with him. How will I recognize him?"

"He is the biggest black man I have ever seen."

Vicky went back into the church without looking back at the pews and the congregation. She was so concerned and preoccupied with him being at the church that she hardly listened to Matt's sermon. She immediately left through the rear door and acted like she needed to go to the bathroom after the church service was concluded.

Wayne sat in the parking lot at the far side, and when Jimmy Sterns walked out of the church, Wayne had to agree that he was hard to miss. He must have been the guy on the motorcycle late Friday afternoon, leaving the judge's home. He got in an older model silver Cutlass. Wayne followed him, called in his license plate, and found out he had just been released from the state prison in Brushy

Mountain, Tennessee. Brushy Mountain had a reputation for being the worst prison in Tennessee, and the worst of the worst men were incarcerated there. He was living in Nashville near Tennessee State College at a gym, the TBI dispatcher told Wayne. "He was arrested for attempted murder four years ago. He plea-bargained the sentence down to ten years and received an early release after four years, with time served for good behavior. He was on a two-year probation. He reported to his probation officer in Nashville weekly. So far, he had not missed a meeting."

Wayne pulled him over as he was headed south on Highway 12, in a wide area in the road. Wayne did not bother to ask him to get out of the car. Wayne figured he would threaten him with more jail time, and that would be the end of him harassing Vicky. He was not going to bother asking for his license or vehicle registration. He knew who he was, and he wanted Mr. Sterns to know that he knew his identity. Wayne had a bag of powdered baking soda in a clear zip-lock bag and pulled it out of his pocket once he got to the driver's side window. He showed the bag to Jimmy as he lowered the window, and Wayne said, "I am the former sheriff here in Butler County, and now an agent with the TBI. I am going to arrest you and make certain you are prosecuted for drug possession." He held up the bag of white powder. He further explained, "Jimmy Stern, you will go to prison for thirty years. You are not only in violation of your probation for having cocaine in your possession but having a firearm would make it all automatic and easy. The gun provides an extra five years." Wayne placed the bag back into his pants pocket very quickly, so Jimmy could not see it clearly. Wayne did not show him a gun. Wayne was aware that baking soda in a bag does not look exactly like cocaine in a bag, but he figured the quickness with which the bag was shown would scare Jimmy.

Jimmy said, "Look, man. I just want to go to church. I saw you following me out of the church parking lot. You know that stuff is not mine. Why are you trying to plant that shit on me? I have no gun."

"Well, listen. I will make a deal with you. You need to stay away from Mrs. Donohue."

Jimmy looked very surprised and turned his head to face Wayne, and asked, "Who is Mrs. Donohue? I need to know who she is first so that I can stay away from her."

Wayne realized he did not know Vicky's name "You need to stay away from Middlebrook United Methodist Church."

"Look, Officer, I do not know Mrs. Donohue. Who the hell are you talking about? I saw some other black people in the church, so I know this can't be because I am black, or is it? I have done my time for something I was not guilty of, to begin with, and now you are starting some shit with me." Jimmy was starting to get mad.

Wayne said, "Look, Jimmy, if you ever come back to the church or get within sight of Vicky Donohue or in any way bother Vicky Donohue, I will see that you go back to prison. I know where you are living, and I can find you. Pick another church."

Jimmy told Wayne that he had been treated poorly by the legal system, and now Wayne was mistreating him. Jimmy hit the steering wheel with his hand, appearing to grow more and more frustrated.

Wayne gritted his teeth, leaned over near the window, and said, "You heard me, and you better listen, or I will have them bury your ass in that prison. You need to also tell that punk, Dillon Hayes, that I am coming for him."

"Who is Dillon Hayes? I don't know anyone named Dillon, and I don't know this female named Vicky Donohue."

Wayne walked back to his car and left, thinking that it appeared Jimmy did not know who Vicky or Dillon Hayes were. He certainly seemed surprised and confused.

***

Monday morning, Vicky headed to the gym to meet Betty for some more work with kicks and exercise. She had noticed, watching Betty work out with a young man who was preparing for a tough-man competition, how quick and powerful Betty was in her punches and kicks. One on one, she could take the guy. She was trying to teach him how to anticipate, what his weaknesses were, and what to expect from the upcoming competition. Vicky thought Betty trained people in Karate in the Army and was a Military Policeman (MP). She no doubt would have been challenged by soldiers twice her size wanting to be able to say that they beat the instructor. Vicky discerned by watching that Betty certainly knew how to defend herself, and she had a great deal more quickness and power than one would think.

Vicky was feeling good about the training. She marveled at how Betty seemed to know all the answers about defending herself and how best for her to improve. After one hour in the Karate class and one hour in a private lesson with Betty, she was always so tired she could hardly walk back to her car. Vicky asked Betty, when they were drinking bottled water after the session, if there were any more suggestions.

Betty said, "Just remember, the best weapon in a fight is the element of surprise, and you need to use it against the opponent. Try to let the opponent underestimate your abilities. Generally, if you break your opponent's nose, he or she will lose the will to fight. The best way to break a nose is to come straight down on the bridge of the nose. It takes, on average, seventeen pounds of forced pressure to break the nose bone, striking down on the bridge of the nose. If you want to kill your opponent, you drive the nose bone straight back into the brain with the palm of your hand or your fist. This is the easiest way to kill someone. Another way is with a throat strike, where you collapse the windpipe. The force to execute either strike has the same basic power level in the stroke to kill an opponent. The throat shot can be either with the side of the hand or the fist, like this." Betty showed Vicky both punches to the throat. Betty then showed her the different punches for the nose, and had Vicky duplicate each one twice.

Betty then said, "There are a couple of other strikes to kill someone, but those are the two easiest to master. A very firm shot to the temple can jar the brain enough to kill someone, but it takes a hard hit, and the strike has to land perfectly to the temple. One additional key is to know the body and the weakest points, and that is where you attack."

Vicky thought, "I hope I never need to break someone's nose." She got in her car and drove to the indoor gun range. She ran into Wayne, who updated her about what the FBI found when searching the judge's home. "There were no girls located, but there was some evidence at the scene. They tested the cage that we had located earlier in the garage, and they found DNA, which had traces of urine from two different girls of Asian descent. They are still running additional tests. The cage had been wiped down with Clorox-based disinfectant recently, leaving no fingerprints, but there were still traces of DNA located in the urine samples where the cage metal was soldered together on the bottom on the cage. Most of the disinfectant had not vaporized, and there is no reasonable explanation for the urine being on the cage except what we know to be true. The cage was not locked. The latch had been broken."

Vicky asked, "What else did they find?"

"I called Darrell and asked him to fly over the home with his drone and take pictures. He went out to the field across the street and flew over the home Saturday morning. The FBI team must have located something at the corner of the property. Darrell told me they had set up tarps to work under, either to hide what they discovered or preserve what they found from getting rained on. He surmised it must be important, for them to set up the canopies."

"I called my boss and told him there was no reason the Feds should not share the information with the TBI. He had already called the FBI office in Atlanta. Evidently, the phone call got a little heated. That is when he was told the FBI used infrared imagining, and they located three bodies in shallow graves, which could be Asian girls. They won't know until additional testing has been completed. The graves were old, no new bodies. The girls appeared to have been buried for more than seven years. The FBI wants all this kept quiet. They said this needs to be kept out of the news. They have leads, and the only way they can catch the culprits was if this was kept quiet. There was more than one suspect, and they are trying to steer the investigation away from the federal judge. If he is implicated, all his prior cases could come under review." He paused and then said, "The only reason the FBI shared that information with us was that we saw the dog cage and the pictures of the girls, and with the flyover we saw them digging where the canopies were set up. They will not share any additional information with us. We at the TBI and Butler County Sheriff's Department having nothing. It just does not make sense; why not enlist our help?"

Vicky was mad at herself. She felt she had lost. "We let the girl down. It is my fault that we did not find her. Do you really believe they have leads, or are they covering this up because it is a federal judge with several hundred cases that would need reopened and reviewed?"

Wayne said, "We did the best we could, and I am not certain what to believe."

"We did not look hard enough. Dammit, I am so mad. I failed. It was my fault. I should have been there sooner."

Wayne looked concerned at Vicky and asked, "What should we be looking for?"

"Pure hatred. We need to look for a corroded container. Whichever container is housing that much hate will be corroded with pure evil. We are dealing with mass murder. This makes five bodies, that we know about. There is no telling how many kids have been killed, or who is involved."

Wayne said, "The FBI is not certain they are all related, but it does appear to me that they are. Since the victims are not citizens, the FBI has not shared any information with us or the media. No one has reported missing Asian girls in the US. There also have been no reports of murdered Asian girls in our country."

"Why will the FBI not cooperate and ask for help?"

"Hell, if I know. I have been asking myself the same question since all this started. When they came to my office at the TBI headquarters, they confessed they had never considered Bill Cramer being involved. It was like they were looking at someone else."

Vicky suddenly had a thought, looking perplexed. "Did you say the latch on the cage was broken?"

"Yes. The latch had been broken. Why are you asking?"

She turned and looked at Wayne, and said, "You know in Sunday School Class, Maggie Burton was talking about Jeff and an old buddy, Ross somebody, and how they loved to fish at nights on the lake. Evidently, Ross loves to drink a lot, but she was saying Ross swears that he saw a naked Indian lady running down the bank and into the woods Friday night. Jeff said he did not believe Ross, and he did not see the Indian. Wayne, what are the chances that it was the missing girl?"

Wayne straightened up and looked at Vicky. "I will ask Jeff where this happened and check into it. I will let you know. I am not going to leave any stone uncovered."

Wayne started to leave, and finally broke the silence and said, "I talked to the boxer. His name is Jimmy Sterns. He just got out of the state prison in Brushy Mountain about three months ago. He nearly beat a man to death in Nashville four years ago. He said he did not know a Vicky Donohue or a Dillon Hayes. Is there any way he did not recognize you? He told me he just wanted to go to church. He seemed to be telling the truth. He got very upset. I threatened him with additional prison time if he bothers you. Then he got really mad and started beating the steering wheel."

Vicky got upset with herself. She said, "This is not what we're supposed to be doing in our outreach program at church. We are supposed to be helping people find a church, leading by example, not driving them away from church and God. I do not see how he could have known it was me. I just assumed Dillon Hayes got my license number off my car when he was following me that afternoon from the grocery store, or somehow knew it was me and told him."

"I made certain Dillon had no way of knowing it was you or how to locate you, but I guess you are right. He could have got your license number, and the two men might know each other. I thought I explained the game plan to Dillon, so he would be too scared to tell anyone, even if he did know. Dillon can't afford to let it get out that he is working with the cops. His partners might kill him. Jimmy may have been telling the truth, and he might not know you. It is a small world, sometimes."

Vicky said, "It is not that small."

"He is staying near Tennessee State College in Nashville, where he is lifting weights, boxing, and working out seven days a week. He works for the gym part-time. He lives in a room above the gym. It is called Box's Gym. He reports to his probation officer weekly. He was released from jail early for good behavior. The gym has a reputation for helping ex-cons once they are released and need time to find employment."

Vicky thought to herself, "Nothing is working out today," as Wayne left. "I am going to drive to the gym and talk with Jimmy Sterns. If he is up to something, I am going to find out, and deal with it." Vicky shot a few additional rounds, with both hands. Mark had turned the switch on, so the target would move across the indoor range from side to side at the back of the range. Mark had instructed her how to aim with both hands, the difference with each hand, and the additional challenges most people are faced with when trying to be good with both hands while at the same time shooting at a moving target. Mark had explained that most people do not realize the process is different and aiming with the dominant eye is different than aiming with the non-dominant eye and using the offhand while hitting a moving target. She put her 9mm Beretta up, and left a few minutes after Wayne left.

Vicky went to see Jimmy, without telling Wayne that she was going. She had plugged the gym's name into her iPhone and retrieved the directions. The drive would take her a couple of hours, round trip.

She pulled to a stop next to the large work out facility, with signs on the door and parking lot reading Box's Gym. The building was an old, red brick building, with two commercial metal dented French doors at the entrance and rusted bars over the windows. The building must have been built in the fifties or sixties, with four stories. It was old and not maintained on the exterior. This area of Nashville was the older section and run down, but the area was starting to rebound with the overall growth of Nashville. Land, any place in Nashville, was becoming a good investment. She walked up the stairs and opened the door. The bell above the door chimed. Large men, predominately black men, were working out and boxing. She saw Jimmy lifting weights at the bench press, with two other large men. The bar had well over four hundred pounds on it. Everyone in the gym stopped lifting weights and boxing, and it was quiet enough to hear a pin drop.

Everyone stared at her. She was the only female in the gym. The smell of men sweating was very noticeable. She had on her dolphin shorts and tennis shoes, with a sleeveless tee-shirt under her unbuttoned, baggy dress shirt. She had her pistol in the back waistband, hid under her shirt, with a bullet in the chamber and the safety on.

As Vicky walked toward Jimmy and got about ten feet away, Jimmy pointed at her and said, "You need to stay away from me. I do not want to go back to jail. Your man said he would put me away next time for thirty years and have the jailer bury my ass in prison. I had no idea who he was talking about until I kept thinking about the church and looked it up online, and I finally recognized you on the cover page of the church web page. You need to stay away."

Vicky said, with a very stern and direct voice, "Let's go outside. I need to talk to you." He hesitated at first and looked concerned, then walked toward the door. Everyone in the place watched them walk out. She told him that she wanted to talk to him about the judge as soon as they exited the door and walked down the stairs.

They went outside, and she asked, "Your name is Jimmy?" After a pause, she followed with, "Right?"

He shook his head yes, after a little hesitation. He sat down on the brick wall next to the sidewalk and the street. He looked around to see if there were anyone close by, like police officers. "I want to talk to you about the judge being involved in child trafficking and slavery. He committed suicide after you left, along with his wife, so they would not have to go to jail." She asked, "Have you seen the news?"

"Yea. I saw the news."

Vicky said, "I was there to take him down and stop him. I agreed to work with the TBI officer and enter the judge's home undercover. We had no backup and were basically flying solo. Without assistance from the FBI, it is very difficult to investigate a federal judge. We did not know about the wife's involvement until right before she hung herself. I never wanted anything that happened at the party ever to be mentioned. I did not have a choice. There was a child in danger."

Jimmy said, "I understand. I didn't have a choice, either."

Vicky then had a tear in her eye and said, "No. I do not believe you do understand. We failed," she said, as she looked at Jimmy.

"We were not able to locate the young girl he had purchased in the human slavery ring. She most likely has been killed by now. There is no way the slave runners would take a chance and allow her to live. We had inside information about a young Asian girl who was in a locked dog cage inside that home. She was brought into this country from an Asian country. We had to verify the facts before another judge would issue a standing warrant on a sitting federal judge, and our source is an undocumented person who will not sign a statement. If she did, no one would believe her. Plus, she is scared she would be deported and separated from her kids. She still could be deported if the other undocumented workers find out she talked to us. They know if they don't tell on her, they also could be deported in retaliation, if the employer finds out that they kept quiet. These undocumented people live by a different code, and they have no rights. She has sacrificed enough by telling us. The TBI officer told me the FBI did locate three graves in the back corner of the property, which might be three young Asian girls' skeletons, but they were old and had been buried for years. They were trying to confirm that the remains were those of Asian girls. This information is confidential, and do not repeat it."

Jimmy said, with a stern look on his face, "I would have been happy to help take down anyone who is hurting a child, especially a crooked judge. You think because I am a black man, that I do not care?"

Then, he added, "If I had known, I would have ripped that house apart looking for the child. Those four security men could not have stopped me. I would have walked right through them. I thought slavery was outlawed."

"Well, we still have some work to do. There are slavery and human trafficking problems in the third world counties that has gone undocumented by the world governments. This problem has just started to become a noted worldwide issue. The children are raped, and then killed. They are treated with the same value as cattle. Once they are used up, they are killed. I wanted to make a difference. I wanted to save that child. I thought I could help. We did not have enough time to secure additional help, and we went with the best plan we had."

Jimmy turned his head, looked at Vicky in the eyes, and said with his deep, harsh voice, "I will help. Just let me know what I can do.

The reason this country struggles so much is because our moral code is not set high enough, and we do not teach the young people vital morals."

Jimmy said, after hesitating, "I knew the judge was bad. He had forced me to fight, and I had just gotten out of prison. The judge helped me with early release from jail, and I thought he was great. I was so happy to be getting out of prison. Then, he forced me to fight. The judge was all about using people. He knew my probation officer, and I have no choice about anything. I would have to go back to jail if my probation officer said I did not report to him when I am scheduled to report. They had me on a leash. I might as well have been back in jail. I figured he was using you in some way, and I could tell you were not into that kind of scene. I am glad to hear you were able to end the judge. I knew the Mexican man was not a fighter. He just did not want to be deported. He was an illegal immigrant. I could tell he was a construction worker. He was no fighter."

Shaking his head a second time, he added, "I have been fighting all my life. I just want to stay out of prison. Brushy Mountain is the worst prison in the state. The jail cell was eight-by-eight with two beds and an open toilet, with no privacy."

Vicky asked, "Why did you drive all the way to Butler to go to church?"

Jimmy said, "My daughter goes to your church. Her mother was pregnant when I went to prison. Some drunk man started putting the mother down when she became pregnant because she is white, and I am black. He started saying ugly things about my unborn child. I hit him, and the next thing I knew, I was in jail. She got married to another man while I was in prison, and the guy is good to my daughter. He is a good man. I met her and held her, but I am not good enough to be a dad."

Vicky said, "So you were at my church because your daughter goes to my church, and you did not know I was at the party and working with the TBI agent to bust the judge?"

"I just wanted to see her; I wanted to be part of her life and spend time with my daughter. She is doing well. Her mother is a good person, and her stepfather is a good man. They take good care of my daughter. Her mother's name is Jeanie Black, and my daughter is Jasmine."

"I do know your daughter, and she is very pretty and well behaved. We are blessed to have her coming to our church, and you are welcome to attend as you please. The TBI officer, I call the sheriff, will leave you alone. I am sorry. I hope God can forgive me of my many sins."

Vicky, feeling repulsed by her action in calling Wayne, then said, "I guess I am a bitch. Look, never tell anyone about what happened at the judge's party, and I might be able to help you."

Vicky then explained, "With the mask and wig on, no one should have been able to recognize me, and I assumed you had. I was there to save a child, and I was going to do what I had to in order to save that child. I still failed. My father used to say, a person needed to pick their crusade and carry their cross with them into battle. I thought I could save the girl, or I was prepared to die trying. I had no way to know what to expect once I entered the judge's residence. We had figured I could move around inside the home, then leave. He had two security men watching me the entire time, except at the end when everyone left."

"Okay, I won't ever tell anyone, and no one will ever know. I promise. I will never mention it."

He then said, very stern and convincing, "I'm sorry it happened. I am sorry you could not locate the girl. You seem like a nice person."

Jimmy thought to himself that he had to respect the fact that she tried to help a child and put her life on the line for someone else. Jimmy, being like any other black male in the United States, could feel his pulse increase at the word slavery. He knew deep down, he wanted to help anyone out of slavery, especially a child from being raped and then killed.

"She just disappeared. I know she was there the day before the party. We just do not know where they took her. The judge never left the house in the past two days. It makes no sense. The TBI found a dog cage in the basement of the judge's home. The hasp part of the latch was broken."

Vicky was upset with herself and looked very frustrated, and she asked, "Jimmy, can I help you? What type of work can you do? Maybe I could assist you in locating a good job with benefits working in construction like asphalt, concrete, brick-mason, or truck driver? Do you want to work in the chicken factory, or work in sanitation?"

Jimmy said, "You mean garbage?"

Jimmy then responded, by shaking his head and saying, "No, thanks."

She said, "Well, to be successful, a person has to love what they do. What do you love to do? I might be able to help."

He seemed hesitant to tell her, but she stood waiting patiently for him to respond. Finally, he said, "I like to sell clothing. I worked in Chicago for a tailor when I was in high school, and then once I graduated from high school, I worked for a few months learning the details of measuring the customers. The manager was married to my aunt. At first, he would not allow me to meet customers. I was assigned to stock the racks and place the clothing items up once they had been tried on; we restock the items every season. I could tell what would work with customers. I later helped people pick out clothes and would carry the items to their cars. I learned that the trick of making the sale is all about being able to connect with the buyer, and always plan for the customers to return. I would keep a list of their names, so I could mention them by their names when they returned. I liked nice clothes. Then, I moved to Tennessee to get away from some bad people, gangs, and stuff. I had an uncle in the area."

Vicky could tell Jimmy did not much want to talk about his time in Tennessee.

Vicky said, "Well, I'll check and see what I can find. What is your number? I might be able to surprise you. I actually know someone that might need a tailor." Vicky then wished she had not mentioned that possibility without first checking with Tiffany. She hoped he did not build his hopes up, only for her to let him down.

Jimmy said, "Call the gym, and ask for Little Jimmy."

Vicky asked, "Who is Little Jimmy?"

Jimmy smiled.

Vicky said, "Okay, Little Jimmy, I am going to get you a job in a clothing store. It might just be a start, and then you can maybe transfer to a bigger town with a larger store."

"Sounds good to me."

Vicky drove back to Butler, knowing Tiffany would not have enough money to hire an extra person. She recalled how Tiffany was worried about buying the business and controlling the costs and the expenses of running the business. The owners were looking to sell the business, and they were not looking to hire anyone, with the sale of the store pending.

Vicky went into Tiffany's store to talk to Tiffany, who had been contemplating buying the business. Vicky walked in, and Tiffany was just finishing ringing someone up at the cash register.

Vicky said, "Hi."

Tiffany smiled and said, "I took your advice. I purchased the store from the elderly gentleman yesterday. Otherwise, I was going to keep thinking about it, and I was concerned they might want to sell to someone else. I have worked in the clothing industry for a long time."

Vicky could tell Tiffany was nervous, but excited. Vicky asked, "Will you do me a huge favor?"

Tiffany said, "Certainly."

Vicky hesitated at first, and then just said, "I need you to hire Jimmy Sterns, a black male who has some experience being a tailor but needs a job. The church might be able to help, initially, with subsiding his salary through the outreach program if you can't afford to pay his salary. We will pay you to pay him. The church will help you and him."

Tiffany said, "I do need a man to work with the men customers, and if he has the experience, that would be great."

Vicky said, "I will make certain he is on the job and is presentable. I am certain he can help you with the male customers. I will have him ready to work tomorrow. I know this is a huge favor, and I will take responsibility for him." Vicky thought she'd better tell Tiffany about his record. "One other thing you might want to know. He just got out of prison. It is a long story, but it had nothing to do with drugs or stealing. It had to do with fighting. He is a nice person, and I believe he will work hard and try to do a good job for you." Vicky clinched when she said it. She knew there was never an easy way to tell someone about the prison time.

Tiffany said, "I trust you, Vicky. If you say he is okay, then I will give him a try."

Vicky took a deep breath, felt relieved, and said, "I will personally guarantee you that he is okay."

Vicky walked out, got in her car, and pulled out her iPhone. Vicky called the number for the gym and asked for Little Jimmy. Jimmy came to the phone, answered, and said, "Hello" in his very deep voice.

Vicky said, without introducing herself, "Can you start tomorrow?"

"Yes."

Vicky asked, "Do you have some nice clothes to wear?"

"I will need to buy some as I make money, but I have some to start."

Vicky said, "Let me give you the address and the information. Tiffany Monday is your boss. She is really friendly."

Little Jimmy took the information and said, "I will be ready to start tomorrow. Thanks." He hung up.

Vicky thought, that was easy. I certainly hope this works out. Vicky then thought she would have to sell Matt on this, so the church outreach program could pay; otherwise, she was going to make the payments each week from her savings account. She was also going to take Matt to the store to buy him some seasonal suits and, specifically, winter clothing.

Steve D. Nichols

Chapter 24

Wayne drove over to Jeff's home at 5 p.m., after he had gone to his office. Jeff was out cleaning his boat in the driveway. The two men said hi to each other. Jeff asked, "Did you come to get the ladder I am storing for you?"

Wayne said, "You can keep it or dispose of it. That case got settled."

Jeff had stored the ladder he and Wayne had found when they were inspecting the water tower to locate the bullet that was misfired in the murder of the young FBI agent during the first of June.

Jeff smiled and said, "I heard the killer was a highway patrolman, and he shot himself in front of you. I guess that is one way of settling a case."

Wayne said, "Yes, he did, and the world is a better place for it."

Wayne walked over to the boat and looked in the boat and said, "That looks like dried, old puke."

Jeff said, "That was Ross's contribution to our fishing trip Friday night. I left it in here, figuring he would come by and clean this shit up. If he had shit in my boat, it would have smelled better. If you had puked in a man's boat, don't you think you should go over to the man's home and clean his boat up for him?" Wayne just smiled.

Jeff said, "He broke my red rod, which is lying over there on the concrete pad, when his size thirteen shoe stepped on the end of it. I heard it crunch under his weight. I had that rod since I was nine years old. It had sentimental value to me. Ross likes to really be comfortable when he fishes. I had pulled the rear swivel boat chair out, and he sat in a fold-out lawn chair from Walmart, with a cooler next to him. The chair collapsed about 10 p.m., and he was stuck in the bottom of the boat like a large turtle on its back. I caught a crappie a few minutes later and let it hit him in the face, while I hoisted it to the front of the boat. Finally, he got up. We switched places in the boat, and he walked to the front of the boat, where he sat down and broke my damn chair. See how the screws have backed out of the fiberglass hull? That is when he said he saw the naked female Indian. A few seconds later, he bent over and puked in my boat. He missed the lake with his puke. I asked him why he did not puke in the lake, and he said he was afraid he might have fallen in the lake while leaning over the side of the boat. He said he thought his toenails came out of his mouth, he puked so hard." Wayne smiled.

Jeff then added, "I like to fish with Ross because he is good-natured, and he is not very good at fishing. I catch my limit and his limit. So, if we ever were checked by a Tennessee Wildlife Agent, we would tell them I caught half the fish, and Ross caught half the fish. However, he normally does not vomit in my boat, and I needed to catch two additional fish to have caught both our limits when he puked."

Wayne smiled again, and then said, "I take it Ross is the name of the man who saw the naked female Indian?"

Jeff looked up from where he was wiping down the steering wheel, "How did you hear about the naked Indian?"

"That is a long story. Where did he see the naked Indian? I understand you never saw her?"

"That's correct, Wayne. I never saw her, and you might want to consider the source. He might have been dreaming, and he obviously was impaired." Jeff kept cleaning.

"Where was this at on the lake?"

Jeff lifted his head up and, with a smile on his face, he said, "We were right off point 17. We were all by ourselves. I did not see a campfire or smell smoke in the area. I looked for another boat tied off at the bank and did not see one. That area is fairly remote. Sometimes people set up a tent and camp along the bank of the lake. The banks, however, in that area are steep, covered with rocks. That would not be a good area to camp. There is not a flat area in the woods. Are there other reports about naked Indians?"

"Could the lady have been an Asian girl?"

Jeff had a surprised look on his face and asked, "Wait a minute, Sheriff, are you taking this seriously?"

"Yes. I am. Can you drive me out there in your boat, and let's look around? I would not be asking if this was not very important and urgent."

Jeff looked up, with sweat dropping from his head, and his shirt was covered with sweat. He had a very sincere look on his face when he looked over at Wayne, and said, "Let's go. Let me get Ross Jr.

wiped up off the carpet first. That puke could really get stuck in the treads of a man's boot. Besides, it is slicker than owl shit on a tin roof."

Wayne could tell Jeff was irate with Ross; he stood back, turning his face away so Jeff could not see him laugh, while he waited for Jeff to clean the indoor-outdoor carpet on the bottom of the boat.

Jeff announced he was ready, after about three minutes.

Jeff backed his truck up and connected the boat trailer to his truck. Maggie had walked outside and said hi to Wayne. Jeff told Maggie he had to show Wayne something at the lake. Jeff asked on the ride over to the boat dock, "So is there a missing girl?"

Wayne said, "There might be. We have to check out all types of complaints."

Wayne asked, "Is point 17 near the two large homes next to the little boat dock?"

"Yes, the crappie are in schools in the middle of the channels this time of year in the cool water, so we troll around the points and track them with the fish finder."

Jeff asked, "Sheriff, how do you like your new job with the TBI?"

Wayne said, "So far, so good."

The two men got out of the boat, once they pulled to point 17 near the area where Ross had pointed, and they looked around on the bank for footprints. Wayne walked toward the small boat dock and the two large homes along the shoreline close to the woods, while Jeff looked on the lake bank for footprints going away from the two large homes.

The bank was steep in this area, and rocky. The lake was part of the Tennessee Valley Authority (TVA) government-run water system management program, whose primary function was to control flooding but also produce energy from the dam, which was located on the Tennessee River about six miles south toward Nashville. The lake level this time of year had been dropping since May. The mud bottom of the lake was now more prevalent and point 17 was a mountain overlooking the lake, with a vast tree forest spreading out for hundreds of acres southeast of the lake. The only road in the area stopped at the small dock. There were no other roads into the forest area. The vast tree forest extended as far as one could see. Wayne and Jeff both noticed shoe prints when they stepped out of the boat near the shoreline from what appeared to be a fisherman who walked the banks while fishing. Jeff said that they must have parked at the small free launch located near the large home, which was next door to the mansion and the judge's large home. There had been no rain in close to a week, and there was no way to tell how old the footprints were. They had agreed to split up, to cover more territory. Jeff walked down the bank of the lake, staying close to the edge of the water. Wayne walked near the tree line, heading toward the free launch dock. After about two minutes, Wayne noticed a bare footprint heading away from the large homes, on the bank near the tree line. He bent down and looked closely at the print, and guessed it was a size three. The predominant part of the ground in this area was shell rocks protruding out from the steep lake bank. In between the rocks in the dirt, he noticed two boot prints behind the bare footprint, going the same direction. He only noticed the one bare footprint. The person had walked or run while stepping on the rocks as he or she hurried along the bank of the lake. The boot prints were very pronounced, with grooves approximately three feet apart. One of the boot prints appeared to have stepped over the top of a bare footprint. The size of the boot appeared to be eleven and appeared to be tracking and following the barefoot person. Wayne had remembered Denny talking about the Army issued boots, and how he liked them. He had talked about how durable and comfortable they were to walk in for long distances in all types of terrain. He had ordered him another pair a few months ago. Wayne was not certain, but he thought this boot print looked identical to the Army issued boot Denny had in the sheriff's office. He slowly stood and looked up into the woods. He looked toward Jeff, who was walking further down the shoreline. He thought to himself, had the FBI had an agent walking the shoreline this far from the judge's home? The distance was a quarter of a mile, and the FBI would not have had an agent walk this far from the judge's home unless there was a reason, but someone appeared to be tracking the other person. He cautiously decided to walk into the woods, with concerns about finding a dead body. The forest was a hardwood forest-type old growth with mostly large oak trees. The underbrush was not thick. He walked up the mountain about fifty yards and looked as he walked. He walked back and forth, a zigzag approach, as he ascended the steep incline, looking for signs of a person walking up the hill. He walked up next to a large white oak and looked up the hill and to both sides. He took the handkerchief out of his pocket and wiped the sweat off his face and head. He bent his head down to wipe the back of his neck, and out of the corner of his eye, he saw a small foot sticking out from under some leaves next to a huge oak tree and a large boulder. He immediately pulled the leaves back, discovering a girl, and he quickly checked the young lady for a heartbeat. He felt a small pulse, and she was naked and unconscious. Wayne picked the girl up and ran through the woods down the hill, hollering for Jeff to start the boat. Jeff had walked down the shoreline and returned to the boat, and then walked the other direction.

Hearing Wayne hollering, he ran over and met Wayne at the boat and wrapped the girl up in his shirt. Wayne held the girl and sat in the passenger seat as Jeff pushed the boat off the shoreline, after untying the lead rope from the rock. He headed wide open for the truck at the dock. He told Wayne they would make the dock in ten minutes. Wayne called Vince and told him to dispatch an ambulance to the dock, as Jeff ran wide open heading to the dock in the Mercury 125 hp. The boat was set for trolling and fishing. It was not made for speed. Jeff hoped he did not have to slow for another boat's wakes, as he was cutting across the choppy surface of the lake. Wayne knew the girl was almost in shock, or actually already in shock. She was not responding. Wayne had slid under the girl, trying to hold her tight and prevent the waves from jarring her, as the boat cut through the wind-driven waves. Bug bites were all over her body, and her feet were cut and bruised from walking barefoot. She was muddy and scratched all over. Wayne thought, what kind of person would harm such a small, fragile girl, and he thought about what kind of hell she had been through. He just was not confident she would make it, and this had happened in Butler County, under his nose, where he had been the sheriff. He felt his anger building, wanting to catch the culprits. Her pulse was very weak, and she appeared to be under weight, undernourished, and not quite five feet tall. He thought, first he would take care of the girl and then locate the people behind this. He knew he was not going to walk away.

Jeff was standing at the boat dock as the ambulance pulled away with the girl and Wayne, and he said to himself, "I cannot believe Ross saw her, and I just did not believe him. He is exonerated." He said a quick prayer for the girl and loaded his boat on the trailer.

Chapter 25

The Spaniard reviewed his incoming text. He liked what he read. He had finally made it to the top of his profession. He was in direct contact with the American that made all the decisions. When his mentor had told him, he was going to retire, he at first was surprised that his old mentor and boss had decided to walk away from the job. He figured the American was the type of person who could never walk away. He was the heart of the network and had developed connections all over the world. He had indicated he would provide the Spaniard's contact information to his boss, the Colonel, who might need his future services. Bill Duff had trained and recruited the Spaniard years ago. He had explained how he could make him a very rich man, and what the job requirements would be. He further took time to explain his physiological views on the world, and that the danger involved in the job was the reason for the high salary. He had been dirt poor, living in the slums of La Coruna, located in the northern point of Spain, and had watched his young wife and two-year-old son die of viral pneumonia because they could not afford to pay for the expensive doctors and medicine. The doctor who worked for the city had misdiagnosed the illness at first, and the antibody had masked the underlining virus. He was very bitter and jumped at the opportunity presented by Bill Duff. He recalled how Bill Duff had explained that it is difficult for most people to kill another person. A killer had to be mentally trained to kill. It was not normal to be able to kill another person without mentally being trained to do the deed and be able to psychologically live with the outcome. He had explained that the job is to kill, and then move onto the next job without looking back or considering the consequences of killing.

He had helped Bill Duff stay hidden, and then helped him leave the country in the dark of night on a boat, after Bill Duff killed the federal judge in Spain. He was so thankful for the training and guidance. He killed the doctor that had misdiagnosed the illness of his child and left with Mr. Duff. After the killing, Mr. Duff had no doubt that the Spaniard was capable of carrying out the task of being an assassin. He had slowly killed the doctor in his apartment, with Mr. Duff watching.

Then, he read the next text a few days later which explained that Bill Duff, who went by the alias Bill Cramer, had committed suicide.

He had never considered Bill Duff as the type of man that would consider suicide. He went online and read the articles, which had indicated Duff was cornered by a sheriff in Butler, Tennessee, for killing three people and instead of going to jail, he shot himself. The Spaniard leaned back in his chair, took a sip of his drink, and thought of the admiration he had for Bill Duff and decided that was the way he wanted to go, by his own hands.

***

The latest message had been received on the Spaniard's secure telephone. The message provided him the address of the Butler County Hospital and the contract for killing the young girl who was still in a coma. The contract needed to be carried out within the next seventy-two hours. He figured he would fly into Chicago, and then fly to Nashville. His air tickets had already been purchased for him. He had a concern with the hit being located in the middle of the United States. He had studied the FBI, and their ability to track someone with their high-tech electronic technology and all the inner-connected cameras.

Biff Duff had trained him well, and how best to move around the globe undetected. The FBI worked with Interpol and all other national police departments in the free world. All modernized countries kept records and tried to track people in his profession. He was a wanted man in several countries. He had been able to keep his face hidden over the years and enjoyed anonymity. He knew he would schedule a visit to the plastic surgeon after this job. There were just too many cameras in the US. His response to the text was, "Contract accepted." He was so proud to be provided the opportunity to work at this level with these people. This signified he had reached the apex of the industry.

He read the report on the flight over. He remembered what Mr. Duff had taught him. Sometimes when killing a person, the assassin needed to send a message, and sometimes the death needed to appear accidental or health related. This contract was neither. The girl quickly needed to be eliminated by whichever means was fastest. Collateral damage was not a concern.

He pulled up the photos of the hospital in an aerial view on his phone. He zoomed out of the map, and noticed it was located in a very remote area in a small town north of Nashville. He read the description of the town provided by the mayor's office, which introduced the small town and activities scheduled in the local community. He was fascinated with the fact there were only four county police officers in the entire county. The second article he noticed was posted about job opportunity in law enforcement. The county was actively trying to hire an additional officer, which meant they were understaffed. He then read the additional information provided by his employer. The report was comprehensive. There was one police officer assigned to watch the room. The report indicated that, if he had to kill the officer to get to the girl, that would be acceptable collateral damage. He thought about wounding the officer and killing the girl. He thought it would be unprofessional to kill an innocent bystander. The late afternoon would be the best time. There were very few people in the hospital at that time. He smiled to himself. This might be the easiest contract he had ever accepted. With a girl in a coma, and only one guard who was not expecting a hit to take place, the county sheriff's department would not be able to respond quickly, with half their force off work at that time of day. He could fulfill the contract and simply drive back to the airport, leaving the car in the overnight parking garage, and fly out on his 8 p.m. flight. This was going to be easy. The big bonus was that he did not have to share the contract money with anyone. He smiled to himself, leaned back in the plane seat, and reminisced. He remembered how poor he was years ago when his wife and son had died. He had tried to make a living as a fisherman, but the competition did not play fair. His small boat was routinely sabotaged. He smiled to himself and knew he would have his revenge on the fisherman who had caused him so much strife years ago. He was now working for himself and could work into his schedule a return home to seek his revenge.

He knew not to ask why. Bill Duff had explained his job over the years was to fulfill the contract and collect the money, and if pulling the trigger to kill a girl was the contract, he knew he would do it. The people paying his fee had a reason. As he sat in the plane seat waiting for it to touch down in Chicago, he wondered about the two physics professors in Germany, he killed about six months ago. He also thought about the politicians in Israel, London, and Russia he had killed, and he understood why; politicians control the countries' purses and militaries. They had the true power in the world. The bankers in Asia and Europe, he could guess why they were targets. This girl must be a witness, he assumed.

He was relieved he did not have to apply torture to try to retrieve additional information on this job or kill her to set some type of example to scare someone else. Unlike Mr. Duff, he did not enjoy torturing someone. His job was to kill the girl and leave the country, hopefully without any witnesses. A bullet would be the fastest method. For two million dollars, he could easily change his appearance after the job, and then he could consider retiring back to the city of La Coruna, Spain, where he could live like a king. Then he smiled to himself, and shook his head no. He realized he enjoyed the work too much to retire. He had become addicted to the excitement of the kill, and the money was too good to pass up.

Chapter 26

Little Jimmy showed up for his first day of work on Tuesday in blue jeans and a nice dress shirt with a tie, looking nice and somewhat professional. He told Tiffany he was very accommodating with the customers, and he would do anything she asked. He told her that his friends called him Little Jimmy.

Vicky was thankful the church agreed to use the outreach money to pay for part of his salary and keep it entirely among the six board members. Matt did a fantastic presentation on selling the committee on the idea, and further explained it was a temporary need. Matt had said, "I do not know of a better way to help a church member and a young man trying to get started. This is what we are called to do, as a church and as Christians. I hope this committee can reflect on this moment at some point later, and realize we made a difference."

Vicky recommended the store to people from the church, along with the Hispanics in the community via talking to Maria. Maria had indicated the Hispanics would come for special events, such as wedding celebrations and graduations, and ask for Little Jimmy. Over the next few days, Tiffany's store was preforming better than Tiffany expected. She kept trying to offer higher end clothes at reasonable prices, to compete with the competition in Nashville. Vicky felt hopeful that Little Jimmy would work out. He seemed to be more analytical than she had first thought and appeared to be a cheerful person.

* * *

On Friday afternoon, Wayne told his boss, John, he wanted to take flex time off for the afternoon, since he had worked several weekends.

John said, "Certainly," and Wayne locked his desk and got into his unmarked car. He called Vicky and told her to meet him at the firing range.

Vicky countered, "How about the gym?"

She had been wanting to buy the one-by-four boards and set a time with Betty, to see if she could break the boards with her kicks. She had been practicing in her basement without the boards in the afternoons. She had purchased a punching bag and told Matt it was a better exercise than taking a workout class, and she could stay at home. She would visualize hitting someone's knee time after time. Matt thought it was a great idea for her to stay at home and exercise, and he told her he was going to start jogging through the subdivision. He mentioned she could join him. He wanted to get some exercise, running with some of the men at church.

Vicky met Betty in the parking lot, and they carried the boards into the gym. Betty had explained to Vicky a few weeks prior that breaking the boards was the next step in her training.

Betty said, "You know, I meant to tell you, I practiced for three months before I tried to break boards when I was in the Army."

Vicky smiled and said, "We will see if I am ready or not, but I have been practicing in my basement, with a punching bag hanging from the ceiling. I hope this is a nonjudgment zone."

Betty smiled and said, "Loosen up, and I will hold the board for you. I am certain you will do great."

Vicky said, "Okay," and did a couple of toe touches; Betty got into position.

Vicky did not hesitate and performed a front kick, hitting the board with all the force in her body, and the board busted in half. The entire process seemed easy and natural for Vicky. She could feel her confidence grow once she saw the board bust into two pieces. She was able to transfer all her body weight into the kick with a shift in her body, which transferred the amount of overall force into the board. She also was able to maintain her balance and reposition herself. Betty had explained that it was difficult to transfer all your weight into a kick, going in a certain direction, and then recoil and maintain balance and prepare for whatever comes next. All fights were different, and a fighter had to be able to reset his or her feet in anticipation for the possible retaliation.

Betty said, "That was a perfect front kick. That would have taken out anybody's knee. The kick had a lot of power, and your balance was perfect. It only takes sixteen pounds of pressure to the side of the knee, and twenty-four pounds of pressure to the front, to drive the knee straight backward and fracture it."

Vicky was somewhat surprised at how easy the board broke in half. Vicky tried three more front kicks and broke the boards each time. Using her left foot to strike the board felt better than using her right foot.

"I want to try the sidekick."

Betty said, "I will hold the board facing to the side."

She used her right leg to balance, and with all her force struck the board with the left foot. The board broke with a loud, snapping noise. Vicky really felt good about her training. Some of the other members started watching. Every time the board broke, there was a loud crack. Vicky felt she could break the boards with either foot but using her left foot to strike the board was easier and felt more controllable.

Betty said, "You only have one more board left."

"I want to try the sweep kick. The toughest kick, as you described it."

Betty started to ask if she were sure she was ready, but she could tell Vicky was going to try it. Betty knew this kick took a lot of practice, a lot of balance, and perfect timing to shift the power into the board. She remembered that when she had practiced, she would lose a lot of her power as she spun in the complete circle. This was a very difficult kick to master because you had to connect the knee perfectly into the side, which would cause the ACL and MCL of the target to be torn and the target's knee to collapse. Betty explained that there were a couple of things that could go wrong. The kicker would lose sight of the knee as they spun in the circle, and the kick had to be performed with both speed and power. Balance was the key, so the power could be transferred through the knee. Speed was also important; the person being targeted could not be allowed the time to anticipate and move.

Betty got in position, and Vicky's foot hit the board too low near Betty's left hand. Vicky could feel the pulsing pain run through her ankle, up her leg, and she knew she hit it too low with her ankle and not her heel. She walked off the pain, then motioned to Betty for one more hold on the board. The second time, Vicky hit the board higher, and it cracked and bent inward.

Betty said, "Good enough," as she finished breaking the board while holding it in front of her. You need to practice, focusing on where the spot of contact should be, and shifting your weight as your foot impacts the knee.

Vicky said, "I am done for the day. Thanks for helping, Betty. I will work on it at home with the bag."

"Glad to help. See you next week."

Vicky walked out with a slight limp, and noticed Wayne pulling into the parking lot.

Wayne asked, "Can we talk?"

"Yes, follow me over to the shopping mall area, and we can talk there."

Wayne started his car and followed Vicky. He pulled in next to her.

She said, "Follow me," as they both got out of their vehicles. They walked into Tiffany's new store, called The Prestige, and Wayne walked through the entrance door and looked up into Little Jimmy Stern's face.

They both stared at each other. Vicky said, "Officer Tipton is in need of some nice clothes."

Before Wayne could protest, Vicky said, "He needs a suit to testify in court, a suit for special occasions, and a new jacket. Wayne, the jacket you've got on was worn out two years ago and it looks like you sleep in it nightly. Little Jimmy is here to help."

Little Jimmy said, "Yes, Officer Tipton. Being on the side of the state in court, you do not want to have one of our real expensive suits. The jury might think something is up. I would suggest a light navy suit with pinstripes, a maroon tie, and a 100% oxford white shirt. Are you a forty-four regular?"

Wayne took off his jacket, looked at the size marked, and said, "Yes. I am."

Wayne tried on the light, gray-colored pinstripe suit, and Little Jimmy measured him and asked, "What do you think, Mr. Tipton?"

Wayne said, "I will take it."

"Now for a dark suit for special occasions," Vicky said, "Like dating."

Wayne said, "I am not certain I need another suit."

Vicky said, "You need another suit."

Little Jimmy went and pulled a charcoal gray pinstripe off the rack and explained that it had more wool material. It was a heavier suit and looked more expensive. Vicky saw Tiffany and walked over to say hello, telling Little Jimmy not to forget the new jacket. Wayne ended up buying two suits, three shirts, and a light-weight brown jacket with pads on the elbows for a total of $1,300.00. Wayne paid with his credit card and walked outside with Vicky, who had said goodbye to Little Jimmy and Tiffany.

Wayne asked, "Did you know Jimmy Sterns worked at Prestige?"

Vicky said, "Yes, I am the one who introduced him to the new owner. That was the least I could do for him, after having you run him away from our church. He is a good man, and I wanted to help him. Did you know his daughter is a member of our church?"

Wayne cringed to himself, thinking about what he had said to Jimmy after pulling him over near Highway 12. Wayne said, "The reason I wanted to talk with you is that I have tried to find out who 'Ed' is. I wish Judge Larkin had provided some additional clues. I have looked locally and nationally. I even asked Dale Hunter and my boss. We checked out possible Mafia connections and most of his friends, but I still do not know who 'Ed' is. There is not even a small clue, and I just can't figure it out. I assume it is short for Eddie or Edward. The judge did not have any friends or family members with the first name Eddie or Edward."

Vicky asked, "Did you ever figure out how the judge could afford something as nice as that mansion?"

"He inherited some money years ago. He was somehow related to the Dupont family."

Vicky asked, "How is the girl you found over at the lake?"

Wayne was surprised Vicky had found out about the girl. Wayne wanted to keep it secret. Vicky was not going to tell Wayne that Jeff's wife had told her about the girl, because she had said Jeff told her not to tell anyone.

Wayne said, "She was taken to the Butler County Hospital and, as for now, she has security posted outside her door. I am not certain how much longer the county and state will pay overtime to watch her. We figured she would have come out of the coma by now. The highway patrol was assisting the sheriff's department since they still were understaffed. We have not told anyone. We have kept the FBI in the dark. We were hoping she would come out of the coma and provide us with some information on who was involved. We need a witness. At some point, we will have to report her to the FBI, but since they have been very reluctant to share anything with us, we will keep it quiet for now."

Wayne thought for a second, and then said, "She is still in a coma. The doctor does not know if she will make it or not. She needs time and rest. The doctor feels she had an emotional breakdown from the trauma, and she is struggling with her inner being. Physically, she should not be in a coma. She had several hundred bug bites, and her feet were bruised and cut. She had been raped, but no DNA could be located from the rapist. She most likely had not eaten in several days. They are continuously providing her twenty-four-hour nutrition and fluids through the IV. She may have been drinking lake water, which is full of bacteria. She is also receiving antibiotics through the IV. The doctors are doing the best they can."

"You know, Wayne, if she saw the people involved, she could be in real danger. The people involved cannot afford to let her tell what she knows. I have been reading up on psychotic killers, and the worst ones follow certain routines, especially when it comes to the enjoyment of the final act, which is killing the innocent person. There is no telling how many girls have been killed and how many people are involved in this worldwide human smuggling ring. Now, you are telling me the only person to survive is not going to be guarded. The information she might provide could be invaluable."

"That is why we have an officer standing watch. The budgets are tight, and I am concerned they will stop paying for the extra officers who are providing the security. I know Butler County will not keep paying overtime. The mayor will not approve the budget. If we tell the FBI, they will protect her, but they will not share any information with us. I want the killers." He looked at Vicky when he said he wanted the killers.

"My God, Wayne, you cannot let that happen. She will be killed. I understand not telling the FBI, but she has to be protected, and one officer may not be enough."

"She might not ever recover, and she might not have seen anyone. How did you find out about the girl?"

Vicky just smiled at Wayne. Wayne asked, "So you're not going to tell me?"

She looked very sincere, "Are you ever going to come to church?"

Wayne just shook his head at the stalemate. "You are a difficult woman."

Vicky smiled, and decided she would go to the hospital and check things out. She kept thinking, and said, "You know, Wayne, the judge may not have meant the name Ed. He might have meant the letters E.D. He was struggling to say anything." Wayne was surprised by this revelation.

"I thought you told me that when he was dying, he had said the name Ed. But what would the letters E.D. stand for? They could stand for a person, maybe a group of people, or maybe a location."

Vicky said, "You know, when I first walked into the judge's home, I noticed a picture on the wall of the judge and another man about the same age but bigger, appearing classier and more refined than the judge. I saw that man at the party with a very attractive blond who was noticeable younger looking. The couple did not look like they were together until they left together. She had to be a trophy wife."

Wayne asked, "I wonder who the judge's friends were? We should have staked out the place and identified everyone at the party. Someone at that party must be involved."

"I could not be seen with a camera, and you said Dillon Hayes had mentioned they normally check for electronic devices. Like you said, we could not stake out a federal judge's home. We could not see the parking area near the garage from the street, and most of the people entered and left by walking around to the side of the home. I may have been the only person that used the front door."

Wayne added, "Most of the cars that drove into the driveway were limousines with dark tinted windows, rented from the airport in Nashville. The people must have been from out of state. I suspect there were a few billionaires present. No one would have approved a stakeout."

Vicky said, with a surprised look on her face, "I believe some of the people at the party were from other countries. They were bilingual. I heard someone speak German and another couple speak French. I did not recognize anyone, but I know someone who might know who the judge's local friends were."

"Who?" he asked, as he shifted his shirt and jacket to his other hand.

Wayne said, "The suits will be ready next week. They are being fitted."

Vicky smiled and said, "You will look very handsome in the suits and jacket. Robert Bowers might know. He has his hand in every land deal in this county. I still have his number on my cell phone, where he called me about helping with the Vacation Bible School, and he was our real estate agent when we moved to Butler. Hold on, let me call him."

Vicky hit his number, and Robert answered, "Hi, Mrs. Donahue, what do I owe the privilege?"

Vicky rolled her eyes and said, "Hey Robert, our church has the outreach program, and we are trying to find out who the judge's family or friends were. I assume you heard about the deaths of the judge and his wife? Do you know any of his local friends or family members?"

Robert said, "He had one very old friend, by the name of Bob Davis, in the area. Otherwise, I do not know of any friends. Bob visited his home at the lake randomly, and no one knew when he was going to show up. I have not talked to him in years."

Vicky asked, "Who is Bob Davis?"

Robert knowing Vicky had not lived in Tennessee for a year smiled to himself and said, "My dear, he is one of our two United States Senators that represent Tennessee. He is over several committees in Washington. They go back a long way. I think they went to law school together, and prior to law school, they may have been in the military together. The senator grew up in Nashville. After high school, he joined the Army. He is a real success story. He went through college while in the military on the GI bill. He had nothing growing up, and now he is thought to be a billionaire. He has been able to hide his wealth over the years, from what I understand."

Vicky said, "Well, I do not believe the church will try to console a United State Senator." She started to say goodbye and then asked, "Do you know someone with the initials ED that the judge might know?"

"Yes, I do."

Vicky was surprised. She blurted out, "Who is E.D.?"

"That is the senator. His real name is Emilio Bob Davis. I did not realize that until I brokered the deal for them, buying their property near the lake. The senator's property touches the judge's property. He may have dropped the use of his first name in college, or he may have never used it at all. He had to sign some papers when I brokered the deal. Neither the senator nor the judge wanted anyone to know who purchased the land to build those big homes by the lake. I remember the senator was very weird about things. I assumed it was because he was a politician, and he did not want the voters to know how wealthy he had become. I had to sign a nondisclosure agreement, outlining that I had to respect anonymity for both of them. I guess the news is out now concerning who owned those two large homes. A few years later, the homes were sold to an offshore corporation, and I have no way of knowing who technically owns the offshore companies. The county tax assessor's office had the sale noted, and the amount of the sale of each home was more than two million dollars, each. The entire deal was kept quiet, with a Quit Claim Deed being the instrument used to transfer the title of the land. The sale of the homes was a cash deal. There was no Deed in

Trust. They were the only ones that ever visited the homes, from what I understand. I assume they still owned them through the offshore companies."

"You mentioned he was weird. How so?"

"He hired a contractor through a friend of mine to build a shell of the home, and then hired someone else from out of state to finish it. I remember going out to the home site when it was being built and noticing the huge basement totally underground, with huge concrete walls. They had to blast rock out of the area to install the large underground bunker in the senator's home. They also had security guards stationed at the home while it was being built, which is not normal."

Vicky asked, "Who built the home?"

"It was a builder out of Nashville. I might have to call you back when I remember. I would call my old friend who recommended the builder, but he passed away a few years ago."

Vicky thanked Robert for his help. "I will see you at church," she said, and hung up.

Vicky looked at Wayne and said, "It is Senator Bob Davis. He dropped the use of his first name, Emilio. He and the judge had been friends for a long time, and Senator Davis was a senator from Tennessee for about eighteen years. I knew I recognized him from somewhere. Now I recall that he has been on TV. That would explain how the girl disappeared so fast from the judge's home. She was taken next door to the senator's home, and she must have escaped. Without Cramer helping, the senator must have made a mistake. They were in this together. I had also wondered where the four security men had gone. They just disappeared. They were not hired by the judge. They were protecting the senator."

Wayne said, "He is over the committee controlling the purse strings for the Defense Department and is on the committee overseeing the CIA and State Department, which is over the FBI in the Senate. He was thought to be a future leader for the White House but decided he did not want to run for president. He supported everything the president did, and they were friends in the same party."

"Did you know the senator and the federal judge each had a large mansion at the lake? I have never heard anyone mention it in church."

Wayne said, "I had heard that they both had second homes at the lake, but they never were seen in the city of Butler. The homes were built prior to me moving to Butler. I did not realize they knew each other. They have never been on TV together, or had any articles written about them knowing each other. They each probably own several homes in different cities and states. I have never driven by the homes. We never have been on a call in that area. The senator's home is located at the dead-end of a small road which turns off Lake Street. The judge's home is located prior to the senator's home, and the two are separated by a large field. There is a small boat dock after you pass the homes that some of the local residents use, but it is small and provides limited parking, from what I have been told. No one would want to drive all the way out there to launch a boat, and then realize there is no area to park the vehicle and trailer after the boat was launched. Past the boat dock is the large forest, which I believe is owned by one of the lumber companies. There are no roads past the senator's home. The senator and his visitors sometimes fly in by helicopter, as I understand it. I still remember when he was elected senator. He was asked if he wanted to be called colonel or senator. He had the name Colonel connected to the top part of his brick mailbox at a home in Nashville. Evidently, he was a colonel in the United States Army. The media made a big deal about his nickname Colonel. Over time people switched and called him Senator."

Vicky said, "We are going to have to get inside that home and verify if there are any signs of girls. The judge and his wife had photos hidden. There might be something we can locate."

Wayne said, "Wait a minute. We can't just break in the home owned by a United States Senator."

"I am going to get inside that home, one way or another. He must have known the man at the water tower who killed the FBI agent. I bet they both were in the Army together."

Wayne said, "This is not like the judge's home, where you technically were invited. You are talking about breaking and entering."

"I am talking about saving some young girls' lives and stopping a monster. We have to finish this. The senator was a colonel, and he is the corroded container full of evil that has been killing the girls."

Wayne thought for a few seconds and could tell Vicky was determined; she was going to need some help. Wayne conceded her point and relaxed somewhat, and said, "The time to break in would be when he was away. I can check around to see when he is scheduled to be back in Tennessee. It will be difficult to get into his house. The home will have the state-of-the-art sophisticated security systems monitored by the Secret Service, and in addition, maybe private security."

Vicky said, "I will ask Maria. She most likely knows who works for the senator cleaning, cooking, and taking care of the lawn. There are only a few maid services in the area."

Wayne said, "I will ask Darrell to see if he can fly his drone over the home and take pictures of the roof and all four elevations. We will need to keep this quiet and under the radar."

"I could look around inside the home, and then if we need, I could always go back and place a hidden camera or listening devices."

Wayne said, "There is no way we could get a warrant signed by a judge with the information we have, and then if we requested a warrant, the senator might find out about the warrant being requested prior to it being served, and no one would ever catch him at that point. I can guarantee you the security team checks for bugs in the home of the most powerful United States Senator on a routine basis, so I am certain that would not work. If planted bugs are found, he would become very careful, and we would never catch him. He is too smart. The only chance we would have to catch him would be when he is relaxed and does not suspect anyone is looking at him. I am wondering if he has contacts inside the FBI and the other federal agencies that keep him informed."

Both paused in thought.

Wayne said, "I will call you. I will see if I can find something out. We will need to be extremely careful with our phone usage during this process."

Vicky went home, changed clothes, and got a large brim bonnie hat to give maximum sun protection, which covered her head and hid her face. She was going to use the hat for hiking and working in her flower bed, and she also had on a baggy long sleeve flannel shirt with sleeves she could roll up. She placed the 9mm in her waistband, on the backside of her jeans, with a bullet chambered and the safety on. She drove to the hospital and parked in the farthest parking spot, under a Pin Oak near the side exit, away from all the security cameras. The parking lot was the size of half a football field, marked off with white parking lanes and a sidewalk, with a curb running the length of the front of the hospital. The main entrance parking lot was connected by a private drive to Main Street, which was also known as Highway 12. There was no activity, with six total vehicles in the lot, one of which was a highway patrolman's vehicle. Two nurses left through the front door and drove off. Vicky noted there was no other activity in the parking lot, and after about ten minutes, she decided to walk in the front door. As she entered the door with her face tilted downward away from the camera angles, she noted there was no one at the front desk. There was a bell to ring for service. The on-call nurse had used the highway patrolman that was watching the girl's room as an opportunity to leave the front desk, to talk with the patients and provide more one-on-one care. The highway patrolman on call would end up greeting the arrivals until the nurse on call arrived at the reception area and took charge. The ambulance employees routinely called ahead, and the nurse would be waiting. The hospital budget was very limited. Vicky glanced down the corridor, and she could see the large officer sitting in a chair, leaning back approximately thirty feet, in the hall asleep. Vicky was outraged. She kept her face down, knowing the security cameras were all mounted on the ceilings, focused downward. She turned and walked outside, calling Wayne as she sat down in her car. Wayne had just walked into his home, and said, "Hi," when he answered the phone.

Vicky said, "Your security man is asleep in the hallway, and there is no one at the front desk. It would be very easy to get to the girl. This is not acceptable."

Wayne smiled to himself, thinking about the patrolman being asleep. He thought that they were not taking the protection assignment very seriously. He said, "I will drive over after I call Darrell."

Vicky asked, "What would I be looking for in an assassin? I assume the person would not be wearing a sign that says, 'I am an assassin'?"

Wayne smiled to himself and said, "They would try to fit in and dress like a delivery person, an elderly person, a nurse, or a doctor. They would wear baggy clothing to conceal weapons. They would not want to draw attention to themselves and would be very inconspicuous." Wayne wanted Vicky to relax. He then repeated himself, and said, "Listen, I will drive over after I talk with Darrell." They both said goodbye.

Vicky thought she would hang around until Wayne drove over, or until the next officer came on shift to replace sleeping beauty. She just had a feeling something was not right, but then again, she thought, "What could really happen?" No one was aware that the girl was in the hospital or had been discovered. Wayne had said this was kept very quiet and away from the news media and the federal authorities. Vicky pulled out her silver windshield interior protection device from her passenger seat and placed it in front of her windshield. She could see out the hole for the mirror cut out. Her car was facing west, and the late evening sun was in her direct vision.

Chapter 27

When Darrell answered his phone, Wayne asked him for a favor.

Darrell asked, "Certainly, Chief, what do you need?"

"I need to meet you somewhere."

Darrell said, "I can run by your home. I am sitting on Main Street behind the large billboard, watching for speeders. I am bored out of my mind."

Wayne replied, "That will work. I will be waiting for you. See you in five minutes."

When Darrell pulled into the driveway, Wayne walked out to the vehicle and said, "I need for you to fly your drone over another home and take photos of the four elevations and the roof at an address near the lake."

Darrell could not control his excitement. Darrell was happy to help his former boss, Wayne, with the photographs. He said he could do it first thing in the morning. Wayne indicated that the home was gated with a security fence, which sat off the road about one-hundred yards. He still did not mention to Darrell that this was the home of the United States Senator, or that the satellite images were all blocked due to federal guidelines to ensure privacy and protection for the senators. Wayne explained to Darrell that he needed to keep this quiet and doing it early in the morning would be the best time. "You need to do this when no one is around, if you know what I mean. It is next door, where the judge lived. The large home on the end of the small road off Lake Street." Wayne thanked Darrell, gave him the address, and watched Darrell drive off.

***

Wayne called Ben Tarwater, the builder who built several homes in the area. Ben told him what he already suspected. There would be no plans filed with Butler County. He said, "I did not start having to file blueprints and obtain building permits until six years ago." The two men hung up.

He then called Vicky and explained that back fifteen years ago, when those homes were built, permits were not required for building plans, and there would be no plans filed with the county. Wayne said, "As soon as Darrell provides me with the photos, I will review them and call you. One more thing; I remember reading the articles about the senator. He also goes by Colonel, and he is best friends with the FBI and CIA. He supports everything they ask for through funding and provides the money to finance their projects, so there is a good chance someone in the FBI is providing him with information about the missing girls. I am going to leave in a few minutes. Goodbye" Wayne heard Vicky say goodbye and disconnected the call. He placed the personal phone in his pocket.

Vicky thought, while listening, that this was why no one would investigate Senator Davis. He had basically paid them off through the funding, and he might have steered them away from the judge and himself in their investigation. The FBI will not share anything with the TBI, and all of this has been kept out of the news media. The FBI must suspect something, thought Vicky.

As Vicky was hanging up the phone, she at first glanced through the opening for the mirror, for the sun protector covering her front windshield, sitting on her dash. She kept watching and noticed a priest drive into the parking lot very causally in a rental car from the airport. It had a sticker with Hertz on the rear bumper. She thought about what Wayne had said about trying to fit in. She unconsciously started rubbing the cross around her neck. She suddenly became very excited. She reached for her phone in the holder and dropped it between the seat and the console in the car floor. She hastily picked it up. She remembered that Matt had checked out the area when they were preparing to move to Tennessee from California, and there were no Catholic churches in Butler County. Most of the churches were Baptist, with a couple of Methodist and a few other denominational churches spread out in the county. She hit speed dial, and Wayne answered, "Hi."

Vicky, with an urgent tone, said, "I am watching a Catholic priest walk into the hospital. You know, Wayne, there are no Catholic churches in this county."

Wayne said, "I will call Officer Henderson and warn him."

Vicky said, "I am going in," and hung up.

Wayne told her to stay put, but his phone line connection had been broken. Wayne still had Officer Henderson's cell number from when he was the sheriff of Butler. He called Officer Henderson, and on the third ring, the voice answered, "Officer Henderson, how may I help you?"

Wayne said, "Look, this is Wayne Tipton. Be on the lookout for a priest. It could be trouble."

"What for?"

"He might be there to kill the girl."

"You've got to be kidding me, Wayne. He just came through the front door of the hospital."

Wayne could hear Officer Henderson say, "Hold it right there," in an intense, commanding voice. He could tell Officer Henderson was excited about something. Wayne listened to the officer say, sounding out of breath, "I've been shot." Wayne ran toward his car and drove as fast as he could go. He called Vince as he drove. He yelled into the phone at Vince, "We have an active shooter at the Butler County Hospital. He is dressed like a priest. One officer is down." The line went dead, and Wayne threw his cell phone in the passenger seat.

Vicky had run across the parking lot, and she knew when she saw the priest enter the front door that this was not going to be good. The priest was about six feet tall with jet-black hair, and was clean-shaven except for sideburns, which extended two inches down his jawbone. He was wearing the normal priest attire, which was black and baggy with a white collar. He seemed very calm and confident as he walked toward the front door. She thought he personified the attitude that he had not a worry in the world. She then remembered he could have multiple weapons and a bullet-proof vest on under his clothing.

Officer Henderson was too late to pull his gun all the way out of the button-down holster. He did not pull the flap back fast enough to fully extend the pistol barrel out of the holster. The priest had a handgun hidden in the baggy sleeve of his robe. With his right hand, the priest pulled a gun from the left arm sleeve of his robe, making the hand-grip easy to locate. The pistol holster was taped to his left forearm and hidden underneath the robe. The first bullet hit the highway patrolman in the center of his chest, and the next one hit him in his right shoulder. The third one hit him in the side of his right thigh. Officer Henderson had realized he was not going to be able to shoot the priest before the priest could pull a gun. He was standing in the middle of the hallway with no options. He decided to jump sideways through the door, into the girl's room, when he saw the pistol emerge from underneath the sleeve of the left arm of the black robe. By doing so, he had dropped his gun in the hall. His momentum carried him out of the hallway into the room, after he had been shot. He was laying on his back on the resilient tile floor, out of breath, and without his only gun. He was still holding his cell phone in his left hand. His gun had fallen in the hallway when he took the bullet to the shoulder. He figured he was going to die. There was nothing he could do. He was holding his chest and fighting for his next breath, where the bullet had hit him in his bulletproof vest in the middle of his chest and completely knocked the breath out of him. He was bleeding from the shoulder and leg. He could hear only two sounds. One was the medical monitor equipment beeping, which was attached to the girl located behind him in her room, and the second being the priest walking toward him down the hallway. With every step there was a squeak from the rubber-soled shoes against the newly polished, resilient tile floor. He looked over his shoulder, while lying on his back, at the girl with the IV and breathing tube lying in her hospital bed, and thought, "I have failed to protect you, and I am sorry." He looked at the door, still trying to capture his next breath. He saw the priest enter the doorway, with a matter of fact look on his face, and he saw the priest slowly point the gun with the long silencer down at him. The last thing he saw was the priest, with a smile on his face. He thought how he looked like the devil, with jet black hair and black sideburns, as he closed his eyes and waited for the final shot. He heard the loud shot, and someone fell. He thought, "I am still alive!" He opened one eye hesitantly, squinted as he looked at the door, and saw the priest lying on the floor in the hall with blood running out a bullet hole in his forehead. The priest had fallen against the door jam, and the door was partially open. He could not believe what he was seeing. It took a second for his brain to register that the priest was dead. He was finally able to take a breath, and looked over his shoulder at the girl, who was still asleep and breathing. He could hear the monitor beeping.

Vicky had entered through the double doors of the main entrance at a full run, using her left hand to hit the horizontal bar to open the door. She squared her body for the shot as she was moving through the doorway. She remembered where the officer had been sitting and figured her target would be in that hallway. As the priest aimed his gun down at the officer, he turned to look at the commotion, toward the front door. She fired one bullet that caught him above the right eye. The force of the bullet pushed his head to the side. Then, he fell dead. Vicky said to herself, "I will be your huckleberry." Vicky knew the bonnie hat with the wide brim would cover her face, and the security cameras would not be able to identify her. She had gloves on, and there would be no fingerprints. She had remembered what Mark, the shooting instructor, had mentioned about his home-made bullets: the shell casings have numbers which can be traced back to the manufacturer, and maybe the buyer, if the records were inputted correctly. She started reaching to pick up her shell casing before the priest had fallen to the floor, and she noticed the nurse running down the hall from the patient's room located in the second hallway to her left, as she was exiting the doorway. She ran back through the front doors, holding her gun under her baggy shirt, and sprinted to her car. She saw no one in the parking lot or on the street. She pulled the sun visor off her dash, throwing it in the back seat, and backed her car down the side entrance and street as fast as the car would go, in reverse. In one motion, she turned the car facing away from the hospital, removed her hat, and drove off. She could hear the sirens approaching the hospital. She turned down the side street, slowed down to look normal, and looped around the back road. Vicky placed her gun under her seat, took off her flannel shirt, and drove back to church for the adult study class. Before exiting her car, she thanked God for giving her the courage to save the girl's life. She prayed the officer would be okay. She knew she would have to throw the gun away; she could not take the chance of the bullet ever being traced to her gun. She walked into the front meeting room, and she sat down next to Matt and listened, but did not hear a word. She was so preoccupied with the senator, and now the priest. She finally excused herself, and she called Maria and asked if she could come to Maria's home early in the morning. She was more determined than ever to finish this. She figured the only person she could trust was Wayne. She knew she did not want her husband involved and was thankful no one was aware of her being the catalyst for now looking into Senator Davis. She knew he must be stopped, and they were going have to kill her to stop her from helping.

Maria indicated that Vicky could come to her home Monday morning. She would be back in town then. Vicky was hoping she could enter the senator's home with the maid service when there were no security guards present. That would be simple. As she waited to meet with Maria, she hoped Maria could make that happen.

***

Vicky met with Maria Monday morning. Maria's home was located off Liberty street, turning right instead of left to go to the Wet Spoon Bar. The house was a small, white vinyl home that had been added onto in the rear. The yard had been mowed and maintained. In the driveway was Maria's old brown Pontiac. Maria met Vicky at the front door and asked her to come in. Maria seemed to be always smiling. That was her nature. She said, "Hi. Vicky. Would you like some coffee?"

Vicky said, "Yes. Thanks, and I need some help."

As Maria was getting the coffee, Vicky asked, "What can you tell me about the large home by the lake owned by Mr. Davis?"

Maria, looked worried, and at once asked, "The senator's home?"

"Yes."

Maria then said, "The security on his house is a lot different from what had existed on the judge's house. What I been told, he is mean to the employees who are all Hispanic. He really is not a nice person, but he seems so nice and caring on TV."

Vicky asked, "How is the security different?"

Maria hesitated.

Vicky then explained, "There are some children who are in great danger. You remember what happened at the judge's home. These two men were best friends. I need your help."

Maria finally smiled and suggested to Vicky that she should talk to Valerie Sanchez, who was the cook and housekeeper at the house, and worked for the senator for years. Maria, however, warned Vicky that Sanchez might not be cooperative in providing the information that Vicky wanted. "She and her family do not have papers to say it is okay that they can be in America. They, like so many families, are constantly concerned about being deported and separated from friends and family members. What people do not understand is when part of a family is deported, or a single person is deported, sometimes they have no place to go. They have made their home in America, and there is nothing for them across the border. They have no money, and no way to obtain help. They have no place to live. A second issue is if the other workers do not tell on them, they can also be deported as punishment for not telling on their coworker. Now, with the death of the lady who had worked at the judge's home, we are all scared. She was just twenty-three years old." Vicky looked sympathetically at Maria. Maria hesitated, but agreed to ride over to Sanchez's home with Vicky.

Maria and Vicky drove to Sanchez's home, which was further down Liberty street, about a quarter of a mile. Maria introduced Vicky to Mrs. Sanchez and explained the importance of the information that they were seeking. Sanchez was a dark-haired five-foot-tall lady that looked to be very able and fit to complete housework. At first, Mrs. Sanchez looked concerned, and would not say a word. She seemed to resent Maria bringing Vicky into her home as she was preparing to leave for work.

She finally said, "You certainly helped my son out at the soccer field a few weeks ago, when he was getting ready to get deported. Thank you. I guess I owe you one favor."

Vicky noticed she spoke clear English, without near the accent of Maria. Vicky said, "You are welcome. We are all in this together, and I really need your help. I will never tell anyone I talked to you. I understand you live with fear of being deported. I will try not to allow that to happen."

Maria said, "We need your help. There might be someone harming children, and we are concerned about the security at the home. You can trust Vicky. She is the one who helped our friends that work at the chicken factory. She is a good person, and I trust her."

Sanchez spoke up and said, "I have never really felt okay with activities in that home." She hesitated, and then explained that the security system shuts down at 9:00 in the morning until 5:00 in the evening in the back of the house area, where they walk when they are scheduled to clean the home. "We enter the home from the rear door to clean the residence. There are cameras in the home in just about every room. We have learned over the years how not to set off the alarms, and where to go where no security alarm goes off. When the yard work is scheduled to be completed, the security system is turned off for the exterior of the home at a remote location, but the yard work is always scheduled a few days in advance. I believe the cameras are still working, and just the alarm has been turned off. So, I am not certain when the electronic security is working. It may just be turned off at the rear of the home for the maid service from a remote location, but when the senator is present, the system is always turned on or off in the house by one of the four security men. There is a trail across the back field for us workers to walk across. We park at the pullover before the small boat dock. We never are allowed to enter through the front gate or front door. The same is required with the yard service; they have to park in the same area." She told them that the help were all illegal immigrants, and none of them wanted to get in trouble. "We would be separated from our families, and we might not see each other for a really long time. We figured the senator did not want to be linked to hiring undocumented workers."

Vicky urged her further. She repeated that the help never entered the house from the front road or driveway. She also told them that there was a section at the home that did not appear to have any security, which is on the outside of the garage area on the side elevation, which had a very high wall with no windows, doors, or cameras. She continued, "There is no smoking allowed inside the home. That was the area where we would take our smoke breaks. If we ventured outside that area, the alarm would sound, and years ago the security would show up. Now, we do not see the security men at the property unless the senator is home. We discovered the smoke area over time, and we stopped setting off the alarm. The security company is a local company out of Nashville. They monitor from Nashville.

Years ago, the security men would be on sight when we were cleaning, but not anymore." She repeated that there were four security men at the home when the senator was staying at his house, and they all carried multiple guns, with radios plugged into earplugs, and mics.

She turned and stared into Vicky's eyes and said, "When Senator Davis arrives, the help must leave. He has a cook that can cook the meals, and us cleaners were sometimes requested back when they had an extended stay. We all walked across the backfield from the parking area at the fence. Sometimes we were only allowed in the kitchen to assist with cooking, and then when the senator left, we were permitted to clean the home. We never could enter the basement. There were two large steel doors with a keypad lock that kept us out, one near the foyer and one in the garage. Again, we only worked in the kitchen, and that was the only place in the house we could be when he was at the home, unless we were asked to make beds and bring in clean towels."

Vicky asked, "What about his wife?"

Mrs. Sanchez looked at her, rolled her eyes, and said, "They do not sleep in the same bed. The wife seems to do what she wants with whom she wants. She seems to have a lot of fun, if you know what I mean. She must be very active. We provide maid service by making their beds and providing additional towels, and that's about it, if they request our help when they are staying in the home. Then, like I said, we clean the home after they leave and do a fast wipe down before they come back, if needed. Except for making the beds and assisting with cooking, we were not permitted in the home when the senator was present. All this was scheduled with my employer, Ron, who calls us when we are needed. I have never met the new property manager who works for the senator. He took charge about three to four years ago. All this was set up years ago with the original management company, and nothing has changed. We are paid by cash through Ron. He is legal and sets up everything."

Vicky asked, "How do you know the wife is not sleeping with her husband at night?"

"Because his bed had been slept in on just one side and hers was very used, and the bedding was all over the place. The sheet covering the bed was always very wet. We had to change her sheets daily. The security detail had their beds downstairs, and they rotated shifts, sleeping in one of four beds in the back room near the garage."

"Who would be visiting her?

"I had no way of knowing. I suspected there was more than one visitor at a time. I believe the company used a helicopter sometimes to visit. I had even discovered a long strand of red hair in the bed sheets, which was not hers. She is blonde. I did not dare tell anyone. She normally does not stay overnight at the mansion. She uses a helicopter to pick her up and fly her back to the Nashville airport."

Vicky did not want to give the impression she was considering breaking into the residence, but she had to ask if the security was more intense when the senator was home. She was hoping Mrs. Sanchez might provide some additional, helpful information if she kept her talking.

Mrs. Sanchez said, "As I said, he had at least four guards when he was present, but when he was not present, there were no guards. The cameras were on the interior and exterior of the home and were being watched and monitored from a remote place somewhere else, maybe Nashville. As far as I know, there were no security guards at the property unless the senator was present."

Vicky thought to herself, so the security was relaxed when the senator was not staying in the home, and the cameras were on the exterior and interior; there would have to be a way in without the camera seeing her. "Did anyone ever come to the home to visit when the senator was not staying at the home?" Mrs. Sanchez shook her head no, and then said, "Never."

Vicky asked, "Have you been scheduled to clean the home this week? I understand the senator was scheduled to be at the home this weekend."

Sanchez shook her head no, and then said, "If he is by himself without his wife, we are not always scheduled to work prior to him staying in the home. But we were asked to complete some yard work, just the normal stuff. We were only scheduled to do a complete wipe down of the interior if Mrs. Davis was coming, or if they were having company stay with them."

Vicky kept hoping Mrs. Sanchez would keep talking and maybe provide additional information. She asked, "So, you never clean the basement area?"

Mrs. Sanchez said, "As I said, there is a keypad lock system to the large metal doors leading down into the basement, and we have never been in the basement area of that home. There are two metal doors leading to the basement, and both have a keypad lock system, with cameras over the doors. One door is located in the front foyer closet, and one is located in the garage. The doors are always closed."

Vicky thought she might wait to talk to Wayne before asking if Mrs. Sanchez could sneak her in the home, but if they were not requested back to the home prior to the senator arriving, she could not help. Mrs. Sanchez also had too much to lose with her family if she was caught trying to help. There was no way her family could be protected. Vicky thought to herself that there must be a way around the security cameras, located on the main level of the home and the exterior of the home. They said goodbye, and Vicky and Maria left.

Wayne met Darrell on Tuesday, after work, and looked at the ten-inch by twelve-inch photos, thanking Darrell for the photos. Darrell had provided seventeen photos, with three photos of each elevation and four photos of the roof. He said, "Do not tell anyone, okay."

Wayne was concerned about getting caught completing surveillance on a United States Senator's home. Wayne asked, "Did anyone see you out there flying the drone?

"No one saw me. It was early in the morning after the sun had just come up. I am certain no one was at home. I did not see anyone, and I stayed across the road in the cornfield. I made certain to keep the drone above the security cameras, which were all focused from atop the exterior walls under the soffit to the ground. I flew the drone over the lake and the wooded area, to hide my intent, just in case someone saw me. They would not know I was securing photos of the home. Whose home is that anyway?"

Wayne knew Darrell could find out without difficulty. Wayne smiled and said, "That home is owned by United States Senator Davis. It is titled in an offshore company name, but he owns it. We felt with it being so close to the judge's home, we needed to complete an aerial survey of his property. The aerial views are all blocked by satellite on a United States Senator's home. My boss had mentioned it to me after I told him about the photos you secured on the judge's property, when the FBI was digging up the bodies. I told him I thought you could secure some photos for us very fast and efficiently, without anyone knowing. I certainly appreciate your help."

Darrell looked surprised that the TBI had wanted him to take the photos. He sincerely hoped this would help him get his foot in the door for a transfer to the TBI. Darrell asked, "Does the TBI or FBI think the senator is involved with what the judge had been doing with the girls?"

Wayne knew he needed to provide Darrell with a plausible explanation. He hated not to tell the truth, but he was in a hurry and felt he had no choice. He said, "With human trafficking happening so close to the senator's home, we just want to make certain there is not a security breach. We all assume his security team is in the know about all possible threats. We just wanted to see if there were any weaknesses. No, we do not believe or suspect the senator was involved with the judge. The FBI is checking into the judge, and they will handle that investigation. They were not certain the judge knew what was happening on his property with the girls. They are looking into employees of the judge and others." Wayne hoped that his explanation would be enough for Darrell, and he tried to be convincing. He then added, "Just keep it quiet, and I will talk to you later. I will let you know what we find. I've got to be going." Wayne hesitated and thought that he might need to sell it a little better, and then added, "I was just making certain the security is okay. It's part of the new job. The satellite imagery over the senator's home is blocked, and the only way to secure photos is with a drone. Thanks for the photos. I will see you later."

Darrell hesitated and seemed to be puzzled, like he wanted to ask something, but said, "You are welcome." He then turned and asked, "Did Vince tell you about the joke being played at the small Baptist Church on Locust Street?"

Wayne said, "No. What happened at South Side Baptist Church?"

Someone in the church acted like they dug up a body from the graveyard, which is next to the church. The church had just had the camera installed to prevent vandalism, and a couple of nights later, someone acted like they were stealing a body. We were betting it was the youth leader and a couple of the youth."

Wayne said, "No. I have not heard of that joke. I may give him a call."

The men said goodbye, and Darrell got in his Jeep and drove off.

Steve D. Nichols

Chapter 28

Wayne called Vicky and explained he had some information from Darrell. He did not want to mention the photos or the drone on his official phone. He also intentionally did not mention the priest. He was not certain who was listening to his phone calls. He said, "I will take this information home and look at it closely. The hospital patient has been transferred to a hospital in Nashville, and she will have a full-time guard. Jerome Henderson is the name of the highway patrolman who got shot three times. He was out of the Nashville office and had worked in Butler County as a backup when needed. He is going to be all right. He thanked me several times for warning him. He said I saved his life, but we both know who deserves the compliment. I thought you and the church would want to pray for the officer and the girl."

He sent Vicky a text, after looking at the photos, and said, "We need to meet and talk Wednesday Morning."

Vicky knew Wayne's schedule, and he would either want to meet before work early in the morning or after work. Vicky texted him back, asking him to stop by the church for youth night, instead. She told him the start time was at 7 p.m. on Wednesday. Wayne replied, "Sure," in the return text. Vicky figured she would ask Wayne to talk to the youth about the laws pertaining to driving and the different court systems, so no one would be alarmed when the former sheriff was visiting the church and her. At least one of the kids would mention it to their parents that Wayne had stopped by the church to see her. She did not want to have church members question her about the single, former sheriff, and now TBI agent, being seen talking with her at the church. At least with him talking with the youth, it would appear she was trying to help the youth, and at the same time, interest Wayne with the church and attending.

Wayne pulled into the back-parking lot near the playground, where there were several vehicles and lots of kids running around outside near the tables. Vicky told Wayne that Mr. and Mrs. Vault were running late and would be arriving in about five minutes. Vicky then asked Wayne to come over to the picnic tables and asked the kids to come over and sit down. She introduced Wayne as the former sheriff of Butler County and now special agent for the Tennessee Bureau of Investigation. She spelled out the acronym (TBI) and announced that Wayne could explain to the kids the difference between the criminal court system and the civil court system. Vicky looked at Wayne and said, "They've been asking questions about the court system, and they may have questions about traffic laws."

Wayne looked a little off balance at first, since he had no idea, he was going to be the guest speaker. He started by explaining that the criminal system was between the state and the individual; whereas, the civil court system was between two individuals, like a car wreck, a divorce, a will, or a property transaction. He went on to explain the importance of the grand jury and how a police officer could make an

The Sinner's Reckoning

arrest, but the preferred method was to go through the grand jury to obtain an arrest warrant. The grand jury would provide an umbrella of protection from a wrongful arrest lawsuit against the police departments because the grand jury represented the people and not the police department. There would be no legal reason to file a suit against the police department for false arrest, since the grand jury had issued the arrest warrant. He also explained that sometimes a citizen could be arrested by the police and also be sued by another person. There would be two separate trials, one for the civil litigation and one for the criminal court. He pointed out that a lot of times, the civil cases were settled with the help of insurance companies, and sometimes people pled guilty to a lesser crime within the criminal court system. In both cases, the trials were avoided. He further explained that there is a federal civil and a federal criminal court system. After about ten minutes of answering questions, mostly about car wrecks and the rules of the road, he thanked them for having him. Vicky turned the class over to the youth leaders, Joe and Brenda Vault. Matt had been to the hospital to visit a church member and would join the Vaults and the youth.

As Vicky walked Wayne into the church office, she acted a little rushed and annoyed. She said, "I thought you might speak to the kids for a couple of minutes. I did not mean for you to get carried away with yourself and talk for more than ten minutes. I figured you would struggle to talk for one minute. You normally never speak more than one sentence in any one conversation. I have never heard you talk that much since I met you."

Wayne smiled at the comment, as he pulled the photos out of a file and showed her the four elevations and roof of the home. Wayne said, "I was not able to obtain a copy of the house plans from the connection at the county. Like I had suspected, there was never a house plan filed when the permit to build the home was purchased. The plans were not required to be filed with the county fifteen years ago."

As she was looking at the photographs, Vicky pointed out to Wayne the wall where Maria's friend had said there was no security. She asked, "So if the judge inherited his money, how did the senator make his money? You said he was a colonel in the Army before getting into politics. A colonel in the Army does not make that kind of money. This home would have had to cost over a million dollars."

Wayne said, "As far as I know, the senator did not inherit his money. He grew up poor or lower middle class. He was able to go through college with the Army paying the bills. The rumor was, he made his money on the stock market and investments, with rumors of insider information being used to make a substantial amount of money once he got out of the Army. He also made a lot of money in foreign countries. All of these are rumors, with no facts. I thought about looking into his finances, but that would have drawn attention from the people who protect and watch out for him. Since we were considering breaking into his home, I did not want to start a security investigation with a trail leading back to me. The FBI and the Secret

Service maintain the security of the senators, and they monitor the internet continuously for people wishing ill will on them. My office monitors our usage of the state-owned computers, and I have no assignment to check into Senator Davis. When my work computer is turned on and in use, the internal affairs office can watch my computer through a mirror system, and they can trace everything I do. The only information I could locate on my home computer was what has been printed in papers. I certainly did not want to pull the IRS information from the work computer. Someone would have wanted to know why. The senator has a lot of powerful friends. I will check a little into him, but I do not want someone wondering why I was looking into his past right before a break into his home occurs. If the break-in is discovered, like I said, the investigation might lead back to me. Senator Davis will have unlimited resources, working inside the government, and unlimited private resources. No doubt he most likely has contacts still in the Army, where he served as a colonel."

Wayne then pointed out that there were no doors or windows, and there didn't appear to be any way to have access through the steep pitch roof in that area where Vicky had pointed to the high wall and no security cameras. "We would have to cut through the roof and drop down into the upper level; but still, we could not gain entrance through the metal doors leading to the concrete basement. The basement is where we need to focus. The maid service would have been aware if there was anything happening on the main level and upper level of the home over the past decade."

"Agreed."

Vicky then asked, "What is the purpose of that vent?" as she pointed to a vent on the upper side of the high wall.

Wayne looked closely and said, "I have never seen a vent like that on a residential home. We can count the brick to estimate the width and length of the cover, which is installed to cover the vent opening."

"You mean the dimensions of the vent?" Vicky asked.

Wayne said, "Eighteen inches high and twenty-four inches wide are the approximate dimensions. A brick is normally eight inches long and three inches high."

Vicky counted and said, "fifty-eight bricks high from the ground, which is fourteen feet, six inches high, and three bricks across would be twenty-four inches,".

Wayne was taken aback by how fast Vicky could determine the height of the vent from the ground. He stared at her for a moment, considering her intelligence.

After a second pause, Vicky said, "I can fit in that vent. That is how I will enter the home. There is no security on that side of the home."

They kept discussing it, and both agreed the only place to gain access into the house unnoticed was through the vent, about fourteen foot, six inches above the ground. Wayne said, "It is on the side of the house where there are no windows, no doors, and no security. The security cameras on the exterior of the home are focused on the windows, doors, and driveway. Darrell said he made certain the drone flew above the lens of the cameras, which were all aimed downward, and most were attached to the soffit of the home."

Wayne asked, "How can you reach the vent? You cannot be seen carrying a ladder across the field, and you cannot climb down from the roof. The roof is too steep. We need to be able to get to the basement. We need to verify where that vent leads."

Vicky did not respond but looked very focused. Wayne then conceded and said, "All we need is some evidence, and then we could obtain a warrant or go back into the home a second time. Like I said before, if someone placed hidden cameras or listening devices, and they were discovered, the senator would be tipped off. He will never get caught if he gets tipped off. This is our only chance, and we may only have this one opportunity."

Vicky said, "I started to ask Maria's friend, Mrs. Sanchez, if I could enter with her and the other maid service employees, but the interior cameras are all connected, and someone in a remote location would be watching the maid service. They are scheduled to complete the outside yard work Friday, but they are not scheduled to complete any interior cleaning. If the security company gets suspicious, the senator will be notified, and we will never catch him. Mrs. Sanchez said the two large metal doors to the basement had a keypad lock system, and she has never been in the basement."

Wayne said, "I can guarantee you that if there are kids being raped in that basement, there are no security cameras operational in the basement area. There is no way the senator would ever take the chance of someone hacking into the security system and discovering the killing and raping of kids."

Vicky frowned, and shook her head in agreement. "What would happen if the power to the home was cut? Would the cameras and security system stop working? I assume the home has battery backup connected to a generator."

"They all are battery backup, and I am betting there is a generator that automatically comes online if there is a power failure. Besides, a power failure would alert the security company. I have never seen a vent like that on a residential home. I would want to talk to a heat and air expert before going any further with the possibility of you entering the home through the vent. That might be the best and simplest way. It would not take more than ten minutes for you to look around in the basement. The only area in the home we need to search is the basement, which is protected by those steel doors. The pad locks are to keep people inside the home out of the basement. The answers we are looking for have to be in the basement."

He hesitated, and said, "I know a man by the name of Henry who would know. I will let Henry look at the photographs. I'm sure he will have some information about this vent, and if he doesn't, he will know who does."

Wayne went ahead and called Henry and asked him if it was too late to look at some photos of a vent installed in a brick wall at a large home.

Henry said, "No, that's fine. Bring them over. I will be glad to look at them."

Wayne said to Vicky, "He lives on a farm near Browns Mountain Road, south of Butler. I will call you later."

Chapter 29

Wayne drove straight to Henry's home, and Vicky went back to the youth meeting. Henry looked like Archie Bunker. He was the same height and weight as the character from the 1970's TV show. He had the silver, thinning hair, and the same build. He looked to be about sixty-two years old. He had worked hard in his earlier years, and now hired other men to do the hard work. He was lonely and welcomed conversation with people. His kids had moved out of state for work, and he only saw his grandkids once a year. He still estimated bids for jobs and scheduled his employees to go from job to job. He had built relationships with contractors over the years, and they would call him on the new construction jobs weekly. His company had been successful, and he had considered selling out. He was afraid he would be bored, with no hobbies, so he kept running the business.

Wayne had used Henry, on occasions, to service his heat pump system. Henry had always arrived on time and got the older unit working in a timely period. Finally, Henry had replaced the twenty-two-year-old unit with a new high-efficiency unit, at a very favorable price. He gave Wayne a heads up on the price increase that was going to happen. The EPA had increased the efficiency ratings, and the

Freon gas was going to be changed and not be compatible with the older units. Both were going to drive the cost up, almost double. Henry and his employee were able to install the older model before the new federal laws went into effect. Wayne had certainly appreciated the savings.

Henry invited Wayne to come into his kitchen, and they sat down at the kitchen table. Henry's wife had died seven years ago, and he never remarried. Henry's home, on the interior, looked like a home owned by a single man in his sixties. It had not been updated in years, and items were stacked all over the table. Henry ask Wayne to have a seat in his office, as he pointed at the kitchen table. Henry reviewed the photograph of the vent and told Wayne that this type of vent was used in big commercial buildings.

Wayne said, "No, this is not a commercial building."

Henry responded that this was a vent that most likely was connected to a metal duct system, that allows air to flow below ground. "There is a fan that circulates air from outside to a basement, through a filter. That is why I thought it was installed in a commercial building that had an underground basement. Homes are not built underground, and there is no need for vents like this in residential construction."

Henry continued, "I have never installed any vents and duct work systems like this, but the contractor must have provided a channel for air in the basement below the ground. There must be an underground basement that is airtight. Most likely, there are solid concrete floors, walls, and ceilings."

Wayne showed him the other photos which Darrell had secured, and Henry pointed out that the different elevations did not have a satisfactory location to install the vent. "The roof line is steep with a slate roof, and could cause leaking issues, and access issues if one had to caulk around the roof vent. They would need to install a cricket behind the high side of the vent to allow the rainwater to be diverted from behind it. The vent would create a dam, and water must be diverted away from the high side or it will leak. Besides, the vent must be open to allow airflow and keep rainwater out, which all would drive the cost up. No architect would design to have an unnecessary opening on a slate roof if there was another option to install the vent. The garage wall was the easiest and cheapest place to install it, and it is on the side of the home, which would go mostly unnoticed. No one would want a vent on the front of their home. It would not be cosmetically appealing, and the rear porches are in the way on the back of the home. There are too many windows on the other side of the home. It looks like the vent runs across the upper garage ceiling, and then there would be a chase, running about twenty-five feet down to the basement floor. The garage appears to be built at ground level, with no basement underneath it. I do not see any signs of a basement and foundation under the concrete pad supporting the garage floor, but it is hard to tell with these photos."

Wayne said, "I have been trying to obtain the plans to the home, which would allow me to verify the linear feet of the duct work."

Henry looked up, with a surprised look on his face. "If the plans are the final updated set, they might have the linear feet of the duct work. Sometimes things get altered, and the plans are not updated. Why do you want to know this, Wayne?"

"For possible security reasons at a home near the lake."

Henry asked, "Was the home built by Robert Knoll, over at our lake?"

Wayne said, "It is the home at the dead end of the small road off of Lake Street, next to the small public boat ramp."

Henry said, "Knoll Construction built both of those homes. Robert Knoll is an old contractor who specializes in big homes out of Nashville. They install elevators, clay tile roofs, one hundred thousand-dollar kitchens, and other upscale furnishings in the homes they build."

Henry explained that he was asked by Knoll Contracting to put a bid in on the project, which he did, but he did not win the bid. He remembered the unusual circumstances about how the house was built. "They only wanted us to do some of the work, and it was the same with the plumber, electrician, and even the builder. Then the job was going to be turned over to another set of out-of-state contractors to finish."

Wayne asked, "Did you ever know who installed the duct work?"

"No. I never was told."

Henry looked like he was trying to remember, and said, "I do recall, I put in a very high bid. I was concerned about getting paid, since I did not know the owner's identity. I was not surprised I did not get the job, and I was okay with not getting the winning contract."

Then, Henry smiled and added, "It takes all the fun out of the work not to get paid, or not to get paid in a timely fashion, and besides, back then I was covered up with work."

"I have learned to be careful over the years. I do recall the contractor, Knoll Construction, recommended me, but they were not going to be paying me or guaranteeing me payment. A third party was going to be paying, and I just did not feel comfortable. I tried to have Knoll Construction guarantee they would pay me, but they would not. That's the way it was most of the time. I would work for the contractor, and the contractor would pay the subcontractors. Knoll Construction got paid a third before they ever started, but us subcontractors did not get offered any upfront money."

Wayne thanked Henry and left. Wayne called Vicky from his truck and told her it was Knoll Construction out of Nashville, and they might have the house plans.

When Vicky got home, she pulled up the web page for Knoll Construction. The construction company had been building homes for over thirty years, and now had a commercial building division. The company had two owners with the same last name, Knoll. She made a note to call Robert Knoll, the President.

***

At about 8:30 a.m. the next morning, Vicky called and asked for Robert Knoll. The secretary said hello and transferred Vicky. He picked up on the second extension and said, "Robert Knoll, can I help you?"

Vicky introduced herself as the preacher's wife at Middlebrook United Methodist Church in Butler. She told him she had some friends come to visit who saw the home on the lake in Butler County and were interested in the floor plan. Vicky explained the friends lived in San Diego, and they wanted the plans to the home at Cheatham Lake. They were going to build a home overlooking the ocean, near the bay. Vicky figured this was not entirely a lie because she did know friends that lived in San Diego and other friends that were considering building a home, just not one this size.

At first, Robert could not recall the project, but when Vicky mentioned that the house was built on the lake in Butler, Tennessee, the second time, he remembered it.

He said, "We started two homes. We never knew the owner of the homes. We just built the shell for the houses, with some of the plumbing, some of the wiring, and some of the duct work. It was then turned over to another builder from out-of-state to complete the project. They used us, the local contractor, to secure all the permits required, which back then were just the state electrical permit and a permit for the septic system required by the health department. We had to use dynamite for the foundation of the one home, to dig out the huge basement. We provided the labor for all the hard work."

Vicky said, "That does sound unusual. Was there anything else unusual?"

"The only time that I had ever heard of a contractor starting the job and not finishing was when the builder got fired by the homeowner during the building process, and that never worked out. We were surprised someone would want to do that on the front end. But our contracts were straight forward, and we got paid from an attorney who controlled the finances. I never tried to find out who owned the homes. I assumed the owner had the property titled in some shell company."

Robert then said, "The large concrete basement under the main level was very unusual for the home located on the end of the road. It was like a bomb shelter. The ceiling concrete was sixteen inches thick with reinforced one-inch steel. The building codes for a commercial high-rise building only required four-inch-thick concrete ceilings. Then, the home had a second basement, which was smaller, and I do remember that the duct work that he had his subcontractor install did lead across the garage ceiling and turned ninety degrees and went straight down to the basement underground. That is what I never understood."

Vicky asked, "What was that?"

"Why have a bomb shelter and not have a safe air supply system that could protect the people in the bunker from polluted air. All that is doing is pulling the exterior air into the basement. The fan system was going to be installed in the duct system to pull the air out of the basement through a small PVC pipe three-inch line, which ran straight up through the attic. The process would also pull fresh air from outside into the basement through the duct work over the garage. There is no basement under the big, attached garage, but there is a stairway down to the basement from the garage, which leads to the large bunker. The only reason, at the time, I could figure the fan was not installed in the main trunk line coming from outside, was because it would have blown like a fan into the basement, and they did not want a fan blowing air into the basement. So, the fan was going to be installed in the smaller PVC line vent system to pull the air out through the attic, and two PVC lines set in the concrete walls at angles to vent to the exterior. I discovered later that this was the same method mines utilized to provide the fresh air below ground in the mine shafts. The fan was going to be installed after we left the job site. I never understood the two PVC three-inch lines set at angles. The architect never would tell me why. He just told me it had to be perfect, and said I had to follow the German engineer's recommendation."

Vicky said, "That is interesting." She asked, "Can you send the plans to me because I want to send them to friends in San Diego? They liked the home above ground, and the way it looked from the lake and the street."

He indicated they had converted all the home plans over the years to PDF folders, in case the plans were ever needed for future projects.

He had learned over the years to keep plans for possible future projects; there was no reason to have to reinvent the wheel, so to speak. He offered to send them to the church. Vicky asked him to send the plans to her personal email address. Reluctantly, he did so. Vicky thought that it sounded like a dungeon, and she knew she was going to find out what was in the basement of that home. She remembered what Maria's friend had said about no one being allowed in the basement. She thought back to Saint Peter, Apostle Paul, Apostle Phillip, and Apostle James, and the pain and suffering they endured, standing up for Christianity. She subconsciously rubbed the cross necklace around her neck that Matt had given her when they had first started living together in college. All four Apostles stood up for what they believed, and they were willing to give their lives for Christ and the good of others. All had accepted death for Christianity, and Peter had even requested to be crucified upside down to show respect for Christ. She was more determined than ever to obtain access into the basement of that home, at all cost. She could not stand to think about young girls being raped and killed. She thought back to Brian, and how he tried to do what he thought was right, which led him to be killed. The guilt she felt was immeasurable. When she saw Brian's parents at church, she felt somewhat responsible for their loss, and was more determined than ever to make atonement for her actions. She wished she had gone to the sheriff and reported the murder she and Brian had witnessed, but she knew Cramer would have hunted her down and killed her. She thought back to what her father had told her when she was growing up, about a person needing to make their decision on what they morally believe, and stamp that into their DNA. She said to herself, "This is my crusade, and I am not going to sit back and allow these kids to be tortured and killed. I may very well be killed trying to help, but I won't be treated any worse than the Apostles who died for Christ." She truly felt she needed to atone for her unforgivable sins.

After reviewing the plans on her computer, she realized they would need a third party. The plan would be simple, with a very small chance of them getting caught; besides, if he were the child molester, the last thing he would want would be the police involved. Wayne would watch the front of the home, while she would need to be lifted, to take the cover off the vent. Carrying a ladder, even a small portable ladder, was out of the question. Mrs. Sanchez had explained that all the cleaning supplies were at the home, and they never carried anything into the home. That was forbidden. The gardeners brought their mowers, weed eaters, and rakes as needed, but the interior maid service carried nothing. They had no work order for a ladder and asking the maid service to assist would be futile. They had too much at risk with deportation. She could enter through the vent, crawl to the drop point, and be lowered by rope with a harness. She could have a two-way radio to talk to the third member of their team. She could exit the same route through the vent. No one would ever know she was in the home. She could look around for evidence and secure photos of the basement.

She was going to need someone strong enough and big enough to lift her and hold her, while she removed the vent. She was going to have to unscrew the vent cover and crawl though the vent. She thought how she had failed at the judge's home at locating the girl, and she was not going to fail this time. She considered one of Wayne's deputies, and thought about how they would have so much to lose. She thought about how Little Jimmy acted when she told him about the judge and the young girls. He seemed to be enraged. If he would not help, which she could understand since he just got out of prison, he definitely could be trusted to keep his mouth shut about the proposal to break into the senator's home. He would have no motive to tell the police. She needed someone now with some experience handling themselves in an adverse situation. He fit the physical requirements, and he was street smart.

Steve D. Nichols

Chapter 30

Wayne kept wondering about what Darrell had told him, about the body being dug up from the graveyard at the nearby church. He had thought he might see Vince and ask him, but he never ran into him. He recalled the FBI had confessed they had located two bodies in middle Tennessee. What are the chances they located another body? He called Vince and asked about the joke at South Side Baptist Church. Vince said, "Yes. Denny and I went out to the church and interviewed the preacher and a deacon. It was quite funny, listening to them tell the story about how they were not missing a body, but a body was stolen. We had the video copied. We are still laughing about it. It had to be a joke. The two males pulled up and knew exactly where to go to pick up the body. They were gone in six minutes. It had to be the youth and the youth leader playing a joke on the minster and deacons."

Wayne asked, "Does it show a vehicle"?

"Yea, a white van."

"Is there any chance the van is the same van that was on video from the hospital where the body was taken? Do the men match the same body type?"

There was a pause. Vince said, "Dammit. I bet it does match. I will go back and watch both videos. The video has the side of the van, and maybe a little area of the front. It was a little blurry. We had just assumed this was a joke. We will look at it closer and call you."

"Can you email me both videos as soon as possible?"

"Yes. I will do it right now. Let me know what you think. Do you have information about a missing body or a homicide? How would they know where to go to find the body? Like I said, they pulled in, got the body, covered the grave up, and pulled out, in six minutes."

"Nothing for certain. I just suspect the FBI is investigating a serial killer and keeping the information internal. Please keep this quiet."

"Will do."

Chapter 31

Tracey and Roger both knew, when they were requested to report to her office, that this was not going to be a friendly meeting. Tracey knocked on the door. Delores opened her door and motioned for them to enter. Tracey sat down across from Delores as she took her chair behind the desk. Roger walked over to the table with the pitcher of water and poured himself a glass of water. Delores looked across her desk at Tracey and said, "I just got my ass chewed out. Please tell me what in the hell is going on in Butler, Tennessee, and why did we, the FBI, not know that an Asian girl had been discovered naked near Cheatham Lake in Butler County. She was taken to the hospital in Butler, where she was in a coma. She was under twenty-four-hour watch by the local sheriff's department and the Tennessee State Police. She had been raped, and she had escaped from the culprits. How the hell did she get taken to Butler County Hospital without us knowing about this? They have been keeping her hidden for two days. We need her statement."

Tracey started to say something. Delores said, "Do not interrupt me." She looked at both men, and then said, "In addition, how did an international hitman, wanted in every country in the free world, who has over twenty confirmed kills, get gunned down in Butler County Hospital without us knowing anything about any of this until this morning, when I got a call from my boss in Washington? How did the assassin get inside our country in the first place without us knowing he was here?"

Roger was short-tempered and was over being kept in the dark, and still upset for being asked to pull back on the investigation. He looked at Delores and asked, "May I ask a question?"

Delores looked furiously over at Roger and said, "Yes. Let me hear your question."

Tracey knew how upset his partner was about the investigation, and that the CIA was somewhat involved. Yet, they were told to pull back on the investigation. He was now concerned Roger was going to say something, and then get fired. He knew everyone was very emotional, and he also was well aware that he loved his partner. They had been friends for years. He always went to Roger's home for Christmas parties and birthday parties with his wife and three kids. Tracey, cutting his partner off, said, "Allow me to ask the question?"

Delores realized Tracey was trying to cover for his partner. She understood their friendship. She looked at both men and said, in a calming voice, "I am sorry for the way this is going down. It has been a long couple of days. What are your questions?"

Tracey started by unfolding his hands and arms and holding them open in a gesture of friendly compromise, and said, "We can't expect the local law enforcement officers to want to share anything with us if we are not willing to share anything with them. We rely on the local state, city, and county officers to work with us. We have alienated ourselves with the Butler Police Department, and now with the TBI.

We have created an impoverished work environment, which does not suggest teamwork. They know we are holding back valuable information."

Roger said, "I know exactly how they feel."

Dolores turned her head and looked at Roger, while Tracey ducked his head. Tracey thought, here it comes. His partner was going to get fired.

Roger said, "No law enforcement officer had ever cursed me in over twenty years while in Chicago, and now with the FBI. I had never been cursed by another law enforcement officer like I was when we demanded the TBI and local officers leave the judge's home. The sheriff yelled at us to check the dog cage for signs of Asian girls, and the judge did not own a dog. What was the cage being used for?"

Dolores started to say something, and Roger raised his hand and said, "Wait a minute. Do not interrupt me."

Delores looked cross at the two agents.

Roger did not care, and he continued, "The sheriff took down Cramer, and we had no clue who Cramer was, or suspected he was involved. We should have been right next to the sheriff, working with him. We should not be stealing our dead undercover officers from the Butler County Hospital in the middle of the night. It is time for you to start telling us what is going on, or I want a transfer to the office of my choice."

Delores now realized this had to come to an end. Either these men were going to trust her and work for her, or they needed to transfer at some point. They both had been excellent FBI agents, and the transfer would be a reflection on her. She also knew she could not allow them to transfer at this time. She could not have additional agents involved in this case. The entire case was highly confidential, with the fewer being in the know, the better. She took a deep breath, and said, "I was told the CIA had a classified undercover operation in play, and we needed to step back. That is all I know. The director told me this, and he did not tell me why, other than the CIA needed time to complete an essential operation. I do not like it, but what can I do? I was told not to tell anyone. I worked in Washington for four years, and I know some people. I tried to find out who is involved. I was told, unofficially, that Cramer was not Cramer. He assumed that name. He did not work for the CIA, but worked indirectly for Army intelligence, as a subcontractor. My contact told me to watch my back and watch my people's backs. My contact told me these are very dangerous people, and if anyone gets in the way, they will disappear. The contact is in operation for the CIA. He is not a desk jockey. It takes a lot for him to be scared, and I could sense fear in his voice. This is some type of rogue operation run by someone in Washington. It may be the military, and now the CIA is somehow involved."

All three stared in front of them at the revelation, and nothing was said for thirty seconds. Tracey finally asked, "What are our orders?"

Delores said, "I am going to Nashville to talk with the TBI folks, and try to build a rapport, but I am limited on what I can say. I have to hold the line. You are correct, Roger. I have always worked well with other law enforcement personnel, but this is not one of those situations. The CIA claims they are not involved in the death of the assassin. They claim it might have been Mussad agents who tracked the assassin and killed him. We hope the girl might lead us to who hired the assassin, and that is why I am so mad. She might be able tell us. Obviously, someone very important wants her killed. The assassin is very expensive. The murder in Russia of the general of the Sixth Army over six years ago was a five-million-dollar contract."

She looked at both men and then continued, "The CIA sent over a report. They believe the person who killed the assassin was a pro from another country. Mussad was the best bet. According to the report, the operative entered the door of the hospital, fired one shot from thirty-two feet away, and exited the same door in less than three seconds. What stands out in the report is the operative had enough confidence to only take one shot, and he was anticipating the discharge of the shell by leaning to pick up the shell as he fired his weapon. He knew he was only going to fire one shot before he crashed through the door of the hospital. The shooter had to have a tremendous amount of confidence and training. As I said, the assassin was an expert with over twenty confirmed kills. He would not be an easy target. The CIA report indicated only Mussad, and maybe Russia, might have a couple of agents that could have executed that shot. The FBI has confirmed, we have no one that has those capabilities. The CIA did not comment if they had someone that good or not. The American elite teams, such as the Rangers, Green Beret, Secret Service and Seal Teams, are all taught to fire several rounds, even in some cases to empty their magazines, to make certain the adversary is taken out. The CIA indicated they were very impressed, but they have no clue who took out the assassin, just a guess. The tape from the hospital of the shooting has been thoroughly reviewed by our experts and the CIA. Friends in London have also reviewed the tape, and they agree it most likely was a hit team from Israel.

We were able to find out how the assassin got into our country. He flew in from Spain on flight 237 to Chicago two days ago, and then flew to Nashville, where he rented a car under an alias. We are checking with our contacts in Spain, but so far, they have no information on him. He had a contact here in America, who provided him the pistol. There is no way he could have brought the gun with him on an international flight. We are trying to figure out who the contact was, and who hired him.

The identity of the operative that killed him is still under investigation; we have no clue how he got into the country. There is no trace of him entering on any flight. After 911, the country scans everyone on every plane coming into and leaving this country, and we have nothing on him. He was a pro. We do not have a face shot of him. He kept his head tilted downward, and his face was hidden under the broad brim hat. We have traced the design of the hat. The hat was made in China. Several stores in America sell it, including Walmart stores. We did discover, by watching the security tapes, that he had entered the hospital nine minutes prior to the shooting, looked around, and exited the hospital. The report indicated he must have been aware of the approximate time when the assassin would be at the hospital. That is why they believe he was part of a team, which tracked him to Butler. It was like he knew where the cameras were located inside and outside of the hospital. The getaway car was never seen. The report indicated the most likely scenario was that the operative was waiting for the assassin to show his intentions. He wanted to make certain he identified the assassin. Otherwise, they could have shot him in the parking lot."

Delores looked at both agents, making eye contact. "I am tired of always being in the dark on this investigation, and I know you are, also. I just do not see how to get out in front of it with all this going on. Please do not repeat any of this. This is all confidential. I cannot grant your transfer now. I cannot allow any additional agents to be involved. This is a highly classified case, and I would ask you two to be patient with me before you start requesting to be transferred. I understand your frustrations. I am very frustrated also."

Steve D. Nichols

Chapter 32

Vicky and Wayne agreed to meet at the church at about 9 a. m. on Thursday morning. Vicky told Matt she would make certain the church was cleaned where the youth had been Wednesday night. Wayne was going to call in to work that he had a doctor's appointment. Matt was going to the hospital in Nashville for a patient visit with one of the elderly members. Wayne drove into the church parking lot, and Vicky opened the door to the office. Wayne started walking into the office and said, "The house is a huge plantation style home, with three levels."

She said, cutting Wayne off, "I am going into the vent and will slide down into the basement with a rope and harness. No one will ever know I was in the home. If the child is in the basement, we will remove her. Then, you and the rest of the TBI can set a trap for the senator. While I am in the home, we can stay in constant contact with a radio headset."

Wayne was surprised with the tone of her conviction and asked, "How are you going to get in and out by yourself? If you open a door or a window, the alarms will go off."

Wayne then calmed down a little, and said, "I want to be extra careful with the planning."

"I will come back out the same vent. I will re-attach the harness and be pulled back up the chase. I should be able to crawl or be pulled across the top of the garage through the chase. There is only a need for one of us to enter the home, and I can fit inside the duct work."

"Let me call Henry again to verify what obstacles we could face."

Wayne called Henry with the speaker on, so Vicky could hear. Henry answered, and Wayne asked whether a person could crawl through a vent that is twenty-four inches by eighteen inches?

Henry thought he was joking and said, "Yeah, but a person would have to watch out for the screws. The vent systems are normally made of thin metal and are screwed at ends and edges. The main trunk line normally has ten-inch supply lines connected, which are also screwed to the main trunk line. This is where the larger screws may be utilized, where the main trunk line and the ten-inch duct lines are connected. The ten-inch lines are connected and running to the registers in each room. The panels are also screwed together with quarter-inch screws, which are smaller screws. The vent system we were talking about the other day, with the photos, should have the same size duct work that runs straight to a wall vent located in the basement from the vent on the exterior above the garage, with no other vents attached, unless they have multiple rooms that need additional air. Then, the air would circulate through a second vent with a fan to pull the air out of the basement and, by doing so, would pull fresh air from outside into the basement. As I said, there should not be any other connection to that main trunk line. It only has one purpose. The heating source, most likely, would be an electric heater, maybe baseboard heaters. There would be no need for air conditioning that far underground. The air, then, is circulated back into the rooms as the fan pulls the air out of the basement rooms. It creates a suction of air from the outside, through the vent above the garage. The air in the basement is constantly being replenished with fresh air from outside. Even if the fan is not turned on, the air will flow and keep rotating. It is hard to explain how this works, but it has to do with the air pressure, and constant flow of air downward and back upward. That is how caves have an air supply. There might be vents in the walls between the rooms to allow the air to flow, or there might be one big room. So, there is always a fresh supply of oxygen in the basement; and the basement, as I said, can be heated with electric heaters. That is why we saw two units on the outside of the home. One for each level above ground, and no heat pump below the ground would be needed."

Henry paused and said, "I have not said that many words at one time in twenty years."

Wayne smiled and said, "Yea, I believe I understand the duct work system."

Henry then said, "Also, a person would have to have a suction pad device to pull themselves through the ventilation system. There would not be enough room to crawl. They better wear very tight clothing because the screws might snag the clothes." After a pause, Henry said, "You know Wayne, someone could get stuck. Also, another problem would be when they get close to the vent filter; they must be able to pry open the filter door, which would be designed to be opened from inside the room. That could be tricky to open from inside the vent in such small quarters. There are two basic types of latches. I am not certain which latch they used."

Wayne asked, "Can you show me and maybe set them up on a panel, so that I can see them?"

Henry laughed and said, "Certainly. I will also show you the two different sized screws used to connect the duct work. The longer screws would make it more difficult to crawl past. The person would need a headlamp. I have a couple of suction pads with the hand-held grips, with the button to release the pad, so that it can be reset fairly easy and quickly. One of my sons used to clean windows for high rise buildings in Nashville, and he would stick it to the glass and release it to move from one spot to another. Hell. There is no way I am ever going to use them."

Wayne asked, "What about the fan?"

Henry said, "The fan, most likely, would be housed in a metal chase and connected to a motor. It should not be located inside the same main trunk line that leads from the exterior vent above the garage to the interior vent in the basement. There would be a smaller duct work system to remove the stale air, which would have a return vent, most likely near the basement ceiling. The main level and the upstairs would have totally separate systems, and the two systems would not be integrated to work with the basement unit or duct work system. The basement system would be unique, and its main function is to provide oxygen to the lower level. It is not like the heat pump system on the other two levels."

Wayne said, "I will be by to pick it up. One more question, Henry?"

Henry chuckled and said, "Only one more?" He then asked, "What?"

Wayne asked, "Will the metal chase support a person."

Henry said, "The metal main duct chase will be laying on the truss system, and yes, that is what supports the metal and the person crawling through it. The person would have to be slim. How heavy is the person?"

Wayne looked at Vicky, and without thinking said, "One hundred thirty to one hundred fifty."

Henry said, "I know I could not fit my big belly through the vent," and laughed.

Wayne said, "Thanks," and hung up.

He looked at Vicky, who had a mad look on her face, and she said, "I weigh one hundred ten, and you better watch it calling me fat. Do I look like I have gained weight?"

He said, "I was not talking about you. I thought you weighed about one hundred seven," as he winked at her. "Meet me here later at about 6 p.m."

Vicky said, "Okay," as she looked at her figure. Then she said, "You need to start exercising. You are starting to get a belly."

Wayne laughed and said, "I will meet you here on my way home."

Steve D. Nichols

Chapter 33

Wayne met with Vicky at the church on his way home that evening. Wayne said, "The senator is scheduled to be back in Tennessee this Saturday. I checked with the airport where he lands his personal jet, on the private airstrip near the International Nashville Airport."

Vicky said, "We must hurry. This might be our only chance to get in and out of the home before he arrives. I believe the girl was kept at the judge's home prior to being delivered to his home. Now with the judge out of the equation, I am betting she is already in the home. She would have to be placed in the home the night prior to him returning to his home. I bet his wife is not coming with him, which means we've got to get this done this Friday afternoon."

Wayne said, "We just do not have any proof to have the home placed under surveillance. My boss would never agree. It would be a career-ending decision if the surveillance team were discovered, and John had approved it. We need a third party. I can stand watch at the field across the street and be ready in case you need backup. I can let you know if the security company shows up. Lake Road is the only access, other than by chopper. I do not see anyone of importance arriving by water from the lake. We need someone to lift you and lower you with a rope, with you in the harness."

Vicky said, "I know the right person, Little Jimmy Sterns."

Wayne was surprised and did not try to hide his disapproval, and said, "Are you certain about him? Why would he care about helping us?"

Vicky had a devious smile and said, "I visited him at the gym in Nashville on that afternoon, after you told me where he lived. I explained about the judge, and he said he would have helped us if he had known what we were doing. He acted enraged with the judge. He said he was all in with the plan. He said he trusted me. Besides, we need someone now. We are in a hurry, and he can handle his part without being scared. He is street smart, and he will be dependable."

Vicky hesitated, and then said, "There is only one way to find out, and we are running out of time. I have already asked him earlier today, while he was working. We can meet him at his apartment on High Top Road."

Wayne realized they were running out of time, and maybe he could help. They had no other alternative. They drove over to meet with Little Jimmy Sterns at his small, one-bedroom apartment, and he said that he would do it. Little Jimmy had no reservations about helping Vicky. Little Jimmy said, "As I told you, I am all in." He hesitated, and then said, "If we are helping kids escape from a monster and crooked politician, I am all in."

Wayne had figured Little Jimmy did not like the legal system and the politicians that ran it, and he understood why, after Vicky filled him in on the drive over about his arrest and conviction.

Wayne said to them, "Good, and let us get the plan down. The plan is straightforward." Wayne showed Vicky the latches and the tools needed to remove the vent cover and release the latch. Henry had set up two different latches on a display, and he showed Wayne what the latches would look like from inside the duct system. Wayne explained, "The vent on the brick wall opens to duct work, which is twenty-four feet across the ceiling of the upper garage. Then, it drops straight down twenty feet and comes out in the basement wall, near the floor. We will use the rope for Little Jimmy to lower Vicky, and I will place a knot at forty-four feet and another one at fifty-two feet, so little Jimmy will know when Vicky will be close to the vent in the basement. I figured an additional eight feet for the exterior wall, with Jimmy holding the rope at six feet from the ground. If the walkie talkies stop working, one pull means to pull her back up, and two pulls means to let her down another foot." Wayne gave Vicky the battery-operated screwdriver and asked her to remove the screws.

She asked, "Is this a test?"

He said, "Yes. The screw could be removed with a socket or a straight-head screwdriver. The socket will stay on the head of the screw better and be easier." Wayne was not certain if Vicky knew how to use hand tools. He was not about to allow her to enter the home without finding out first.

Vicky showed Wayne she knew how to use the miniature battery-operated screwdriver with the socket. The screws came out, and then she reset them on the board. She also used the knife to open the latch to the vent, which would be located in the basement wall cavity.

Wayne said to Vicky, "When you arrive at the drop point, you need to drop down the chase and not turn to go through another chase. I am not certain the plans for the system have not been altered, and you might have to improvise. We will not know the exact layout, and there is no way to predict what you will be faced with, inside the duct work or the basement. They could have modified the duct system during the construction. If you turn the wrong way, you most likely will not be able to backtrack. The turn could lead to the fan or a smaller duct work system. Then, you will be stuck. It would be almost impossible to move backward in the chase. You will have to use the suction pad to move forward. You will not be able to turn around. There just won't be enough room. You go straight across the garage ceiling, and then drop straight down. The fan is connected to the duct work for the air to be removed from the basement into the three-inch PVC line, which pulls fresh air into the system by pulling the stale air out first. It is a circular system. Also, there are two security doors with a keypad at the top of the stairs to the lower basement, near the foyer on the main level and the garage. We will by-pass the security doors by going through the vent system. We are hoping there are no security warning trip-switches in the duct work. If I see anything coming on the front road, I will call you, and you can abort the mission. You should have time to exit the home anyway you can. The alarm will have sounded, so use a door on the rear and run across the back path to the side rear gate. The security door can be opened from the inside of the lower basement without the security codes." Then, Wayne added, "At least that is the case with all other security systems. They are trying to keep people out, not keep them in, with the security system."

Vicky said, "Maria's friend said both metal doors have a camera located above the doors, so we will try to avoid the metal door entrances. Little Jimmy, you will need to pull me back up the chase when I am ready to leave. We will leave the rope and harness in place. I will contact you by radio when I am ready. I will place the vent cover back over the vent in the room once I have entered the duct system. I will also install the vent over the exterior when we leave. No one will ever know anyone entered the basement of that home. If the security system videos two people running across the rear field, it will be no big deal. They will never know anyone was in the home."

During the meeting, she asked if Little Jimmy could hold her up, so she could unscrew the vent screws and remove the cover.

Little Jimmy smiled and said, "That will be no problem. I understand my part. I won't let you down Mrs. Vicky."

Vicky said, "The plan is simple. Wayne will be on the headset and radio us if anyone shows up from the front road. There is only one way to reach this home by car, and that is Lake Street. Little Jimmy, you and I will cross the field when the immigrant workers are leaving at 5 p.m. The alarm will be off, and no security personnel should be on the property. The one camera that is focused on the pathway will be covered by the lawn serviceman, Maria's friend."

Vicky hesitated, and then said, "Maria has got that straight with one of the workers. He is her cousin. He will remove his shirt and place it on the lens as soon as we cross the halfway point in the field. This is a precautionary measure. The best guess is that no one is watching. This should take us within three seconds to remove the shirt. We will stay up against the brick wall and out of the camera viewing range. This particular camera is aimed toward the rear yard, coming into the pool area. The camera is not pointed in the area close to the home or toward the garage area. The second camera is covering the rear door and windows, which is focused up close near the home and spans the rear yard and hot tub area. We will be more than halfway across the field when the shirt is placed over the camera lens. After we cross the halfway point, the camera would be able to pick us up. We figure the range of the camera into the field is approximately thirty yards. When we leave, we can cut the wires to the camera, we can cover the lens again, or we can run by the camera through the field to the gate. They have several other cameras. We want to make certain the security system to the home will remain on and not be triggered. And, we do not care if they know someone was around the home. They won't know we were in the home. They will have no way to determine it was us. Little Jimmy and I will both wear gloves. No fingerprints. There is no way anything could go wrong."

Wayne said, "One more thing. If there is not a girl in the basement, that does not mean we lost. All we need is probable cause for me to enter as a police officer, doing my job. If you find something, you can leave through the back door and leave the metal door ajar leading to the basement. I can say I saw something suspicious at the home, and I entered and inspected the basement. At that point, I can call the TBI for backup and be legal, and we can set a trap and catch the responsible party. The senator, at that point, would need to answer some questions. You may not want to use your camera until you are aware of what is in the basement. Any photo could be used against you as evidence you broke into the home."

Vicky said, "That sounds like a good plan. We have all the bases covered."

They agreed to meet on a Friday afternoon to execute the plan and enter Senator Davis's home. Wayne gave Vicky the rope, harness, headlight, small camera, and a pouch which could fasten around her waist.

Wayne said, "You should be in the home for no more than ten minutes. You should be able to cross the garage ceiling and drop down the duct work within two minutes. Open the latch and vent cover. Inspect the basement, enter the vent, and put on the harness for Little Jimmy to pull you back up and out, in six minutes. From what we understand, the walls, floor and ceiling are all concrete. There should be no hidden areas."

In order to feel good about the task, she repeated, "What could possibly go wrong?" They all nodded in agreement.

Wayne then said, "I bet the camera is not being monitored at the remote location, but if an alarm goes off, we will abort. None of the security companies watch the feeds from the cameras twenty-four hours a day, seven days a week, unless the alarm is tripped. Then, they will view all the feeds from the cameras prior to sending out security personnel. If we trip an alarm, the senator would not be allowed to enter the home by his security team until the home has been cleared, and the reason for the alarm going off has been confirmed."

Wayne made eye contact with both Vicky and Little Jimmy, and they both agreed, they would abort. "We are not here to be heroes. We will live to fight another day. So, abort." Wayne knew Vicky would never abort the mission if she thought a girl was being held in a cage in the home. He had to say his piece, and he hoped for the best.

Wayne then said, "Otherwise, it will take security personnel at least an hour to drive in from Nashville. They most likely will not call the sheriff's office locally. They never have before when I was the sheriff. I will listen in on the scanner to see if a call is made to the sheriff's office. If they are raping and killing kids, the last thing the senator would want is a police officer at his home. If a call goes into the sheriff's office, I will call Vince and tell him I will cover it for him. I will tell him I had my scanner on, and I was checking this large cornfield across the road from the home for a possible opportunity for dove hunting in September, and I wanted to make certain doves are flying into the field. I will pick you up Friday at your home, Vicky, at about 4:30 p.m."

Vicky said, "That will work. Matt will go out to eat after he has a church meeting."

Little Jimmy said, "I've got three questions. Why are you not checking out the main floor and the upstairs?"

Vicky said, "We have talked to the cleaning people, and they would know if there were any kids being held on the two upper levels. The basement is built like a dungeon. They are being kept in the dungeon. I know it. The senator is scheduled to arrive Saturday night, so we should be safe."

Little Jimmy then asked, "You mentioned the child is being dropped off in the senator's home the prior night. Who is dropping the child off?"

Vicky said, "We do not know. We had a witness at the judge's home who described the two men as being European. The witness only spoke some English, and she was scared of being deported. She has nowhere else to live. Plus, she was worried she would never see her family again. I understand that when the families are sent back across the borders, they can get separated in the transportation process and never see each other again. South America is a big area. We want the senator. If we stop the vehicle with the girl, no doubt the senator would be notified, and we would never catch him. These men would never confess what they know."

"What happens if the senator has the basement set up for a motion detector or sound alarm system?"

"We figured I would be in and out before anyone could respond if the alarm is triggered. I should be in and out in ten minutes or less. By the time someone could respond, we should be gone."

Wayne said, "We have no time to look into who might be dropping the kids off. In order to catch the senator, we will have to catch him when he is not expecting it. He has most likely been doing this for a long time. He has been too smart to get caught. This might be the only opportunity we have, and I want the senator. I suspect he is the evil corroded container the FBI is trying to catch."

Chapter 34

Little Jimmy showed up at the parking area, at the field entrance near the boat ramp, on a big Harley motorcycle, wearing a black vest and jeans with sunglasses and a pair of black gloves. He intentionally was early and figured he would sit on his Harley, watch the pretty view of the lake, and wait.

Wayne picked Vicky up in his old truck and said, "I can't believe we are actually doing this, but I can't figure out a better plan. This should be very simple, in and out, Vicky, in ten to fifteen minutes, no more, no less."

Vicky said, "Yes. It should be simple. I've got my part down, and there are very few moving parts to this operation. If the alarm goes off, we still have at least fifteen to thirty minutes to abort. It is like you said, they would not call the local sheriff's office, and if they do, you will know it. Besides, the Butler County sheriff and deputies are the only ones that can respond to that location in a reasonable time. This is going to be very easy. There is no way anything could go wrong."

Wayne glanced at Vicky and thought, "I hope you are right." Wayne said, "One other thing." Vicky turned her head to look at Wayne. He said, "The TBI had to share the hospital video of Officer Henderson being shot with the FBI, since the officer was shot while on duty. The FBI was very upset we had not told them about the Asian girl in the hospital. This all happened way above my pay grade. John just mentioned it to me in passing. He said, when the manager of the FBI came to meet him, his boss, and the State Attorney General, he asked since when does the FBI share anything with them on the state level, and he smiled when he said it. The FBI manager stated they had full jurisdiction, and John smiled even bigger. He finally told them he was not going to share shit with them. At that point, the State Attorney General and the Regional Director for the FBI, some lady out of Atlanta, got into a heated debate. The FBI finally agreed that they need to share information with us, and we are all one big, happy family."

Wayne paused and smiled, and then said, "I believe John set them up. They indicated they had shared everything with the TBI folks in the room and the Attorney General. John then showed them the video of the van taking the body at the hospital, and then showed them the same van at South Side Baptist Church taking a body from a shallow grave in Butler. They then indicated they could not talk about the pending investigation. That was the fifth Asian girl within the last three years that they have located. They would not tell John how they knew the location of the body. They left the TBI in charge of the Asian girl in the hospital because, technically, no one is certain where she is from or of her identity. They actually do not have jurisdiction until she can be identified."

Vicky said, "There have been five dead girls in the past three years and one alive in a coma, one dead FBI agent, and three dead girls from approximately seven to eight years ago. Someone knows a lot more and is not telling. We are fighting ourselves."

Wayne said, "It gets better. The FBI concluded, by the action of the shooter that killed the priest, that we are dealing with a professional hit on a hitman. The dead priest was a hitman from Europe who was on every watch list in the world. He was able to keep his face hidden over the years. No one knew what he looked like. INTERPOL thought the assassin was from Greece, but now they know he was born in Spain. No one knows where in Europe he lived. They timed the shooting to be 2.7 seconds once the person busted through the front door of the hospital, took the one-shot, picked up the shell casing, and exited. The FBI accused the CIA at first, and then the CIA pointed out that the Israel Government had a reward for this assassin, for five million dollars. The FBI now believes the assassin was followed by a Mussad agent or agents, and the Asian girl was used as a trap. The team, which is part of the Mussad from Israel, came into America and carried out the killing. They somehow were aware of the girl, and where she was located. They knew he had been hired to kill her. The CIA was also suggesting Mussad did not know his identity or his description. They just knew of the contract on her life. So, they waited and used her as a decoy. The Israel Government is disclaiming involvement. The gunman was too fast and efficient not to be a professional killer. The gunman only shot one bullet, and he was reaching for the shell casing before the assassin had hit the floor. They concluded only a pro would have that much confidence, to use only one bullet from that distance and reach for the shell casing that fast. Without the shell casing, we cannot locate the manufacture of the shell. The bullet was fired from a 9mm pistol. Most agents and assassins would have fired multiple shots. The assassin was very expensive to hire and had killed over twenty bankers, politicians, businessmen, and other government officials around the world. He was a bad man. I thought you would want to know."

Vicky asked, "Who really hired him, and how did they know about the girl in the hospital?"

Wayne said, "No clue, but it had to be someone well connected."

Vicky said, "Like a United States Senator who was in the Army. I can't help what the FBI or CIA is doing or not doing, but I am going to help that little girl. I might get killed, but I am going to do everything I can to help that child. We might be the only hope she has. No one is looking out for the children. They are being used as bait and killed by the sadist killer."

Wayne said, "We might find out, with our home invasion this afternoon, if the senator hired the assassin. My sixth sense radar is going off. There still must be something else going on, which is not related to the girls. The FBI has never acted like this in the past. They know something and are not telling. John mentioned there is no reason the CIA would be involved unless there is something else going on with foreign intervention inside our country."

They both looked at the senator's home, as they slowly rolled past the front fence and gate. Vicky said, "I do not see anyone." He pulled around the corner, facing toward the public boat ramp several hundred feet ahead. Little Jimmy was sitting on his Harley, looking over the lake, next to an older truck owned by the lawn care workers. Wayne dropped her off at the side rear entrance with Little Jimmy and told them he needed five minutes to get set up and be in position. He said, "Good luck and may the force be with you," as he drove off.

Vicky slightly smiled and thought to herself, "Who would have ever thought Wayne would be a Star Wars fan?"

Little Jimmy noticed the smile on Vicky's face, and said, "I want to be Chewbacca."

Vicky almost burst out laughing. She thought, that certainly was random, and it somewhat eased the tension on what they were getting ready to do.

Wayne had parked in the edge of the cornfield, down the street and across from the senator's residence. He had backed his truck into the side area of the field along the tree line, about fifty yards off the road. His plan was to act like he was surveying the field for possible dove hunting in early September in case anyone asked. He could see the road approaching the senator's home. He was considering getting out of the truck and walking behind the large trees, about twenty-five yards from the street, directly across from the senator's driveway. He decided to stay in the truck close to the police scanner, to listen in case a call was made to the sheriff's department. He held down the button on the walkie talkie and said, "It is clear. Do you copy?"

Vicky replied, "We are a go."

The Hispanics helped Vicky and Little Jimmy get through the side rear gate. The workers were ready to leave, and got in their vehicles, ready to drive away. They passed the last worker, without a shirt as he was running toward the gate. Vicky thought, Maria must have gotten them all to agree to help, and all of them are sacrificing their ability to stay in America.

Vicky and Little Jimmy moved fast across the open field, which was close to four hundred yards to the large wall. Little Jimmy removed the shirt from the camera lens off the camera facing the trail. They knew to stay clear of that camera. Little Jimmy was out of breath and sweating uncontrollably after the run across the field. The sun had not set yet, and the heat index was above 90 degrees. Vicky was also very hot and perspiring. Her face was red from the heat and the run, and she had run around to the high garage wall. She had already taken off her clothes and was down to the tight-fitting black leotard and her sockless feet. She decided to go with the black, more dependable gloves, which unfortunately were also going to be hotter. She understood what she was on the verge of doing, and realized she was slightly edgy with an increase of nervous energy. She knew she had to keep her emotions in check.

Wayne had gone over part two of the plan several times. Little Jimmy would hide her clothing, after he lifted her to remove the vent cover. He would then hide behind the two large Hemlock Pine trees, which would provide him a vantage point to watch the rear of the home and the side where the vent was located, after Vicky had entered the home. The rope would be left in place, with it hanging down the wall from the vent. Wayne thought about the options, and there just was no way to conceal the rope. The rope was Vicky's only way to exit the home without anyone being aware of the break-in. Once Vicky tells Little Jimmy to start pulling her out, he would pull her out one foot at a time until she reached the top of the metal chase, and then she would pull herself across the top of the garage ceiling area with the suction pad. To enter, she would crawl to the drop point and descend through the vertical chase to the vent, with Little Jimmy dropping her one foot at a time until he had the knot in the rope in his hands, which marked the correct depth. Vicky would enter the basement, look around, and leave through the same vent, with Little Jimmy pulling her back out the same way. He then would hold her up until she placed the vent cover back in place. No one would ever be aware they were inside the home. Wayne would meet them at the rear gate and provide Vicky a ride home. Wayne had reviewed the plan several times with Little Jimmy and Vicky.

Vicky had finally announced, "We've got it."

Vicky was ready for action. She did not want to talk about the mission anymore. Wayne was wanting to be cautious. He was well aware of the perils of home invasions. People were arrested daily for breaking and entering, and none had felt they would get caught. Wayne also knew that most of the arrests occurred after the break-ins. It was when they were caught selling the stolen items, which would not apply in this situation. This operation was just too simple, in

Vicky's mind, to spend any additional time reviewing it. Little Jimmy seemed to lean with Vicky. He, also, was ready.

Vicky and Little Jimmy were in position at the wall, and Vicky had relaxed her nerves and focused on saving the child. She kept pushing away the negative thoughts, like being trapped in the duct work or being shot by security personnel. She said, in a relaxed tone, "Little Jimmy, it is game time. Let's get this done and get out of here."

They tested their 2-way radios, and all three checked out. Wayne had explained they needed to keep the talking to a minimum on the radios because another 2-way radio in the immediate area could hear everything that was being said. The line was not secure. Little Jimmy bent down on his knees and allowed Vicky to step up onto his shoulders. Then, as he stood up, Vicky placed her feet, one at a time, in the palms of his large hands. He extended his arms straight up, while Vicky kept her balance by touching the bricks as she reached for the vent. He held her steady, and she reached around to her pouch. She immediately pulled the battery-driven screwdriver out of her strapped-down pouch. She had attached the pouch to the small of her back and started with the bottom screws. There were four screws on the bottom and four on top, with three up each side. Wayne had told her that Henry mentioned that she needed to start at the bottom, removing the bottom screws; otherwise, the vent would start leaning, and could bend. She was able to reach the vent, and successfully unscrewed the screws in less than thirty seconds. She handed Little Jimmy the vent cover, the pouch with the screws, and the drill, while he was holding her with one hand. The heat was making the entire process more difficult. Vicky knew from cheerleading that sweat made her slippery, and she could feel the wetness in Little Jimmy's hands.

There was a rope attached to her, which was tied to a climbing hook and harness to her waistband, that wrapped around her shoulders. Wayne had, at the last second, given her two darts which could knock a man unconscious. He had confiscated the darts from Bill Cramer's trunk, before the deputies showed up along with the TBI agents, at the water tower where Cramer had died. He felt the darts might be needed, but he hoped not. She had secured them to her upper, inner thigh with a black strap made with Velcro. The Velcro made it easy to secure the strap to her left thigh. As she was fastening the darts, she recalled how they worked. Wayne had said the darts were a precautionary step. He had explained when he was shot with the dart gun, he had fallen to the gravel driveway, paralyzed within a second, and unconscious within another second. He explained the darts worked similar to a syringe, and once the tip enters the skin, the drug flows into the body automatically. He told her to take the cap off the needle and stick it in the body of the other person. The knife would be used to release either style latch. The knife could also be attached to the lower calf, similar to a scuba diver. The pouch which housed the battery-operated screwdriver and handheld suction pad might get in the way and could be taken off once the vent was removed. Wayne was worried about the unknown. He was concerned about Vicky getting to the latch and not being able to open the latch, and then she might be stuck unless Little Jimmy could pull her out backward. With the ninety degree turn inside the duct work, being pulled backward with all the screws, Henry had mentioned, would be very difficult. The metal duct work was screwed together from the outside with the sharp screw ends extending into the inside of the duct work at the intersection and turns in the duct system. He knew they could cut through someone's skin very easily. He also finally understood that he was more nervous than either Vicky or Little Jimmy, and he was not even entering the home.

Vicky thought about the girls and what they must have gone through. She felt that her little bit of sacrifice was nothing compared to what they must have endured. She felt motivated, and recalled what Wayne had said, "I am not certain about this plan, but it is the best we've got."

Vicky thought to herself that if the senator was coming in tomorrow, they had to get this done today. A little girl might already have been smuggled into the home. The senator would not allow the girls to be seen outside his home and traced back to him. He must have been doing this for years and had never got caught. He had to be very careful and ruthless not to be caught. She wondered how many people could be involved. Wayne had mentioned a syndicate when he had described the network. If the child were not in the home, there might be other signs in the basement that she would have to discover and secure photos quickly of the entire basement. Why have a dungeon in the first place? She remembered the pictures of the young Asian girls concealed in the back of the armoire at the judge's home. She knew the senator must be the child molester and killer. The judge and the judge's wife both said the same thing; they have not hurt anyone. Vicky knew they had raped the girls, but according to them, that was not hurting anyone. These people were sick, and they were all friends. Vicky felt calm and had no reservation, just a feeling of absolute commitment. She entered the vent, adjusted the head lamp, and turned it on. She used the suction pad to pull herself across the garage ceiling in the metal duct work by setting it and then pulling herself across the metal, two feet at a time, then releasing the suction and resetting the suction pad. The sweat on her body actually was a blessing because it enabled her to slide across the sheet metal surface without any resistance. She was careful not to get too close to the sharp screw ends holding the main duct work together. Since there were no smaller duct work runs attached to the chase, the main trunk line had very few screws once she started across the garage ceiling. She noticed the screws connecting the main chase at the entrance. They were located on two sides and the top, but none on the bottom, which made the initial entrance easier. She could look forward with the head lamp and see the additional screws at the ninety-degree turn, going down vertically toward the basement. She engaged her mic and told Little Jimmy she would need to crawl over and beside some of the longer screws. She indicated she would let him know once she had cleared the screws. She knew she was going have to be very careful not to get caught on the screws while crossing the top of the garage and the vertical drop point. As she got closer, she could see the screws protruding into the shaft at the turn in the metal duct system, from all four sides. She knew she would have to negotiate her way through the screws, which would be tricky in the close confinements.

Vicky got to the drop point, where the duct work dropped straight down. She tilted her head, so the head lamp shined straight down. She could see the filter in front of the vent at the bottom of the drop. She had to climb across the connection point, where the horizontal duct was screwed to the vertical duct and avoid the three sharp screws coming in from both sides, the top, and the bottom. She knew her entire life rested with Little Jimmy not dropping her. She had to be lowered headfirst, with the harness holding her, suspended, inside the metal duct work. Little Jimmy understood he had to lower her down by the rope, one foot at a time. During the planning stage, they configured that she needed to crawl twenty-four feet across the top of the garage, and then the vent dropped down twenty-two feet. Little Jimmy would need to lower her on the rope and hold her suspended, so she could reach the filter and then open the vent cover while hanging upside down. The vent cover was connected to the wall with hinges, and once the latch was released, the vent cover would open into the room. The plan was simple. They tied a knot at fifty-four feet on the rope, so Little Jimmy would need to keep the knot at six feet above the ground at the exterior wall.

In order to maneuver across the screws pointing up through the metal at the drop point, she raised up on her feet, lifting her midsection, and wedged the suction pad on the far side of the chase, dropping down and slowly walking forward until she could spread her legs, to avoid the sharp screw in the middle. She realized they should have brought some cutters or padding to cover the screws. On the way back out, she would cover the screw tips with her gloves to prevent getting cut. She could tell the muscles in her arms and legs were straining to get her midsection across the screw coming straight up in the middle of the chase. She had pushed so hard to move forward with the plan, but they had not considered one of the obvious hurdles would be the screws. A pair of handheld cutters could have made the process a lot easier. She had already started to dread the trip back up the chase and across the screws.

Vicky hit her earpiece to engage her mic, to tell Little Jimmy she had arrived at the drop point, and the measurements appeared to be correct. Right after the call to Little Jimmy on the headset for him to start lowering her down to the vent, the radio system went offline.

Vicky had made the turn and was hanging suspended, upside down. She hung in midair for a couple seconds. She finally felt the rope dropping her, one foot at a time.

Wayne was listening, and he heard the connection go dead. He started changing channels and saying, "Can you hear me?" He then realized that the Secret Service or private security were jamming all phone and radio signals; the senator and his protection detail were pulling down the road and passed him in the two black Suburbans with the windows tinted. This was normal procedure by the Secret Service, and now private security firms had started the practice. The government security personnel had been doing this for years around the world, to eliminate or disrupt the communications of possible groups wanting to inflict harm on a government official. They had arrived a day early. Wayne felt panicked. He had no way to notify Little Jimmy or Vicky that the senator and his security detail had arrived and were entering the driveway through the secure gate at the front of the residence. The radio and phone signals were jammed prior to the vehicles coming into sight. They had not considered this scenario. Wayne started to contemplate his options. He had no workable plan. He hoped Little Jimmy could hear them arriving and somehow pull Vicky out, and then they could run for cover. Wayne knew the security detail for the president and United States Senators could kill on sight if they felt an immediate threat. Their guns were always required to be cocked, with a bullet chambered.

As Vicky was approaching the filter vent, one foot at a time, she pulled the knife out of the strap holster on the inside calf of her right leg, and bit down on the blade to secure it. She wanted to be ready as soon as she got close. One foot at a time. She hoped this would be a fast trip in and then out, within a couple of minutes. She had figured she could climb up the rope once she reversed herself in the room if Little Jimmy tied off the rope. She had no way to tell Little Jimmy when to stop and hold firm. She pulled the cardboard filter toward her and folded it into half, while pushing it out of the way into the inner corner. She pulled the knife from her mouth and shoved the blade behind the latch, and the vent opened into the room. She unlatched the harness and pulled herself through the opening, into the room. She stuck the knife with the knife holster behind the vent with the harness and extra rope. Her camera was attached to the harness. She figured she could return and retrieve the camera if she needed it. She wanted to look around first and verify what was in the basement. She wanted to locate the girl. Wayne had mentioned the possibility of a sound alarm system and a motion detector. She had tried to be as quiet as possible as she crawled through the duct system. Now, she stood still and listened. She did not hear a sound. The basement was perfectly quiet, and she could hear the central air-conditioner running on the main level.

Vicky entered the lower basement below the main floor near the garage and walked to the hall, which led to some stairs going upward to the garage. She was surprised the basement had several lights turned on, attached to the nine-foot-high ceiling, connected by conduit. She had figured the basement would be pitch dark. She took her head lamp off and left it hanging on the back side of the doorknob to the room with the vent. She realized she needed to move back down the hall to locate the main basement room. If there was someone hidden in this home, it would be in the bottom basement bunker. The plans of the basement they had received were not updated and accurate. The builders had switched plans, and the plans had not been updated. She hesitated and listened in the hallway. She thought she heard the upstairs air-conditioner turn on. The two air-conditioners running would be normal, with the heat index above eighty-five degrees. Vicky had to figure out where to go to locate the other main room on the bottom floor in the basement.

Chapter 35

Wayne had seen the senator arrive, but there was nothing he could do. He hoped that Little Jimmy and Vicky would not be detected. He hoped they realized the plan needed to be aborted. He had no way to tell them to abort. Wayne waited about five minutes and watched as another black Chevrolet Suburban pulled down the road and passed him, and then turned into the open gate and drove toward the senator's home. The gate started closing immediately as the vehicle cleared the threshold of the driveway. He had just enough time to hide behind the big tree next to the cornfield. There was a total of three vehicles. The windows were tinted very dark, and Wayne could not tell how many people were in the vehicles. He considered firing his pistol in the air in hopes of a warning, but he knew if he fired a shot, he would never be permitted to enter the premises. There was just no way, after hearing a gunshot from the road area or field across the street, that a team of security personnel would ever allow him access to the property with one of the most important senators in the home. Plus, they would be on full alert for possible trouble. He became very distraught. Wayne ran back to the old truck and put his ankle holster on under his pant leg and made certain the small pistol under his pant leg could not be seen. He ran and hid behind the roll of trees across from the senator's home. He knew he had to do something. There was no sign of Vicky and Little Jimmy. The way the home was built, the garage wall, where Little Jimmy should have been positioned and Vicky had entered, could not be seen from the street. Although it was on the side elevation of the home, it was facing more to the rear of the home. He listened for Little Jimmy's motorcycle to start up. By this time, he figured Vicky was still in the home and had not gotten out.

***

Vicky kept quietly looking from room to room, but suddenly met a large security man who was about 6'6", 270 pounds. He must have come down the second stairway. She recognized him from the judge's home, and she wondered how did she not hear him. He was huge and dressed in a dark suit and tie. She was surprised to see someone in the home, and by the way he looked at her in her black leotards, he was also surprised. He smiled and stepped forward, and Vicky remembered what Betty had said, that when they placed their weight on the front foot was the perfect time to strike. Betty had told Vicky, "To be successful, you cannot hesitate. You will only have one clear shot. The foot will not slide backward, with the body weight holding it in place." She also remembered to be calm and show no signs of being a threat. She hit with speed and power, and she pushed the knee backward with all her strength. She remembered Betty smiling when she said, "The bigger they are, the harder they fall." She knew she had to act fast before he saw the Velcro strap holding the two darts around her inner thigh. She used the instructions she had received when taking her Karate class and took his left knee out from under him by rotating her body to the side, planting her left foot under her, and striking his left knee with her right foot. He appeared not to register for a second, that his knee was fully fractured, and he was falling. He had a grimace on his face and cussed as he fell. She had immediately rotated her body backward and moved back down the hall, allowing him to hit the concrete floor in front of her. Then, she jumped on his back as he was reaching for his knee. She reached for one of the darts, and she removed the cap off the dart while moving forward. She then plunged one of the darts into his neck, while pulling his mic out of his ear, covering it up in the palm of her hand. She wanted him to be quiet and not alert the other security men. The dart had rendered him unconscious in less than a second. Vicky realized there must be a problem. She wondered, did this man come from upstairs? Are there security men in the basement that the maid service knew nothing about? She had to make a decision. Proceed with the plan and try to locate the girl, or retreat and try to escape. She was not certain she could escape at this point without being able to radio Little Jimmy. She also realized this was the only chance she had to save the girl. She walked past the big man in the hall and turned the corner. She heard a voice from upstairs and saw the back of another security man dressed in the same type of clothing, who was looking in the direction of the voice.

She immediately pulled the second dart from the Velcro band on her upper thigh and approached him from behind in the narrow hallway. He didn't see or hear her. She removed the cap from the second dart and plunged the second dart in the back of his neck, while she pivoted to kick him in the back of the knee. She stepped into the back of his knee with her left foot and grabbed the mic from his ear as he was falling. She ran down the hallway. She hoped the kick to the back of his leg would delay his response enough for the dart to work. Wayne had told her the dart and the drug would work about a half-second faster if it was shot into the body, and not the extremities. The dart worked within half a second. He tried to turn to see what happened, but he stumbled from the blow to the back of his leg. He reached for his gun, but his right hand could not hold the grip. The pistol fell to the floor. He fell on the concrete floor as he was turning. He made eye contact with Vicky as he hit the floor. He was trying to talk, but no sound was coming out. Vicky retreated down the hall, but then turned to make certain the dart had worked. To avoid being shot, she stood and turned at the end of the hall, and she was prepared to step into the other hallway. She removed the Velcro strap, and left it with the cap of the dart.

She then stepped back into the hallway, and went past him into the main basement room, which looked like a dungeon, with a hook in the center of the ceiling and a rope tied off at the wall. There was a large drain in the middle of the floor. There were additional iron rings randomly bolted to the walls, ceiling, and floor. The room was all concrete, walls, floor, and ceiling, with four large lights. The ceiling throughout the basement was nine-foot-high and all the walls, floors, and ceiling were painted white. She saw something like a box covered by a large cloth pad, like U-Haul uses to protect items when moving. The box was about four-foot-high by three-foot square. She knew she had to hurry. She ran across the room and pulled back the cloth pad and saw a young Asian girl in a large dog cage. The girl had a gag in her mouth, and her hands were tied. She looked like she had been crying and had given up trying to escape. Vicky was surprised by what she saw. She could smell urine. Her heart went out to the child. Then, she got mad. She tried to locate something to open the lock on the cage door. She knew she was not going to leave the girl in the house, and she could not carry the cage up the steps without someone seeing her. She ran back across the two guards lying on the concrete floor in the hallways, and up the stairs leading to the garage. Wayne had been correct. The door at the top of the stairs to exit the basement into the garage was not passcode protected or locked. She opened the door about three inches. She recalled what Maria's friend had said about there being a camera located above the door, which would be pointing away from her position inside the doorway. She ran back down the stairs and picked up the mop in the small closet. She ran back up the stairs and eased the door ajar. She carefully pushed the camera lens straight upward with the mop handle. With the door open, she could see a pegboard with several tools. She listened, but she only heard the two air-conditioners running. The garage was very neat. She saw two bolt cutters, one large and one small, hanging on the pegboard near several other hanging tools. She made certain the cameras in the garage were focused on the garage doors and the exit door. She then used the mop handle to block the door open so the door would not shut, while she ran across the garage and grabbed the large bolt cutters. The lock on the large dog cage was a small lock and should not be too difficult to cut off with the bolt cutters. She also knew she could exit through one of the garage doors with the child and run in the direction of the road. She ran down the concrete stairs, across the two guards lying in the two separate hallways, but when she turned into the doorway to the main room, there was a third guard who had just entered the room from the foyer stairs. The guard had seen the little girl in the cage, and walked by her, and now he saw Vicky walk around the corner into the doorway. Vicky realized he had to have noticed the girl in the cage, and he had made no attempt to try to check on her and open the door to the cage. He was not there to help. They had to be using the other set of stairs, and these men had walked down the foyer stairs. Vicky had to hold her temper in check. All these men knew the girl was in the cage. She dropped the bolt cutters behind her in the hallway, with the rubber hand grips hitting the concrete floor last, to limit the noise as she entered the room. He did not have an opportunity to see what she had been holding, and she smiled at the guard as she walked up in front of him. She wanted everything to appear normal, like she was a guest in the home. She considered using the bolt cutters as a weapon, but she knew once the guard saw the bolt cutters, he would pull a gun. She felt surprise was her best option. She wanted to make certain he was not anticipating her strike to his knee or registering any kind of threat from her. He was standing with his weight evenly placed on both legs and appeared to be very confident in himself. He was about 6'2", 200 pounds, and appeared to be in excellent shape. He was built like a fighter in a large weight division. She sized him up as quickly as she could. She was more concerned with this guard than the other two guards. The big man was too slow and too overconfident in his size. The second guard was ambushed from the rear and had no opportunity to resist. This man, like most men, would notice her perfect figure, in nothing but the leotard, and make the critical mistake of allowing Vicky to get too close. She walked up to him with a smile on her face, staring into his eyes. She stood within two feet of him and made her smile even bigger. She immediately performed the sweep kick with everything she could muster. She knew she was too low at practice with the board on her first attempt, so she aimed high. She caught him in the perfect spot. The right knee collapsed inward, toward the left knee. He had not considered her a threat and must have thought the other two guards had met her and allowed her to pass. The senator sometimes provided his men certain benefits, and pretty women were always appreciated by the guards. She rotated her body on the concrete floor and jumped backward. He was able to grab her hair by her ponytail and pull her backward toward him. Vicky remembered what Betty had said about the kill shot to the nose. If you wanted to break the nose, hit down on the bridge of the nose; but, if you must kill someone, drive the nose bone back into the brain with either the fist or the palm. Vicky thought, he knows the girl is locked up, and he is part of the crime. He had fallen almost all the way down. He had, out of reflex, reached for his injured knee with one hand and pulled Vicky toward him by her ponytail with the other hand, when Vicky turned and used the momentum to her advantage. He had no way to block or to protect his face. She stepped toward him, with her head tilted down, lifted his chin with her left forearm, and with all the force of her right hand drove the nose bone straight backward with a palm shot. His head tilted backward, with his eyes stuck wide open. He fell, dead before he hit the ground. Vicky looked at his body lying on the concrete and noticed he was not moving. She knew she had to hurry. She pulled his jacket open, unsnapping the strap, and grabbed his gun from his shoulder holster. She immediately went back and picked up the bolt cutters, returning to cut the lock. She thought, if she could just get the girl out of the cage and up the stairs, they could make it. Wayne will be close by to help.

She bent down, set the pistol on the top of the cage, and was prepared to force the hand grips together and cut the lock, when she heard a deep southern accent from directly above her and behind her say, "I will blow your head off if you move one muscle."

Then, another younger but very fit man entered the basement and walked over against the wall, with his gun pulled, aimed at Vicky. Vicky put her hands up, slowly turned, and looked at the man with the gun who had walked up behind her. He looked to be about fifty years old, with a deep dark tan and no wrinkles. He had very dark brown eyes and stood about six feet tall. The other man was not as heavy but looked like a fighter. Neither man showed any emotion. The foreign-made pistols had silencers. Vicky did not recognize the brand of guns. The older man stepped backward two steps to increase the distance between himself and Vicky, and then motioned the younger man to pull Vicky over under the hook in the ceiling with a rope, which was tied off on the hook in the wall. The man with the gun stepped to the side and aimed the gun at the side of Vicky's head. The younger man worked fast and tied her tight around her wrists and hands with the gloves in front of her. He then walked over to the wall and pulled the rope that ran through the hook in the ceiling. The ceiling was at least nine feet high, and he used his weight to pull the rope tight, forcing Vicky off her feet and leaving her hanging in the air, swinging back and forth. The man with the gun pushed, with his left foot, a small stool under her feet. When she could reach the stool standing on her toes, the younger man tied off the rope on the hook in the wall. The older man motioned for the younger man. The younger man ran through the rear door where Vicky had entered. The older man walked over to the security guard on the floor and kneeled on one knee. He checked his neck for a pulse. He glanced at the girl in the cage and around the room. He hesitated in thought. The younger man reappeared through the door and said, "Basement is clear. Two down but not dead." He held up the empty dart casings and the Velcro strap. "A/C vent is ajar."

The older man glanced up at Vicky and said, "This one is dead". He stood up and looked at his partner and tilted his head toward Vicky as to suggest she was the only one here. He placed his gun in his holster and pulled a small hand towel from the table, using it as a gag, very quickly, sticking it in her mouth from behind her and tying it in the back of her head. They heard a shout from upstairs that someone was coming to the front door. The two men were very efficient and decisive with their actions. The two men looked at each other and walked up the other set of stairs to the front foyer, without saying a word. Vicky realized the bottom basement was actually all concrete, with drains in the floors of the rooms, and was built under the main level of the home, with no rooms built under the main garage. There were basically two rooms in the basement, with four or five smaller rooms off each of the two bigger rooms, all divided by one hallway. She was located under the front section of the home, near the foyer. There was an extra room, with a back stairway from the foyer. The plans she had reviewed had been altered. Vicky thought, if she could get the gag out of her mouth and yell, that it may be her only hope in the short term. She looked at the girl in the cage, who was crying. The girl started kicking the cage, making a slight moaning sound. The girl was limited to what she could do, with her hands tied behind her. She was completely nude, and Vicky could tell she was still a child.

She knew Wayne would not leave her in the home without doing something to help. She figured Wayne would approach the home through the front door. She knew Wayne needed to be alerted and call for backup, and he needed to do this before he approached the home. She also knew Little Jimmy had not signed up for this, and she could understand if he had retreated across the back lawn and left. The gag was loose fitting. She thought, if that was Wayne at the front door, she had to yell and warn him. He might be her only hope. There was no way, with the girl in the cage, they were going to allow her to live. She had seen the evidence.

***

Wayne knew he had to do something. He thought he might bluff his way into the home. So, he drove up to the gate and used the intercom to request to see the senator. He explained that he worked for the TBI and needed to discuss the judge's death. There was something important that he needed to review with him about the death and the property line between the two properties. The senator was the only person on the main floor of the home. He walked over to his monitor when he heard the buzz from the front gate, and he looked at the video screen. He listened, and figured the man in the old truck, who mentioned the judge and the property line, was going to have to be handled. He knew he would need to figure out a plausible excuse, and have the intruders killed inside his home. He could not afford to take chances out in the open. There could be other witnesses. He answered the intercom and told Wayne, "Certainly, come on through the gate, and I look forward to meeting you". When he wanted, he could sound very pleasing and charming. Wayne had no way of knowing what happened to Vicky and Little Jimmy. He felt, with him announcing he was a state police officer, they would not try anything. He hoped Senator Davis did not realize they were together.

The gate opened, and Wayne drove up to the front of the house. He walked up the three steps to the front door. A middle-aged, very tan man opened the front door and smiled, as he stepped to the side to allow Wayne to enter. He motioned for Wayne to proceed into the living room to the left and mentioned Senator Davis was waiting. However, once inside, Wayne turned to his left, looking for the senator. He started to walk toward the living room, but the security man, who had stepped to the side, partially in the way, hit Wayne very hard, twice, in the right rib cage. The man had positioned himself, so he could drive his right fist full force into Wayne's rib cage, once Wayne had gotten even with him. Wayne heard and felt his ribs crack and knew immediately that some of his ribs had been broken. Wayne fell to the floor with piercing pain running into his right rib cage. The pain in Wayne's side was horrible. The senator walked into the foyer with the younger man and told the security men to drag Wayne to the basement. The two men searched him and pulled out his two guns. The older man bent even with Wayne, gritted his teeth, and said, "Don't make me hit you in those ribs again."

At that remark, Wayne was able to stand hunched over to the right, holding his ribs, and he walked down the stairs with the gun pointed at the back of his head. Wayne was certain at this point the plan had failed, and they were either going to be arrested or killed, depending on what Vicky had discovered. Wayne knew the two punches to the ribs where punches meant to debilitate, so he could be controlled and not be a high-risk threat to fight. Wayne stayed hunched over, holding his ribs, and noticed, to his dismay, Vicky was hanging from the ceiling on a hook, tied off with the rope leading to the wall. She was standing on her tiptoes, and finally had been able to rotate her mouth and chin back and forth, which allowed the gag to drop out of her mouth, and it was hanging around her neck when Wayne was pushed into the dungeon. Wayne yelped in pain as he was being pushed. He tried to keep his body turned to keep his hurting ribs away from the men. He did not know if he could take another punch to the ribs. He could feel the cold sweat pouring over him with the nauseating pain. He noticed the security man lying on his back on the concrete floor and was not certain if Vicky had drugged him with a dart or what had happened. He stared at the man for an additional second, did not see his chest moving, and wondered if he was dead. When they pushed Wayne on the floor against the wall across from where Vicky was hanging, he looked up and saw the hook with the rope used to tie Vicky and hold her above the floor. He figured he might be able to untie it, but he would need twenty to thirty seconds, by the time he stood up and started working the knot loose. The man was watching him, with a gun aim directly at his face. With every breath, he could feel the pain from his ribs pulsating through his side. Wayne had not noticed the cage for a few seconds after sitting on the floor. The large blanket was lying in the floor, and he could see the naked back and black hair of the young person leaning against the back of the wire cage. He could not tell if the person was an Asian girl, but he assumed she was part of the kids being kidnapped by the syndicate. He then realized, by knowing the kidnapped girl was present, he was going to die. There was only one hope. Wayne realized Little Jimmy was their only possibility of living through this. He conceived that he should have called Vince, but then he remembered his phone signal would not work with the jamming equipment these men had used to block all calls in the approximate quarter mile radius.

The senator walked into the room and said, "We need to kill them, and be fast about it. She has broken into my home." He looked down with neutral expression at the security guard lying on the concrete floor. "She is nothing but a common thief, and that will be the result of the investigation, when the police find her dead body upstairs. No one will question the shooting of these two in my home. One is a dirty cop, and the other is a thief. We can make it look like they shot each other." He then looked back at the security guard and said, "You will need to dispose of his body, and I will hire another guard."

Vicky hoped Little Jimmy had gotten away. She understood her fate, and because of her, Wayne would also be killed. The senator evidently did not realize they were on the same team, or that there was a third member of the team. She was facing the hallway leading to the foyer stairway. She could turn her head and see the entrance to the hallway and the stairway to the garage. She had not noticed the long wooden table with hooks hanging from the side, sitting in the shadow of the room. The table actually looked like a table from the medieval time period. It was sitting under a large light, in front of the back wall located behind her. The back wall was covered with a mirror. The two large lights had just been turned on by the senator. There was a drain under the table. She knew there was only one thing the table could be used for, and with the little girl in the cage, she hoped they killed her before the girl. She did not think she could stand to watch the child being raped and mutilated.

***

Meanwhile, Little Jimmy, who had positioned himself behind the large Hemlock evergreen pine tree, was watching a security man, who had walked out and looked around the pool area and had glanced his way. He had not moved. He knew movement was easier to discern than being perfectly still. He was behind the trunk of the Hemlock tree, which had very thick, low-hanging branches. The trunk in no way could conceal his entire body, but with the thick low-hanging branches, his dark pants and vest, he blended in. The security man was on the back deck, standing behind the table. The tree was a perfect cover. It was about fifteen feet from the rear corner of the home and was most likely planted to hide the garage elevation from view from the rear of the home, or the east elevation from the small boat dock area. The top of the tree was nearly thirty feet high, and the diameter at the bottom of the tree trunk was approximately fourteen inches. With all the limbs fully extended, with the green pine needles, the tree limbs stretched about twenty feet across at the bottom. There was a second Hemlock, that must have also been planted right after the home built next to this one. Little Jimmy knew if the man walked around the side of the home, he would see the rope hanging from the vent to the ground. He also knew he did not want to let Vicky down. He had to pull her out or hold the end of the rope so that she could climb out. He looked at the rope to see if it was moving, as a signal from Vicky that she was coming out. He had realized the situation, but figured with Wayne being a state police officer, they would be okay if they got caught. He also knew at this point, if the man saw the rope after walking around the corner of the home, he had only two choices. He could give up, or he could make a run for his motorcycle. Little Jimmy also knew the man would pull his gun and radio for the security team inside. The radio transmission was coming in and out for the security guard. The security man got suspicious that something was not kosher inside the home. He knew from the past that the radio signal would not be clear if it was coming from the lower basement area. There was too much concrete and steel rebar used in the basement ceiling that blocked transmissions. He was focused on the interior of the home. As he stood looking to see if he could notice an irregularity through the large French doors, Little Jimmy took the opportunity to swiftly walk around the base of the tree and ease up behind him. The lights in the family room were off, and the man placed his hands on the sides of his face to wall off the ambient light from the porch. He was squinting looking through his hands. He suddenly noticed a reflection of something large in the door glass and turned, and his eyes went wide open when he saw Little Jimmy and his right fist. Little Jimmy had reached his shoulder with his left hand and spun the guard around. The right cross landed square on his chin. The security man was unconscious before he landed on the concrete tile-covered pad. He fell straight backward, with his head striking the hard surface first. Little Jimmy hesitated at first to pick up his pistol. He remembered what his probation officer had said about him staying away from guns. He knew he could get an additional five years in prison for holding a gun. Little Jimmy went ahead and picked up the pistol from the holster, stepped over him, and entered the back door. With the gloves on, he could not stick his large finger through the trigger gap in the small automatic pistol. He held the pistol anyway. He figured it might come in handy for Vicky or Wayne. He looked around through the door and did not see anyone. He then proceeded to walk through the hall into the garage. He noticed the mop handle held the steel door ajar, and the camera lens had been pushed upward and was focused on the ceiling located directly above its position at the door. He thought he heard voices coming from the basement steps, and he started going down the concrete steps to the basement from the back-entry area in the garage.

The door to the basement was left open by someone with the mop handle. Little Jimmy thought to himself, this had to be Vicky that had left the door ajar to escape. The security guards and the senator would not need to leave a mop in the door to hold it ajar. Little Jimmy thought Vicky must have found the child, and she might need help. She must have figured this was her way out. He thought to himself, the safe move would be to leave and just drive off. He figured he was not going to let Vicky down. He could hear a man's voice coming from the basement as he descended the stairs. He tried to be as quiet as possible, as he took one concrete step at a time and the voices got louder and louder.

The younger security man came up behind Little Jimmy and stuck a gun to his head as Little Jimmy was on the last step. The young security man had gone up the stairs near the foyer and walked around; and, noticing the security man lying on the exterior tile pad, he followed Little Jimmy down the stairs, one step at a time. He walked down the stairs behind Little Jimmy and caught up to him on the last step. He told Little Jimmy if he didn't do as told, he would blow his head off. Little Jimmy thought, "Shit, I forgot to look behind myself coming down the stairs." He wondered where this man had hidden, and how he did not see him. He resigned himself to the fact that he had let them down. He dropped the gun at the bottom of the hallway and thought, "I hope Wayne can help. He is with the TBI; everything will be okay."

The young security man nudged the gun barrel against the back of Little Jimmy's head and forced him to walk around the corner into the concrete room where the others were being held. As soon as Little Jimmy walked through the door opening from the hallway with his hands up, he saw the middle-aged man standing, facing Vicky, and Wayne, who was sitting against the wall. The middle-aged man turned in their direction and pointed the gun at Little Jimmy. Vicky noticed the middle-aged man suddenly change his focus, and Vicky looked over to her left and saw Little Jimmy. Vicky yelled, "Do not shoot him," as she stuck her leg out in the way while standing on one foot, trying to stop the man from shooting Little Jimmy. The pistol was now aimed at the chest of Little Jimmy.

The man hesitated and motioned for Little Jimmy to proceed and sit on the floor next to Wayne. At that point, the younger man appeared, with his gun aimed at the back of Little Jimmy. The older man gave the younger security guy a signal, and he immediately placed his gun in his shoulder holster and started dragging the dead security man out the door and down the hallway. They could hear him carrying the man up the stairs. Vicky had not realized the young man had left the dungeon until he came back into the room, with his gun pointed at Little Jimmy. She had been so focused on the man with the gun, Wayne, and the senator, and he had walked up the foyer stairs without her realizing he had left the room.

Little Jimmy was surprised and disappointed to see Wayne sitting against the wall. He would never had dropped his gun in the hall if he had known Wayne was being held at gun point. He knew he would have taken his chances on the steps. Little Jimmy had hoped Wayne would be their salvation. He had no clue Wayne had been captured. He had assumed Wayne would have been able to see the vehicles entering the residence from his lookout position in the large cornfield, and not get caught. He sat down next to Wayne, and said in a whisper, "I hope you called for backup."

Wayne grimaced in pain, and he shook his head no. Wayne now realized this was his fault. He should have known better. He was the experienced officer. He should have had several other officers in play on this job. He thought Vicky was right all along about Frank Vitola, picking up on the fact he was a killer. She had built a rapport with the undocumented people in the Butler community, and through them was able to set a trap for the bank robbers and killers from Arkansas. She was right about Judge Larkin, Senator Davis, and the assassin from Spain. She was very intelligent. When figuring out the height of the vent on the senator's home, she had figured the math, fourteen feet, six inches high, without a calculator, in less than a second. Now, Wayne concluded they were all going to die. He started getting angry, knowing this was his fault.

Vicky assumed they all three were going to die. She looked at the cage, and her heart went out to the girl. She felt she had failed again. Her only hope now was the man with the gun. She knew the senator wanted them dead. She wondered if he was a CIA agent, or was he a mercenary? The older man, who seemed to be in charge, just did not act like a mercenary. These two men were not part of the security detail who watched the senator. All the older man's actions seemed to be very well calculated, and the two men had communicated by signaling to each other without talking. She figured they would already be dead if they were mercenaries or hired guns. Vicky kept trying to develop a strategy. She could not understand why they were not already dead. She wondered, could these two men work for the CIA? They were either private contractors who worked for a large arms contractor, or CIA agents. The older man did not appear to be an agent from a foreign country. His southern accent would be difficult to duplicate. She had to figure out an angle. She felt responsible for Wayne and Little Jimmy, and she could not stand to think about what would happen to the girl if she did not do something. She kept running the scenarios through her head. Then, it dawned on her. They had to be CIA. They were so focused on their mission; they had not noticed her figure in the French cut leotard. Every male she had ever met or dated had always talked about how pretty she was. Even her girlfriends' boyfriends would look her up and down, but these two men had not even noticed. They were totally consumed with their very important mission. A hired gun or mercenaries, who were going to rape and kill her, would have looked at her with lust and talked about doing the deed. These men were not concerned with her.

The older man pulled out of his right-side cargo pants pocket, and handed the senator, a bundle of $100 bills that were taped together. Vicky thought there might be $50,000 or more. She thought, why now? Why the girl? This guy had to be an undercover agent. Who else would be giving a United States Senator money? This had to be an undercover investigation.

The senator smiled, took the bundle of money, and said, "Thanks." He gently set the money down on the small table, with towels stored in the underneath doorless cabinet.

She took a chance and said, "I know you are a CIA operative."

The man walked up next to Vicky and stayed to the side of her, so she could not kick him. Vicky thought, he is very experienced at this. He seemed to be well trained. He showed no emotion, and he seemed to have a second agenda.

Vicky said to him, "I looked into your eyes. I know the eyes of a killer, but please show mercy and allow the child to be released unharmed. She does not deserve to die by the hands of this monster. He has raped and killed at least eight kids." She looked at Senator Davis when she said monster, and then looked back at the man standing near her, with the gun aimed at her.

Senator Davis said, "I am growing bored by all this. Kill them all. If you want to have some fun, you and your man can enjoy her before you kill her," pointing toward Vicky.

The senator then said, "Besides, you (looking at Wayne) killed a very good friend of mine."

Wayne looked up, while holding his ribs, and said, "I did not kill that bastard judge."

The senator laughed and said, "I am not talking about Judge Larkin. Hell, I owe you for killing the worthless coward. I am talking about Bill Duff, the dear friend of mine for over thirty years."

Wayne looked surprised and asked, "Who is Bill Duff"?

The senator said, "He was the highway patrolman."

"You certainly have some sick friends, and you are a sick bastard and a disgrace. Why did you not start a rock band and call yourselves The Psychos Are Us? You could have been the lead singer. You son-of-a bitch."

The senator grimaced and said, "Bill Cramer was the alias for Bill Duff, the rogue highway patrolman that killed the young woman at the water tower with the machete. Mr. Duff was a natural killer. No question about that fact. He had killed hundreds of people over the years. Mr. Duff and I met in Afghanistan, thirty years ago, when we were serving our ungrateful country. We accomplished more in Afghanistan than the entire Armed Forces and Coalition Forces combined. We were able to force the adversaries to understand that, if they did not work out a ceasefire, they were going to die in a very unpleasant manner. They were going to have to watch their children and wives die, by being cut up with a machete. That is how our country was able to pull most of the troops out, because of me and Mr. Duff. The American people have no stomach for war, and do not understand the need to kill the maniacs who threaten our country. I was a captain in Army Intelligence at that time, and I discovered Mr. Duff had an appetite to torture people, which was very handy in that type of war. Mr. Duff went too far and was caught red-handed, and I was the young Army captain that got him out of the charges, by lying for him. I had enough wisdom to realize we needed soldiers like Bill Duff. I helped him obtain a cover, and got him out of the Army, where he worked as an independent contractor in the region. Whenever the Army needed information and needed to torture someone without anyone knowing, Mr. Bill Duff would step in for the task. After I was promoted to colonel, I set him up with several aliases. I hired Mr. Duff to manage several foreign operations, and he also helped me by supplying me with my needs, in the form of young Asian girls. Mr. Duff had set up quite a network in Asia and Europe." He pointed toward the cage and said, "Their parents sell them for hardly anything. The trick is having them delivered to me in good shape, and not all used up. There is an increasing market for them, and the competition to buy them is growing greater and greater."

Senator Davis paused, and said, "I had also covered up the actions of my subordinate, the judge, when the judge also worked under my command in Army Intelligence. I took a promotion to colonel and transferred to South Korea. The judge was a captain and had been caught visiting an establishment where his wife had worked as a call girl, and they had indulged in perverted activities with young Asian girls. The judge had met his wife in South Korea, where she was the main attraction in the business, working as a whore, and the damn fool fell in love with her. His career and future were in my hands, and I helped him. He felt obligated over the next thirty years to return the favor and help me. He and his wife, in turn, also introduced me to the pleasures of the young Asian girls."

Wayne said, "So you three set up and established quite a network of human trafficking. You set Bill Duff up with the job with the Tennessee Highway Patrol, and this gave Mr. Duff the perfect cover to assist in handling the young Asian girls. After the judge and his wife were finished with the girls, they would turn them over to you to be raped additionally, and then Mr. Duff could torture them to death and dispose of the bodies. You are a bunch of sick, perverted assholes."

The senator looked like he was going to say something else, appeared to be a little surprised, and then said, "I know you killed my friend. He would have never killed himself. He did not have that type of personality. He was a survivor, and he knew I would help him if he ever needed it. You lied on your official report. I know you executed him, and now you walked right into my home, which I will consider a blessing, for the opportunity to impose my revenge for my old friend. He was an American hero, and he deserved better than to be killed by you."

The senator then looked at Wayne with a very arrogant smile, and said, "They pay me all this money and provide for my needs. They do whatever I command. You are nothing but a dirty cop, and these two are nothing but common everyday thieves."

Wayne asked, "What about the assassin from Spain you hired to kill an innocent child?"

The Senator smiled and said, "He was a fool. He was going to be the replacement for Mr. Duff, but he never was going to be near as good as Duff. He should have checked, and he would have known there are no Catholic priests in Butler, Tennessee. I never met him or talked with him. Do you know who killed him?"

Wayne could feel his ribs throbbing with pain with every breath. He shook his head no.

There was a pause, and then he continued, "I have some fun pending, and I need for you all to go. I am on a tight schedule. I know you're a dirty cop and you killed my friend, so my men are going to kill you. I assume these other two are just everyday thieves who happened to be in the wrong home at the wrong time. We will execute them also, and by doing so, help the community."

Wayne said, "I have backup. Several officers with the TBI know I am here. You can't kill all of us and expect to get away with this."

"You have told no one you are here. You are on your own. I recognize a maverick when I see one. If there were other officers involved, they would already be here. By the time they do get here, you and the other two will be dead, and we will make it look like you three shot and killed each other. The jamming equipment would not allow you to make any calls, so I know you are lying. I recognize the man next to you. He was the boxer at the judge's party. He must have cased out my home that afternoon. Nothing worse than a damn thief, which is punishable by death in my home."

Little Jimmy did not move. He knew the man with the gun, watching him and Wayne, was an expert and would shoot him dead if he tried anything.

The senator looked over at the cage that held the young Asian girl. She was bound and looked pitiful, and he walked over and carefully placed the quilt back over the cage.

At that point, the other security man walked back into the room. He motioned to the man with the gun. He was finished with whatever he had been doing, which sounded like loading up the three injured security men and the one dead security man in a vehicle in the upstairs driveway area.

Steve D. Nichols

Chapter 36

Vicky spoke up and said, "You're a monster, Senator. You deserve to burn in hell."

The senator said, "And you are a thief that got caught in my home. The crime is punishable by death. I have turned off the security cameras, so we can make the killings look like a double homicide and a suicide." He looked at the middle-aged man and said, "Go ahead, and carry out the sentence."

Vicky determined the man with the gun was with the CIA, and he seemed to have paused and had reservation about what he had discovered in the basement. He also was their only hope for survival. She said, "This is all wrong. You need to do something. You took an oath to protect our country against foreign and domestic threats. A young girl is being held in that cage, under the blanket. She has done nothing wrong. She is an innocent child. Let her go. If you want, kill us, but let her go. I am begging you."

He asked, "How do you know I'm with the CIA?" At that point, the senator's expression seemed to change. He was surprised by this revelation. Vicky took that as a cue to talk more to the man with the gun. She knew he was the only hope they had. She also knew the CIA had made mistakes over the years.

"The CIA has done bad things over the years trying to help our country, while the meek in those other countries have been sacrificed.

The CIA has supported dictators and other leaders over the years: The Shah of Iran, Ferdinand Marcos in the Philippines, and Manuel Noriega in South America. To stand back and close your eyes to these unnatural and unjust acts to the innocent makes you just as sinful in God's eyes as the senator for allowing that young girl to be raped. You should go ahead and rape her yourself. Our Lord will judge us all."

The man walked up to her and looked her directly in the eyes, and Vicky knew she was going to die. She stared him in the eyes without blinking or fear, and she said, "I am the good shepherd, and the good shepherd lays down his life for the sheep."

"Are you quoting Apostle John to me?", he asked, as he gently pushed some hair out of her eyes. Vicky thought about kicking him, but she knew she could not provide enough force to cause any damage, standing on her toes on one foot and trying to kick with the other foot. She just could not produce any power, and the other man now had a gun on Little Jimmy and Wayne. Vicky had given up, and she said, "You are welcome to visit my church. I am certain your soul needs to be cleansed and forgiven. Maybe our Lord will be merciful to you, unlike what you are doing for the child."

She looked at him with disgust, and then he turned and walked back over toward the senator, while pulling a syringe out of the left side of his cargo pants pocket. The senator could not see the syringe. He quickly holstered his pistol, grabbed the senator's left wrist, and slammed the syringe in the senator's upper arm, injecting, through his shirt, its contents.

He gave the motion to the second security man, for him to get ready to leave. He then turned and told the senator that he was not as important as he thought he was, and justice had just been served. He stared in disgust at Senator Davis and said, "I am ashamed that you rose to the level of colonel in the United States Army. The senator fell on his knees and then on his back on the concrete floor, holding his chest with an anxious and surprised look on his face. The senator started to plead for help. He said, "You don't understand what you are doing. We are about to make revolutionary-type changes in the world. Please stop."

The middle-aged man stepped over the senator on the floor, and then looked at Vicky, and said, "He just had a massive heart attack, and will be dead in a few seconds. The autopsy will reflect a heart attack of natural causes, and we will take care of the others." Vicky looked at Wayne and Little Jimmy, with a surprised look on her face. She had been hoping they were ready to try something, but this was unexpected.

He smiled at Vicky and said, "I would cut you free, but I cannot afford to lose my only man. You have already laid out three highly-trained private security men, and the big man laid out the fourth one." He smiled, picked up the bundle of money from the table, and swiftly left through the door leading to the stairs and the garage.

Steve D. Nichols

Chapter 37

Vicky urgently said, "Untie me."

Little Jimmy jumped up, released the rope from the wall, and ran over and untied her wrist.

Wayne said, "Check the senator's pockets. He must have a key."

Vicky ran over to the senator to find the key to unlock the cage. The key was in his front shirt pocket. Vicky looked into the dying man's eyes with total disgust and felt no pity for him. The senator said, "Help me. I have plenty of money, which I can give you. Please don't leave me here to die. You do not understand what I know and who I work with to significantly change our future. I don't deserve this. I know important things."

Vicky said, in a very low, soft voice as she smiled at the senator and gently rubbed her fingers across his face down to his chin, which appeared to be a loving gesture, "I pray our Lord will provide you more compassion than you did these young girls. I am trying to seek atonement from our Lord for what I have done, and I might very well see you in hell."

The senator looked into Vicky's eyes, with the realization that his time on earth was coming to an end. He said, "Beware of the Zipline Vortex Effect."

She took the key from his shirt pocket, and she quickly unlocked the lock, and helped the girl out of the cage, removing the plastic ties on her wrist and the cloth rag from her mouth. Vicky hugged her. The girl could not stand at first, and Vicky asked her if she could speak English. The girl just stood and looked like a zombie. Vicky slipped a tee-shirt from the cabinet over her head and hugged her a second time.

Vicky said, "Little Jimmy, pick her up and carry her up the stairs to the kitchen. She needs something to eat and drink."

Vicky then asked, "Can you walk?"

Wayne said, "Yes," and Vicky helped him stand. She looked at the senator one last time as they left the dungeon, into the hallway to proceed up the stairs to the foyer. He had just died. She and Wayne turned and walked up the stairs, with her holding him up under his arm as they walked up the stairs. She wondered what the senator meant about the "Zipline Vortex Effect." What could he had been talking about when he said a new revolutionary world-altering event?

Wayne was trying not to moan, with the pain from his ribs. Vicky located a bottle of Ibuprofen in the kitchen cabinet, and Wayne took four Ibuprofen. Wayne just sat there, watching the girl eat some bread and drink some water Little Jimmy had given her. Little Jimmy found a coke can in the refrigerator and gave her a small glass.

Wayne said, "I will call Vince and my boss, John, on the landline. You two need to leave before the police arrive."

Wayne made both calls, and then said, "Vince will be here in six to seven minutes." Vicky did not want to leave the girl, but she knew she did not want to be found in the home and be involved.

Wayne said, "You will need to put the vent cover back on as you leave and take or hide the tools. Try to leave no trace."

Little Jimmy nodded and said, "Mrs. Vicky, let's get this done."

Vicky ran back down the stairs and opened the vent cover, where she had left the harness attached to the rope. She disconnected the harness, reset the damaged filter, and closed the vent cover, leaving the suction pad behind in the duct work at the ninety degree turn where the duct work dropped straight down. She figured no one would ever find the suction pad. She grabbed the headlight from the doorknob and headed for the back door. She threw the mop in the garage and allowed the door to close behind her.

She ran outside, where Little Jimmy was waiting to hold her to install the vent cover. He handed her the screwdriver and the screws he had laid on the ground next to the rope. He had already pulled the rope through the duct work and made certain the cameras were turned off, blinking red, and not energized, viewing the backyard area before Vicky came around the corner of the home. They could hear the sirens getting closer, as Little Jimmy lifted Vicky and held her as before. She placed one screw in each side of the cover to make it look like it had never been removed. Little Jimmy lowered her, and she told him to get moving. She would catch up. She wiped the tools off for possible DNA and fingerprints and threw the tools, rope, harness, and fanny pack with the unused camera under the pine needles under the Hemlock tree. She did not want to take a chance of getting caught with them, and no one would see them under the pine needles. She forgot to ask Little Jimmy where her shirt, shoes, and shorts were located. She did not have time to look for them. She had assumed they were lying on the ground near the trees. They might have been under the second tree. The sirens blared from the police cars as they got closer and closer. She had to leave, and she noticed Little Jimmy was about halfway across the field. She ran across the field in a sprint, passing Little Jimmy up at the exit gate. She struggled with removing the gloves where they had stuck to her skin from being hot. She threw her gloves in the bushes next to the parking area and tried to catch her breath. The road was gravel, and she tried to avoid the rocks with her bare feet.

***

Wayne carried the young Asian girl out the front door with his opposite arm, holding his ribs in pain. The four Ibuprofen were starting to work. He sat on the front porch steps, and noticed Vince coming up the driveway in his cruiser. He could hear Darrell or Denny's siren not far behind. The TBI was also on their way, along with the local Tennessee highway patrolman. Wayne said, "The calvary is coming. He reached over and kissed the girl on the head and hugged her."

For the first time, the girl produced a small, friendly smile as she looked at Wayne. She had eaten some sliced turkey, cheese, and bread that Little Jimmy had provided for her from the refrigerator. He told her everything would be okay. Even though she did not speak English, she seemed to understand the circumstances, and what was said.

Steve D. Nichols

Chapter 38

The black Suburban had pulled out before the call to the police had been made, and as they were exiting the driveway, the older man asked the driver if he had gotten the bolt cutters. The driver nodded, yes. The man in the back seat, that Little Jimmy had punched, appeared to have a concussion. He was sitting behind the driver, with dried blood on his face and hands. He kept mumbling about needing to go to see his mother, that she was waiting on him at home, and other nonsensible words. The younger man kept telling him that they would take care of him in a few minutes. The older guy pulled his pistol with the silencer out of his shoulder holster from under his jacket with one fluid motion, with no hesitation, and shot the man in the forehead, as they turned on Lake Street. He then turned his upper body around, and shot the unconscious man sitting up in the back seat directly behind him, with his head leaning forward, in the top of the head.

He said, "Stop the damn car."

The young man looked over at his boss and understood what he was going to do. He stopped the vehicle at a wide area in the street once he turned the curve, after he passed the driveway to the judge's home. The older man opened the passenger door, walked to the rear of the vehicle, and opened the hatch. He pulled back the tarp and shot the unconscious man and the dead man each in the head. He got back in the passenger seat and said, "You can drop me off at my car, and take them to the Butler County dump; go in the back entrance, and cover the bodies up, with my gun, in the trash. They should have known better than to work for that asshole, and they had to know what he was doing. We just cleaned up our mess."

As he pulled over and dropped the older man off, the younger man said, "I will see you back in Washington. I will upload the dead men's photos to headquarters. They will want to know who they were. I am glad I secured the photos while they were in the home; otherwise, well, hell, you know what I mean." He smiled at the older man, knowing all four now had head shots.

"The older man said, "I have got to call in and report the status. We still have nothing, and I am not certain the senator was our man. I am certain he was not going to provide us with information about the leak in the CIA or information leading us to the syndicate. With all this other stuff he has been doing with these kids, he needed to be stopped, and we did our civic duty. Those three did not deserve to die. The lady was right. We needed to make a moral decision, and I made it."

He dropped the older man off at his vehicle on the side of the road. When he pulled up to the gate, which was located northeast of Butler, about ten minutes later, he got out and cut the lock, opening the gates to the back area of the landfill. The area was very remote, with no homes in the area, and there was no security. The road leading to the rear of the dump was a gravel road, with large potholes. The large garbage trucks exited this way during the workweek after dropping off their loads of garbage. Of course, this time of day, there were no workers present, and there was no security needed at the dump. No one would want to steal the trash. He drove through the back gates of the landfill to the area with newly dumped garbage. He looked around to make certain there were no witnesses, and hurriedly pulled each dead man out of the Suburban and laid them in a row next to one another, covering them in a large amount of trash, with the pistol laid next to the man on the end. He wiped up some of the blood in the vehicle and left the towels in the trash. He immediately left through the gate that he had just cut the lock on. He assumed no one would ever find those bodies.

The older man took out his cell phone, as he started driving south on I-24. He wanted to stay in Nashville, and he needed time to think. He hit speed dial for his boss, Max Doran, on his cell phone. Max answered his phone by saying, "Operational Director CIA, Max Doran. How may I assist you?"

Scott Bonier had always admired Max for his cheerful sense of humor. No matter how bad the shit was piling up, he always kept a sense of humor. Scott answered by asking, "Is this a secured line?"

Max, realizing the tone in his top agent's voice, turned serious and said, "Yes. The line is secure. What do you have, Scott?"

"The senator had a heart attack, and he is dead."

There was a pause. Max knew Scott had killed the senator with that remark, and Max said, "We better have this meeting in person. I am not certain how secure this line really is."

Scott said, "Johnny and I met some good Samaritans. I was very impressed with what they were able to accomplish, their dedication and loyalty to each other, and their fortitude to fight for what they believe. I had to make a decision. The senator was involved in some bad things, dealing with kids and rape, but I am not certain he is our guy. I believe he was involved, but he was not in charge. I mentioned I had his money, and he said he would have to check with someone else. I will be back in town in a few days. I am going to stay in Nashville this weekend, and I will see you Monday. Johnny is driving back separately, and he will be back in town to meet you tomorrow."

Max asked, "What happened to the four security men that always traveled with the senator? From what I understand, they were the best-of-the-best private security team anyone could have. One of them was from the secret service, one was a former seal, and two from the Army. They were the best."

"Max, you are not going to believe what all the senator was doing with kids, but the four security men you are referring to were dealt with by the three good Samaritans. You may want to hire them. Johnny can fill you in on what happened. They can be trusted, and are not part of the syndicate or linked to the traitors and moles in the CIA. You need to hire someone you can trust outside the programs.

You just do not know who to trust, and I am getting old." Both men said goodbye.

Max knew, when he asked Scott to return from retirement, that it was wrong. People retire for a reason, and Scott had deserved his retirement. Max also knew the CIA had been infiltrated by the syndicate at several different levels. He just did not know who he could trust.

Steve D. Nichols

Chapter 39

When Little Jimmy exited through the gate, he was breathing hard, and sweat was pouring down his face. Vicky then realized, to her surprise, that the 'getaway car' was a Harley motorcycle with choppers. Little Jimmy walked over, picked up and put on a dark pair of sunglasses he had left on the handlebars, and started the Harley up, handing Vicky an extra pair of sunglasses from the saddlebag on the side of the bike. She thought, "I have never been on the back of a motorcycle, and I am in black leotards." She rubbed her head and said to herself, "You've got to be kidding."

She then asked herself, "What choice do I have?" as she climbed on the back of the bike. She noticed how big Little Jimmy was, and how tall and wide his shoulders were. She also noticed he was covered with sweat and decided to lean back in her booster seat. She wanted to avoid contact. She could hardly see around him, even with the rear seat elevated above his. She could feel the hot air coming from the tailpipes on her bare legs and feet as they started out. She pulled her legs up and set her bare feet on his thighs. She hoped no one would see her, the preacher's wife, like this. She figured she would look the opposite direction when they either pulled by or passed another vehicle. She asked him to drop her off at the neighbors', located behind her home, because she knew the Caldwell family was out of town. She figured someone would see her being dropped off in her driveway. There were always kids out playing Frisbee or Wiffleball in the road of the subdivision, and older couples walking or jogging. She still would have to run around the home to retrieve the hidden key. She told Little Jimmy that she could jump the fence and get to her house without anyone knowing. She thought to herself, "I am more nervous about being seen like this than I was breaking in the senator's home and dealing with his guards." As they drove west on Lake Street, they passed two highway patrol vehicles, with their sirens going and doing speeds in excess of 70 mph. She made certain to look the other direction as the police cars flew past. She felt relieved this little girl was going to be okay. She said a quick prayer for allowing God to provide her, Little Jimmy, and Wayne the fortitude and courage to help the child.

The sun was setting; the motorcycle came to a slow roll at the Caldwell's driveway, and she jumped off. She did not bother to say goodbye to Little Jimmy. He turned and drove away without ever coming to a complete stop. The motorcycle was very noisy, and she hoped to make it close to the fence around her pool without being seen. At least then, the neighbors might think she had been swimming at her pool in a one-piece bathing suit and not realize she was on the motorcycle. She looked around and did not see her neighbors. There was no way she would be able to come up with a plausible reason, being the preacher's wife, wearing nothing but black leotards, and getting off the motorcycle of a single male who just got out of prison. She ran through their side yard to her back gate and around her pool, unlocked the door, and let herself in with the hidden key. She prayed that none of her neighbors could see her. She should have never allowed Wayne to pick her up at her house. As thorough as Wayne was at planning this operation, he had not figured she would have to ride on the back of a motorcycle home, in leotards. Both her neighbors were Baptist, and she knew they lived to spread this type of news. Vicky noticed Matt was not at home and said, "Thank God." The church meeting and dinner must have lasted longer than expected. Vicky took a very quick shower and put on her Micky Mouse tee-shirt. She looked out the back window of the home, to see by chance if anyone had seen her running from the neighbors. She did not see anyone. She went and sat down on the couch, leaning back. She heard the garage door opening.

Matt walked in soon after Vicky had leaned back on the couch. She got up and met him at the door. He walked in and complained about how hard his day had been. Vicky asked him how the meeting went?

Matt said, "They are still deciding if they need to hire temporary help, part-time help, or another full-time preacher."

Vicky did not want to mention her day, and the stress that was built up in her body. She knew she needed her husband to be a man. She took off her tee-shirt and said, "Maybe I can help you feel better."

***

The next Sunday at church, Vicky walked in, knowing that the church was growing. She saw Little Jimmy talking to some of the young women, about clothing no doubt, and when the new items would be delivered to the Prestige Retail Store. She saw Jeff Burton, the man who worked at Butler County Water Company and fishes most every weekend, with his wife, Maggie. Next to Jeff was a blond headed, pale-skinned, bigger man, and a woman next to him, and many others. Holly and Cindy were sitting with their boyfriends. There were other high schoolers in the area talking to the girls in the youth group, and additional friends. Vicky thought to herself, this is more than double the size of the congregation than when we got here. She felt good that the boys were now showing up with the young girls, and she could now see the growth in the youth group. She was so proud of Matt. He really understood how to grow a church, and his preaching was excellent. He always focused on love and grace, and never on hellfire and brimstone. He would mention in his preaching to do things out of love and not fear. There is no fear with perfect love. He also, always mentioned the importance of the church members helping each other, and how this action would always be noticed by others in the community. "We need to lead by example," he would always say. Vicky sat down on the second row from the front, near the isle.

Chapter 40

Matt was getting ready to start the church service, the organist sat down, the choir stood, and everyone who was standing and talking located their seats. Vicky was sitting in the second row to the side and noticed the older tan man from Friday night at the senator's home walk in the back of the church. There was always someone arriving late, but his presence surprised her. She thought, why would he be in attendance? He killed a United States Senator and acted like it was a normal thing he did every day. She figured he would not be visiting the church for revenge purposes or to harm someone. She slid her hand inside her large purse and placed her hand on her pistol. She knew a few of the men carried their guns, and that was part of the church security plan. Given the threats and the state of the Middle East, the Methodist Church Organization had warned the churches they should be on alert for terrorist acts, especially during Sunday morning assembly. The FBI had told all church organizations after 911 to be on a lookout for terrorist acts. The FBI had provided a profile of possible terrorists, and some of the descriptions were a male, a loner, a non-member, and a non-recognized person from the community. The church council had asked a select few to watch out and be prepared. Other churches across America had been given the same warning and were also implementing specific plans of action. She knew the new sheriff, Newsome, and his deputy, Darrell, were in attendance, and her shooting instructor, Mark, had volunteered to keep an eye out. She remembered quoting Apostle John when she thought he was going to kill her, Wayne, and Little Jimmy, and he had recognized the quote. He knew the bible, and he was here for the church service. She remembered that she asked him to come to their church. She motioned for her husband to hold off on the start of the church proceedings, and right before the service started, Vicky walked back to the mystery man and introduced herself and asked him to come to the front of the church and sit with her. Matt waited for her and the man to be seated before he started to pray. He started the service, which led to the choir singing, then the church announcements, then the second opening prayer, with concerns from the congregations. Then the offering plate was started at the rear and passed down the rows. After they passed around the offering plate and it arrived, the man pulled from his jacket pocket and dropped the bundle of hundred dollars bills that he had at the senator's home into the offering plate and smiled straight ahead.

The ushers kept looking at the large sum of money. Matt noticed, and looked at his wife, as if asking, "Who is he?"

After the service, Matt smiled, and abruptly stepped down from the podium to meet the man sitting next to his wife.

Matt said, "I see you have met my wife."

The man said, "I met her Friday, and she asked me come and visit her church. She said the preaching was excellent, and my soul needed the grace of our Lord."

He then said, "Preacher, I have sinned, and I was in need to hear a good sermon." He thanked Matt for the very inspirational church service, which focused on love and grace. He thanked them both and shook Matt's hand a second time, thanked Vicky for inviting him, and he abruptly turned and quickly left. Matt watched him walk through the church doors to the parking lot and asked, "What is his name?"

"I have no clue."

"Where did you meet him?"

"Near the lake, while I was jogging."

Vicky then said, "I will see you after lunch. I need to run by the store for our dinner."

Matt kissed her and said, "I will see you about 2 p.m." He then turned and started talking to the people standing around after the service.

Vicky had driven separately. She knew she was going to be busy all day, but while sitting in the church, she just could not stop thinking about the routines of psychotic killers. In the middle of the night, she had awoken with a nightmare, and sat up in bed. She started thinking about the Asian girls, and what they must have endured. She wanted to bring them justice, and she started remembering what she had read about this type of killer and the ultimate question of why? According to four out of five case studies, the sadist killers had the same routine. They received pleasure and gratification from a specific, perverted act. The act of killing a person was not the reward. It was the circumstances that led up to the killing. The killing of a person was a means to finalize the event, and then the culprit would need to move on to the next person. Watching another person suffer, plead, and beg were noted in four of the five studies. To inflict mental torment and physical pain was preferred by all the sadists.

Matt had started the sermon by mentioning to the flock what he most wanted when he was asked to meet his maker. He said it was really simple, "I want God to tell me the job was well done." He paused, and allowed that to settle in with the audience, and then started in another direction with the sermon. Vicky had been listening to Matt, who had started preaching from the Book of Genesis on how Jacob stole his brother Esau's blessing from Isaac, their father's wealth, when he tricked his blind father with fur gloves, so he could pass as Esau. Matt had made his point about how we all trick other people. It is easy to trick other people. Sometimes it is a group effort to deceive, and all will be held accountable before God. There is no tricking God. He switched to the New Testament to reinforce the point of his sermon. We need to condition ourselves and our hearts to know the difference between heaven and hell. The devil has made hell to appear, at times, on earth very close to heaven, to trick us.

She stopped listening and was overwhelmed with a memory and a feeling something was missing. Her sixth sense was on full alert. She thought, have we been tricked? What am I missing? She remembered the three girls located in the shallow graves had no fingers missing, but the more recent discovered bodies had signs of being tortured over several days, repeatedly raped, and having fingers removed. Why would Cramer pull Wayne's toenail off, and not cut his finger off? The senator had a funny look on his face when Wayne said Cramer had tortured the girls to death. How could Cramer have been in Nashville, Chattanooga, and Butler, while working a full-time job with the highway patrol? That was it. There was another player who was killing the girls after the judge and the senator had finished with them. The senator could not have gotten away from his security detail to kill and bury the bodies. He never stayed in Tennessee long enough to carry out the torture, which lasted for days. He then would have to bury the bodies, which would have taken additional time. She did not want to believe the judge when he said he and his wife had never hurt anyone, but they also were not in town long enough to carry out the gruesome killings. The way the judge looked, when he said they had not hurt anyone, was like he was truly sorry. She knew she had to talk to Wayne as soon as possible. As soon as church was over, Vicky watched the older man leave, and she said goodbye to the church people standing close by and told Matt she would see him later. They hugged and kissed. She called Wayne from her car seat, while sitting in the church parking lot in traffic, and told him she was coming over to his home. It was very important. She pulled in his driveway, and he walked out his front door, barefoot in blue jeans with a white tee shirt, drinking a beer as she got out of her car. He could not help but notice how pretty she was dressed up in her dress and heels. "Hi. Wayne. How are the ribs?"

Steve D. Nichols

"There are two small fractures. I went by the hospital, and they x-rayed them. They hurt like hell. Pardon my French."

"I guess that is why I did not see you in the church today. How are the girls doing?"

Wayne smiled and said, "It has been a long week, and I thought we were going to be killed Friday night," as he set the empty beer can down on the front steps to his home.

Vicky looked at the empty can and asked, "Is it not a little early on Sunday morning to be drinking. Besides should you be mixing your pain medicine with alcohol?"

Wayne smiled, glanced at Vicky, and then looked across his yard to the woods. He said, "The one we found at the lake came out of her coma, and she is doing a lot better. The one from Friday night has been taken to Washington. They said they are going to do what is best for the girls. The parents may have sold them. One of them was somehow taken from North Korea. The other one, I do not know."

Vicky said, "The parents thought they were helping the children relocate to a better situation. I can guarantee you they had no way to know their kids were going to be raped and killed. They need to be taken back to their parents. Can they locate which country the other child is from?"

She paused, and Wayne did not answer. She then said, "You will never guess who I sat next to in church."

Wayne just stood staring, and figured she was going to try to make him feel ashamed about not attending church and drinking beer on Sunday morning. She had asked him to attend church several times.

Vicky smiled and said, "The middle-age man from the senator's home was at our church, and he sat next to me on the second row. He really surprised me, Matt, and the men passing the offering plate. He dropped that big bundle of money in the offering plate."

Wayne was totally surprised and turned to look at Vicky. He said, "You've got to be kidding! The guy that broke my ribs? That son of a bitch hit me when I was not looking."

"He must work for the government, most likely the CIA or one of the other agencies. We never had an opportunity to talk at church, and he left immediately when the service was over. You need to start coming to church more often. It really is amazing who you might meet. But that is not what I came to tell you.

Wayne said, "While I was sitting in the senator's basement, I excepted we were going to die. I have been wondering, and I asked Little Jimmy if he knew or suspected those two men were agents for the CIA. He said he had no clue. How did you know they were agents for the CIA? What tipped you off?"

Vicky did not want to tell Wayne that the final clue was that the men did not seem to be interested in her. She said, "It was literally a shot in the dark."

Vicky hesitated, while she glanced at her outfit and heels, rubbing her hand over her thigh acting like she was removing small debris, to see if Wayne noticed. She smiled when she noticed that he also looked at her. "You remember I told you I had been reading several case studies on psychotic killers. They follow routines. They almost never change the routine that gratifies them. The girls found in the graves on the judge's property had no fingers cut off. They had been buried for years, with no signs of torture to their bone structure. The other two girls the FBI had mentioned to you had missing fingers where they had been tortured over several days. I believe you said the burned off appendages had been cauterized over a few days. Why did Cramer, or Duff, or whatever his name was, pull your toenail off and not cut your fingers off? He would not have changed his routine. I am not certain we have the killer of the girls. I believe the killer is a sadist, who tortures the girls by cutting their fingers off one at a time. The original killer did not torture them in the same manner. I believe Cramer was involved and made arrangements to transport the girls, and maybe he was the money handler, but I just do not see how he could have been traveling back and forth between three cities, worked full time, and had time to torture and then dispose of the bodies of the girls. The bodies were miles apart, located around Nashville. We all assumed he was the killer. I believe you said the girls were held captive for several days, tortured, raped, and then killed. You can work out the logistics with the senator, the judge, and Cramer, but it just does not add up."

Wayne stood in shock, looking at nothing but the woods and field. He finally said, "It never made sense that Brian would pull over and stop on Highway 12 in a remote area, for a highway patrolman he knew to be the killer of the lady at the tower. Now that I think about what Cramer said at the tower, he did not say he pulled Brian over. He said Brian was surprised when he walked up to the car. I have always wondered if someone else had him pull over, and then Cramer came to the scene. That would make sense, and what you are suggesting is plausible. Brian would have pulled over only for someone he knew because he was in a hurry to meet me then fly back to California. We still have a killer out there somewhere, and maybe two, and he will kill again. It might be months from now, or years later, but the sadists always keep killing until they are caught. So, you think the girls found in the grave at the judge's home were killed by someone else, and a different killer now is raping and torturing the girls prior to killing them."

Vicky said, "Yes. Maria's friend, who cleans the senator's home, indicated she had never met the new property manager and her boss had never met him, either. He took over about three years ago. The new property manager for the senator would call her boss and leave the money in an envelope at the home, pay in cash for services rendered, and they would go clean the home. He called the lawn servicemen, and they would go cut the grass or whatever they were asked to do on the exterior. I never followed up on who that might be. Whoever that person is must be inspecting the home at some point and have access to the interior. He could be a local person. There might be a money trail. Could you find out who the senator was paying to watch his home?"

Wayne said, "No. The senator has his wealth set up in shell corporations located all over the world, and we at the TBI would have no way to track his income stream on a worldwide level. The FBI has taken over the case.".

"One more thing, if you walk into a room and see a spider web, what do you see?"

Wayne looked confused at the question, and he said the first thing that came to his mind. "I see a web, and sometimes a spider. Why are you asking me that question?"

"Because in my research, I discovered a test to verify if a person might have a sadist personality with psychopathic tendency, and that was the number one question on three separate tests. The sadist killer always said they saw the captured prey either dead or struggling to break free before certain death caused by the spider. The focus of the sadist killer was on the slow death of the prey. The articles further explained the sadist almost always traumatizes, humiliates, tortures, insults, and abandons the person they eventually kill. The sadist does all these terrible things over a certain period of time. We may be dealing with a group of sadists."

The end.

ACKNOWLEDGMENTS

***

To my editor Tracy Neal for all the hard work.

To Chesnie Nichols for the book cover and advice.

To big sister, Sherrie Rutherford, for all the loving help in writing book two.

www.ingramcontent.com/pod-product-compliance
Lightning Source LLC
Chambersburg PA
CBHW050023030726
47506CB00001B/86